The Tribe: A New World

A.J. PENN

CUMULUS PUBLISHING LIMITED

Published in 2011 by Cumulus Publishing Limited

Text Copyright © 2011 A.J. Penn

The Tribe Copyright © 2011 Cloud 9 (The Tribe) Ltd

ISBN: 978-0-473-19938-8

Visit The Tribe's website at **www.tribeworld.com**

Contact addresses for companies within the Cloud 9 Screen
Entertainment group can be found at www.entercloud9.com

This is dedicated to you, the reader.
And to the spirit of the Mall Rats
and all those who share it.

PREFACE

Amber walked graciously down the aisle. Bray spellbound, focused on her. She looked beautiful. The crisp white wedding dress reflecting the sun that shone through the stained glass windows of the tiny church.

For a moment Bray almost forgot that there were other people gathered for the wedding. So intent had he been on his bride to be.

Sitting on either side of the aisles that Amber passed, were faces Bray knew all too well. His grandparents. His uncles and aunts. Family members. Many from other parts of the world, who had come to witness this special day.

But most important of all, Bray exchanged a look with his parents, his father nodding in understanding and support. They looked so well. Healthy again. Bray's mother dabbed a tissue to one eye, emotional and proud of the day their elder son was going to marry, setting off on a new chapter in his life.

"Nervous?" Martin whispered in Bray's ear.

Bray turned to his younger brother, looking immaculate in a black tuxedo.

"Martin! What are you doing here?!"

"I'm your best man - remember?"

"No!" Bray responded.

"Oh, yes! Brother!" Martin smiled coldly, fixing Bray's tie, adjusting it to perfection, a trace of venom in the tone of his voice.

Stunned as he was to see Martin, Bray's attention once more fell on his bride, as Martin indicated Amber approaching the altar, ever closer.

With each step she took, Bray's heart almost faltered. He was overcome by it all. His love for Amber, the monumental day of the wedding - and the fact that so many dearly loved ones, Martin included, were somehow there to experience it with him.

Behind Amber, her two bridesmaids followed, holding the long trail of the wedding gown in their hands. Their faces beaming bright smiles of their own, Patsy and Chloe were thrilled to be involved in the special day of Amber and Bray's betrothal.

And then she was beside him. Amber looked up to Bray as he lifted the thin veil off her face so she could see into the eyes of her husband to be. The delight on her expression was clear for all to see.

It was her smile which had always captivated Bray. With that one longing look she gave him, her eyes locked on his own, her expression one of contentment, peace, togetherness. If he could freeze a moment in time forever, this would be it. Her gaze, her smile spoke volumes about the love she felt for him, reassuring him that they would always be together. No matter what happened in this God forsaken world. Everything would always be alright.

"This is a day that will be long remembered," Tai San spoke up loudly to the assembly.

Bray stared absently at Tai San. Amazed also to see her there. Presiding over the ceremony. But there she was, like his brother Martin, his parents, the dearly loved friends and family who were all there around him. She was very much real. Wasn't she? Or had Bray's memory betrayed him? Was he losing his mind? He certainly began to doubt his senses. He thought so many of the people had perished. Yes, died. Was he now in Heaven?

"It's okay," Amber whispered softly, clutching Bray's hands in reassurance.

Feeling a little more at peace, Bray focused again on Amber, putting his faith in her. Like he had always done before.

"We are gathered here today for the union of Amber and Bray," Tai San continued. "Two spirits. Drawn together. Destined to be united for all eternity."

Bray cast another glance at Tai San. Beneath her smile, he noticed her eyes seemed to be cold, vacant.

"Amber - do you take Bray to be your husband?" Tai San asked.

"I do," Amber said, gazing once more longingly at Bray.

"And Bray - do you take Amber to be your loving wife?"

Amber waited for Bray's answer, the words she was obviously so desperate to hear, yearning in her heart, from the very depths of her soul.

The doubt about what was really happening resurfaced in Bray's mind. He had spotted Dal, sitting in the audience. Amber's best friend from the days before the adults were wiped off the face of the Earth. Dal, too, had met an untimely end. What was he doing - at the wedding?

"Are you alright, brother?" Martin asked quietly, so the assembled crowd could not hear.

"Do you take Amber to be your wife?" Tai San repeated once more in a monotone, her voice almost robotic. Certainly not the spiritual and emotional Tai San that Bray had known from his past.

3

"Answer her, Bray!" Martin shouted out, seizing Bray by the arm.

Squirming to get out of Martin's iron grasp, Bray was horrified by the realization that Martin was no longer wearing the immaculate tuxedo as before - but had turned into the visage of Zoot, complete with the leather jacket, goggles resting on his black cap, his hair long and scruffy, his eyes burning in manic intensity.

"Do you, or don't you take Amber to be your lawful and loving wife?" Tai San asked again, an element of impatience and threat in the tone.

"Let me go!" Bray shrieked out, desperate to escape from the hold of his younger yet powerful brother. Zoot clung tightly, his firm grasp restricting Bray, struggling to get away.

"You're not leaving! You're staying put - brother!" Zoot yelled contemptuously.

"Well?!" Tai San probed, trying to contain her anger.

"Do it!" Zoot shouted.

Were they going to forcibly put a wedding ring on Bray's finger?

Unable to free himself, Bray was powerless, looking on at Amber, Tai San, the assembled loved ones who gazed impassively from the aisles, ignoring his pleas for help, assistance.

Amber reached into her wedding gown - and rather than presenting a ring, she now held a long medical syringe in her hand.

"Oh, I do. I do, I do, I do," Amber repeated, carefully moving the syringe into position above Bray's arm. "Till death do us part!"

"Power and Chaos!" Zoot roared, urging Amber on, a look of complete madness in his darting eyes, fierce with energy.

"Amber - no!" Bray shouted out.

But it was no use. Amber suddenly plunged the needle into Bray's outstretched arm, Bray yelling out in intense pain as the syringe penetrated deeply into his vein.

"Please help me!! Amber!!!" Bray cried out, desperate.

Calmly, Amber pulled back the top of the syringe, the needle gradually drawing up blood.

Terrified at what he was experiencing, Bray felt his heart racing, and he was overwhelmed with nausea at seeing Amber taking the blood sample from his arm, examining it coldly as the syringe filled up.

"Amber!" Bray called out, trying to make contact, get through to her.

It was hopeless. Amber ignored his pleas, focusing on the syringe.

"Martin, help me!" Bray begged, looking now to his brother, to see if he would help get Bray out of this nightmare.

But Zoot still held onto Bray tightly, refusing to yield.

"Keep going," Zoot insisted to Amber, more blood being taken out of Bray's arm, entering into the syringe.

"Why?" Bray cried out, tears welling up in his eyes at the cold, calculating nature of it all. The unwillingness of anyone to come to his aid, the brutality being bestowed upon him by those he cared about the most, his friends and family, Amber, his loved ones who didn't feel the same way about him, tearing him apart.

Bray was feeling faint, increasingly light headed. Yet he fought to keep consciousness. To listen to his brother's explanation for the macabre turn of events.

"You are me, Bray," Zoot went on. "And I am you. We are one!"

"His pulse rate is high," Judd spoke calmly. But from his tone it was clear he was concerned at the health of his patient.

Bray was laying on an operating theatre table, a reality space visor attached to his face.

Though he was strapped down, his body convulsed, shaking, the nerve impulses causing his fingers to twitch rapidly, his head thrown from side to side by invisible forces. He was attached to a bank of monitors displaying his vital signs, pulse rate, temperature, blood pressure.

Two girls stood nearby wearing reality space visors, the shorter of the two holding a long medical syringe in her hands, removing more blood from Bray's arm.

"It's getting dangerous!" Judd insisted. Dressed in white, Judd was like some mad scientist, his eyes now gazing at the complex instrumentation all around him as he stepped away from Bray, examining the equipment readings.

"That's enough. For now," the taller of the girls, Eloise, agreed, reluctant to end proceedings but submitting to the advice of Judd.

Removing the reality space visor from her face, Eloise shook her head, readjusting to being back in reality. Her cold blue eyes surveyed Bray. That had been an intense session. They had really gotten through to Bray that time. Pleased with her efforts, Eloise smiled, stroking Bray's hair reverently.

Taking the reality space visor off her own head, the shorter girl holding the syringe filled with blood, carefully passed it to Eloise, bowing in respect to her leader - and to the deep red contents of the syringe.

Judd began to unfasten Bray's own reality space visor, Bray murmuring in pain and confusion.

"Brothers and sisters!" Eloise called out suddenly to the viewing gallery.

The operating table on which Bray lay was in the middle of a surgery theatre, bright lights shining down in the centre, illuminating the patient for all to see.

In the gallery - which was more like a sealed chamber divided by glass - there were about twenty observers, most about the same age as Bray. They had one thing in common, however, that united them. Every single one of them wore Zoot style hats, complete with goggles. And they gazed at Eloise in excitement, an air of collective tension and anticipation as Eloise held the syringe in her hand up to the light.

"The blood of Bray. And of Zoot!" Eloise uttered in awe, as if she was holding an artefact of immense value.

Judd had unfastened Bray now from the bed. Bray was barely conscious.

With the shorter girl assisting, the two of them supported Bray, his arms draped over their shoulders, and they began to drag him away towards the exit doors.

"Martin... Amber..." Bray quietly murmured in distress to himself, ravaged, tears streaming down his face.

Eloise turned from Bray to face the gallery of observers.

"We have communed with the Mighty One," she said. "Visited his realm, the plane of other existence."

"Zoot will lead us, we will obey," the gallery chanted in unison, in reply.

Eloise emptied the blood into a glass vial, which she held up for all to see.

"The blood of the brother. The blood of Zoot!" Eloise intoned, staring at the vial with fascination, her blue eyes intense.

"We are of one blood. We are one with Zoot," the gallery chanted in unison, in response. All were now staring in reverence.

"He will lead - and we will follow!" Eloise shrieked.

Approaching the exit door, Bray was drifting in and out of consciousness. His body was weak, his spirits low, his mind confused, all a scramble.

Repelled by the bizarre goings on, Bray just about had the energy to turn his head to one side to look behind him.

To his horror, he saw Eloise sip from the vial, blood overspilling around her lips.

The gallery erupted into loud, rhythmical chants which resonated in the medical theatre, as if shaking the very foundations of the building itself.

The last thing Bray was aware of was the continuing chanting of his brother's name from the gallery before he lost consciousness...

"Zoot! Zoot!! Zoot!!!!"

On the opposite side of the gallery in a private viewing platform, a figure stood in the shadows surrounded by his fellow council members.

They were all wearing blue flowing robes.

One, The Guardian, gazed intently at the proceedings. And slowly broke out into a manic smile.

CHAPTER ONE

The little trawler pitched up and down as the ocean waves carried it ever onwards. But to where, Amber wondered, the spray from the side of the boat drifting into her face.

She was standing at the stern, staring out to the endless horizon of water surrounding them in all directions. She had always loved the sea. Her Dad had taken her to the beach many times when she was a little girl, and she had an appreciation of the beauty of nature, a respect for its awesome power. Nature had a way of putting things in perspective.

If this was any other occasion, Amber would have been soaking up the experience, enjoying every moment of it. The sound of the waves. The sun beaming down, bathing her in its warmth. The ocean, Amber reflected, wouldn't have changed for thousands of years. Despite the loss of the old world, the demise of the adults, this was one constant. And Amber took comfort from that. From the notion that there was one thing unchanging in this completely changed world.

Amber's thoughts turned to the plight she and the others now found themselves in. She needed some time away from them. A moment alone to consider everything that had happened since they fled the city that had been their salvation.

How many days had they been at sea? And where were they, Amber wondered. It must have been several weeks, with land now being a distant memory. Jack had tried to keep track of the number of days of their voyage but as time passed, gave up.

Their close confines had led to frayed nerves. Nineteen of them, cramped together in a little fishing trawler designed for a crew of eight.

Amber knew the situation was dire but she and Jay tried to keep everyone else's spirits up. Which was easier said than done. A feeling of unease had taken over the vessel. Of pointlessness. Despair. Arguments erupted over the most petty issues. Everyone got on each other's nerves. With all the bickering, it hadn't been easy for Jack to concentrate and despite his best efforts, he hadn't made any progress in trying to work out exactly where they might be.

The original plan was to head for the outer islands in Zone 4, which they calculated would be about a thousand miles from their previous home in the city. Jack had charted a guideline course. Even at three miles per hour then they should have hopefully approached land within ten to fifteen days.

But now their very survival was at stake. How ironic. To be on a fishing boat, but to have no fish, and hardly any food. The trawler had long ago been looted of nets. And other equipment. Salene, Jack and Ram had tried to fashion together makeshift fishing lines but with no bait, there hadn't been any bites so far.

The only food they had was that stored on the boat by Zak, the trader who the boat belonged to back in the city. Zak had been one of May's contacts. Someone she could go to if she needed any kind of supplies. And it was thanks to Zak's boat that Amber and the others had a means to embark upon their voyage.

The key to the food locker had been given to Amber, voted the leader - or the 'Captain' of the vessel by the others, and she had been carefully rationing the small amounts of food and stored bottled water accumulated by Zak. But supplies were running dangerously low.

Jack had tried to fix the fresh water issue by rigging together a rain water collection device using a tatty plastic tarpaulin. But he had been unable to test the ability of his invention to collect water since it hadn't rained.

Water, water, everywhere - and not a drop to drink. Amber recalled the line from Coleridge's famous poem about a doomed ship, shaking her head at how cruel fate could be, putting them in such a predicament.

Their physical health was further endangered because the one toilet the boat had was blocked and no longer working. A terrible noxious odour had begun to fill the air in the cramped cabins below. Most of the Tribe had started to sleep on the outer decks.

The issue of where they were going had caused many a fierce argument. When they had first escaped, Ram wanted to head out to open sea to get away from the pandemic which they thought had infected the city. To sit it out. But Amber and the others knew that their only hope for survival was to try and settle in a new land.

A couple of days into the voyage, it became apparent that Zak wouldn't be any help to them in practical terms of navigating. He had admitted, bashfully, that he knew nothing about the ocean or how to sail. It wasn't even his boat originally. As always, Zak had an ability of 'acquiring' things. Items, even people. It was only by a miracle that there had been a small amount of fuel in the engines, that it hadn't been siphoned off by the Locos or some other tribe in the city. Zak was a trader, not a sailor, and though the boat had been his home, he wouldn't be of any use in the Mall Rats finding their way.

Ram gloated at this. Sure his plan had been the better. If they had anchored a safe distance off shore, then they could have assessed matters. Perhaps even explored the land along the coast. He had explained his worry that out in the ocean, they could get caught in currents and end up lost.

The others agreed with Amber that staying in the region was tantamount to committing suicide.

Besides, she didn't quite trust Ram. And was never too sure exactly where he was coming from.

Some in the party - especially Lex - blamed Ram in the first place. Had he not devised the computer program which had connected to Mega's chemical arsenal, then the Mall Rat tribe - along with other tribes in the area - had a chance, however slim, of building a new world. Now they had no choice but to look for somewhere else to settle.

As it became apparent that the little boat was lost, Ram had been all too eager to say "I told you so" and had rubbed up the others, irritating them deliberately. And clearly hoped he could persuade them to return. Without a compass, no GPS, nobody able to navigate by the stars (though Jack was trying to teach himself how)... they were directionless, drifting. The only question was - to where?

Amber's mantra had been to keep heading north. Her resolution was that they use the sun as it rose each day as their compass. It's how Amber had learned to keep her bearings when she was in the eco-Tribe, living in the forest, gauging where east or west was to identify the time of day, reliant on the position of the sun.

The helm still worked. So they were able to at least steer the boat. Jack had thought it wise to preserve what little fuel they had. Amber agreed, the power to the engines had been cut a few days out into their voyage.

The others looked to her as a leader because so often she had the right idea at the right time, a solution for every problem that confronted them in this world of no adults. But now, Amber realized that she had no solution. She was as scared as everyone else. Here they were, stuck in the middle of nowhere, supplies and morale running out. But they had no choice. And she was determined that they would survive. Somehow. Somewhere.

"Amber?" Jay asked, wrapping an arm lovingly around Amber's shoulders, having just emerged from the cabin to the outer deck at the back of the trawler. "Are you okay?"

"Yeah, I'm fine. I just needed a bit of space."

"Whatever happens, we will get through all this. I promise," Jay encouraged her, giving her a tender kiss on the side of her face.

But he sounded more convinced than he looked. The two of them stood hugging for a moment, staring out at the endless expanse of ocean all around, confronting it, as if they would never back down from any challenge it presented.

* * *

At the bow of the boat, May patted Zak's back. He was leaning over the side of the trawler, coughing and spluttering, throwing up into the sea. Again. And again. He had been ill for days now.

"That's it, get it all out," May encouraged, trying to help Zak, though being in such close proximity to someone vomiting was hugely unpleasant to her, her face scrunched up in disgust at the awful smell and heaving sounds coming from Zak.

May had known Zak back in the city and respected him for his survivor skills. He was a rogue. From the streets. Like she was in many ways. A resourceful and persuasive type who somehow was able to make deals with others and come up with food, batteries or other worthwhile items. He was a tough negotiator. And might sell his soul if he could benefit. But May liked him. She couldn't help herself. Except for Pride, she had always been attracted to guys who weren't exactly squeaky clean. And she knew that somewhere within Zak's flawed psyche, he wasn't devoid of any feelings. He clearly liked her.

"Has he got the virus?" Gel shouted loudly, staring at Zak and May from within the front of the cabin interior.

"He better not, or else he's outta here," Lex threatened, trying to ignore the proximity of Zak and his seasickness.

Gel was sitting on the sculpted carbon fibre interior bench with Lex laying down, his head resting on Gel's lap as a makeshift pillow.

"I guess the good thing about not eating is you get to lose weight," Gel said out of the blue, prompted by the rumbling of her stomach. She, like the rest of them, was always hungry, trying to get by on the small amount rationed by Amber. "At least I've got a slimmer figure," she added, glancing down in admiration of her more slender than ever frame.

"Yeah, well the bad thing about not eating - is you die," Lex scoffed.

Sammy, along with the others, also watched May try and comfort Zak.

It made Sammy heave. And he threw up all over the floor.

"Man - that's gross!" Darryl said, looking as if he might also vomit. "If you're going be sick, get out there with them. Don't do it in here!"

Trudy stared intently at the pool of sickness, spreading across the deck. And suddenly lunged, scooping some up, forcing it inside her own mouth, savouring the taste as if it was a welcome feast.

Ram blurted out in uncontrollable laughter. While the others stared in a mixture of disbelief and disgust.

"What the hell are you doing!?" Lex asked.

"Trying to survive. And I don't care how I do it. This is mine! All of it! I saw it first," Trudy spluttered, mouth full, the vomit overspilling from her mouth and drooling across her face. She forced it back in, licking her fingers.

"You're welcome to it," Lex said, gazing at Zak, who was vomiting again. "Hey - save some of that for Trudy! She's hungry."

"Shove it!" May yelled.

"No, you shove it!" Ram shouted impatiently to May. "Why don't you tell your loverboy that if he owns technology... even a boat... he should have at least figured out how to use it!"

"Cut it out, Ram," May countered. "If it wasn't for Zak and his boat, where would we be right now?"

"Anywhere would be better than being stuck here. On a boat full of idiots," Ram sighed to himself.

"That can be solved easily, Ram," Lex replied. "If we throw you overboard, then at least there'd be one less mouth to feed."

Ram considered Lex, realizing he was quite capable of carrying out the threat.

"If you're bored, Ram," May admonished him, "go and troll somewhere else. I'm sure the sharks would appreciate you annoying them!"

"Ram winding people up? Well there's a surprise," Jay joked, trying to lift everyone's spirits as he moved inside through the cabin, with Amber beside him.

She glanced at Trudy, now licking the floor.

"Trudy - what on earth are you doing?"

"Having some 'seconds'. Of vomit," Gel said, disgustedly.

Amber helped Trudy up and sat her back on the bench.

"I know how you must feel, Trudy. But that's not the way. Come on, now. Everything's gonna be alright. There'll be enough food and water for everyone. As long as we keep rationing it."

"If not... we'll just have to look for other 'things' on the menu," Lex suggested, casting a threatening glance at Ram, who ignored it, but felt deep within that he wouldn't put it past Lex to resort to cannibalism.

With dry lips, a thumping headache, but an iron will not to give up, Amber had called the Tribe for a meeting. Every few days the group met to go over their plight, see if anyone had any ideas to improve their situation. Amber was above all concerned that with Ram's dissent she could have a mutiny on her hands. She wanted to keep everyone focused. And calm. Especially Trudy. She was never the type that needed much encouragement to panic, with her histrionics.

Sammy was asked to join Lottie, who had already taken Trudy's daughter, Brady, and Amber's baby to the cabin below so the rest of the Tribe could meet, despite his protestations at being a baby sitter.

"Sorry I'm late," Ebony said, reaching the top of the stairs leading into the main cabin area. She was followed by Slade. There was a cool and tense air between them.

"Make yourself - comfortable," Jack said, a hint of humour in his voice. They were all so cramped, squished together in the cabin that there was little room for them all.

"Mind if I sit here?" Ebony asked Slade, settling next to him.

"Do what you want. What do I care," Slade replied coldly.

The others could see that their relationship was still strained and that they must have been arguing.

The meeting went ahead. And once again, Ram stated strongly that they should turn the boat around and head back in the direction they had come from, intent as ever to return to their old home in the city.

Ram was outvoted. The overwhelming majority chose to keep following Amber's recommendation, sure they were bound to reach land eventually.

"We might be dead by then," Ram cautioned.

"You have such a way with words," Salene admonished him, while discretely indicating Trudy, who was staring vacantly into the distance, tears welling up in her eyes.

"I don't feel so good," she said, her voice a fragile, hoarse whisper.

Salene sat beside her, trying to provide some emotional support. Trudy had been on a rollercoaster ride of emotions of late. Amber and the others were always aware of her vulnerable state and moodswings, even at the best of times. Amber suspected that she probably suffered from clinical depression. She had been through so many traumatic experiences in her young life. And always found it difficult to cope.

"She needs a drink," Ellie suggested.

"We all need a drink," Lex said. "I could sure do with a shot of Jack Daniels."

"Same here, Lexy-boy," Ram quipped, eager to ingratiate himself to Lex. "And Trudy here looks like she needs - a psychiatrist."

"That's enough, Ram," said Amber, steeping forward, offering Trudy Amber's meagre water ration.

Salene held the bottle to Trudy's lips but Trudy didn't seem to notice it there. She was lost as if in a vision, in another world. Her eyes transfixed.

"What's up with her?" Gel asked no one in particular as Trudy suddenly began to sob uncontrollably, her shoulders heaving.

"We should get her downstairs," Amber said, concerned for Trudy's wellbeing, thinking she might feel better if she rested for a while.

Salene tried to encourage Trudy to stand up, Ellie going to the other side of Trudy to support her.

"Get your hands off me!" Trudy wailed hysterically.

"Trudy, it's gonna be okay," Salene whispered.

"Come on, Trudy. Try and keep it together," Amber said. "Everything's going to be fine."

"No. It's not! You know it. And I know it!" Trudy screamed. "We are doomed! All of us! We're all going to die!"

CHAPTER TWO

His eyes closed tightly, Bray imagined himself in another place. A different time. It was the only refuge he had right now, his imagination. The only way he could escape from the predicament he had ended up in.

His thoughts drifted back to Amber. To their life together back in the city. He loved her with every fibre of his being and the pain of their separation ached deeply to his very core. He could picture her, looking back at him with love in her eyes. She was the kindest, most gentle, sincere person he had ever met. He thought they were destined to be together, starcrossed lovers in a fairy tale ending, living happy ever after.

Yet were those many precious memories of Amber - themselves real? Had his life of the past with her even happened at all? Or was it all some part of a virtual reality program? Was he even sitting, in solitary confinement in his cell, like he perceived he was?

Bray had been subjected to so many simulations that he was beginning to doubt his own mind, losing sight of what was real and what was illusion.

He was even in danger of losing himself, his sense of self-identity, his very being. All the barrage of information he had suffered, the sensory stimulation, the virtual worlds he had been trapped in, the experiments he had endured. It was now taking its toll. He felt as if his spirit had been drained. And that he wouldn't be able to keep going on for much longer.

But he had to try. What little dignity and essence he still had, Bray now consciously clung on to. He wouldn't give in, or give up. Somehow, if he could only find the time to think, separating the real from the illusionary, he hoped he could discover some way of getting through this living nightmare that fate had thrust upon him.

So immersed in his thoughts, Bray didn't notice the guards entering his cell, the iron door creaking with rust as it was unlocked, swung open.

They surveyed their prisoner. Bray lay on the ground, covered in dirt, his brown hair matted in mud. He hadn't been washed for some time.

One of the guards tried to suppress the body stench as he carefully approached, placing a tray on the ground beside the prisoner.

"Breakfast," the guard whispered caustically, staring at Bray with contempt.

Bray snapped out of his reverie and returned to the stark realization of the hell he was in. He looked at the 'breakfast' plate. A bowl of cold gruel, flies crawling and buzzing on the foul rotting food.

Bray met the guard's stare with his own, his eyes full of resistance.

"Eat!" the guard ordered, keen to watch Bray consume the disgusting meal.

"I'm not hungry," Bray lied. He was starving. But he realized this was almost a power struggle between him and his captors and he was determined to not give his jailors any satisfaction.

Suddenly the guard lifted the bowl and rubbed Bray's face in the contents. Bray struggled to resist but with his feet and hands bound, there was little he could do. He found himself choking, inadvertently inhaling the oats, the flies up into his nostrils and mouth.

"That's enough!" barked the all too familiar voice as a tall girl entered the cell, the guards bowing their heads in respect. She was about the same age as Bray. And he recognized the voice. It had haunted him since the first time he had arrived at the compound. Now he felt an involuntary shudder as she strode purposefully towards him, her piercing blue eyes studying him.

Tall, with flowing black hair down over her shoulders, Eloise was an imposing sight, a commanding figure who exuded natural authority and charisma. Her black uniform clung to her body and she swayed seductively while surveying her most important prisoner, the burly guard nearby stepping away to allow her some space. She was aware of her good looks and in a camp full of many male guards as well as prisoners, she was always happy to use her natural attributes to get her way. But being firmly in control of the compound, didn't need to rely on anything other than her status. And power.

"Leave us!" Eloise ordered the guards.

Nodding in deference to his leader, the huge jailor ushered his fellow guards out of the cell, the thick iron door shutting behind them.

Every day was full of many ordeals, Bray wondered what had been planned for him this time.

Eloise smiled, her impeccable white teeth leering as she leaned over him and began to stroke his hair gently, wiping flecks of spilt oats away, scoffing her displeasure at seeing Bray this way.

"How are you feeling?" she asked out of care, but Bray picked up her tone was obviously not as sincere or genuine as she was making out.

"What do you think?" Bray spat out an oat of gruel which landed on Eloise's shoulder.

Casually, Eloise brushed off the gruel. "I think you are a stubborn human being. But you will learn - that you are not as stubborn as I. So why don't you and I become allies? We could do great things together," she pouted seductively.

Bray stared back at her. Eloise was clearly an intelligent individual who took delight in mindgames, Bray reasoned. But he wasn't about to play. Not now. Not ever. He wasn't about to give in.

"Come on," Eloise encouraged, casting a coy glance at Bray, playing the temptress. "Give a girl a break. Surely I'm not that bad in your eyes? You must find me... even a little bit attractive?"

Bray appreciated Eloise's obvious external beauty, her blue eyes staring into his own. She was certainly attractive. Yet he was repulsed by her. Who she was as a person. He fully knew she was in charge of his imprisonment and would have been the one to order the guards to act so mercilessly, let alone subjecting him to so many reality space experiments.

"Leave me alone," Bray demanded.

"My dear Bray, surely you don't mean that," Eloise said in mock-hurt at his words. "I mean, look at you and me here. Together. We're one with Zoot. Aren't we?"

"What do you want with me?" Bray snapped, angered at the mention of Zoot. He never agreed with the path of his brother. But still felt outraged by anyone manipulating Zoot's name and reputation, distorting his brother's life and legacy.

"I want you. For one night. That's all. You and I to spend one night together," Eloise smiled disarmingly.

"You're crazy!" Bray scoffed.

"Crazy for you, you mean. Praise Zoot!" Eloise added, playfully mentioning Zoot's name once more.

"I'd rather die! Than spend one night with you, Eloise!"

"Both can be arranged," Eloise cautioned. "If you're nice to me, I can be nice to you. But if not..."

Out of nowhere, Eloise slapped Bray hard, in the face.

"You think I really care about you? Or your stupid brother, Zoot? The 'Zootists'? Any of that? If so, you're very much mistaken. You're nothing more than a very valuable commodity, Bray. Worth more to me alive than dead. As long as you father a child. My child, that is. Either willingly. Or maybe... in our next trip into reality space!"

"You're mad!" Bray protested.

Eloise seized Bray by his jaw, pressing down on both sides of his face with her hands, digging her nails into his cheeks, her blue eyes intense, inches away from Bray's face.

"One night, Bray. And one child, that's all. Don't let down all those who put their faith in 'Zoot'. Let's give them something real to worship! My baby... Our child!"

And with that, Eloise kissed Bray passionately, Bray squirming to avoid her but unable due to being tied down.

"Think about THAT," Eloise said, pulling herself away from Bray and scrambling to her feet.

Snapping her fingers to her guards, the iron door creaked open and Bray braced himself as the guards entered.

"I'm patient but you don't have forever, Bray!" Eloise said.

Spinning on her heel, Eloise headed out of the cell, a guard closing the door behind her.

"Show him what happens. When I run out of patience," she called back to the guards who remained in the cell.

Defiant to the last, Bray gritted his teeth as the guards descended on him quickly, their fists flailing.

CHAPTER THREE

Despite thinking the situation couldn't get any worse, Amber realized that they were now moving into a more difficult state than before.

That morning, the last of the food supplies had run out. Amber carefully rationing a small tin of rice pudding, giving most of the share to the youngest, Brady and baby Bray. She had done her best to stretch the rations as far as she could during their voyage but there were too many mouths to feed, not enough food - and now, there was no food.

The final bottles of drinking water had also been used up first thing that day but thankfully the boat had passed through a rain squall during the night. Jack's improvised water collection had done its job well, a little pool from the rain being held in the tarpaulin, which Jack was trying to carefully drip feed into the empty bottles.

Amber's lips were sore. They kept cracking open, resulting in a number of little cuts which bled from time to time. Her physical condition was deteriorating, as it was with the others, and she wondered if they had the onset of scurvy or God knows, what other kind of illnesses. This is how sailors in the old days must have felt, Amber considered. She had studied elements of the European voyages of 'discovery' at school in history and in a way felt an affinity with the explorers, a connection. After all, she too was on her own epic adventure. Except at least the sailors knew what they were doing, whereas Amber and her Tribe had limited nautical skills. And now were hopelessly lost. Running out of hope.

Baby Bray was fast asleep in Amber's arms. She cradled him protectively and tried to keep calm. She knew that panic was the last thing they needed right now. But it was hard to keep a level head with the constant tension in the air and anxiety of all the others. The stress of their dire situation was getting to everybody.

Amber focused on her baby. He was so beautiful. Pure and innocent. But hungry. And without any more food... Amber dreaded to think.

Most of the Tribe sat on the outer decks. It had been too hot and humid to be down below lately. There was no air circulation and it was more comfortable, relatively speaking.

Various people reacted in different ways to the situation. Their only routine was that they had no routine. Each day was just like the day before. With the boat drifting. A collective delirium was almost setting in. Some were bored, others tried to find ways to pass the time. But all were worried about what the future lay in store for them.

"I spy with my little eye - something beginning with S," Gel said to Lottie and Sammy playfully, for the umpteenth time.

"Sea," Lottie blurted out unenthusiastically.

"You could at least try to enjoy it," Gel complained.

"I spy something beginning with I - Idiot," Ram scoffed disdainfully at Gel, as he paced back and forth.

Lex immediately sprang to his feet, pinning Ram by the throat to the wall.

"And I spy something beginning with L. Loser about to go overboard!" Lex glared menacingly.

"Let him go, Lex," Amber demanded, crossing to them. "Come on. Let's not make matters worse."

Slade and Jay moved to Ram and Lex, separating them.

"Back off, Lex. Now's not the time," Jay said.

Lex released his grip but glared as Jay and Slade led Ram away.

"Just don't turn your back on me, pal. I mean it," Lex threatened. "You're not even a Mall Rat. And after all you've done in the past - you have no right to even speak!"

"We're all in the same boat now though, Lex," Salene said gently. "And we've got to look out for each other."

"Or how about we all leap over the side? End it now!" Trudy suggested.

"Don't give up hope, Trudy," Amber said encouragingly, while casting a knowing glance at Salene.

Amber had mentioned earlier to all of them that they especially needed to keep an eye on Trudy. If she lost hope, then with her precarious state of mind, who knows what would happen. She might try and harm herself. Amber hoped that her suspicions would prove to be inaccurate. But deep down thought it was wise to implement a suicide watch.

At the bow, May and Zak sat next to each other, talking. Holding hands. They had been chatting the whole morning. For all that they had known each other back in the city - they were bonding more throughout the voyage.

May had never been lucky in love. Those she had lost her heart to before had either fallen for someone else, like Pride with Salene, or something had gotten in the way of May having a close relationship. Maybe this time it could be different? If they all survived, of course.

On the upper deck, Ebony had been trying to find some shade and get some fresh air. She stared at Ruby and Slade nearby, who were themselves engrossed in conversation, reminiscing about people and adventures shared in the past in the town of Liberty, where both had spent some considerable time.

Earlier that day, Ebony had tried to make up with Slade again after their previous arguments. Slade wouldn't accept Ebony's apologies, however, instead wanting her to stay away from him. As far as possible within the limited confines of the tiny trawler.

He couldn't forgive the things she had said about his brother, Mega, the insensitivity she had displayed at his death. Yes, it was true that Mega had been responsible for many terrible things as a leading member of The Techno tribe and was instrumental in releasing the 'virus' causing them to flee the city. Slade was still trying to come to terms with it all and had difficulty reconciling Mega's actions with the emotional sense of loss he felt as a result of his brother's death.

But what really got to Slade was the fact that Ebony seemed to have selective moral standards. She was the last person to criticize anyone. He was sure that she was no angel, being a past leader of the Loco tribe. And her hypocrisy repulsed Slade. He needed time to go over it all in his mind. But primarily, space away from Ebony.

In her mind, it seemed like Slade was spending too much time with Ruby, rather than time alone mourning his brother and thinking over things. Including their fractured relationship. Maybe she was being paranoid though and wondered if Ruby and Slade were just idly talking? Or was he deliberately being with Ruby - in front of Ebony - to teach her some kind of a lesson? Make a point?

Whatever was going on, Ebony felt pangs of bitter jealousy. She was angry at Slade and resentful toward Ruby. Ruby was a survivor who made the most of her opportunities. Ebony didn't trust her. Her mind calculating, Ebony wondered the best way how to win back her man.

After the altercation between Lex and Ram, Salene moved along the deck to dangle an improvised fishing line in the water. Her Dad had taken her fishing many times as a young girl but so far she had caught nothing. It was almost as if the ocean was empty of fish.

"You really think you're going to catch something?" Darryl asked as he sat beside Salene, looking out over the side of the boat.

"If I don't try, I'll never know - will I?" Salene responded, concentrating on the fishing line. A little piece of dried rice pudding had been tied to the other end of the line. Salene hoped something would take a bite, though the notion of a fish eating rice pudding was quite ludicrous to her. What would her Dad have thought of using that as bait?

Darryl inched closer to Salene and smiled suavely.

"There's plenty of fish in the sea."

"What's that supposed to mean?" Salene asked but suspected Darryl wasn't just interested in her fishing.

"Oh, you know. I'm single. You're single. Everyone else round here pretty much are couples. There's Jack and Ellie. Amber and Jay. Ruby - or Ebony - and Slade. May and Zak seem to be getting on okay. Gel thinks she and Lex are an item. And, well, it's just a pity to be alone. I dunno. How about you and I...?"

Salene, flustered, unsure how to respond, sighed.

"That's lovely, Darryl. And you're sweet..."

"So are you," Darryl quickly beamed.

"But the answer's no. No offence. But... it's not the time for this. And you're not my type."

"Oh, come on. A good looking girl like you. A good looking guy like me," Darryl insisted.

"Right now, I would rather kiss a good looking fish. I'm sorry but no, Darryl!"

The line tugged in her hand. "I've got one! I've got one!"

Suddenly she stumbled as the trawler engines roared into life and the little boat arched dangerously, spinning about 180 degrees.

"What the hell?" Jay shouted, trying to steady himself along with Amber, nearby.

"Where's Ram?" she snapped, realizing Ram was no longer there.

Jay and Amber rushed to the upper deck bridge to the helm where Ram stood like a man possessed, turning the wheel, his teeth gritted in determination.

"Ram! What are you doing?" Jay shouted.

"Saving us!" Ram called out. "We're going back!"

"Turn the engines off!" Amber roared, aware that the precious little fuel they had was being used up. She reached out for the ignition key but Ram pushed her away and continued clutching the wheel tightly.

The trawler banked on a steeper angle, causing all the others on board to scream in mounting panic, wondering just what was going on, the horizon tilting, Ram spinning the wheel, cackling crazily.

Jay and Amber grabbed Ram, forcibly removing his hands from the wheel, yanking him away.

Amber corrected the helm, the trawler boat gradually righting itself level.

"Witch!" Ram hissed at Amber. "Don't you see? A few more days of this and we'll all be hanging out with the angels."

"In your case, Ram - I think you have an appointment with the devil!" Amber said.

Ram glared defiantly at her.

"We should have gone back to the city when I said. Now, we're doomed. We're all going to die. And you know something, Amber? It's all your fault!"

* * *

Amber stood at the front of the little trawler, staring up in wonder at the stars that twinkled above her. It was a magical night. There was a sense of peace. Even the ocean was calm, as smooth as glass, barely a ripple all around as the waves gently lapped the side of the boat, the crescent moon shining down brightly, reflecting on the water's surface.

They had come so far, Amber reflected. Back in the city, in the days after the 'virus', Amber and the others had fought so hard to bring order, to create a new society and to overcome many challenging obstacles from Zoot and his Locos to the religious fanatics of The Chosen, to the invasion of the Technos. And now, stuck out here, stranded on the boat, it just didn't seem fair. They had all given so much effort. They had tried so hard. But life wasn't always fair, Amber knew. Were they drifting to their doom, like Ram said? And if so, was she responsible?

"Can't sleep?" Jay spoke quietly as he walked up and stood beside Amber.

"No."

"Lex's snoring?"

"I wish. I thought it was bad when we lived in the mall," Amber reflected, thinking of Lex's snoring, which was indeed very loud and the source of many a sleepless night for the others. "I was thinking more of Ram."

"That was quite a day, wasn't it," Jay sighed in marvel as he took in the breathtaking starlit sky.

Amber nodded. "Four fish caught. Thank goodness for Salene's fishing skills... and let's see, six arguments... one potential nervous breakdown with Trudy... one near capsize due to Ram... one major mutiny," Amber counted on her fingers.

"At least Ram's quietened down. Must have been in the sun too long. Something's gotten to him."

"You mean... me?"

"I wouldn't pay any attention to what he said, Amber. All of this... it's not your fault."

"I just don't understand why he's so intent on trying to get back. It doesn't make any sense. Surely he knows we didn't have a choice. You know him better than anyone. Any ideas?"

"Nothing. If he's got a hidden agenda, he's hardly the type to reveal it. The only thing anyone can ever know about Ram, Amber - is he's a person of extremes. A true enigma."

"As if I needed any reminding," Amber replied bitterly.

Ram had been a scourge to Amber, all of the Tribe, in the past. The entire city. He had caused so many problems, heartache. Though he claimed innocence, not knowing what had happened to explain Bray's disappearance, Amber couldn't help but doubt him. She felt distrust.

Thrown by circumstances into working together to try and defeat Mega's tyranny, Ram and Amber had never been friends or gotten close. They had been allies of convenience. And now there was no common enemy, Amber felt an unease that of all the people she would be stuck with, drifting on a boat in the middle of nowhere, one of them was Ram.

A moment passed as Amber and Jay stood, the only noise the sound of the water lapping the boat as the two of them searched the stars.

"It's beautiful, isn't it?" Amber breathlessly said, in wonder at the view. "Makes you think. Here we are. A tiny boat on a vast ocean. Itself on a little planet. We're just a dot in the universe, aren't we? I mean, what's it all about?"

"Who knows?" Jay responded. "I guess that's the mystery of life. What makes it interesting. We don't know."

"Do you think there's something greater out there?"

"Like God or something?"

"Mmm," Amber assented. "My Mom... she was religious. But I couldn't understand if there is a God - then why was there so much pain and suffering in the world? How could that be? How could what happened to the adults - be allowed to happen?"

"There were certainly enough problems in the world when the adults were around. And now it's up to us, isn't it? How do you think we've done so far? Is the world a better place?" Jay asked.

"Not for us, so far it isn't. But we've got to try, don't we?" Amber replied, with complete conviction. "If we don't try to make it a better world, who will? How can we expect anyone else to? We've just got to do our best."

"In the past, our ancestors would look for answers in the night sky," Jay suggested. "That what you're doing?"

"I guess so. I've got enough questions. Such as why are we on this boat? What's going to happen to us... Are we ever going to get out of this thing alive? What about my son? What future do we have? So far, it's not as if any answers or solutions are jumping out at me."

"You've been amazing, Amber. And you're doing great. If it wasn't for you trying to help everyone else, we might not even have got this far."

Amber smiled bashfully, touched by Jay's words.

"I don't know if we decide our own fate," Jay went on. "Or if destiny is set out for us already, and what will be, will be. But what I do know is, I love you, Amber. And whatever happens the rest of today, tomorrow - I couldn't be happier right now than being here with you. There's no other place, and nobody else, where I'd rather be."

Tears welled up in Amber's eyes. She certainly hadn't expected that tonight when she stepped out to gaze at the sky. She was so touched by Jay's words, the honesty of them. The magic of the moment, there under the night sky.

Was there anyone else she would rather be with? Once, she thought it would have been Bray. But after he disappeared - and presumably died - Amber was happy to have met and then fallen for Jay. She hadn't chosen Bray to vanish - and had he lived, she would have always been faithful to him. But there they were, her and Jay, under the Heavens. Perhaps it was fate after all, outside their control.

Unsure what words to say, she leant forward, tenderly kissing Jay, wrapping her arms around him, hugging him tightly, the two of them together but alone as the millions of stars shone, glimmering above.

Whatever their destiny, in her heart Amber was glad Jay was a part of her life - however much time she had left to live, whatever the future had in store.

CHAPTER FOUR

"For what you've been through, you seem in remarkably good health," Judd said, feeling Bray's pulse.

They were in the medical theatre and Judd had been checking the condition of his prized patient to make sure Bray's body would be up to the stresses and rigours of another reality space interface that Eloise had planned.

"Your pulse rate is steady, your blood pressure's good. I just wish there was something more I could do for you," Judd said, looking sympathetically at Bray, who sat on the bed in the medical theatre. He was dazed, staring lost.

"Thanks for looking out for me. You're the only one who has round here," Bray replied, his voice quiet, weak.

"If you want to know the truth - I don't entirely agree with all that goes on around here," Judd stated. "Science and medical advancements are one thing. Human experiments are not something I can ever sanction."

"Then do something about it, Judd."

"Like what? I'm a scientist. Not a fighter, Bray. I'm not a warrior like you."

"My dear Bray," Eloise called out, striding into the medical theatre, in an air of eager anticipation. "Our guest will be ready for tonight's initiation, Judd?"

"His body's ready. Whether his mind is in order, that's another matter entirely."

"Such a pity he wasn't being more co-operative," Eloise said, caressing her fingers gently down the side of Bray's face.

"I'll be on my way then," Judd suggested.

Nodding out of respect to Eloise, Judd walked away, guards flanking the entrance to the medical theatre opening the door for the scientist to exit.

Bray cautiously glanced at Eloise, her blue eyes examining his own tired, beaten features. He wondered how she would react to what he was going to say.

He hoped Amber wouldn't be disappointed in him. He hadn't had many relationships in his life. And was close at once with Danni. But Amber was different. His one true soulmate. He would never willingly be unfaithful to her. Dishonour her. But he was out of options. Running out of time. Hope. He had no other choice. At least that's what he wanted Eloise to believe.

"You win, Eloise," Bray said, his voice a whisper.

"Say that again?"

Eloise's eyes narrowed, concentrating on him. Had he really just said what she thought he had?

"I'm beaten. I'll do whatever you want of me. Everything you ask..."

"Everything I want of you?"

"Everything," Bray admitted reluctantly, turning with shame to look at his conqueror before him.

Eloise grinned. She couldn't suppress the delight welling up inside. If Bray was serious - if he would give her what she wished for - this would elevate her to a whole new level. Her hold on the 'Zootists', her influence as the Mother continuing

Zoot's bloodline, would put her into a great position to powerbroke. With those in authority. After so much stubborn resistence from Bray, she was finally going to be victorious. And it felt delicious.

"You've made the right choice, Bray. I will be - honoured - to carry your child. Together, we can achieve so much. Perhaps more than either of us can possibly imagine."

Eloise's eyes were lively, dancing with energy, excited at the promise of what that night would bring as she looked over Bray's body in anticipation. At last. He was completely her's.

She called out to the guards.

"Wash him. Clean him up. Then bring Bray to my quarters. Tonight - he and I will... make history!"

* * *

Two guards, flanked either side of Bray, escorted him from the cells to the living quarters of the compound, their heavy boots echoing on the metallic floor.

Bray hoped he knew what he was doing.

His wounds from his beatings had been tended to. And he had been showered. Some guards had even dressed Bray in a dinner suit, and he almost felt like he was going on a date to some high school ball. It was very surreal and for a moment he wondered if this was another reality space program.

Now clean, smartly presented, Bray almost felt human again on the outside. But inside he felt empty, used, exploited. Like a walking piece of meat. A possession. No longer in charge of himself. Or his life.

They reached a double doorway. One of the guards politely knocked.

"Send him in - and then leave us be!" Eloise's voice rang out from the other side of the doors.

The door was opened. Bray was pushed inside, the door quickly clicking shut behind him.

Eloise's quarters were lavish. A huge log fire burned, providing an ambient light. There was a buffet of food on the table. Bowls of fresh fruit. Blood red wine in decanters. At least Bray thought it was wine. A thick fur rug lay on the floor. And the air was punctuated by a rich perfume.

It was strange to see such comfort, after all the deprived conditions he had been exposed to for so long in his cell. Bray expected Eloise to live well - but not this well.

And there, gazing at her reflection in the mirror, stood Eloise.

She was squirting herself around her neck with scent, but she didn't really need to embellish her allure.

Bray was taken aback by her. She looked beautiful. There was no doubt about it. Her long black hair brushed carefully over her shoulders. Just the right make up. She wore a silk gown but in the light, Bray couldn't help make out the naked contours of her body, the enticing natural silhouette revealed through the thin silk.

She was Aphrodite. A goddess.

She was his. And he was her's.

"It is finally time," Eloise whispered, putting down the perfume and extending her hand as she walked towards Bray.

"You look stunning," Bray admitted, dry mouthed.

"So do you," Eloise smiled seductively.

Bray's hands had been firmly bound but Eloise began working on the ropes, untying him, her long nails clattering away as they worked on his restraints.

She was so close to him now, Bray couldn't deny the natural physical attraction he felt to Eloise.

"There - that's better now, isn't it?" she whispered.

With the last of the knots untied, the ropes around Bray's wrists fell to the ground.

"And there…"

Eloise dropped her dressing gown, the light silk collapsing to the floor revealing Eloise's natural form.

She led Bray by his hands to the large bed nearby in the centre of her quarters and began undressing him. His jacket. Undoing the tie.

Her expression one of longing, to her delight Bray began gently kissing the side of her neck, Eloise closing her eyes in complete bliss at what was transpiring.

"Oh this will be such a pleasure," Eloise murmured appreciatively.

"Absolutely. A real pleasure," Bray said, seizing her arms forcibly.

Eloise recoiled in shock as she realized Bray was using the rope from his bounds to tie Eloise's hands together behind her back.

She struggled to free herself but it was no use as Bray fastened the ropes tightly around her arms.

"Sorry about tonight. But I'm already spoken for," Bray said matter of factly, placing the dressing gown over Eloise's otherwise exposed naked body, covering her to protect her dignity. Despite all the wrongs she had given him, he was ever the gentleman.

"Guards!" Eloise screamed out, enraged at Bray's deceit.

The double doors burst open.

Two guards swept into Eloise's quarters.

Initially, they were surprised at seeing Eloise sprawled on the bed. They were not used to seeing her in anything but her usual uniform. But suppressed their urge, aware of the consequences.

The distraction she unwillingly provided them was just the opportunity Bray needed.

He sprung into action, striking one of the guards with a powerful punch. The huge guard fell to the ground, knocked flat out cold.

The other guard leapt at Bray.

Bray moved to kick the guard, who raised his arm to block, before Bray suddenly spun on his heel in a feint, unleashing a rapid blow into the groin, the guard collapsing to the ground in agony.

Out of the corner of his eye, Bray noticed Eloise rushing toward a control panel, and backing to the wall, she adjusted her bonds to press an array of buttons.

Suddenly a pulsing and piercing alarm echoed as Bray rushed through the doors and into the metallic corridor outside the quarters.

He now had a chance. However slight. He just had to take it.

* * *

In the maternity wing, female disciples in the midst of giving birth and groaning in pain at the height of their labour, gazed panic-stricken as did the white gowned medical team, looking around in concern at the sound of the alarm and the pulsing lights.

Guards immediately sprung into action on high alert, rushing out of the ward.

In the manufacturing infant wing, hundreds of new born babies started crying, awoken by the alarm. Their attendants exchanged concerned glances in confusion, watching other guards reacting, rushing away.

The complex he had been imprisoned in was huge, Bray considered, as he raced down the metallic corridors. And once again he wondered if this was real or if he was trapped in some virtual world. Amidst the noise of the alarms, he was sure he could hear the distant sound of babies crying, their anguish echoing throughout the cavernous compound.

He had no knowledge of the geography. Or what other gruesome events ever took place in the complex. All he had seen were the medical theatre, the cell he was kept in, the virtual reality space simulator rooms.

With no idea where he was going, Bray was running on pure instinct, hoping to find the fire exit. He had noted it earlier en route from his cell to Eloise's quarters. But there were so many corridors and he was unsure of just exactly how to retrace his steps.

He knew from talk amongst the other slaves and disciples that no prisoner had ever escaped the compound. Or even tried to.

Rushing around a corner, he almost collided with Judd.

"I thought that alarm might have something to do with you!" Judd said, indicating. "That way to the very bottom, you'll find another corridor veering off to the right. And some emergency exit doors. You'd better move. In a few seconds this area will be overrun by the militia."

"You've got a chance as well, Judd. If you want to take it!"

Suddenly two guards approached.

Judd pointed to Bray.

"Seize him!"

The guards confronted Bray, who exchanged blows.

Judd removed a hypodermic from his white lab coat pocket and plunged the needle into the back of one of the guard's necks. Within seconds the guard slumped unconscious to the ground, while Bray unleashed a blow into the gut of the other guard, doubling him.

"Follow me!" Judd yelled.

They ran in full flight as more guards converged from other corridors, pursuing Bray and Judd, who disappeared through the emergency exit fire doors.

* * *

Bray gratefully breathed in the cold night mountain air. He was thrilled to be outside once more. With Judd beside him, the pair ran on in full flight towards the lush forest environment surrounding the compound.

Behind them, the sounds of guard dogs barking and yelping suddenly accompanied the pulsing distant alarm. Bray could hear guards shouting and was now aware of spotlights arcing, sweeping all around, illuminating the area.

For a split second, Bray still wondered if this was all really happening. If he was once more in a reality space program of Eloise's - without even knowing it.

"This is real - isn't it?" Bray questioned Judd, the two of them scrambling towards the dense foliage.

"You think reality space air smells this good?" Judd replied, panting as he ran. "This is real, Bray. Believe it. You've made it back out to the real world. And so have I. Thanks. I owe you one."

The bright glare of a spotlight suddenly outlined Bray and Judd's silhouettes, their shadows momentarily trapped by the beam of light.

Pushing themselves on from the pursuers gathering behind, and fuelled by adrenalin, Bray and Judd quickly avoided the spotlight glare, racing away, disappearing deeper into the forest. Into the night.

CHAPTER FIVE

There hadn't been a breeze for days. The little boat was motionless. With no noticeable current pushing it along. All around, the ocean itself was now lifeless. There were no waves. None of the movement of the boat, pitching and rolling, that had been so much a part of their voyage so far. There was an eerie silence. Not a sound. Even from the calm water all around them. Except for the noise of static.

Inside the trawler, Jack leant over the radio in the wheelhouse, twisting its dials, concentrating as he listened intently. Each day Jack had turned on the radio for a few minutes at a time, hoping to preserve its battery for as long as possible. But today, just like all the other times he had tried - all he had gotten back so far was the sound of radio silence.

"What are you hoping to get? The top ten best selling songs? The weather forecast? There's nothing, Jack," Ellie said as she sat beside Jack wearily, her voice hoarse and dry.

"There has to be something out there. Someone still transmitting. A ship?..." Jack insisted, though he seemed less convinced as each frequency he tried resulted in squealing static. "Someone else... Some land, somewhere."

"You don't give up, do you?" Ellie said admiringly, kissing Jack on the side of his face through her cracked, dehydrated lips.

They were in the doldrums. The heat from the blazing midday sun overhead glared down onto the boat. The rest of the Tribe took as best shelter as they could, lounging in the shade to conserve their energy.

Apart from Jack and Ellie in the wheelhouse, the others were all taking refuge around the upper deck.

Darryl was trying to entertain Lottie, Sammy and Brady, doing impressions of famous adults from the old days, who Darryl had hero-worshiped in his dreams of becoming an actor. Though neither Lottie, Sammy or Brady knew who Darryl was impersonating, being too young to remember the adult celebrities of the past, they were entertained by the odd voices he was making, the strange expressions on his face. They had difficulty focusing in their state. And there was no enthusiasm in Darryl's performance. He just didn't seem to have the strength. And his twisted facial expressions took on a surreal haunted element, his eyes drained of hope, almost life.

May and Zak were half asleep, leaning on each other for support. May had felt elated, suspecting she might have found a soulmate at last, though she wished this had happened in another place, another time, where she might have had more time to enjoy their growing relationship.

Slade rested his arm on Ruby, her head on his chest as she slept. Stroking her hair tenderly, Slade had enjoyed the renewal of his friendship with Ruby since they embarked on the boat.

He and Ebony still hadn't spoken further about their fallout over Mega's death. Neither had the energy or desire, not wanting to risk conflict with one another - especially in front of the other Tribe members. And not now, when their very survival was at stake. All were intent on conserving their precious life force.

Ruby had kept Slade company the past day or so. Not saying much, just being there, with him. That's what friends were for, wasn't it? It was just that, friendship? Nothing else? Slade couldn't help but feel there might be something more than friendship though on his part. But his thoughts were dominated by the recent loss of his brother. And whether he was also about to confront his own mortality.

Gel seemed to be drifting in and out of semi-consciousness.

Lex was keeping an eye on Ram, who was preoccupied, lost in some secret thought.

Ebony was fast asleep.

But as Trudy stared at her, she wondered if Ebony was actually dead.

Trembling with anxiety, Trudy wiped away tears filling her eyes. She was deeply concerned about Brady but she tried to keep herself calm, holding her emotions in check. She didn't want Brady to see her so upset. The others had tried to keep Trudy's spirits uplifted. To support her. But she knew, there was nothing anyone could do to help. It was just like the days when the adults were wiped out, Trudy worried. Though this time, she was sure it was their turn to face their doom.

Part of her hoped she would succumb before Brady. But another part of her couldn't bear to think of Brady left on her own. Perhaps it would be better for Brady's end to occur first. In Trudy's fragile state of mind, she was beginning to consider if it was her duty as a mother to take back the life she had given her child. To end her suffering.

On the outer deck, Salene once again dangled the fishing line out of the water. They hadn't caught any fish for a couple of days, with none visible in the silent ocean, it felt like even the fish had abandoned them, leaving them to their isolation. Except for a few sharks trailing the little boat. Salene seemed too weak to have noticed the fins protruding on the surface.

It hadn't rained for a while. The last of the water collected by Jack's tarpaulin invention draped on the roof of the boat had been used up earlier that morning.

With no food, no water, it was the hardest part of their voyage since they had left the shore. Everyone was starving... sunburned... dehydrated. It was just a matter of time. Surely they just had a few days left.

Everyone knew it. Though nobody voiced it. But it was like all of the Tribe were mentally preparing for it. Coming to terms with the possibility that they might be experiencing what could be the last few days of their lives. None of them wanted to give up. They weren't ready for the end. But so much of what they faced was out of their hands. If they didn't get food or water soon, they knew deep down they would all perish.

They were all in the same situation, united in adversity. Their fates bound together. The quarrels and disagreements that had so characterised the voyage had now ceased. They had lost energy even for that. Whatever conversations they did have, brief as they were, were ones of encouragement. Not conflict. Support. The stark situation they faced was bringing them all together closely. They may have not had much hope. But they still had each other.

Ram was still a source of irritation to all, however, which he brought about himself. He could never relate to the Mall Rats. His was a different ideology.

Amber glanced at baby Bray fast asleep with Jay cradling Amber's child in his arms, Jay himself deep in sleep on the deck of the trawler. Like Trudy, Amber worried greatly about the future for her own child. As parents themselves, Trudy and Amber had a perspective nobody else could fully appreciate. But where Trudy was a single mother, Amber was glad to have Jay in her life.

With her own survival in jeopardy and that of her son, Amber's thoughts turned once more to Bray. The father of her child. Was he really dead? Or was he out there, somewhere, and had survived? Maybe he had met someone else, like she had with Jay, and began a new life? Whatever the situation, he would always remain precious in her thoughts, her entire being. She would always care for his memory, but Jay was Amber's present life. And her future. If they would only live to see it.

Ram began cackling quietly to himself. He was trying to restrain his giggling but in spite of his efforts, he couldn't help but erupt into manic laughter.

"What's so funny?" Amber asked.

"I was just thinking... Dead men tell no tales," Ram said.

"What the hell's that supposed to mean?" Lex snapped.

"Don't know about you, Lexy-boy, but it looks as if all my secrets will be going with me to my grave. Along with everyone else around here."

"You're pathetic!" Amber exclaimed.

Something suddenly caught Amber's attention out of the corner of her eye.

She turned to look at the ocean - and for a moment thought she was seeing things. Perhaps it was a vision brought on by her weakened physical state.

Amber stared, open eyed, making sure what she saw was real.

"Oh my God!" Amber yelled excitedly, her mouth dry.

"What is it?" Jay awoke with a start, carefully standing up with Amber's child in his arms.

"Everyone! Look!" Amber screamed, delirious, pointing out to the ocean.

And there in the distance, on the horizon, the outline of a massive ship loomed.

CHAPTER SIX

Bray ran for his life, terrified. Panic-driven. He was racing through the thick undergrowth of the forest, trying to keep his balance as he sprinted, stumbling over the twisting tangle of branches and tree roots he sped through.

In the distance he could hear the pursuing group of Eloise's forces. They were shouting out for him. Hunting him down.

Bray and Judd had parted ways soon after they left the compound, thinking that they had more chance to escape by splitting off, hoping to divide the guards tracking them. Bray wondered how Judd was getting on, ducking below a thick tree branch, nearly scraping his head as he hurled past.

Eloise would be furious at his escape, Bray realized. In the time he had gotten to know her, he had been totally unsettled by her vindictiveness and brutality. How one human being could treat another so cruelly, exploit them, he just didn't understand. If he was caught, he didn't expect any mercy. Which only added an extra dimension to the adrenalin pumping through Bray's body as he fought to overcome the fatigue and breathlessness threatening to stop him running on, ever onwards.

Bray had experienced being chased in the city many a time. Be it from Locos, Demon Dogs, The Chosen, or a host of dangerous tribes.

But here, in the forest, Bray was on unknown ground. He had no knowledge of where geographically Eloise's mountain complex was located. Sprinting as fast as he could, he also had no idea of what dangers lay ahead. Whatever it was, Bray only hoped it was a better prospect than the threat posed by Eloise and her guards relentlessly pursuing him.

* * *

On her orders, the guards had themselves split up into several groups and they would catch their prey, Eloise knew. There was nothing Bray or Judd - the traitor - could do to escape their fate.

Eloise and some of the guards were on quad-bikes, daring to hit the thick undergrowth at speed as they tore through the terrain, searching for any sign of Bray or Judd.

Ahead of Eloise another group of security guards used sniffer dogs, following the trail.

And all around, the Zootist' initiates sprawled out through the forest searching for Bray, their 'demi-God'. They were all capable warriors. Manufactured in the image of their master. All chosen for their fighting skills. The sight of so many seemingly cloned figures of Zoot joining the hunt was a chilling and sobering reminder of the 'research' being conducted at the compound.

With the help of the extra personnel scouring the terrain in the shape of the 'Zootists', obsessed with Bray and the legend of his brother, it was just a matter of time, Eloise promised. They would find him. And she would make Bray pay for his deception of her.

In the event they were unsuccessful, Eloise, ever calculating, had already devised an extravagant excuse to give to her superiors. Judd was certainly to blame. But she would embellish that she was attacked by him and Bray during the escape. But at least she could still manufacture the bloodline and DNA of Bray, even if it meant her becoming impregnated by someone else. How could anyone ever know?

* * *

Up ahead, Bray realized a group of guards were gaining on him. He could hear the tree branches and vines snapping as his pursuers closed in. And he could hear the sound of the 'Zootists' chanting his name, then the name of his brother, Zoot.

Bray was all consumed with adrenalin. Fear. This was madness. Crazy.

The sound of sniffer dogs howling and barking excitedly, getting closer, ever nearer, meant Bray didn't have long before his scent gave him away.

Bray had only one chance...

* * *

Judd was exhausted. He felt as if his legs couldn't carry him any further. But he had to go on. He knew helping Bray escape wouldn't be tolerated. His betrayal would be punished. He pushed himself. Don't give up, don't stop.

Behind, the revving of the quadbike engines grew louder and Judd knew he needed a miracle to avoid being captured.

Making an instant decision, he began to climb a tall tree, hoping it would offer a form of protection, a place to hide. Perhaps the pursuers would be so busy looking around, they wouldn't think to look up.

* * *

In another part of the forest, the guards with the tracking dogs smiled leeringly. The dogs were on the trail, tails wagging enthusiastically as the pursuit went on, surely now nearing its end.

"We've got him!" one of the guards called out as a sniffer dog barked out at a tree, altering its master.

The hunting party swarmed around the base of the trunk.

"Got you!" the main guard shouted, the dogs yelping, teeth snarled.

Another guard pointing, noticed something up in the bough of the branch.

The main guard stared in the direction indicated, looking forward to seeing Bray - or Judd's fearful expression.

He bellowed in frustration.

Instead of either, all the main guard could see was Bray's shirt, tied to a branch, blowing in the breeze.

* * *

Bray was close enough to hear the guards' shouts and curses of disappointment. He was glad he had the quick thinking to leave a trace of his scent behind as a decoy for the sniffer dogs.

Onwards he raced, wondering how long the forest would continue, what lay ahead. At least the forest offered some form of visual protection, the thick foliage obfuscating Bray, keeping him hidden from his pursuers.

Bray nearly lost his footing again, tripping over a thick fallen branch.

He had to keep going. The guards wouldn't catch him, he vowed, as the sniffer dogs resumed their pursuit.

* * *

Eloise screeched her vehicle to a halt, a cloud of dust and twigs flying as the tires skidded across the ground.

"One of them's around here somewhere!" she shouted, her icy blue eyes manic, obsessed with revenge, realizing the howling dogs were onto something.

Eloise smiled. She had him. Question was, which one?

In the tree above, Judd looked down on Eloise. He dared not breathe, make a sound, his chest heaving after his exertion. He closed his eyes, clutching the branch that he sat on, hoping to blend into the tree itself, becoming invisible, his heart racing with fear.

Casting her gaze upwards to the huge tree, Eloise was thrilled by what she saw.

"Well, well well...," she giggled jubilantly.

Judd felt as if he was staring into the personification of all his nightmarish fears, now come true.

"You did well to escape, Judd," Eloise shouted, congratulating him, the guards around her dismounting their quad-bikes, getting ready to reel in their prey.

Eloise indicated. A guard tossed an AK-47 to her, which she caught.

"I surrender!" Judd yelled in growing panic.

"Oh, I don't think so, Judd. No can do!"

Eloise took the safety latch off, aiming the weapon in Judd's direction like she was targeting a shooting game with an electronic gun she used to play as a girl in the arcades.

She grinned, taking careful aim.

"Noooooooooo!" Judd screamed.

"Yes! This bullet has your name on it. Game over, Judd!"

* * *

Bray stopped running, distracted as he heard the explosive sound of gunfire suddenly crack and Judd's agonized screams in the distance.

The forest erupted as flocks of birds quickly took flight, their wings beating rapidly as they soared to the sky, squawking in protest at being disturbed.

Bray said a silent prayer for Judd. He hoped the ending had been quick, that he hadn't suffered. That Judd was now at peace.

But hearing engines being revved ominously, signalled that the hunt was far from over.

He didn't have long, Bray knew all too well, and he sprinted off, a renewed sense of urgency in his stride. He had to keep running - but to where?

CHAPTER SEVEN

Ellie looked up. It was huge. The massive bulk of the cargo ship Amber had first noticed cast its shadow over the little boat that had been their home for so long, while Jack carefully did his best to manoeuvre the trawler, drawing it alongside the giant vessel.

"I love you!" Ellie cried out to Jack, giving him one more look before she took her turn. If these were the last words she would ever say, they seemed appropriate, giving her comfort as well as courage.

Jack dared to look away from the cargo ship for a fleeting second, nodding to Ellie, giving her an encouraging smile.

"I'll see you there!" he called out from the trawler's wheelhouse.

Given a renewed surge of confidence from Jack's assurance, Ellie prepared herself, Jack carefully steering the trawler a few inches closer, the gap between her and the container ship closing. Ellie climbed onto the roof of the wheelhouse where Darryl was crouched, balancing himself with the motion. He had volunteered to remain to steady everyone. The elevation of the wheelhouse providing a better 'launchpad' to bridge the difference in height between the roof of the trawler and the open deck of the cargo vessel.

Ellie took a deep breath, then leaped.

The Tribe had decided to head towards the cargo ship to see if anyone might be able to help them, using the last of their fuel, the engines of the little trawler coughing and spluttering as Jack had earlier steered the boat towards the mysterious vessel. Yet despite calling out for help as the two boats see-sawed side by side, it seemed as if the cargo ship was deserted. Nobody had responded to their shouts.

Realizing they couldn't stay on the trawler forever, now it was out of food and water supplies - and very likely was to run out of fuel - the Tribe quickly resolved that they had to take their chances on the container ship. Hopefully, they would stand more likelihood of survival on it than the trawler.

Ellie gripped at the safety railing of the mammoth container vessel.

Slade and Lex pulled Ellie up by her arms, hauling her onto the open deck.

"Well, look what we've caught here," Lex joked.

"Thanks," Ellie smiled appreciatively.

So far, most of the Tribe had made it. Jay had been the first to make the leap of faith and had rigged some ropes, bound as an extra safety for the others to cling to in case they missed the railing.

Amber was so relieved that destiny had played an opportune card. She dreaded to think of the Tribe trying to cross the gap from the trawler boat to the cargo ship if the waves had been rougher. Thankfully, although the wind was picking up, it hadn't affected the evacuation from the trawler so far.

It was hard enough as it was for Jack to manoeuvre the tiny ship alongside the mammoth vessel. They didn't have any ladders for the transition. It was just their tired and exhausted bodies they had to rely upon to physically traverse the distance between the trawler and the container ship. Boarding at the open deck level. The prospect of leaving the trawler had given them all a renewed sense of hope, a surge of energy. They were nearly all safe, Amber thought, with two more to go.

"See you on the other side," Darryl shouted to Jack, struggling to keep the two vessels close enough, doing his utmost to minimize the distance between them. Jack wondered if Darryl was referring to the afterlife rather than the huge vessel.

Darryl jumped - and just made it. Slade and Lex's arms ached as they pulled Darryl up over the safety railings, onto the deck, massive metal containers stacked all around them.

One more to go, Amber thought nervously, her stomach churning with tension.

So far it had been a miracle they had all made it across, Amber felt. The most difficult challenge had involved Brady and baby Bray. Trudy had been hysterical when she had lifted up Brady, pushing her with all her might, to the safe arms of the others who had already made it, reaching out toward the child from the deck of the cargo ship.

And Amber had felt the intense stress of the moment when she made her own leap, her little son clutching to her. They had coiled a safety rope around each of the youngsters as an extra precaution if they fell. Baby Bray had been also tied to Amber in a makeshift harness made from the tarpaulin that served as Jack's improvised rain collector. They were all safe, so far. But now it was Jack's turn. And Ellie couldn't bear to look, comforted by Sammy who noticed a shadowy shape in the water of what he knew was a shark and turned Ellie away, hoping she wouldn't catch a glimpse.

Inside the little trawler, Jack only had a few moments, aware as he cast his eyes towards the back of the trawler, its engines coughing and heaving, that the precious fuel was running out. Jack had volunteered to be the last to go, feeling he was the best helmsman of them all, given his innate technical skills. He just hoped he had made the right choice. But all the tribe had confidence in him. He had always been the tribe's 'Mister Fixit', able to turn his hand to all things mechanical.

One last time, Jack thought, idling the engine of the trawler, getting one final spurt of power to help him steer the little boat, inching it closer, closer, to the cargo ship, the two vessels almost touching.

"Come on, you little boat," Jack urged, getting in 'tune' with the trawler. Mechanical objects, as well as computers, almost had their own personality to Jack and he exhorted the trawler not to let him down, not now, when they'd been through so much together.

Judging the trawler was as close as he could make it without causing a collision, Jack let go of the wheel and climbed onto the roof.

From the cargo ship, Ellie jumped up and down nervously, hardly bearing to watch for signs of her loved one. And the others all watched breathlessly.

Now the trawler began to inch away from the cargo ship, with nobody left to steer it, to keep it level.

Jack gritted his teeth. He was going to have to give it all he had. He stepped back a few paces, then sprinted, leaping, taking flight across the divide, soaring from the little trawler towards the mammoth cargo vessel. It felt like everything was in slow motion, as if he was flying. He was all too aware of the growing gap that had now opened up, his arms flailing to reach out to the vessel, sensing the distance widening, like an invisible force was trying to pull him down into the unforgiving ocean below.

Ellie screamed. Jack wasn't going to make it.

Jack felt himself descending, sure he'd mistimed his jump. As he desperately reached out, extending his arm, in that split second, he knew he had got it all wrong, it was too late.

And then it was over.

Jack's arm nearly snapped as he felt the strong grip on him, quickly reversing his momentum. Jack clattered into the side of the ship, pain searing through his body as all his weight concentrated on his shoulder, his feet dangling, gravity trying to pull him into the watery abyss.

Slade called out a primal yell of fury, urging himself to hang on as he leaned over the side of the railing, every tendon in his body aching, struggling to grip Jack's arm.

Lex and Jay held onto Slade's legs to stop Slade from himself falling over the edge of the vessel.

Tears streamed down Ellie's face. She couldn't take the anguish, and the others around her could also hardly bear to watch either.

Jack managed to get a foothold into the safety ropes Jay had rigged, propelling him upwards.

With a mighty heave, Lex and Jay pulled Slade towards them, Slade continuing to bellow in determination.

And there, in Slade's strong arms, Ellie and the others could see that Slade had saved Jack, who was now on the deck, shaking in fear, Ellie racing over to give him a hug.

"You always... been this good at catch?" Jack quipped to Slade, trying to make light of things, though he was visibly shocked by his close escape.

"Oh, Jack, thank God you're okay," Ellie said in relief.

"Thank Slade, you mean," Jack replied, looking at Slade in all sincerity, cradling his arm Slade had been holding, hoping it hadn't been dislocated.

"We all owe you, Jack. If it hadn't been for you steering the trawler - none of us would have made it onto here," Slade responded.

Jack looked around at the Tribe, gazing at him with a mixture of concern, gratitude and relief.

"So I'm a hero," Jack smiled, in mock self-adoration.

"My hero," Ellie beamed through tears, kissing Jack lovingly on the lips.

Amber was so grateful they had all made it. Just. But made it to where? What exactly was this ship?

She watched the little trawler boat drifting away on the current, taking all the memories of what they had experienced. Now there were many questions that needed to be answered.

* * *

The Tribe decided to split up into two groups to explore the massive ship that fate had put in their way. They had boarded roughly in the middle of the vessel, with several hundred feet of hull going each direction either side.

Amber suggested that one group go to the bow to examine the open deck and metal containers stacked high, while the second group headed to the towering structure at the aft of the ship which Amber suspected was the crew living quarters, and where the bridge would no doubt be located at the very top, beneath the satellite dishes and golf ball-shaped radar visible on the roof.

Just what was this vessel doing here, out in the middle of nowhere? Was there anybody onboard? And if so, were they friendly or hostile? Was there any food? Any useful supplies they could use?

The wind had begun to pick up and it roared at the front of the ship, howling like a banshee, as the first group picked its way cautiously through the gaps in the containers piled high all around them.

"It's like being in a big maze," May whispered, giving voice to her thoughts, peering up at the containers.

"Wonder what's inside them?" Zak questioned, patting the outside of one.

Some had United Nations logos displayed on them. Just what was the cargo being carried inside?

Slade was on edge, treading carefully in case they bumped into anyone. Surely the crew of the ship, if there were any, wouldn't take kindly to the Mall Rats inviting themselves aboard.

"Relax, Slade," Ruby insisted, putting her hand on Slade's strong arm. "I think the only people here are us."

"Better to be safe," Slade countered, his eyes vigilant for any movement, any sign of life.

Slade and Ruby rounded a corner, peering ahead, the wind whistling between the metal containers.

"Wait!" Ram said in an undertone, putting his finger to his mouth to signal the others to be quiet. "I can hear something," he continued, a look of panic on his face.

* * *

At the back of the cargo ship, Amber and Jay led the other group as they carefully made their way towards the main accommodation structure, treading cautiously through the walkway between the metal containers stacked highly each side.

"Think anyone's here?" Salene asked, looking around nervously, the wind increasing in strength, making her shiver in cold, as well as fear.

"We'll find out - one way or the other," Jay answered.

The ship's hull groaned and creaked as it rode through the waves, the ocean gathering strength, pitching the ship up and down like a massive pendulum.

"So far so good," Ebony said, studying the tall accommodation structure they had now reached. It must have been four or five stories tall above the outer deck.

"Hellooo?" Gel called out, as she, too, looked up at the crew quarters.

"Shut it, Gel!" Ebony ordered. "We don't know who's in there! Duh!"

"We don't know if anyone's in there," Lex retorted. "And nobody tells Gel to shut up - except me."

"Pig!" Gel blurted to Lex, sticking her tongue out, making a face at Lex.

"Please, cut it out!" Amber implored, hoping to focus the others.

"Look... up there," Trudy said, squinting, distracted by the sun reflecting from the windows of the accommodation structure looming above. "I think... I can see someone."

* * *

At the front of the vessel Ram was absolutely terrified. He stood, trying his best to hide against the side of one of the stacks of metal containers. The others froze, eyes wide open, wondering what - or who - Ram had noticed.

Slade tensed, anticipating someone to leap out from behind one of the containers at any moment. If there was going to be a fight, he'd be ready.

The wind shrieked, the creaking steel of the cargo ship hull reverberated as the waves struck the bow. Adrenalin coursed through the group's veins, all gripped by anxiety, their senses heightened.

"Booooooo!!!" Ram suddenly shouted, leaping forward, causing the others to nearly jump out of their skins in fright.

"Ram, you idiot, what the hell are you doing?!" Ruby shouted, gasping for breath.

"You nearly gave me a heart attack!" May protested.

Ram burst out laughing, enjoying his little trick. "I got ya! All of ya! You should have seen the look on your faces!"

"Is he always like this?" Zak stared disdainfully at Ram, cracking up manically at his practical joke.

"On a good day. On a bad day he can only get worse. A lot worse," May shook her head in disapproval.

"Was that really necessary?" Slade asked, clearly irritated as much as all the others.

"Oh, come on, Slade-y boy. You gotta admit. That was funny!" Ram grinned gleefully.

Slade stared Ram in the eye.

"Well done, Ram. If there is anyone else on board, you'd better hope they think so. Because your little joke might have just alerted them to our presence!"

Ram's chuckling faded as he appreciated Slade's words and realized he might just have made a grave mistake.

* * *

About fifty feet up above the outer deck, Amber held tightly onto the rails of the fire escape they had climbed, taking them to the top floor of the accommodation structure tower. With the ship now heaving in the waves, she felt dizzy, engulfed by a sense of vertigo as she looked down at Darryl and Salene far below, the two of them looking after the little ones as Amber and the others reached the top of the emergency outside stairwell.

They were now at the bridge. It was difficult to see inside due to the angle of the sun shining brightly, a white reflection of light dazzling off the windows, though that didn't stop Trudy in particular from staring at the bridge, sure someone was inside.

Jay tried the doorway to the bridge leading in from the outside fire escape. It wouldn't budge.

"It's locked," he pointed out, trying the handle again.

"Leave it to me," Lex suggested, taking a step back down the fire escape. "I always travel with my - 'keys'."

Suddenly Lex charged forth like a bull, bashing into the door with all his force, shouldering it open. Then he collapsed in a heap to the floor from his own momentum.

Jay took a combat stance and jumped through the doorway.

Amber followed Trudy in.

Trudy stopped as soon as she stepped through the doorway, her eyes wide with deep fear. And screamed, petrified.

* * *

Slade and the rest of his group heard Trudy's cries and raced towards the back of the boat as fast as they could. The others were in trouble - and they needed help.

"Up there," Salene pointed to the top of the accommodation tower structure as Slade raced past, clambering up the fire escape stairs. Salene and Darryl stayed put on the outside deck with Amber's son and Trudy's daughter. They had promised Amber they wouldn't move, in case Amber and the others encountered danger up in the bridge. Salene's face was contorted in worry. She wondered what was going on up there but did her best to comfort Brady, who was weeping into her shoulder, worried at hearing her mother's distraught scream.

Slade raced through the doorway into the bridge, with Jack and the others not far behind him.

Skidding to a halt, he first noticed Trudy passed out, laying on the floor of the bridge.

Anxiously looking around, Slade saw Amber, Jay and Lex, startled and unsure, recoiling from what Trudy had noticed.

There, in front of them all, sat the adult crew of the cargo ship. Or at least what was left of their rotting, skeletal remains.

CHAPTER EIGHT

Bray's feet and legs ached as they pounded the ground, his heart beating rapidly. His entire body felt like it was going to give up due to exhaustion but Bray's sheer power of will kept him going, running further, pushing him on. And on.

He wondered if Eloise was still after him. He hadn't been aware of any guards in pursuit or heard the quad-bikes, the sound of the sniffer tracking dogs, the 'Zootists', for some time now.

The forest he had been fleeing through was vast, the undergrowth thick. Who knew what lay around the corner, past the next group of trees. He was constantly vigilant, ever attentive to the slightest sound or visual clue signifying if danger was approaching.

Bray hadn't slept for a couple of nights. He believed the worst thing to do was to stop running and make a camp somewhere. If he fell asleep, he was so tired he worried he wouldn't wake up, wouldn't notice Eloise's guards moving in on him, if indeed they still were hunting him down. He couldn't risk that. Stopping wasn't an option.

Filthy, Bray had earlier covered himself in dirt, rubbing plants and mud all over him. He hoped the conflicting smells would be a way of distracting the sniffer dogs from his scent.

Tired and hungry, Bray survived - just - on nothing more than handfuls of berries grabbed from plants. He looked around, hoping to find something he could eat.

Suddenly, the forest began to clear. There were fewer trees, and Bray stopped running as he reached the boundary.

The terrain was opening up. Ahead lay nothing but barren wilderness, a bleak looking landscape - with no cover, nowhere to hide.

Had the area been subject to a natural phenomenon? Some kind of disaster? It certainly looked as if it had, with only charred tree stumps remaining. Had there been a fire? Or was it due to a clearance of the vast area by man at some point in time? And if so - why?

Confronted by the choice of heading back or taking his chances in the wilderness that lay ahead, Bray decided the best thing he could do to further his escape was to put as much distance as he could between him and the forest.

After taking a few precious seconds to catch his breath, Bray sprinted forward towards the open barren land, covering the ground much quicker than before, no forest and myriad of trees to slow his progress this time.

He wondered just exactly where he was. What lay ahead. And if the danger from Eloise and her forces was still lurking behind. Fighting overwhelming fatigue, Bray just hoped he could keep going long enough not to find out.

* * *

Back in the forest, Eloise examined Bray in the crosshairs of her binocular lenses. She could see that he was stumbling. He looked weak, in a terrible state.

"Should we go after him?" one of the guards asked, almost afraid to question Eloise or pre-empt her orders - but was also clearly afraid and uneasy to continue with the pursuit.

"No need. He's in the 'wasteland zone'," Eloise replied.

The 'Zootists' and guards gathered around her, gazing intently, as she lowered the binoculars from her eyes.

She was preoccupied, deep in thought, her blue eyes sparkling in the sun.

"It seems our master, Bray, has gone to join his brother, Zoot - in the afterlife!" Eloise cried out.

"Zoot, Zoot, Zoot!" The Zootists erupted into a frenzy of chanting at the news, circling around Eloise, some bowing to offer their allegiance, displaying their loyalty.

Basking in the adulation, Eloise lifted the binoculars to her eyes again for one last look at her former prisoner, racing off into the wilderness. He must be at least two or three hours away.

"So long, my dear Bray," Eloise spoke to herself smugly.

Perhaps revenge came in different shapes, she considered, and this is how it was meant to be. Out there in the 'wastelands', Eloise knew Bray didn't stand a chance. Not if he became contaminated. Bray's suffering would be slow, drawn out. Delicious. There were some punishments worse than even she could devise. And the best thing of all, she reasoned, was that Bray didn't even know what he was getting himself into. He had no chance whatsoever of survival.

CHAPTER NINE

The Mall Rats stood on the open deck of the cargo ship, the vast stacks of metal containers all around them, their contents still a mystery - as was what had happened to the ship's crew, causing their demise.

The crew had been laid out on the deck. Their remains covered in blankets and linen found in the cupboards and cabins of the accommodation tower structure.

Amber thought of Bray suddenly. She wished he was here. He was so wise, philosophical. He would have known what to say in this situation. But now it was up to Amber. To preside over the funeral of the ship's crew.

Following the gruesome discovery in the bridge, the rest of the accommodation quarters had been explored and Amber and the others were convinced that there was no one else alive on board the ship except themselves.

A few more bodies had been found, lying in beds inside cabins, another in the kitchen galley. The bodies couldn't be left there forever so it was partly a practical decision to bury the dead. More than that though, Amber felt they owed it to the crew, whoever they were, to give them a dignified send-off, and to pay their respects.

Some of the others looked at Amber, waiting for her to speak, while the rest stared at the shrouded bodies before them, contemplating their thoughts.

Salene had her arm around Trudy in an encouraging hug. Trudy fought back tears. She had been freaked out by the discovery of the dead. Really spooked. It reminded her so much of the old times, when the adults first passed away. Many memories, painful to her core, flooded back as she looked at the covered remains of the crew, images of her parents and family flashing before her eyes. Though she was showing the most visible signs of emotional distress, she was not alone - everyone was feeling much the same as her, thinking similar thoughts, encountering the ghosts of the past.

"We stand here to pay our respects to those who have gone before," Amber began. "We do not know who they were. Where they were from. But one thing was for sure. They would have been someone's son... or daughter. Perhaps parents themselves. Brothers. Sisters. Whatever happened to them - we hope that they are now at peace and I would ask you to all join me in a moment's silence before committing their souls..."

The wind drifting in from the ocean began to pick up, howling in gusts through the gaps in the metal containers stacked throughout the mammoth vessel. It was as if the ship was haunted by an unknown presence, causing Trudy to steal uneasy looks around. And she wasn't the only one. Some of the others, including even Lex, were just as uneasy.

This was such an unusual place for a funeral, Amber thought, waiting for the wind to subside so she could continue. They had all endured loss, said their goodbyes to loved ones, in many different places back on land. And now they were doing so again. Amber hadn't expected to ever encounter adults. Now in a way they had to bury the past all over once more.

"Everything has its beginnings and endings," Amber went on. "Life is no different. We are all born. And we all, one day, will meet our end. But we live on forever, in memory. And though we didn't know the crew of this ship... they have touched us and reminded us never to forget the adults. All those from our past, who were special to us. Who will always be a part of us. Out of the ruins of the old, we will create a new future. We owe it to them, to those who have gone before. But most of all, we owe it to ourselves..."

Amber looked at her son, a symbol of hope for the future, being cradled in Jay's strong arms.

"Life will continue. It will endure. There will be challenges to meet. But we'll face them. Head on. We promise you this - whoever you were," Amber addressed the covered crew members. "Your passing will not have been in vain. The old times, the adults - none of it will be forgotten. We'll pass down the stories of the past to our children. We will ensure there is a future. Somehow. Humanity will survive. May God bless you. And I'm sure I speak for everyone when I say our only hope now is that you all rest in peace."

Amber nodded to the others. One by one, the covered corpses were carefully lowered over the side of the ship and dropped into the ocean below.

Stepping forward, Amber helped lift the last of the crew members, grabbing hold of the linen shroud. She thought of the others from the past she had buried. Her parents. Her best friend, Dal. And her heart ached for those she had lost. Her lover, Bray.

Life was so precious, beautiful. As the final crew member was released overboard, Amber vowed that somehow, for the sake of her son, for the others, for her, they would get through this. They would survive. She would do everything to make sure of that, give all that she had so that they wouldn't end up suffering the same fate of the crew. Their destiny wouldn't be to end their days on the vast cargo ship.

Or so she had hoped.

* * *

It would take several days for the Tribe to explore every inch of the container ship. It was that massive in scale. They had checked every cabin, store room and most compartments on all the decks but would need to assess all the containers and contents, to confirm that there was indeed nobody else on the ship. Just them.

Then they would need to identify some kind of a plan. And to see if Jack and perhaps even Ram could work out a way to navigate the vessel to a destination, whatever that destination might be.

The issue now was to settle in to daily life in their new home. It felt strange at first. The living quarters, in the five story accommodation tower structure, still had the personal remnants of the crew, with everything left in the same state since each item was last touched. It was like the Marie Celeste, seeing the chairs, the cutlery, dishes left in the kitchen galley... and clothes hung in cupboards, almost like time had been frozen since the adult days, with everything unchanged.

Compared to the little trawler that the Tribe had survived in for so many weeks, the enormous cargo ship was like being in a floating palace. Now, everybody had their own bed. There were more than enough cabins to go around. Just so much space.

Settling inside their cabin, May and Zak were putting their own personal touches to their temporary new home. Zak was making the beds while May was inside the en suite bathroom.

It was no secret what their priority was. Being alone. They were now a couple. So rather than having their own individual cabins, they were going to share one.

She looked a mess, May thought, examining her reflection in the bathroom mirror. No one had washed for weeks. They all stank, filth all over them, their hair mottled. May could hardly bear to look at herself. But she took comfort that she aroused something in Zak. Not just sexually. It was clear that he was also interested in her as a person.

Twisting the tap on the shower, May hoped that by some miracle, the ship would have some running water. She heard the pipes connected to the bathroom creaking and grinding. Nothing. Not a drop came out of the shower.

"Is that normal - you making so many noises going to the bathroom?" Zak quipped, calling out from the bedroom as he made the beds.

"Ha, ha. It isn't me," May smiled, twisting the tap on the shower further clockwise, disappointment showing on her face as her hopes were dashed.

Suddenly, water exploded out of the shower head, hitting May in the face. She yelped out.

Zak rushed in to see May leaping up and down for joy in the shower, as cold, clear water flowed all over.

"You never told me you wear your clothes in the shower either," Zak beamed as he cast an admiring glance at the wet garments clinging to her shapely body.

* * *

The morale of the Tribe soared with the discovery that the massive ship still had running water. Everybody felt so much better having taken a bath, washing their clothes.

And it wasn't just the water. In the kitchen galley, they discovered that the storage cupboards were stacked with tins of preserved food.

"This feels like Christmas!" Ellie said elated, opening a tin excitedly. Most of the tins had Chinese writing on their labels so nobody knew exactly what was inside. Ellie squealed in delight as she realized she had a can of peaches. "Fruit! Oh my God! Fruit!"

"At least we won't go hungry," Ebony sighed gratefully, holding up a tin to the others. "Anyone like fish?"

"How'd you know that?" Darryl asked in admiration. "I didn't know you could speak Chinese."

"There's a lot you don't know about me, Darryl," Ebony said, her demeanour cool, pointing to a large picture of a fish on the can in her hand, tapping it. "What do you think would be in there? A banana?"

"There's no need to be sarcastic," Darryl shrugged, his pride wounded.

"I hear there's some food around here," Slade said, entering the kitchen galley, with Ruby not far behind. Ruby and Slade had obviously just both had showers in their respective cabins and got cleaned up, Ruby fiddling with her hair, the two of them arriving by coincidence at more or less the same time from different parts of the ship.

Ebony wondered if they had both had anything as an 'aperitif' before arriving for their main meal.

She and Slade still hadn't had a chance to reconcile with each other over their falling out about the death of Slade's brother.

"We've got piles of food," Lottie spluttered between mouthfuls of tinned spaghetti, tomato sauce all over her face.

"You wouldn't believe how hungry I am," Ruby smiled.

"I'll bet," Ebony scoffed, giving a disdainful look.

"This is delicious!" Sammy said, cramming chocolate liquid into his mouth.

But Ebony ignored them all. She was far too knowing in the male female game not to pick up the soupçon of flirtation between Ruby and Slade, who was feeding Ruby a mouthful of the chocolate dessert.

Throwing the can of fish at Darryl, Ebony snarled.

"Suddenly, I've lost my appetite!"

And she stormed out of the galley.

* * *

Out on the open decks, Salene was assisting Amber, Lex, Gel and Jay, trying to solve the mystery of what cargo the ship was carrying. They had found some crowbars and were using them to wedge loose the doors to the metal containers.

Earlier, they had discovered a few of the containers housed medical supplies inside, with untold amounts of bandages, wound dressings, antiseptic, paracetamol and other pain killers.

It was like providence had provided them with a bounty, something to help them in their time of need, Amber thought. She was also touched by the irony that the medical supplies hadn't been enough to help the adult crew originally on board.

Gel was ecstatic. She had personally discovered a container stacked full of toiletries, with thousands of bottles of shampoo, liquid soap and shower wash.

"I think I've died and gone to Heaven!" Gel said.

"Stand back - or you just might if this door smashes into that pretty little body of yours," Lex commanded as he braced himself, with the crowbar stuck in a gap in the metal container, Gel giddily ambling around him.

"How do you think I should have my hair?" Gel asked dreamily, imagining all the ways she could impress Lex and look good.

"It might be an idea to try and keep it on your head," Lex replied, prying the container door open.

Inside, it was full to the brim of more preserved food, with boxes stacked, hardly room to spare. There had to be thousands of tins of food in that one container alone.

"There's just one problem... deciding what to have for dinner," Lex said.

"Have you always got nothing but food on your mind?" Gel teased.

"Oh I don't know. I can think of something else I might be interested in tonight," Lex winked to Gel.

"Then I'll go and make myself look prettier," Gel beamed, scampering off toward the accommodation tower structure where the cabins were, her arms laden with toiletries.

Lex watched her go. She was sure scatty, he smiled. But he found her attractive enough. And she might help him pass the time rather than face a long, lonely night.

Right now though he was thinking about the mysteries of the cargo ship. So far they had discovered a lifetime of food and supplies on it. But why? Where had it been going? Where were they now? And what had killed the crew?

Amber and Jay shared the same concerns. There were so many questions. And they just hoped they would come up with some answers.

* * *

An hour later up in the bridge, Jay entered, carrying a tray full of processed tinned meat, cold beans and canned vegetables, laid out on three plates.

"I've brought you lunch, one plate each," Jay said, putting the tray down on one of the empty swivel chairs. "It's not much but it's the best I can come up with."

"Not much? It's a feast," Amber smiled, tucking into the meal appreciatively.

She had gone to the bridge to meet up with Jack and Ram, who were examining the controls and instrumentation.

"Did you wash your hands?" Ram asked warily.

"For you, Ram, always," Jay replied, well aware of Ram's germ fetish.

"Thanks," Jack said, putting up a spoonful of cold creamed corn up to his mouth - which dribbled down his shirt, to his bemusement.

"So how's it all going?" Jay asked.

"Everything seems so complicated," Jack answered between mouthfuls. "It's like being on the bridge of an alien spaceship. We're still trying to work out what each symbol means - none of it is in English."

"I have utmost faith in you, Jack," Amber said.

"What about me?" Ram cut in, clearly offended.

"That all depends. On the results. What you can contribute."

Every dial and control panel in the bridge was written in Chinese. And compared to the little trawler with its simple helm and gear to throttle the engines up or down, this was far more complex, Jack explained. There were so many dials and symbols and he didn't know exactly what they all did.

"But you still think you'll be able to figure it out?" Amber asked, the tone of doubt obvious.

"I don't know about Jack. But arr, me hearty. Shiver me timbers. Ram'll succeed alright. And we'll be back home again before ye know it!" Ram said.

"Maybe we don't want to return, Ram - remember?" Amber pointed out.

"How could I forget," Ram scoffed. "But I'm warning you, I'm not used to taking orders from anyone, let alone landlubbers forcing me to live on the high seas."

"Please, Ram - no more pirate speak," Jack pleaded. Ram knew it irritated others and he was always more than happy to indulge his mischievous side.

"Then let's try some - geek speak," he considered Jack, as if throwing down the gauntlet.

"You're something else, Ram. You really are," Amber said. "There's no time for power struggles - or competition."

"With my brain," Ram replied, supreme confidence in his manner as he pointed at his head, "my special brain - and Jack's help, we'll work it out eventually. We just have to be careful. We don't want to press the wrong button and lower the anchor or something. Or we could be in the same position as we were on the trawler. Stuck in the middle of a vast ocean with nowhere to go."

The last sentence was a clear dig at Amber.

She didn't take the bait. But decided that it might be to everyone's advantage to further nourish the competitive spirit between Jack and Ram. She was fully aware of Jack's natural abilities. And as much as she loathed Ram, she was aware that where Jack had an aptitude for all things mechanical, as well as computers, Ram was an experienced and talented programmer. Surely between them they could work out all the systems on the bridge.

"I could steer the trawler but this," Jack pointed all around him. "I mean, look at the size of it. It's on a completely different scale."

Jay and Amber appreciated the difficulty of the task, with the mammoth length of the container ship stretching out the front windows of the bridge for several hundred feet ahead of them.

"That has to be the dial showing the wind speed, shipmate," Ram said, pointing at one of the control panels.

"I don't think it's just the wind speed. I think it's something more to do with the strength of the currents," Jack said.

"Don't doubt my intelligence," Ram snapped.

"Oh - and it's alright for you to doubt mine, I suppose. I never thought you could be so stupid," Jack replied.

Jay glanced at Amber and cast a slight smile. The logic in her trying to pit Jack and Ram together in a technical battle might have motivated them both to get a quick result in understanding all the charts, maps and instrumentation on the bridge but if they weren't careful, it might just fuel a bitter argument and them falling out.

"Settle down guys," Jay said. "You've got to try and work together - right, Amber?"

Amber didn't reply. She was focused on a journal she had discovered and was now flipping through the pages. It was written in English - and what it had to say was mind blowing.

"Did you call me stupid?" Ram bellowed to Jack.

"Yes. Right now you're being stupid," Jack argued.

"Amber - can you tell Jack to stop calling me names?" Ram asked. But Amber ignored him, preoccupied by the journal. "Amber!?" Ram called out, insisting he would be heard. "The only name I will accept is - brilliant!"

"Come on, guys. Let it go, will you?" Jay said, crossing to Amber.

"What is it?" he asked her.

Amber snapped out of her reverie, her eyes wide open in wonder. She shook her head as if dazed, trying to take it all in, absorbing what she had read.

"Is everything alright?" Jay questioned, noting Amber's uneasy demeanour.

"I'm not sure," Amber replied, indicating the journal in her hand.

* * *

"My name is Doctor Jane Gideon..." Amber began, reading aloud from the journal she had found. The others had been summoned to the bridge and were now listening intently, desperate to know what Amber had discovered, except for Lottie and Sammy, who were in one of the cabins babysitting Trudy's daughter and Amber's son.

"Aren't you gonna start with Once Upon a Time?" Lex chirped up, chuckling at his own sense of humour, the others hushing him in response, telling him to be quiet.

Amber gave Lex a look that said all that she thought about his joke.

She cleared her throat, and continued.

"... I'm a Lieutenant, one of the medical personnel on the USS Theodore Roosevelt, part of the United Nations Emergency Task Force, Pacific Fleet. I have been helicoptered in to the Chinese merchant vessel, Jzhao Li, and will be recording my notes on my investigation in this journal in case I need to refer to my findings. The Captain of the Jzhao Li had radioed for immediate medical help. So my team and I have been deployed to assist. The Jzhao Li is carrying invaluable supplies which will be crucial to the success of the rendezvous and it is imperative the ship proceed.

So far I have examined all the crew. The engineers have shown symptoms of the pandemic sweeping the world but none of the other crew are infected. Yet. I have recommended the engineers be quarantined. Also that the results of our findings be marked classified."

"Classified?" Salene asked. "That's odd."

It wasn't exactly a secret that the 'virus' had spread as an ominous pandemic around the entire world.

"Assuming she is referring to the virus," Amber replied.

"What do you mean - there was something else?" Lex asked, as confused and concerned as were all the others.

"Could be. I don't exactly know. What follows next seems to be measuring the health of each of the crew, recording their medical records," Amber said, flicking through some of the pages in the journal. "Here we go," Amber said to herself, finding the spot she had been looking for. "This is another entry a few days later."

She continued reading aloud.

"Sadly the engineers have passed away. Predictably succumbing to R18SYT. Which is accelerating within its mutation. So ends my observations of them in this journal. May they rest in peace. I will request evacuation for post mortem study back at Base 12."

"Base 12? Wonder where that was?" Slade pondered.

"Probably near Base 11," Gel said, causing the others to exchange frustrated glances at her.

Jay couldn't help but notice Ram's expression clouding.

"Any idea?" he asked.

"Not a clue," Ram responded.

"Go on, Amber. Keep reading," Ram urged.

"As for the rest of the crew, they are now displaying symptoms and we are all suffering. Myself included. The main mystery to me is how this is spreading when the engineers had been isolated 180 degrees north, 27 degrees south. I am referring, of course, to the survival grid identified through the global initiative rather than any nautical bearing.

The pattern emerging seems to illustrate the diagnosis and treatment originally identified to be inadequate. And our separation from the rest of the Task Force continues. We are isolated, as with the other ships that have now been infected. So many questions, but so little time. God knows how much longer we have left before we, too, succumb..."

"Suddenly I don't think it was such a good idea coming on board this ship," Gel said, gripped by fear.

"Shut up, and listen!" Ebony chided.

"This is a couple of days later," Amber went on...

"I am finding it hard to record my thoughts. The pain in my head is intense.

Over half the bridge crew are now dead.

The tissue samples I have taken show a foreign origination. Coupled with the broadcasts received from the other ships of the Task Force, this proves conclusively that the beta serum now being tested will not work as it was originally intended, and outlined in our briefing papers provided to the military authorities. As a consequence, we are all suffering here on this very ship. And I am at a loss what to do!"

Amber skipped forward a few more pages. There was utter silence in the bridge, the only sound that of the churning ocean waves outside as the cargo ship, the Jzhao Li, they now knew it was called thanks to the journal, continued drifting, the sea wind rattling the windows of the bridge.

"I don't understand why the requests for evacuation have been denied to the isolation sectors of the Task Force. Protocol clearly states that all those quarantined should not be ignored. Yet radio contact has been lost. And we are seemingly left alone to die. I sit here, in the bridge, my pen and journal my only companions, as I look out at the ocean. And the occupants of the Jzhao Li are passing away.

My fingers ache. My body has convulsions. I, too, am not for this world much longer.

The survival of our civilization is at stake. It is ironic how this curse upon our planet, something we cannot see... can reek so much devastation, pain and suffering. But this pales in comparison to a feeling of being misled. If the governments of the world were truly aware - as I suspect they might - hopefully history will discover and record this act of utter sacrifice and betrayal.

I have lived my life well. I have tried to help others. But I now know that help will not reach me. In time."

Amber squinted her eyes. The handwriting of Dr Jane Gideon was increasingly hard to read, no doubt due to the difficulties the Doctor was encountering at the time.

"This seems to have been written less than a day later," Amber explained...

"This will surely be my final entry. To my family, I love you. If you have survived this catastrophe, then I hope my words bring you comfort, if they ever reach you. If not, if you too are subject to the plague of our age, then I will see you again, if the good Lord is willing. Nothing can separate us, not even death will keep us apart.

I sense the call and I am ready. I pray our humanity will survive. And that whoever is responsible will be held to account. I leave this world as I came into it - Jane Gideon."

"And that's it," Amber said quietly, taking it all in as she put the journal down. The others around her were quiet as they also tried to assimilate what they had heard.

It had been an eerie experience, reading Doctor Gideon's words, holding the very same journal that she, too, had once held, hearing the account of her last days on the face of the earth. It was all unsettling, tragic, though Amber took some comfort from Doctor Jane Gideon's obvious kindness and humanity to others.

"We're going to be okay - aren't we?" Trudy asked hopefully, breaking the silence in the bridge, the anxiety in her voice obvious.

"I dunno about that," Lex replied. "All that stuff that Doctor wrote... it sure as hell doesn't give me much hope."

"We all have a resistance, don't we?" Salene added. "That's why we survived the virus in the first place."

"Who knows?" Jack said, muttering his thoughts aloud as he tried to make sense of it all in his mind. "That doesn't sound to me that she was just referring to any kind of 'virus'."

Trudy broke up, sobbing, as Salene comforted her.

"Well done, Jack," Ellie said, giving him a dirty look.

"What did I do? I'm just trying to help."

"I think we should all calm down and try and go over it all together later," Amber suggested. "Rather than jumping to any kind of conclusions."

"Oh really?" Ebony said coldly. "Well, I'll tell you this for nothing. I've already arrived at my conclusion. And we're in it. Deep. Right over our heads. Just like those crew we buried. This isn't a ship. It's a floating tomb."

CHAPTER TEN

Bray trudged through the barren, charred wilderness, every muscle in his tired body aching, urged on by sheer willpower alone. Fatigue threatened his progress, tempting him to give in.

Losing his footing, Bray tumbled and just managed to catch his fall, scratching his hands as he tried to land in a controlled manner, his fingers hitting some gorse plants, their bristles cutting into him.

Bray winced, cursing his luck that out here, wherever 'here' was, in the middle of nowhere, he should trip and fall onto one of the few plants that did manage to survive in this forbidden wasteland. The only question was, could he survive too?

Once more, doubt entered his conscience. Give up, give in. What's the point in going on?

Fighting back, dismissing the notion of surrender, Bray pushed himself up, regaining his footing. His right leg searing with pain, Bray yelled out in agony.

He had cut himself in an earlier fall the day before, on a jagged rock. Feeling his gashed thigh gently, Bray guessed he had probably got an infection by now. He had tried to fashion a makeshift bandage out of his clothing, wrapping the ripped material on his wound. But there was little more he could do. Every so often, his wound resumed bleeding, his improvised bandage covered in red.

"With the bloodline of Bray, we are one with Zoot!"

Bray shook his head, dismissing Eloise's voice, the image of her cruel expression, embedded deep within the recesses of his imagination. He hoped more than ever he had finally got away from her, would never see her again - or her crazed 'Zootist' followers.

Her experiments, the invasion of his very mind, through the many forays into reality space, sharing a virtual fantasy - they had all been insufferable. And even now, had an effect. Bray once again had difficulty deciphering if his current predicament was real or if he had been caught and was now trapped in a virtual reality simulation.

What Bray had found even worse, harder to stomach, was the distortion of how he viewed his brother's legacy and life. Compared to how others he had encountered throughout his imprisonment seemed to think of Martin. Was Zoot a God? What had he done to deserve such worship? He was certainly troubled, disturbed. Extolling his mantra of 'Power and Chaos'. But Bray knew he was no monster. Deep down inside, 'Zoot' was still 'Martin', Bray's brother. He had good in him. And they enjoyed a close relationship growing up. Surely the deep bonds of two brothers could never disappear? For all of the confusion, having been subjected to all the simulation programs, Bray was sure he was close to Martin once. Wasn't he? Or had that all been programmed, a fantasy?

To Bray, Martin would always be the quiet, shy young boy who loved his family and idolised his older brother. Martin would have been disgusted at the world that was taking shape after the adults had perished. With people like Eloise, manipulating, pursuing selfish agendas, all too happy to trample on others to get their way.

A warm breeze blew in Bray's face. Dry as he was, dehydrated, it only intensified his discomfort. As did the intense sun, beating down. So used to being inside, the bright outdoor light hurt his eyes, the sun burning his skin. There was no shade or protection.

There had been trees here in a different time, no doubt a continuation of the forest that must have grown there once before. Now, only endless tree stumps remained, the ground charred in places. Ashen. The topography was truly post-apocalyptic. Bray noticed what he perceived to be a huge, deep crater and bypassed it, for many hours, rather than risk scaling down and crossing the mammoth divide. It was as if some thermonuclear explosion had occurred. Or a meteor strike. Something had happened. Parts of the soil were crystalizing. Swirling circular shapes rippled as if fossilized by an ominous shockwave.

Bray felt in a way he was the only person left in the world.

Though he had regained his freedom and was overjoyed to be away from Eloise, the isolation he now felt, his painful solitude, the awful predicament, was difficult to bear.

There was nothing in this wilderness. Just the great likelihood of a slow, painful death. Either starving. Or succumbing to his infection.

Continuing onwards with a limp, dragging his infected leg and trying to put most of his body weight on his other side, Bray's thoughts of his own mortality... and his brother... led him to recalling the funeral of Zoot. The memory was so clear to Bray - like he was there, remembering every detail, even though he knew it was all in his mind. Was he going to join his brother soon? Would anyone mourn his likely passing - or even know of it?

What had happened to Amber, Bray wondered as he trudged on. She had been such comfort to Bray then, at Zoot's funeral. And not long afterwards, throughout their time together as a couple, when they were very much in love. Had she survived the Techno invasion? What of the baby?

Last he saw, going through it in his mind, Amber had gone into labour, before the Technos captured him. He had left her in the barn, hearing the sounds of the Technos' planes as they flew over the city, beginning their invasion.

Recognized by Techno forces, Bray had been dragged, kicking and screaming. Taken from Amber. Away from the life he knew. The life he cherished.

Bray had encountered many other fellow prisoners. He met up with KC and Alice in a slave camp prior to them being shipped to various locations for laboured servitude. And he heard tales from them that the Guardian had resurfaced. Somewhere. Even that Ryan was still alive and had been transported somewhere overseas, where he had met up with Paul. In one of Bray's own camps, he was sure Tai San had been there previously - the description Bray's fellow slave gave, certainly matched Tai San.

News of Bray's tribe, the Mall Rats, had also spread to so many other areas and he was proud of their reputation and primarily, aspiration of building a new world order out of the ashes of the old.

Bray himself had been passed from one group of oppressors to another, traded as a slave, exchanged like he was a piece of merchandise, not a fellow human being.

He didn't know how long he had been under Eloise's sway at the compound in the mountains. His mind, his memories cluttered. Conflicting images, sounds, assaulting his senses, creating almost a new reality. With the only constant being he was unsure if he could rely on his recollections.

But Amber had been real. Their love. He wouldn't forget her, even with the mental and emotional turmoils he had been subjected to under Eloise.

He never knew what happened. There were rumours, word that Amber had perished, as well as lived, passed on from other prisoners he had encountered in his incarcerations. Alice and KC had heard talk that Bray had a daughter. In another camp as Bray desperately pressed for more information, other prisoners remembered hearing something about the leader of the Mall Rats having a son. Twins. Others said the baby hadn't made it. Some told him Amber had died in childbirth. Bray would only know for sure what had happened to Amber and the baby if he saw them for himself. And he was determined, for them, to do so, to make it out of this hell he now found himself in.

He couldn't yield, he had to survive.

"Come on!" Bray urged himself through cracked lips, his voice dry and hoarse. He was so thirsty. His last drink had been when it had rained the day before - he had walked around with his mouth open, catching the drops. He must have looked so stupid doing that, Bray laughed. How Amber would have laughed as well, he felt. But there was desperation in the tone, a manic intensity.

As he pushed himself on he gazed up at the Heavens and screamed angrily, amidst his almost hysterical laughter.

"Thank you for the rain! I couldn't have survived without it! But it'll probably kill me now!"

In his confused state, there was an element of truth. He had slipped and stumbled onto the rocks trying for even a drop of moisture, causing the very gash now painful in his leg.

His skin agitated and sore, blistering in the dry sun... if only there was somewhere to get out of the baking heat. A tree to provide shade. A shelter.

"You gonna help me with the tent?"

Bray suddenly smiled fondly, recalling Martin's voice, his question that was asked frequently in the times he and his brother had struggled putting up the family tent, often in the pouring rain, on their camping vacations. He could almost imagine Martin in front of him now, in the wilderness, looking for a place to set up camp, Bray ready to help out.

He had loved the outdoors when he was younger. The family would go away on vacation and he would have many adventures, exploring all that the great outdoors had to offer with his brother, Martin.

Bray recalled how back in the city he had longed for the natural world. How he had missed it. As a Mall Rat, his life had been a fight for survival in the urban jungle and he had always felt an affinity with nature. The purity of our mother Earth. The purity of his relationship with his brother. Once. In a different time. Now he felt as if he was almost in a different world, almost on another planet.

How he missed him. He felt the pangs of separation still to this day. A sense of loss. Not just at Martin's tragic passing. But what Martin had done to his own life, reinventing himself as the city tyrant, Zoot.

Could Bray have done more to stop the transformation of Martin into 'Zoot', the frightening and unpredictable force that had terrified so many?

Was it something he had done? Had he contributed to Martin's fall? Heaven knew Bray had done all he could, given everything in his power to bring the real Martin back, to get rid of Zoot. And Martin had been close to coming round. The humanity in him returning, before his sudden death prevented any chance of Bray saving him. He would never forget his younger brother, he would carry his memories of the good times with him for the rest of his days. Even as he was perplexed and saddened by the many bad times and experiences with Martin... the tragedy of Zoot, his love for him remained.

Was Bray now being punished? For having the same bloodline? Was he now in purgatory?

Suddenly Bray heard a noise behind him, a rustling, and froze in his tracks, his body coursing with tension. Was it Eloise? The 'Zootists'? Some other threat? The devil?

Spinning around, Bray spotted some gulls, waddling around on the ground, pecking for bugs with their beaks.

He smiled initially as the birds' heads comically bobbed up and down, curious at what they might find, their eyes searching the terrain. The only living creatures around, apart from himself. In a way they were like him, out here, in the great unknown, fighting to survive and he felt an affinity with that struggle.

But then as he focused his gaze, he wondered if they could somehow even be vultures. Just waiting. Biding their time. for when he would succumb.

In his heart, Bray knew he was dying. And through his disorientated state, wondered who he would be reunited with, if there was an afterlife. Martin? Or did Zoot live on, in Heaven?

* * *

Time went on. How many days, Bray didn't know.

"Don't give up," he muttered to himself, dragging his infected leg. Every time he moved it, the pain was excruciating. His thigh had swollen up. Felt like it would burst.

The agony of his isolation was nearly crippling. He was going mad. Out here on his own, with only fear and uncertainty as his companions.

And he wondered if what was right in front of him was even real. Or another hallucination. All in his mind. It had loomed on the horizon at first and Bray had headed towards it, fascinated by what he saw - or thought he could see.

He reached out to touch it.

There. It felt real, poking his fingers through the wire mesh.

It was a barbed wire fence. Perhaps a dozen feet tall, with wicked twists of sharp wire knotted all around it.

The fence ran the entire length of the land in front of him, as far as the eye could see. And he could see no end of it. No beginning. Just the barbed wire bisecting the entire wilderness. An impenetrable barrier.

And there, just visible through the mesh on the other side of the fence, in the middle of nowhere, was a military style truck. Half buried in the dusty dirt. With its sand coloured dessert camouflage, the vehicle looked like some ancient artefact, a relic from a bygone age, sticking out of the ground. At the back of the truck, a tattered door flap billowed in the warm wind that blew across the desolate landscape.

Perhaps the wreckage would work out as a makeshift shelter from the burning sun? Maybe there were supplies inside he could use.

Putting his hands on the mesh, gathering his strength, Bray began to slowly climb the wire fence.

He gashed his fingers on the barbed wire, crying out in pain, his dry skin bleeding profusely from the fresh cuts being inflicted. His tired, weak body urged him to let go. The agony was unbearable. Like he was being tortured.

But he kept climbing, reaching the top, where the barbs were especially tangled.

Yet as with Eloise before, Bray wouldn't yield. He had come too far. Fighting his natural urges to release his grip, he forced his fingers to keep clinging on to the wire, willing his infected leg to hold his body weight, in complete inner torment as the wire bristles sharply cut into his body again, blood now dripping to the ground.

It was then, at the top of the fence, that Bray spotted the castle, further away. And for a moment, struggling through his weakness to hold on the jagged wire, he felt that it was too late. He had surely lost a grip on his sanity and was seeing things.

But there it was. It was real. The castle stood in the distance, the sun setting on the horizon.

Bray gazed, transfixed, clutching the fence. Staring at the castle. Was it Heaven? Was this what death was like? Did he have the will to let go? Propel himself to the other side.

With the sun continuing to set on the horizon and the light growing dim, Bray was now becoming engulfed in darkness. Illuminated slightly by fading beams.

Trapped at the top of the wire and weakly balancing precariously, Bray's life force felt as if it was ebbing away, disappearing with the setting sun.

He yelled out in bitter frustration, pain. A sustained wail of anguish. Realizing he wasn't going to make it.

The vulture-like birds he saw earlier swooped, their wings fluttering in a frenzy as they began pecking at the wounds oozing blood, dripping from his leg dangling over the fence.

CHAPTER ELEVEN

Stop it, Amber thought to herself. She couldn't help it, and gazed one more time at her reflection in the outside window on the ground floor level of the accommodation tower. How did she look?

Eyeing her image in the window, the sun shining on it so it was like seeing into a mirror, Amber had a look of concern, rather than checking herself out vainly.

Since the discovery of Dr Jane Gideon's journal, Amber and the others had all been anxious about their health and the questions posed by the journal.

"I look fine," Amber said to herself. Didn't she?

She focused again, studying her appearance.

So far nobody had been showing any obvious symptoms. Of any illness. Other than being cast adrift at sea for so long.

Amber tried to tell herself to stop worrying. She knew that once you allowed fear to take a grip, it would never let go and she didn't want to allow herself to be driven by her worries, taking counsel of her anxieties. This was the approach she had always taken in the darkest days back home in the city, when the adults perished and the world fell into the abyss, looking like the survivors wouldn't be far behind with the future grim. Amber had always fought her fears, she had tried to keep calm, level headed. It wasn't easy though.

And she could see how voodoo was such a potent force. If someone was ever told they were cursed, then that's all that was needed. The torturous power of the imagination would do the rest.

"I'm okay..." Amber insisted, thinking positively, forcing herself to turn away from her mirror image. She looked - like she always looked. She felt fine. She just hoped that for the sake of her baby and the others on board that they wouldn't meet the same fate as whatever happened to the crew of the Jzhao Li.

So many questions remained unanswered. Who were they? And most importantly, what was their mission? The journal had mentioned Dr Gideon was part of a so called United Nations Task Force. The Pacific Fleet.

What exactly was the United Nations Task Force doing in this region in the first place? The Tribe had talked at some lengths about it all, wondering what Dr Gideon's journal had recorded. None of them remembered hearing about a United Nations fleet assembling anywhere in the days when the adults began to die out. There was nothing about it mentioned on the news. Had they perhaps stumbled by chance upon something that had been top secret?

Dr Gideon had indicated in her writing, Amber having studied it, re-reading it several times, that the United Nations fleet was part of an effort to combat and escape - something. Which certainly could have been the so called global 'pandemic'. But she had referred to so many elements being 'classified'. And Amber wondered if there was something more to it all than the 'virus'.

During the days in the city, the Mall Rat tribe thought they had the answers surrounding Pandorax as a result of all the investigations when Ellie spearheaded her enquiry and published her newspaper, The Amulet.

Amber had never been a particular fan of conspiracy theories, believing many of them to be far fetched, sources of unnecessary worry. The mysterious journal of Dr Gideon only fuelled a seemingly inexhaustible amount of potential reasons. Was the Task Force dealing with the pandemic or onto something else? If so, it would pose to be an almost impossible challenge trying to decipher just exactly what.

One thing for certain though. There they were, living on a vast container vessel, a remnant from the adult days, a ship that was part of a fleet intended to 'save humanity', as Dr Gideon put it in her words. Had the governments of the world, the United Nations, known more about the pandemic than they had let on to the public? Was there something more to it all than the information that had been released?

The priority was to formulate some kind of a plan. Dealing with what they knew to be fact. Opposed to any pointless speculation.

It seemed to Amber, along with all the others - except Ram - that their only option was to try and steer the ship to some kind of destination on the assumption that they were in a position to do so, of course.

Amber had every faith in Jack and Ram's technical skills, and she wondered how they were getting on up in the bridge.

Though she didn't trust Ram as an individual, suspicious of his true motives, believing his past actions had shown him to be nothing but a selfish tyrant, Amber was well aware that he was a genius after all. At least with computers. Nobody doubted that. Ram's intellect and wizardry were clearly off the scale. Jack's technical skills had always been incredible and he too had an aptitude for computers though he lacked Ram's programming flair. But if anyone could reactivate the instrumentation on the bridge, then they could.

Such a pity Ram wasn't able to channel his many gifts into something positive for humanity, Amber felt. Maybe this was a start, an opportunity for him to change, continue as he meant to go on. She hoped so. He certainly had a lot of ground to cover, amends to make from his past wrongs.

"How are they getting on?" Amber asked as Jay entered the cabin. "Any breakthroughs?"

Jay had just been in the bridge checking on Jack and Ram's progress and Amber could see that something was troubling him.

"Is everything okay?" Amber asked.

"Difficult to know. They managed to get a Sat Nav signal for just a few minutes. But the grid just doesn't make any sense, Amber. The co-ordinates show that we are somewhere near the Pacific islands. But the grid readings don't refer to any by name. Only zones. And no matter how hard Ram tries to cover it up, it seems to be freaking him out big time."

"Why?" Amber replied. "If this was part of a United Nations fleet, maybe they just used zones for their charts rather than any geographical names. The military would often do that. Wouldn't they?"

"Maybe," said Jay. "But Ram's still going on about using this ship to head back home, to the city. I could understand in a way when we were on that trawler. But on this ship, we have a real chance. And I don't get it. Why he can't see."

"You don't think he knows something - we don't?" Amber considered.

"If he did, he's not exactly the person to be very forthcoming, Amber. You know that."

"What about Lex and the others? How are they getting on?"

Apart from Sammy and Lottie, who were looking after the little ones, all the others had been deployed in shifts to check out more of the containers, crack them open, see what else they could find.

"I'll go and catch up with them for an update," Jay said. "Amber, there is one more thing though."

"What?"

Jay kissed Amber on the cheek tenderly. "I love you."

"Thanks," Amber smiled. She suddenly felt a whole lot better.

Jay left and Amber sat, re-reading Doctor Jane Gideon's journal again. Trying to fit together any piece of information which might shed light. But she was more preoccupied by Ram.

That she still so doubted him, was unable to trust him, only added to her unease at the Tribe's dependence on Ram in their time of need. He had proved in the past he could be a dangerous individual. And if he was holding some secret of any kind, then they would all have to be careful.

* * *

Slade pounded the rusty steel beneath him as he jogged on the outside deck of the cargo ship, passing Lex and his team examining the containers. He was due to take the next shift. And in his break, welcomed the opportunity to have a work out, determined to keep his fitness levels up.

But it also helped him to spend some time alone away from the others, his mind wandering as he jogged, considering all kinds of issues from the passing of his brother back in the city, his life before the 'virus' when the adults were still alive, to what the future held out for him and the others. And his relationship with Ebony.

He had calculated a circuit for his jogging, weaving in and out of the stacks of containers piled all around. Each lap must be a third of a mile.

This was some jogging track, he thought, as the massive cargo ship pitched up and down on the ocean below. He must have jogged a good three miles, Slade added in his mind, with just a few more circuits to go. He was trying to achieve a target of five miles.

Slade rounded a corner, accelerating his stride. It was time to pick up the pace over the last laps and get the cardiovascular system really pumping.

Ebony stepped out from a stack of containers on the opposite side of the ship where Lex and the team were working and Slade took a momentary fright as he nearly collided into her, stopping immediately in his tracks, his chest heaving from his exercise.

"Ebony! Always full of surprises," he said, gathering his breath.

"I've been trying to find you, Slade."

"Well, you have... what is it you wanted?"

Ebony seemed bothered. Agitated. She cast furtive glances around, making sure nobody was listening to them.

"I want to talk with you! This is a death ship! You heard what was in that journal. It isn't safe on board. There's two lifeboats, back there" Ebony indicated the two small boats hanging from the accommodation tower structure at the back of the ship. "We've got to get out of here!"

"What do you mean 'we'?" Slade asked.

"Who do you think I mean? I mean us. Me and you."

"Ebony... there is no 'us' anymore, in case you haven't noticed. And I'm going nowhere. I'm not leaving the others, getting off this ship. And neither are you."

"I thought we had something special going. That we were an item?"

"Yeah... we had something. At one point. Long ago."

"So what is it?" Ebony implored, her eyes welling up with tears.

"It's you!" Slade snapped. "You... mystify me. First I lose my heart to you. Falling head over heels in love. Then you rip it to shreds, as if you don't even know who I am. I've come to realize you're not the person I thought you were."

"If it's about Mega, once again - I'll say it, I'm sorry. What more can I do to show you - I was wrong about what I said."

"You're right about that. I remember every cruel word. "He deserved what he got," you said. You were glad. "Happy," I think was the word you said. "Happy" that he had died. That I deserved more than him for a brother."

"What did you expect me to say? That you should feel really proud of his achievements, unleashing all those chemicals into the city?" Ebony snarled.

"You don't get it. No matter what Mega did - he was still my brother! All that I had left of my family from before!"

Slade looked at her. It wasn't just hurt in his eyes. But regret, pity. And utter loathing.

"From what I've learned about some of the things you've done in your life, Ebony, especially as Queen of the Locos, you're hardly in any position to criticise anyone. At least I had feelings for my brother. Unlike you with Java and Siva. I mean you weren't exactly a loving sister now, were you?"

"It's Ruby, isn't it? She's lured you in. I've seen you both together. The way you look at her. She's always trying to impress you. Tarting herself up. Constantly fiddling with her hair. She can't take her eyes off you!"

"Is that all you've got to think of with everything we're going through?" Slade asked disdainfully.

"There is just one other thing," Ebony snarled. "Is she good? In bed?"

Suddenly Ebony sprung forward, her arm a blur as she took Slade by surprise, scratching the side of his face with her fingernails, deep scratch marks visible on his cheek.

"You keep the hell away from me from now on!" she screamed. "And you'd better tell that bitch to do the same!"

Giving Slade a filthy look, Ebony stormed off.

Slade watched her leave, feeling the cuts in his face.

And she had gone, doing her very best to put as much distance between them, getting away from all the thoughts and feelings she once felt for him, leaving Slade far behind her.

* * *

"Jack - you'll never guess what I can see?" Ram asked, peering through the binoculars he held to his face, staring out of one of the windows in the bridge.

"I dunno. The Easter bunny. The Loch Ness monster. No - let me guess. It's blue, wet and starts with the letter W?"

Jack sat on the floor with his back to Ram. The two of them had been arguing - again - about what the different instrumentation meant on all the equipment in the bridge.

"It is blue and wet but it starts with the letter O - I see nothing but Ocean," Ram said.

"Enough games, Ram," Jack replied, flicking through some print outs recovered from the engine room. "We've got work to do."

"You still sulking, Jack? Now I know how Ellie feels when you two have been arguing."

"We do not argue, thank you very much, Ram. And no, I am not sulking! Can't we just - get on and try and get all this to work?"

Ram put the binoculars down and looked at Jack. He enjoyed winding him up, really took delight from Jack's reactions to Ram's never ending practical jokes and barbs. But he realized Jack was right. They did have a lot to be getting on with, working out through a process of deduction what some of the dials and readings must mean. They knew the speed of the ship - it was drifting about 3 knots per hour. They knew the direction it was headed. North west. They had reactivated the Sat Nav signal for a minute or so. Now they were trying to engage the engines and auto-pilot system.

Ram had his view about what buttons to press to achieve a certain result, while Jack interpreted things differently. Both shared common ground that nothing should be touched or activated till they were confident what the item in question would do. They didn't want to endanger the ship, releasing ballast which might cause it to capsize or something.

Ram was in high spirits. He was lapping up every second of it. The task they faced was a difficult one. There was just so much complex equipment in the control room. But Ram found it a stimulating mission, something to challenge even him, his mental powers, his own self-declared 'genius'.

By contrast, Jack was getting frustrated not just by Ram's arrogance, but the pressure was getting to him. It was up to them to try and make some use of the ship, to figure it out, how it ran, if they could steer it. There were so many 'ifs', Jack thought, as he went over the engine room diagrams.

"Cheer up, Jack," Ram said, slumping down in one of the tall swivel chairs at a control dashboard, spinning around merrily in circles for a moment. "Enjoy it - this is fun!"

"This is not what I would describe as fun," Jack said.

"Well, I'll be..." Ram mumbled to himself, holding the binoculars up to his eyes again and staring out of another window.

"What is it now? You found Gel and the girls out sunbathing on the front deck?" Jack chirped up.

"Jack - would I do that?" Ram said in mock protest, a wicked grin on his face.

"Yes, you would. And you have."

"No, not this time, Jack. I've got my eyes on some other 'scenery'."

"What do you mean? A dolphin? A mermaid? Tell me."

"If only it was one of the girls sunbathing..." Ram pondered in disappointment at what he observed.

"Ram, you've spent far too much time on computers," Jack jested. "You've gotta get out more."

"Look who's talking. No, what I can see... How did they used to say it in the old days - that's right. Land ahoy..." Ram said casually.

Jack dropped the engine room charts and scrambled to his feet, Ram passing over the binoculars so Jack could have a look.

Ram was right. Out there, in the distance, Jack could barely contain his excitement as he saw the unmistakeable signs... the outline of land on the horizon.

And unbeknownst to Jack, rather than hope, it clearly filled Ram with an awesome dread.

CHAPTER TWELVE

He was alive. For how much longer, that was another matter, Bray thought, feeling the agony in his infected leg, the pains all over his body, ravaged from the many barbed wire cuts when he climbed the barrier that had so challenged him.

Drawing weakly on his fading strength, he had managed to scramble down the other side of the fence before finally falling to the ground.

Spending the night in the wreckage of the overturned vehicle, Bray had rested up, regaining what was left of his energy following his trek through the wilderness.

The military truck had provided a welcome though temporary refuge, nothing more. There was no food inside it. But to Bray's delight, there had been an out of date can of cola left in the front seat glove compartment, that had sustained him during the long night, the foul tasting liquid nonetheless truly appreciated by his dehydrated body.

And now with the sun beaming down overhead once more, the temperature rising, Bray was thrilled to be alive still. He had dug deep, summoning everything within his spirit, his very core, to get that far on his flight from Eloise.

He had made it to another day.

Now he would find out if it was worth it. If all the suffering, the risks he had taken, would pay off.

Heading towards the 'castle' and buildings that he had spotted the previous night, Bray discovered a long section of tarmac. It must have been a runway at one point, Bray was sure in his still confused state. It was sheer joy to walk on such a surface compared to the rugged terrain in the wastelands, though the tar had melted in places. With lots of cracks, the runway was damaged, in a state of disrepair, almost mirroring how Bray felt himself with his body so weak.

The runway stretched for some time. Approaching the 'castle', Bray noticed other buildings in the distance in the perimeters. And every quarter of a mile, parallel to the barb wire fence, there were warnings signs displaying: DANGER. BIO HAZARD.

Hours later, nearing his goal, Bray was able to identify that the buildings formed part of what had to have been a military base.

There were massive hangars, with airplanes still inside. The strange thing was, Bray considered, the planes were from different time periods. Was this a war museum? He had his doubts. The majority of aircraft were modern day fighters, their sleek aerodynamic forms resting at peace, in contrast to the high speeds they had been designed to attain.

Was there anyone else there? Or just himself?

And yes, once again Bray wondered if he was inescapably trapped in a virtual reality program.

He pushed himself on, finding stamina to examine other parts of the base.

There were several outbuildings. Construction machines sat idly, like prehistoric monsters, frozen in time. Fossils from a bygone era.

Some hangars were incomplete, obviously still being built by whoever had worked on them before they had been abandoned, presumably left part finished in haste when the 'virus' spread around the world.

Bray noticed dozens of buildings which he was sure had once been barracks. Inside were empty beds, rusting lockers with doors open, cupboards bare. There was nothing of value for Bray to use. Just the ghosts of the past. Remnants of what had once been.

Nature was now reclaiming the base. There had to be water somewhere. Perhaps under ground, Bray reasoned. Above the ground, young trees grew in random patches, bursting through concrete paths, their roots making the paving slabs uneven. Plants of all shapes and sizes dotted the dusty soil, wild vines extending up walls as if nature itself was reaching out. But Bray was aware since entering the wastelands that apart from the vultures he was sure he had seen, this entire area looked to be devoid of any other birds or animal life. Perhaps their natural instincts were keeping them away. Did they knew something Bray did not?

Having checked out several of the buildings in the outer perimeters of the base, Bray turned his sights on the mysterious 'castle' that loomed nearby.

Maybe it would have the answers Bray was looking for, as well as something inside that could aid his struggle to survive.

* * *

Bray entered the castle through its open portcullis, the jagged metal tips of it pointing down at him threateningly. His boots scrunched down on broken glass and debris which littered the floor.

This was no castle, Bray had come to realize.

It was a shop.

Treading warily, unsure of what or who would be inside, Bray continued to cautiously examine his surroundings. The 'castle' was a facade, covering the shop inside. Most of the shelves had fallen down, the building had been ransacked, but one shelf in the store still held up, a few toy dragons sitting on it, their mouths wide open angrily, breathing out little orange plastic breaths of fire.

A knight wearing a suit of armour stood in the corner, its gauntlet empty of where it had surely once held a sword. The knight had been sprayed in layers of graffiti, strange whirls and symbols that seemed like an alien language, Bray unable to decipher any of it. He stared at the knight, who wore a crown at the top of his helmet. A plaque stuck to the base of the stand the armour stood on read 'King Arthur'.

Going outdoors through the 'castle' entrance, Bray identified that he had stumbled into an amusement park. What was left of one.

All around him were decrepit, decaying rides. There was no sound, just that of his breathing and his feet as he walked around, checking out his environment. To his left was an old merry-go-round with plastic horses that no longer carried any riders, the heads of the horses smashed, missing legs and hooves. On his right was what had once been a charming fairy-tale themed restaurant, its windows broken, chairs and tables upturned, toppled over like a hurricane had tore through. And he couldn't help but notice all the buildings seemed to have been charred.

Bray tensed, the pain in his leg throbbing as he spotted a small roller coaster in the distance beyond the buildings in front of him. Its frame looked as fragile as he did, the skeleton of its wooden struts marked by burn marks where it had once been on fire, great gaps visible in the loops where its carriages had once twisted and turned.

It was a strange, haunting place. Bray could all too well imagine how it would have been in its day, a fun place, where kids of all ages would have enjoyed spending their time, being together, Mums and Dads frolicking with loved ones. If only any of them knew of the 'virus', the catastrophe that had been waiting to transform the world that once was into a nightmarish hell.

It was the first time he'd been to a theme park, Bray smiled slightly to himself, thinking how ironic it all was. His family didn't have a lot of money when he was growing up which is why most of the time they had gone camping on vacation. His brother, Martin, had always wanted to go overseas, visit one of the famous destinations he had seen only in brochures or in commercials. And now here he was. Bray had made it to an actual amusement park.

Bray cautiously hobbled around the ruins, vigilant in case those who had graffitied and damaged the place still remained. He needed to find food. Drink.

Walking through the fairy tale-themed fantasy village, the cozy storybook buildings with their plastic wooden beams and atmospheric arching roofs, Bray spotted a vending machine inside one of the houses, itself another shop.

Entering slowly in case someone was inside waiting to ambush him, Bray saw toy cuddly knights and damsels in distress inside the machine, waiting for someone to rescue them.

In another section there were some chocolate bars. Bray picked up a witches broomstick left on the floor in the shop and used it to smash through the glass. Then he grabbed the chocolate bars inside, left well past their sell by date. And ravaged, began to consume the bars, savouring the food, the sweetness, even though the chocolate was stale and tasted horrible.

Bray suddenly heard laughter. The sound of young children, giggling.

Was he imagining it? Was this whole theme park nothing but a dream?

The high pitched squeals of delight rang out again and Bray knew that he wasn't hearing things. There were definitely some children around somewhere nearby.

He stealthily stepped out into the twisting fairy tale street, taking cover as he carefully made his way toward the source of the sounds of laughter.

Skirting the sides of the buildings, Bray peered around the corner of the street, poised in case he needed to put up a fight, his body tense with adrenalin.

He noticed a young girl and boy. They had to be no more than seven or eight years old. They were sitting either side of a see-saw in the shape of a dragon, bouncing happily up and down, laughing merrily as they took turns soaring vertically. The boy wore a far too big fighter pilot's helmet on his head, the girl a tattered, filthy fairy tale princess dress.

Bray breathed out a sigh of relief, his body relaxing. They would be no danger to him, but he had to make sure there were no other threats around.

Stepping out into the street slowly, so as not to frighten them, Bray approached, his hands held up as if in surrender.

"Hello," he smiled, his lips dry and cracking open.

The two kids stopped swinging on the see-saw. Turning to see Bray before them, they screamed suddenly in fright, terrified by him.

"I mean you no harm," Bray said, hobbling toward them, his leg searing in pain.

The girl and boy took off, panicked expressions on their faces, determined to get away from the stranger in their midsts.

"Please! Wait!" Bray yelled out and began to chase after the kids. He must look threatening, he thought, having been in the wilderness for so long, his face unshaven, hair matted, his filthy clothes torn, covered in dirt, blood.

Moving as fast as he could, Bray gained on them.

"Please stop! I'm a friend, I mean no harm," Bray called out, though it did nothing to reassure the terrified kids.

The young girl and boy raced through the entrance of what must have once been the foyer of a large administrative-looking type of building and he quickly followed.

"Hello?" he called out, his voice echoing as he paced around.

"Please - is there anyone there?" Bray shouted, his eyes darting furtively, trying to catch a glimpse of the kids, of anyone.

Spotting movement, just a tiny shadow, Bray walked up to a reception desk in the large foyer, his feet scrunching on the floor, trampling broken glass and layers of dust.

Peering over the side of the reception, Bray saw the younger girl and boy huddling together, doing their best to hide.

"I am begging you, please help me," Bray implored.

They looked up at him, terrified that he had found them. Maybe they didn't speak English, Bray reasoned. They might not understand him. What could he do?

He stretched closer, his hands held out wide open, showing he meant no harm.

The kids recoiled, screaming.

And Bray noticed their eyes were looking not just at him, but at what was behind him.

Bray turned to see - but it was too late.

Struck on the back of the head from behind, Bray collapsed in a heap, losing consciousness.

CHAPTER THIRTEEN

"I can't believe it's really out there!" Salene said excitedly, peering through the binoculars at the outline of land, still several miles away.

"And it's all thanks to me - I saw it first..." Ram said distantly to himself, slumped back in his seat, deep in thought, his feet resting on another chair. But from his tone, he was hardly elated.

"I'm so happy I could nearly give you a kiss!" Salene enthused, putting down the binoculars and turning around to face Ram and the others, the group assembling in the bridge to discuss the news of land being discovered.

"If your lips are willing - my face is ready to receive," Ram grinned.

"I said 'nearly' give you a kiss," Salene backed down.

Darryl blushed. He had developed a crush on Salene and all this talk of her kissing anyone made him feel awkward.

"I don't see why everyone seems so happy round here," Trudy spoke up, agitated, indicating the bridge all around them. "Haven't you forgotten where we are? The bodies we found here? Whatever happened to that crew might happen to us! Especially if it's a mutation of the virus! And who knows what dangers could be ashore!"

"Trudy - I agree," Ram said. "You're talking a lot of sense."

"Rubbish," Lex interrupted. "It's land, Trudy," he continued. "We've been dreaming about getting back on land for who knows how long now. And finally, there it is!"

"Trudy - I know what the journal said. We all heard it," Amber replied, trying to keep Trudy calm. "But I honestly don't think that any of us are infected by whatever killed the crew. Look at us all. We all seem fine, healthy."

"Physically anyway - if not mentally," Ram said, casting a cool glance at Amber.

"Shut it, Ram," Lex ordered. "In the Mall Rats, majority rules. We've all voted to try and head ashore. And that's the way it's going to be."

"There's no chance in hell we'll get to that land, Amber," Ram scoffed.

"And why's that?" Amber asked suspiciously.

The two stared at each other, their mutual antagonism obvious.

"It's simple. How do you suppose we get there, Miss know-it-all?" Ram explained, raising his voice in hostility. "We don't know how to even control this ship yet, do we?"

Amber smiled, unflustered by Ram's outburst. "That's your and Jack's department, Ram. I guess we're just lucky to have such a 'smartypants' like you among us. Unless - you're not as smart as you keep telling everyone."

Ram glared, agitated by her deliberate provocation.

Just like she hoped he would be.

"Prove me wrong," Amber said. "That you can help Jack get this ship working. Or aren't you up to the challenge?"

* * *

Amber and the others reasoned that if they could find a way to reactivate the ship's propulsion, it would at least get them closer towards the land, with little risk of the ocean's current taking them away from their objective. Then they might have a chance to use the small lifeboats to tender ashore.

The rest of the Tribe left Jack and Ram alone so they could concentrate and work together on the bridge - but with the two of them interpreting what all the great swathes of buttons and readings before them meant, they were at odds with each other and achieved very little. It felt like they were going nowhere.

"Ram - can't you see? This must be some form of ignition," Jack said, from where he was standing. "I can't believe you can't see it."

Ram growled in frustration at Jack, thumping his fist on the outside of the control panel.

"Careful!" Jack tensed, worried Ram was going to hit some buttons without first knowing what each of them did.

Ram peered out of the window of the bridge to the outer deck below, as Jack returned his attention to understanding the myriad of buttons stretching before him.

"Jack - I think Ellie's looking for you."

"I didn't hear anything."

"I heard her shout from outside. You must have been absorbed in your work. She just waved at me. By the look on her face, she must be needing you."

"She could have at least come up here and asked. She know's how busy we are," Jack flustered, heading out of the door to go and see what she wanted.

A leering grin appeared on Ram's face, thrilled at his deception.

With Jack out the way, Ram studied all the instruments in front of him.

He would show them. Especially Amber. Ram felt she was self-righteous. Had they forgotten? He had been a Tribal leader. And not just any Tribe. But the Technos. He had achieved so much and the others treated him like he knew nothing, Amber in particular.

For all their sakes, especially his own, Ram was determined to use the mighty Jzhao Li container ship as a means of transportation. But not to go ashore. Ram was still intent to get back to their homeland.

And away from the island that beckoned.

He resolved that once he kick-started the engines, then he would alter the auto-pilot compass to turn the immense cargo ship around and point it in the opposite direction.

Ram had the answer, like always. Everything was simply a process of elimination, deduction. He knew he could meet the challenge that now faced him.

"It's elementary, my dear Jack," Ram spoke softly, dangling his finger over a button, the Chinese lettering keeping hidden what the button did - though for no longer, Ram thought. He had worked it all out.

Pressing the button firmly, then several around it, Ram stepped back, waiting for a response from the ship.

A few seconds passed.

Then suddenly a loud grinding sound could be heard coming from the very depths of the ship, the noise of grating machinery moving, the hull vibrating as the once mammoth and dormant mechanisms of the Jzhao Li sprung to life once more.

A look of triumph was on Ram's face.

"Told you so," he said smugly. He had done it.

The rumbling noise bellowing from below continued, a whirring, the screech of metal high-pitched as it resonated.

And then Ram noticed something was wrong.

The front of the ship stretching out from the window ahead of him was not pointing straight, as it had since they first stepped aboard. Nor was it altering course.

The ship was beginning to lean, ever so slightly, on an angle.

Ram wondered if his eyes were playing tricks and he stared, fascinated, trying to understand what was happening.

There was no doubt about it, the cargo ship was tilting.

With the imminent danger, suddenly the land on the horizon seemed very far away.

Jack burst in the door of the bridge panting, out of breath from running up the stairs.

"Ram - what the hell have you done!?" Jack shouted.

Ram looked despondently at Jack, the worry on his own face all too visible.

"I don't know..."

Sammy and Lottie gazed eagerly out of the cabin window. They had been excited at the prospect of going ashore with visions of playing parts in a real life adventure, similar to some of the tales they had read in the old books. Sammy's imagination was coloured and distorted in experiencing what it might be like to be a modern day Robinson Crusoe. But now he and Lottie were deeply concerned by the angle of the ship. Behind them, Brady played with baby Bray, oblivious to the threat which was now occurring.

Trudy appeared out of the bathroom. She had just taken a shower. She stared through the window, transfixed.

"Oh, my God! What's happening?!"

* * *

"I don't like it down here," Darryl whimpered as he followed Lex, Ruby, Jay, Salene, Ellie and Amber.

"None of us do," Amber whispered, her voice echoing in the metallic corridor.

She had suggested that they examine the ballast tanks while Ram and Jack continued on investigating the bridge.

May and Zak had been sent to check on Sammy and Lottie, who were caring for the two children in the cabins - but also keeping an eye on Trudy. Amber had reinforced that May and Zak try and keep Trudy calm when they explained what Ram had done. She didn't wish to add to the danger they were clearing facing with any unnecessary histrionics, suggesting that Trudy then work with Gel, May and Zak gathering food and supplies.

As an added precaution, Amber had deployed Ebony and Slade to check out all the lifejackets and make sure there was enough for everyone in case they needed to use them quickly, along with inspecting the lifeboat stations.

Amber's group was creeping along in the engineering room section in the bowels of the ship, several decks beneath the waterline. The corridor was dark, the electric lighting that had once lit it no longer working, and Jay used a flashlight to illuminate their way in the gloomy depths.

"This is creepy!" Darryl muttered.

"Darryl, would you calm down? You're freaking me out!" Salene snapped.

"Be quiet - please!" Jay insisted, trying to concentrate.

The beam of the flashlight in his hand cut through the darkness that lay ahead, with its spotlight falling on metallic walls, illuminating signs in Chinese text.

It was very humid and there was a lot of moisture in the air, with water dripping down.

"Do you hear that?" Ruby asked.

She could hear a rushing sound. Perhaps it was the ocean outside on the other side of the hull, the waves crashing against the sides of the ship.

The group arrived at a watertight door that stood in their way.

Through the other side they could all hear the torrent flowing louder and they were soon up to their knees and ankles in water.

It was unmistakeable. The door was straining to hold the mammoth weight of the unforgiving ocean.

"I dunno about you guys - but I think it's time we got out of here," Lex said, rightly concluding that the ship was taking in water.

* * *

Ebony peered at the ocean below, the waves rolling against the side of the ship. At least it wasn't too rough, she thought.

News the Jzhao Li was taking in water had spread like wildfire among the Tribe and a mood of panic had set in. Here they were, so close to land but so far. The island was still several miles away, the jagged outlines of the terrain now visible, and who knew how much longer they would have.

Ram had accidentally tampered with the ballast of the ship, flooding it with too much water, activating the watertight doors in the process. The huge doors did their best to stem the flood of water flowing in but with the ship listing, minute by minute, the situation was clearly precarious for the entire tribe.

Amber had sent out the alert for all to be on standby to abandon ship.

Which is exactly what Ebony had in mind as she jumped onto the gantry attached to the side of the vessel, towards its stern, harnessing the lifeboats.

It was now the moment to look after number one.

Ebony expected the small lifeboat to still have some fuel in it. Surely the crew of the Jzhao Li long ago, would have left the lifeboats on standby, ready to go, with supplies of food and water, enough fuel. She was willing to take that chance.

Spotting a handle on a little panel at the edge of the gantry, Ebony shifted it and to her relief, the lifeboat began to gradually swing out, dangling high above the water. At least something worked around here still, Ebony smirked.

Hitting a green button on the control panel in front of her, the lifeboat started to lower, suspended by the ropes it was attached to and Ebony knew it was time to take a leap of faith.

Jumping onto the lifeboat as it rapidly descended, she landed on its deck with a clatter, well balanced, using the feline agility she had been born with to full effect, finding her footing quickly.

It was only now Ebony appreciated the sheer scale of the Jzhao Li, towering above the lifeboat, angling dangerously above on its tilt. If it leaned any further, Ebony worried that the massive cargo ship would capsize and suddenly come crashing down on her.

The lifeboat reached the surface of the water and bobbled up and down on the current.

Pulling out a knife she had taken from the kitchen galley, Ebony cut the ropes that dangled, tethering the lifeboat to the mother ship. With the last of the threads torn away cleanly, Ebony realized she was finally free.

"Come on!" Ebony pleaded, turning the rusty key left in the ignition of the small lifeboat that she had placed all her future in, her very life.

The engine coughed and spluttered, smoke bellowing, diesel fumes filling the air.

The propeller at the back cut into the water as Ebony shifted the throttle, steering the lifeboat away from the monstrous cargo ship leaning above her.

The lifeboat sped away. Ebony let out a shrill yell of delight. The relief of her escape, her continued survival in this crazy world, was almost fun and she was engulfed by a feeling of jubilation. Just like how she had felt in the days when she used to drive around in Zoot's police car, back in the city.

She was ready for whatever adventure lay ahead. Bring it on!

Looking back behind her at the Jzhao Li as it continued its tilt precariously to one side, the distance opening between it and the lifeboat, Ebony grinned.

"So long, suckers," she hissed, turning forward to the mysterious land that lay in the distance ahead.

* * *

"Do something!" Ellie pleaded, as Jack frantically scanned the buttons and dials in the bridge.

"Like what?!" Jack shouted, panic on his face.

"Anything!"

"I'm trying, Ellie!"

Amber burst in. "Any luck?" she asked, but already knew the answer as she watched Ellie, Ram and Jack gaze despondently.

It was getting hard to stand and move around now, with the ship badly listing.

"Looks like we're running out of time, Jack," Amber continued. "It might be an idea to get your lifejackets on and join the others. I'll alert them. We really should all be on standby. This thing feels like it could go over any second."

"Looks like Ebony's already abandoned ship, Captain," Ram said, indicating.

Amber and the others noticed Ebony in the lifeboat, speeding away and Amber sighted to herself. Typical. Ebony didn't waste much time.

"There has to be something we can do!" Jack shouted, fastening his life jacket on, along with the others.

"Oh, to hell with it!" Ram snapped, and he began pressing buttons randomly on the console in front of him.

"Ram! Haven't you learned anything?" Amber said.

"I guess you're right, Amber!" Ram replied. "I'd better go and gather a few things up if we're leaving."

He crossed to the door and exited.

Jack focused on all the dials on the bridge. Each item on the instrumentation panel had to do something, perform some function. It was just like using a computer, albeit a very big computer. One that was sinking fast.

"Just give me one more minute, Amber. I promise!"

Amber nodded and watched eagerly with Ellie as Jack took the plunge and pressed a button. He waited with baited breath, in an air of anticipation.

Nothing happened.

Plan B. Another button pressed. Nothing.

"Oh, come on," Jack uttered, looking up to the Heavens above, imploring. "Give me a break."

Jack pressed a few more buttons.

Suddenly it was like the entire ship was struck by enormous vibrations as far below, a rumbling sound swept upwards, shaking their very bones. An ominous noise, the hull shuddering, reverberating as a powerful force exerted itself.

Jack stepped back, unsure. He had certainly done something, and he looked around at the others to see if they knew just what.

Amber raced out onto the outside fire escape stairwell, leaning over to see the back of the ship.

Down below, the water was churned into a white froth of foam as the powerful back propellers spun, driving the ship forward, the Jzhao Li slowly picking up speed.

Pumping her fist triumphantly, Amber ran back into the bridge.

"You've done it, Jack! You've done it!" she grinned.

Jack leaned back and gave a huge sigh of relief, Ellie hugging him, whooping for joy, and all three exchanged hi-fives.

The remaining members of the Tribe, assembled on deck, looked up at the bridge and also whooped it up, relieved as the ship was now gathering speed, which was also helping stabilise the mammoth vessel.

* * *

Ebony cursed her luck, the engines of the lifeboat spluttering in protest as they misfired, the boat slowing down, like its very life force was fading.

Ebony urged the lifeboat on, gripping its wheel with one hand while the other struggled with the gear, trying to coax the last remnants of power from its engines.

It was so typical, Ebony thought, her teeth clenched in a mixture of frustration and determination.

"Come on!" Ebony shouted, desperate. "Don't run out of fuel on me! Not now!"

The unknown land was still some way ahead of her. Ebony could make out rows of palm trees on the horizon, some sandy beaches. Just where was she?

Behind her, the Jzhao Li was quite a distance away but powering through the ocean towards the land, heading away at an angle on a different course.

Ebony wondered how on earth the others had managed to get the ship going again. She resented their success while she struggled, the lifeboat failing her in her time of need.

She thought about swimming to shore, calculating how far away it was, if she would make it. She had never been an expert swimmer. And who knew if there were sharks, rocks or other menaces lurking beneath the surface. Besides, with the powerful currents, she might be swept further out to sea while struggling to reach land. Swimming to the shore would be a last option, only if she had to.

The small lifeboat might have abandoned her, but she wasn't about to abandon it.

* * *

"The good news, I can see some sandy beaches - the bad news, there seem to be reefs surrounding the entire coast. And cliffs," Salene commented, staring through binoculars at the land straight ahead.

"That's just what we need," Jay said sardonically.

The Jzhao Li was moving at some speed now. It had been hurtling through the water at about 20 knots per hour and at that rate they would reach landfall in about 12 minutes, Jack contemplated. He had suspected that it was increasing speed, set by the auto-pilot. Problem was, Jack didn't know how to disengage the system. And consequently had no idea how the vessel could ever slow down.

If they couldn't find a way to steer the ship, the huge cargo vessel that had been their refuge would be their doom as the Jzhao Li, speeding towards the landmass, was clearly on a collision course, out of control.

Amber stood transfixed, the ship rapidly approaching the land which was looming closer. Closer.

"Jack - you've done well. But that's enough!" Amber said.

"I can do it, Amber! I'm sure I can!" he protested.

"No!" Amber replied emphatically. "Our only hope is with the lifeboat."

Unwilling for a moment to give up his efforts, Jack looked out the window of the bridge at the landmass stretching beyond them. He knew Amber was right, there was no other option. They only had a matter of minutes before the ship would run aground. Or worse still, hurl ashore.

* * *

"Is everyone here?" Jay asked, looking around, doing a headcount.

"Everyone except Ebony - bitch!" Lex answered. "Talk about every man - or woman - for himself!"

"What about Ram?" Slade asked, glancing around.

Suddenly they noticed Ram in full flight approaching along the deck towards them. He had for some reason changed out of his Techno uniform and was now wearing clothes he had recovered from the Jzhao Li crew.

"Well - how do I look?" Ram asked, as he arrived.

The others stared open-mouthed. It was macabre. And Trudy was especially repulsed.

"How could you, Ram?" Trudy said. "Wearing the clothes of a dead man?"

"Never know who we might meet ashore," Ram explained. "Thought I might try and make a good impression, make myself presentable."

The Tribe were assembled at the back of the ship, clambering into the remaining lifeboat, which wasn't easy, given the angle the Jzhao Li was still tilting on.

Ahead of them, they could see the land very clearly now, countless rows of palm trees, the sandy beaches, the reefs in shallower waters bordering the coast, rocks protruding menacingly.

Jay and Slade stood either side on the gantry while the others boarded.

"Well, what are we waiting for?" Jay said, yanking the lever on the gantry control panel to lower the lifeboat. "Let's get out of here!"

Slade nodded as the lifeboat edged out, the hydraulic lift grasping it shifting position, dangling the lifeboat high above the water. Slade climbed on, joining the others huddled together.

"Green must mean go," Jay said, pushing the green button on the control panel, the wind rustling his hair as the cargo ship sped through the waves.

He leaped into the lifeboat, which descended toward the water and hoped, as they all did, that it would lower quickly enough so they could get away from the massive vessel before it struck the land.

And then without warning, the lifeboat stopped dead in its ropes, dangling in mid-air.

Trudy and Gel shrieked in fear. Everyone in the boat exchanged panicked looks, wondering what had happened.

"What the hell?" Ram asked, looking up at the rope attaching the lifeboat to the cargo ship.

It was as they all feared. The mechanism was stuck. They were all stranded, nearly three stories above the ocean, the lifeboat swinging on the ropes, the waves beneath rushing past.

"I'll be back!" Slade shouted.

"Where are you going?" Ruby called out.

Slade didn't answer and clambered up the rope, his arms straining to haul himself upwards.

Following in Slade's trail, Zak, too, suddenly began to climb up the rope attaching the lifeboat to the Jzhao Li.

"Careful, Zak!" May shouted.

Swinging onto the gantry, Zak joined Slade, the two examining the control panel to manoeuvre the lifeboat.

Looking up at Slade and Zak on the gantry, Jay and Lex stood up, determined to lend their assistance. But the lifeboat wobbled and they lost their balance, Amber grabbing hold of Jay as the rope shifted, lowering the lifeboat a few feet nearer the water.

Slade pressed the green button again, hoping the lifeboat would resume its descent, but to no avail. The lifeboat was stuck.

"The handle!" Zak shouted, pointing, clutching the gantry as the wind bellowed, the cargo ship picking up speed.

Slade looked at what Zak had noticed, spotting the manual release handle on the other side of the control panel.

"Jay!" Amber cried out in worry, as Jay stood up again, struggling again to keep his balance. He held onto the rope, steadying the lifeboat, ensuring it remained taught in the pulley above. Lex assisted, both straining with all their might.

"We've got it!" Slade shouted to Zak, as he cranked the handle as quickly as he could.

Suddenly the taught tension in the rope was released. No longer stuck in the winding mechanism, the rope eased through the pulley it was fed through, the lifeboat descending at speed toward the water.

"Hold on!" Jack yelled.

Thinking quickly, Jack turned the key, throttling the engine of the lifeboat, which thankfully came to life, with a splutter. He knew as soon as they hit the surface, they would have to speed away from the momentum of the massive cargo vessel, with the land looming ever closer.

"Come on, boat, don't let me down!" Jack muttered.

"Slade! Zak! Jump!" the others shouted at the top of their lungs, gazing up at the gantry now five stories above them, the lifeboat striking the surface of the water, throwing its occupants with the force of the impact.

Revving the engine for all it was worth, Jack tried to keep pace with the speed of the Jzhao Li to give Slade and Zak a chance.

But they were stranded on the stricken vessel.

Having spent its life crossing the oceans of the world, the Jzhao Li was now making its final journey.

In the lifeboat racing away in the other direction, Jack struggled to steer with jagged rocks beckoning, tantalizingly close.

The others could hardly bear to watch what they knew was about to transpire. They were powerless. There was nothing they could do, though Jack tried to alter course and head closer toward the vessel.

Slade closed his eyes and jumped while Zak clutched the railings of the gantry, staring with horror into the abyss, aware that impact was inevitable.

The Jzhao Li ran aground, striking the reefs at speed, the ship screeching and shrieking as its steel hull peeled open. Over a hundred thousand tonnes colliding with an enormous underwater landmass. Like a lumbering leviathan, the mighty propellers at the back of the vessel kept spinning, cutting into the submerged reef while at the front of the ship, the Jzhao Li was literally torn apart. Groaning in an agony of twisted metal, debris strewn everywhere, the stacks of containers on its outside decks tumbling, crashing into the water. The noise was terrifying. Like a monster of the sea meeting its end, metal rending, grinding.

"Slade!!" Ruby cried out.

May gazed around for any sign of Zak, while the others surveyed the area in mounting panic as they clung to each other desperately.

Jack cursed as the lifeboat skuffed against the side of another rock, a scraping sound revealing that though they had escaped the Jzhao Li, the lifeboat was far from safe.

A mighty explosion suddenly erupted at the back of the huge container vessel, tearing through the Jzhao Li, punching a hole in the hull, flames soaring into the sky as the fuel caught alight, roaring upwards, smoke billowing into the deep blue sky.

The shockwave sped across the surface of the water, the occupants of the lifeboat struggling for cover as the massive cargo ship met its doom before their very eyes.

CHAPTER FOURTEEN

Bray felt the cold water impact as it struck his face, awakening him with a start. He instinctively gasped at the shock and shook his head, water flying in all directions from his wet hair, droplets dripping down his face.

His body felt weak and his mind totally groggy as if he was still fast asleep and hadn't fully woken up yet. In a stupor, Bray took a moment to try and make sense of his surroundings - and what had happened to him.

His vision was blurred and it was then he felt the throbbing pain in the back of his head where he had been struck.

Adrenalin filling his body, he blinked his eyes rapidly to try and clear his vision. He would have wiped his eyes but suddenly realized he was unable to do so - both his hands had been bound tightly behind his back. He tried to move, to get up from the prone position he found himself in - but his legs had also been bound, tethered at his ankles. So he was a prisoner once more, he thought, slumping his head back - on a very comfortable pillow. This was no ordinary prison, Bray thought. Just what exactly was it?

Though he felt like he was still in a deep sleep - and for a moment, wondered if this was all a dream - Bray finally was able to take in details of his environment, the blurred vision he had first experienced on waking up beginning to dissipate.

He was in some kind of living quarters. Laying on a bed, the mattress inviting and supportive. The ceiling above his head was missing the customary graffiti that had been so evident in the post-adult world and there weren't any obvious signs of vandalism or damage. Scanning his line of vision downwards, the walls around him were also in good condition. It felt as if he had almost gone back in time, to how living conditions used to be. But he also noticed a bank of security monitors, displaying outside images of the runways and various vantages of the barbed wire perimeter.

It was then that Bray spotted the young boy he had followed earlier... when? How long ago? The boy was staring at Bray from the other side of the room, examining him with fascination like he was an animal in a zoo.

Beside the boy stood the little girl Bray recognized from his previous encounter with them in the ruins of the theme park and administrative building. She was now holding a large bucket in her arms, watching Bray with curiosity, a hint of anxiety in her eyes. So she must have been the one to give him his wake up call, Bray figured.

"Hello," Bray began, trying to strike up a conversation, giving a friendly smile to the young boy and girl before him.

"Don't speak to them, talk to me," a warm voice spoke, determination in its tone.

Bray turned to where the voice was coming from and another girl, taller, obviously much older than the other kids, was slowly approaching him, one of her arms touching the bed as she edged nearer, using it as a guide, running her fingers along the side of the mattress. Bray couldn't make out much of her features. She was mostly in darkness, that side of the bed in shadow from the dim table lamps doing their best to illuminate the room.

"Be careful!" the young boy called out protectively.

"I'll be fine," the much older girl reassured him, moving forward towards Bray.

Stepping out into the diffused light, Bray could see that this girl was not that much younger than him. Tall, standing with good posture, her brown hair tied in a long ponytail that swung behind her back. She had a gracious air about her. A few freckles on her face, she was pretty.

It was her eyes though which were so striking. Full of expression. Yet opaque as if staring into the distance, the realms of an unknown world. Bray recognized that this girl was blind.

"Who are you?" Bray asked, looking up as the blind girl sat by the side of the bed.

"The one asking the questions," the girl replied matter of factly.

Bray winced as the girl touched his infected leg, pain shooting up his body. He wondered if he was about to be tortured, just what she meant to do with him.

"I'm sorry. I was just feeling your wound. To see if your infection is healing," the girl said, her fingers gently caressing around the wound on his leg. It had been bandaged, Bray only now appreciated, feeling the gauze fastened over his infection.

"Thanks," Bray said, the pain in his leg subsiding from her gentle touch.

"We could have left you to die. But we've cleaned you up, tended your wounds. Given you antibiotics. My younger brother has even given you a shave," the blind girl said.

Bray felt alarmed at the thought of the young boy being anywhere near a razor blade - let alone one near his neck - but it was true. He could feel the air in the room on his face, which was now smooth, the stubble he had grown during his time in the wilderness shaved clean.

"What do you want of me?" he asked.

"Answers. Like - who are you?"

"My name is Bray."

"Why were you following my younger brother and sister?"

"They were the first people I had seen in ages. I've been lost, wandering around for some time and if I hadn't found you - this place - I'm sure I wouldn't have made it."

"Where are you from?"

"That's a long story. Another land, originally. Least of all, I think. But now? I've been on my own for some time, trying to survive." Bray omitted any details about being an escaped prisoner, on the run from Eloise. He had to find out who these people were. For all he knew, they might hand him back in to Eloise's forces, or be in some sort of contact with them.

"Are you saying that you travelled over the wastelands?" the blind girl asked in disbelief.

"Just believe me. I'm a long way from home."

"That's very hard to believe. That you made it here. Some of our people climbed the barrier. Tried to head to the north. Across the wastelands. But none of them ever returned. Did you have anything to do with it?" the blind girl asked, a sense of anger now in her demeanour.

"No, I promise. I'm on my own. I haven't seen anyone else and I don't know what happened to the people you're talking about."

"Neither do we. And if you are responsible in some way...?"

Bray could only guess that whoever the blind girl referred to must have encountered Eloise's forces, if they had even made it that far through the unforgiving wilderness.

"Where are your markings?" the blind girl asked suspiciously.

"Markings? I don't know what you mean."

Without saying a word, the girl leaned forward and placed her hands on Bray's head, her fingers gently feeling his face.

"I can't identify you..." she said, reading Bray's features. "You have no markings anywhere." Then she ran her hands around his powerful arms. "No barcode?" she continued.

"He has a small tattoo on the side of his face, Emma, but I don't recognize the sign," the young boy advised.

"Well?" Emma asked Bray, who was still keen not to give too much information away.

"It's just something I got done a long while ago. Do you like it?" he smiled to the younger girl, who nodded shyly and received a kick from her brother.

"Are you really - free?" Emma asked, finishing her face reading and leaning back, dropping her hands onto the surface of the bed.

"Free? Free from what?" Bray replied.

"Nobody... owns you?" the blind girl questioned, Bray spotting a hint of surprise in her tone.

"Owns me? No, no one owns me at all."

"Then your presence here gives us much to think about."

The blind girl stood up and backed away from Bray, feeling her route with her hand, touching the bed as she moved on.

Bound and tied, unable to go anywhere, Bray began to feel a sense of injustice and the fighter in him began to emerge as he struggled with his bonds.

"Aren't you going to tell me anything?!" Bray called out, frustrated.

Emma turned to him, hearing his voice, her opaque eyes staring in his direction.

"You need to save your energy. And so do we. Get some rest. While you still can. We'll talk again. Later."

With that, Emma opened the door and exited, her brother and sister following, the younger girl flicking off the light switch by the door as she departed, extinguishing the room in darkness.

Bray struggled to keep awake but feeling tired, confused, his body weak and head still hurting from where he had been struck before, the last thing Bray heard before he fell asleep was the door to the room being locked from the outside.

CHAPTER FIFTEEN

"I claim this land for the Mall Rats!" Jack spoke in mock grandeur, standing on the beach of this unknown world, surveying his surroundings like an explorer of old.

"I still can't believe we made it!" Trudy exclaimed, looking up at the clear blue sky to thank her lucky stars, hugging Brady protectively in her arms.

"Don't speak too soon. Not until everyone is accounted for," Amber replied and instructed those who had survived to search around the beach until they had checked that everyone was okay, found. Also to see what could be salvaged. Then they would need to make some kind of shelter.

Splitting up, the survivors spread out around the beach, the waves rhythmically lapping as the tide rolled in, hitting the shore and bringing in all sorts of debris from the Jzhao Li.

All around them, the sandy beachfront was strewn with pieces of metal, plastic bottles, drenched tins of food, many of which spewed out their contents into the ocean, having been damaged, crushed when the mighty vessel ran aground.

Jay stood in the water, knee deep, wading around to see if they could find anything useful. Or if there was a sign of any bodies.

The surface of the water must have had thousands of items floating in it, bobbing around, having fallen out of the containers which had once been on the outer decks of the cargo ship.

The Jzhao Li itself was several hundred metres away, breaking up, its burned out hull creaking as the tide came in, engulfing the damaged superstructure, gradually shaking loose whole sections of the riveted hull, the occasional loud shriek of screeching metal audible from so far away. What was left of the ship lay on a severe angle, the wreck collapsing into the growing depths of the ocean, the last remaining metal containers it carried tumbling into the waters with a mighty crash, like ice falling off a glacier.

"Anything, Ellie? You okay?" Amber asked loudly so her voice could be carried from the beach to the lifeboat, still out in the water.

"There's nothing more in here, no sign," Ellie shouted back to the shore.

She and Lex had been checking out the splintered lifeboat they had escaped in, a massive dent on the front from where it had collided with a gigantic rock. A gash was visible in the side of the small vessel and it was taking in water. The lifeboat was still stuck fast, as it had been when it first struck the rock that held it pinned in its grasp, Ellie and Lex standing on the rock and leaning into the lifeboat, trying their best to keep their balance.

"Be careful, Ellie," Jack called out from down the beach, concerned, then he gazed around for signs of the others.

Satisfied that there was no sign of those unaccounted for still trapped in the lifeboat, Lex traversed, leaping from the boat to the rock, joining Ellie, and began swimming to shore.

It had been so close, such a lucky escape and they both hoped all had made it. But they were beginning to have their doubts.

Ram sat on the beach, cradling his head in his hands, lost in another world of his own.

"Ram? Are you hurt?" Amber wondered, walking among the cluttered assortment of debris, her eyes scanning the beach for any sign of absent friends.

"Leave me alone, Amber. I'm thinking," Ram grumbled.

"You can save your thinking till later, once we've found everyone. Why don't you get off your butt and help, start looking around?"

"Fine! If you insist!" Ram snapped, getting to his feet - and lashed out petulantly at a pile of shampoo bottles that had washed ashore, kicking them venemously, venting his frustration.

Just what was his problem, Amber thought to herself as Ram waded into the shallow water and began searching through the myriad of items floating around him.

Amber shook her head, mystified as always by Ram and his behaviour. But now wasn't the time to be concerned by any of Ram's histrionics. There were lives in danger, missing people to find.

May sat further down on the beach, her legs tucked up as she rocked back and forth, crying. Amber crossed to her and sat down beside her to offer some comfort, wrapping an arm around May, her shoulders heaving in emotion.

"There, everything will be okay," Amber said, doing her best to give some reassurance, to help with the hurt May was feeling.

"Really?" May blurted out doubtfully, her eyes welled up, wet with tears.

"We'll find them. Zak and the others. I promise you."

"What if he didn't make it?" May asked, dreading to ask the question. "What if he's - "

Unable to finish, May choked up and buried her head in Amber, wailing at the potential loss of her loved one she so painfully expected, Amber hugging her tightly, trying to absorb May's pain.

* * *

"Oh, my God - Darryl!" Salene called out. Far away from the others, Salene noticed a figure and ran towards it, finally reaching Darryl, his body lying inert face down on the beach.

Concerned, Salene knelt above Darryl, casting her eyes up and down at him, wondering if he was alive.

"Oh, my God, oh, my God," she repeated over and over again, hesitating, lost in her fears.

Following her instinct, Salene slowly pushed Darryl onto his back. He didn't react.

Behind her, Jay and Lex were sprinting along the sandy shore, making their way towards her to lend assistance.

"Relax, Sal, remember?" Salene urged herself, telling herself to keep calm and trying to recall the first aid lessons she had taken at school.

Leaning over Darryl, she could hear his heart beating in his chest. So he was still alive. For now.

Opening his mouth to free up the airwaves, Salene gave Darryl the kiss of life, breathing into him, willing him to live. He responded, poking his tongue into her mouth and she recoiled in amazement.

"I didn't know you cared!" Darryl said, looking up at Salene.

She was shocked by the immediate transformation in Darryl's health, then the truth dawned on her.

"You were faking it?!" she asked, in disbelief.

"I saw you heading my way, thought I'd play possum. I had to do something to get a smooch from you."

"You'll get a punch in the mouth!" Salene retorted angrily, and she began to hit Darryl, furious at his deception, as he shielded himself, yelping out.

"Easy. That's a weird form of lifesaving, Sal - it won't work. You look like you're going to kill him!" Lex said, out of breath as he and Jay arrived, the two of them stunned at seeing Salene pounding Darryl.

"He deserves it. Idiot!" Salene shrieked, and with one more hit, she stormed away, heading to another section of the beach.

"Women, eh?" Darryl sighed despondently to Lex and Jay as they helped him to his feet. "I can never figure them out."

* * *

About another hundred metres ahead, Ruby and Lottie gazed around, examining the beach for any glimpse of the missing others.

"Ruby!" Lottie shrieked, suddenly noticing someone, and pointed ahead.

Racing over, as Ruby and Lottie neared the figure, they identified Slade laying still on his side, a gash on his head, dried blood caked on the wound. Ruby and Lottie's expressions were full of concern as they crouched behind him.

"Hello, Ruby," Slade whispered casually.

Ruby grinned in delight that Slade had survived. "How'd you know it's me?"

"I can smell your perfume."

"You're alive!" Lottie shrieked, thrilled.

"Either that, or this is some afterlife."

"Are you hurt?" Ruby asked, examining Slade's body.

"I'm okay, don't worry."

"I wouldn't be too sure about that," Lottie replied.

Stepping over him to get to his other side for another look, Ruby suddenly put her hand to her mouth, gasping as she, too, noticed what Lottie had seen.

Slade's right hand was covering a gaping wound in his side, a jagged piece of metal sticking in his stomach, below his left ribcage, blood oozing through his shirt, flowing through his fingers.

Lottie could hardly bear to look at the sickening wound and turned away.

"It's that bad, huh?" Slade wondered, groaning at the pain.

Holding back the tears, Ruby's silence told Slade everything, confirming the worst fears he suspected about the extent of his injury.

* * *

"Of all the places we could have ended up, trust us to find one without any hotels," Gel complained, dropping palm leaves onto a pile, gradually getting bigger.

She had been deployed, along with Trudy and Sammy, to gather some leaves to build a makeshift shelter.

"What's the matter? You missing your hair conditioner? Shampoo?" Sammy scoffed, adding some palms of his own to the collection, Brady beside him, throwing her own small bundle on top.

"Stop thinking about yourself for once, Gel, and get your priorities straight," Trudy said.

"I was only talking," Gel mumbled.

"Exactly! Try thinking as well, for once," Trudy snapped.

Gel stuck her tongue out at Trudy, making a face behind her back.

Noticing, little Brady retaliated, poking her own tongue out at Gel, sticking up for her mother as Sammy cast a glance at Heaven.

Tempers were beginning to fray within the entire group as the reality of the situation they faced was beginning to dawn on them.

There had been no sign of Zak, who was still missing.

Slade's injuries were horrific, a source of concern to everyone, especially Ruby.

And with the day advancing on this strange land they found themselves in, Amber had realized they had best start making a shelter before it got dark or the weather turned.

As well as gathering a pile of palm leaves, branches and sticks to construct a shelter, they needed to erect some kind of cover for Slade. They felt he was too injured to be moved from his current location.

There was concern also at exactly where they were. And if this land was populated. They would need to check out their environs. All hoped, if there was any other form of life around, that the inhabitants were friendly. Not hostile.

The priority though was to consolidate their base, gather supplies, search for any sign of Zak, and tend to Slade.

After a brief catch up to identify the next stage of their plan, Darryl was to accompany Amber, who was going to join Ruby to offer what assistance they could provide to Slade, now that they had recovered medical supplies.

Lex, Salene, Lottie, Sammy, Gel and Trudy were to assist Jack erecting the makeshift shelter.

The little ones played nearby in the sand. Young Brady was having the time of her life, racing around Trudy, eagerly picking up leaves fallen from the palm trees like it was some game, and playfully kicking sand in the air. Trudy's daughter had rarely seen sand before and this new world was so different to the concrete jungle of the city that had been their home in the past.

Though upset by all that had happened to them, Trudy herself seemed overall more content than she had on the

Jzhao Li, her spirits lifted as she found joy at the delight of her daughter in their new environment. But this was marred by the injury to Slade and concern at Zak being missing.

Jay was to catch up with Ram and search the opposite end of the beach in case Zak had washed ashore elsewhere.

"I've never seen so many trees," Darryl said, keeping his good humour, indicating the palm trees lining the beach, as he crossed with Amber towards Ruby, crouched by the injured Slade.

"We're certainly not in the city anymore," Amber said.

"Palm Tree Rats rather than Mall Rats? Maybe we should change the name of the Tribe. What do you think?" Darryl grinned.

"First things first. We've got more important matters to deal with," Amber replied.

For all of her concern, Amber couldn't help but notice - as had Darryl - that the landscape was beautiful. In another time, another place, she would have been thrilled to be here. In this strange land. In some ways it seemed like the perfect holiday destination, somewhere you would go on a honeymoon. The aesthetic straight out of an exotic brochure. But this was no vacation. The reality of their situation was that they all had to survive, Amber resolved. Get through their predicament, one minute, one hour at a time, then each passing day.

As Amber and Darryl approached, they could hear Slade's groans, his teeth clenched as he tried to ride out the agony he was feeling from the wound in his side.

Ruby knelt beside him, cradling his head tenderly, doing her utmost to pacify, take away the pain, her expression one of complete concern at Slade's suffering. She resolved that she would never leave him.

"How's it going?" Amber whispered to Ruby.

"Good, real good," Ruby lied, her face contorted in a grimace of worry. She was doing what she could to put a positive light on things so Slade wouldn't be any more in distress than he already was. But she needn't have bothered. He didn't hear Ruby or Amber. Slade was in a world of his own, fighting the pain he was going through.

And as Amber exchanged concerned glances with Ruby and Darryl, and Slade groaned again, Amber cringed at his discomfort, wishing there was something she could do to alleviate his suffering. She examined what medical supplies they had but realized that they really needed to come up with something more substantive. The problem was, with no apparent help around, she was at a loss what else they could do.

"Steady him - we're gonna have to remove this and bandage him," Amber said, referring to the piece of metal still embedded in Slade's side.

Ruby gently caressed Slade's hair, then glanced as Amber took a deep breath and gently, carefully, removed the piece of metal.

"Pass me those bandages, Darryl. Come on, as fast as you can!"

Darryl was rigid, his eyes gaping at the blood oozing from Slade's side. The colour drained from Darryl's face and he fainted, collapsing onto the sands.

Amber sighed. That's all she needed, though she too felt queasy as she tended to Slade's wounds, bandaging him.

* * *

"Ram, so there you are!" Jay called out as he ran up the beach. "I've been looking everywhere for you."

"Nice to have been missed," Ram said, his back to Jay as he sat on the wet sands, the tide lapping around his legs.

"We need all hands to try and search for Zak."

"You can all manage without me, I'm sure. Amber's still in charge, isn't she? You usually get by without my involvement.

I may as well speak to myself half the time, nobody ever listens to me anymore."

"That's not true," Jay said, smiling slightly at Ram's sulking. Despite being such a genius, Ram could act so childish sometimes. "Come on. We need you."

"I'll wait a little longer, if you don't mind."

"Why? What are you doing?"

"Trying to catch fish."

"With just your bare hands? Now this, I've got to see."

"Let me be, Jay. Please."

"What is it? You still harping on that we should have gone back to the city? That you were right all along? If so, now's not the time to be out here throwing tantrums, making a point. What is, is. We're shipwrecked on this land and we've got to make the best of it."

Ram scoffed, unconvinced.

And it was then Jay noticed the blood in the water, the waves slowly lapping around Ram as the tide moved in.

"Are you hurt?" Jay asked in sudden concern, aware now that Ram had kept his back to Jay this whole time.

Leaning forward to check Ram out, he realized that in reality Ram was up to something. Hiding, keeping something from Jay.

"Get away from me!" Ram exploded, shifting position in the sand to keep his back to Jay.

"Enough games!" Jay shouted.

Grabbing Ram by the shoulders, Jay physically spun Ram around.

He was astonished to see blood pouring from a recent flesh wound on Ram's forehead.

"What? The wound? I tripped, bashed my head on a rock."

"You're lying" Jay said, curious and angry at Ram's strange behaviour.

For Ram's 'accidental' injury was confined to one part of his head.

"We need to talk, Ram!" Jay insisted.

To all intents, the wound looked self-inflicted. And that Ram had been trying to scratch away his 'Techno' symbol markings from his forehead.

CHAPTER SIXTEEN

Ebony was gripped by panic as the lifeboat she was in continued its inexorable drift out to the open sea.

She had given up trying to restart the engine, which had long ago spluttered out the last of its fuel in a cough of fumes. Since then, all she could do was steer the helm, trying to angle the tiny vessel back towards the land.

Ebony had never been too knowledgeable about the sea, she was a city girl. Whatever explained the changing current though, one thing was for sure, it was taking the lifeboat and Ebony with it, further and further out towards the vast emptiness of the ocean.

She had always been a survivor. From the streets.

Now, for one of the few times in her life, she was vulnerable. Exposed. Helpless. It had been agonizing being so close to the landmass, the promise of escape, after so many days at sea. The lifeboat was drifting away, as if fate was teasing her, toying with her feelings.

At one point earlier she had jumped into the water and tried to swim to shore when she realized the danger she was in. Unable to make much headway against the prevailing current, she had swam back and with all her efforts, just made it onto the lifeboat. It had been a frightening moment when she had truly felt like she was alone in this unforgiving world, worrying she was going to drown.

At least the lifeboat afforded her some sanctuary out here, in the middle of nowhere, but for how much longer, she couldn't say. Ebony had precious little in the way of food or water supplies due to her hasty escape from the Jzhao Li. Everything she tried to do now to survive seemed like it was hitting a dead end, with the tide driving her further towards the open ocean.

For a moment Ebony wondered what had happened to the others - and to Slade. Last time she saw them, the Jzhao Li had been hurtling towards the land on a different course to her's. She had been drifting for several hours since then. The Jzhao Li was now far away, out of sight.

Had they survived? What did she care, Ebony felt. Slade had made his choice. And she couldn't help but hope that Ruby was suffering, pinning the blame on her for Ebony's break up with Slade. If Ruby had been dealt a cruel blow of fate, then it served her right. Bitch.

As far as her own fate was concerned, Ebony started to sob. She wept for herself, her plight, the cruel and unfair way that her destiny was unfolding. She wondered if this was a punishment for all the bad things she had done in her life, if what was happening to her was some form of divine retribution, God paying her back in kind, causing her to suffer. With the expectation that all that lay ahead for her was a long, lingering, painful death, Ebony struggled to come to terms with it, sure she would end her days on this floating tomb.

But Ebony didn't believe in karma, she thought, through teary eyes. She had got away with a lot in her life and surely she would make it, somehow. Maybe the tide would change and her lifeboat would drift back towards shore once more.

It wasn't over till it was over, she thought, trying to raise her fading spirits.

She was alive, for now, and as desperate as the situation she faced, Ebony tried to dismiss her fears, clinging to her instinct for survival. She'd been through hell before, when the adults first perished and she had been forced to use everything in her considerable arsenal of tricks, cunning, guile to endure in the city. She had to keep going, she urged herself. Somehow she would survive.

For all that she was trying to provide herself with some form of hope, she felt utter despair, misery welling up inside. And she wailed at the injustice of life and the situation she was in.

Tears flooding her eyes, overwhelmed and exhausted, Ebony cried herself to sleep.

* * *

Hours later, it was the sound of the approaching engine that woke Ebony up with a start.

Reacting quickly, she poked her head above the side of the lifeboat to find out what was going on, doing her best to keep herself hidden.

All she could see, all around her, was the ocean. The land was barely visible on the distant horizon. She calculated that the current must have obviously taken her miles out to sea while she had slept.

Suddenly she noticed a white cruiser approaching at high speed. It was still some distance away. Ebony shook her head in disbelief. It was unbelievable. Out here, in the middle of nowhere. Who were they? What the hell were they doing?

More importantly, what should she do? Try and attract their attention? But clearly she already had their attention and she felt like a sitting duck, exposed. She had no idea who was in the cruiser, where they were from, and what reason they had to move towards Ebony's lifeboat. Maybe they would be friendly and were simply going to rescue her. Or worse, the occupants of the boat could be hostile.

Ebony always looked to cover the worst case but now had no option, being stranded, other than to pull one of the blankets that had been stored in the lifeboat over her head. Maybe it would turn out there was one person on the cruiser and she could take them out, whoever they might be, overpower them and take the cruiser for herself. She just didn't know. For now, it seemed like the best idea was to hide, assess her options until she knew what she was dealing with.

Peeking through the blanket, Ebony tried to catch a better glimpse of the cruiser as it approached, closer, closer. Then it circled like an animal viewing its prey, before striking.

Adrenalin pumped through Ebony's body, her mind racing to decide what she should do. Stay hidden or show herself?

The engines of the cruiser were deafening now.

Ebony risked another look, poking her fingers through the blanket, lifting it up so she could try and check out just exactly what was happening.

The cruiser idled its engines, mooring itself at the front of the lifeboat. From her angle, Ebony still couldn't see how many people were involved.

She hid again at the sound of someone jumping aboard, heavy-footed, telling Ebony it was obviously at least one person. But then her heart sank as she heard more people bounding on deck.

Suddenly the blanket covering Ebony was whipped away, exposing her.

She noticed four powerfully built-guys. About the same age as her. They were dressed all in black, wearing balaclavas rolled up into berets which covered their heads, their hair close shaven as if they belonged to some kind of military. Their leader indicated his subordinates in a ruthlessly cold and efficient manner.

"Check the identification plates. Commander Blake will want details of where the Jzhao Li was registered!"

"Yes, sir!" the subordinate said, then scoured the lifeboat, punching in details of the brass plaque on the instrumentation panel into a small mobile device he was holding.

The others yanked Ebony to her feet.

"Identify yourself," the leader ordered her.

"I'm a mermaid, lost at sea," Ebony replied seductively.

She knew she was attractive and could turn it on and off when needed. She had never been afraid to use her allure to get her way with guys in the past. And thought she'd try this time. But it wasn't working. The leader considered Ebony, then turned to his team, with more important matters on his mind.

"Any other stowaways?"

His companions were methodically checking to see if anyone was hiding under the other seats or blankets.

"Doesn't seem like it, Sir," one said.

The leader indicated and two of his men assisted Ebony to her feet.

"Keep away from me!" she yelled, striking out, punching one in the face, kicking the other with all her might into his groin.

It seemed to have no effect whatsoever.

They were impassive and didn't react to her attack other than grabbing Ebony by the arm, which they forced up behind her back to restrain her so she couldn't move.

These guys knew what they were doing, Ebony thought, and quickly realized that she'd better back down and go along with them. For now. They were obviously well trained in the art of combat, unlike some of the tribes she had encountered in any battles on the streets.

Her oppressors led her onto the deck of the lifeboat where they transferred her to the cruiser. It was much bigger than Ebony had envisaged and could hold several passengers.

Ebony noticed a girl, again about her age, also dressed the same way as the boarding party. She had hideous scars across one side of her face and must have been in a bad accident at some point, Ebony thought. After the first wave of revulsion, Ebony even managed to garner a degree of sympathy. Since the darkness descended in the post adult world, life was hard enough without having to face it behind a disfigured mask like that.

"Welcome aboard!" the hideous girl said contemptuously.

Ebony gazed around in growing fear. Members of the boarding party were securing the lifeboat with ropes, presumably to tow the tiny vessel somewhere.

The hideous girl tossed a fishing net over Ebony, then extended one leg, pushing Ebony to the floor with ease like the martial arts expert she clearly was, before yanking the net, tightening it and leaving Ebony unable to move her limbs, her movement totally restricted by the bonds.

She braced herself, petrified, wondering just what lay in store for her as the cruiser was revved and sped away, hurtling through the ocean, towing the lifeboat in its wake. But to where?

CHAPTER SEVENTEEN

The Mall Rats decided to call their new home "Camp Phoenix," naming it after "Phoenix Mall," the shopping mall that had been their home back in the city.

It was an appropriate name, given the hope everyone shared that like the mythical bird, they too would rise up and survive, life would go on, from facing doom at being shipwrecked in this strange new world. The image of a phoenix conjured up flames and that too was applicable, Amber felt, given the intense searing heat that seemed to cook the very air around them.

Amber was like a bee, buzzing from one place to the other, as she tried to encourage everyone and bring some semblance of order to Camp Phoenix, which was still more a name only than a proper camp.

Her thoughts drifted to Jay. And Ram. They had been gone now for what must have been a few hours, though Amber had no way of exactly telling the time, relying only on judging the position of the sun in the sky.

Jay had left with Ram to explore the perimeters.

Before they departed, Jay informed Amber what he had discovered, with Ram trying to remove his Techno markings.

Ram had maintained to Amber and the others he had accidentally hurt his head and there was nothing more to it than that.

But Amber's constant distrust of Ram prevailed. To Amber, he had always proven from his actions in the past he was capable of being up to something, usually no good.

Throughout their entire time on first the trawler, then the Jzhao Li, Amber had been unsettled by Ram and his insistence on going back to the city. It just defied all sense, wanting to return to a city gripped by pandemic.

Was there some connection between his extreme moods, changing out of his uniform and trying to dismiss any sign of his markings, and desire to go back home? Or did he know something about this strange land that the others didn't know?

If anyone could find out the answers, it would be Jay. He'd coax the truth out of Ram, somehow, and Jay told Amber he had been quietly hopeful that if he could talk with Ram in a one-to-one conversation, away from Amber and the others, he would discover what it was that had so troubled Ram since the moment the Tribe had fled - and why he was so eager to get back to their doomed home city.

Ram was a dangerous individual though. As much as Jay was skilled in combat, able to handle himself, Amber hoped he would still be safe going off into the unknown undergrowth with Ram. You could never be too safe with the former leader of the Technos. Amber tried to dismiss such thinking, instead looking forward to Jay's return, with Ram - and hopefully the unearthing of any secrets Ram had been trying to keep from them.

Jack and Lex had been deployed to search another area and agreed not to venture too far. All were just keen to gain more insight into the perimeters of their environs.

As the oldest male left behind while Lex, Jack, Ram and Jay were away, Darryl had sincerely tried to 'man up' to his responsibilities and was pouring sweat as he sorted through great piles of palm fronds, branches and sticks to use in the construction of their shelter, Lottie, Gel and Sammy helping him out.

Amber was somewhat surprised and displeased by Gel, however, who Amber spotted laying in the sun like she was lounging on the beach in a luxury resort on holiday.

"Gel - what do you think you're doing?" Amber asked, walking up to her.

"What do you think I'm doing?" Gel replied, as if it was all so obvious.

Amber shrugged, her confused expression showing Gel she didn't know what she was talking about.

"I'm sunbathing - duh!" Gel petulantly explained, deliberately ignoring Amber, and went on with improving her suntan.

"Gel - if you stay there one more minute, I swear I'll-"

"Amber - give me a break!" Gel called back. "You're not my mother!"

"Thank goodness. This isn't some kind of break away, Gel. You either get up and pull your weight or you get out of here and have nothing to do with our camp. It's up to you."

Amber stormed off, pacing down the burning sands and behind her, sighing like a spoilt child, Gel reluctantly went to help Darryl, Sammy and Lottie in constructing the shelter.

Slade was asleep now, Amber could see as she approached, his dreams a refuge from the pain he felt in his side when he was awake.

Like before, Ruby was steadfastly by his side, watching over him.

"You should try and get some rest yourself," Amber whispered to Ruby, so as not to disturb Slade.

"I can't leave him," Ruby replied. She looked like an emotional wreck, which she was, her make up smeared over her face from the tears she had shed.

"I'll stay with him, make sure he's okay," Amber insisted. "You've been here for hours. What would Slade say? He'd want you to take care of yourself. Go and take some time out, gather yourself together."

Understanding the sense behind Amber's suggestion, Ruby smiled, appreciating the help, leaving Amber in charge of Slade.

Salene and Ellie were continuing to assist May in the ongoing search for Zak, his disappearance causing all great concern.

In another area of the beach, Trudy had lit a fire with some fallen branches and was carefully holding improvised skewers of tinned meat over the flames as Ruby arrived and sat down to join her.

"Hungry?" Trudy asked. "This should be ready in a minute."

Ruby nodded gratefully.

Some of the canned food from the Jzhao Li had been gathered into a pile of stores. There had been no can opener so Trudy had to bash the tins open with a coconut.

It had been ironic using food to open food, she thought. Brady was crawling on the sand, pushing one of the coconuts like a toy while Amber's baby lay asleep under the shade of some palms.

"This is kinda fun, isn't it?" Trudy said.

"I wouldn't call this fun," Ruby protested, "with Slade injured!"

"We're all worried about Slade," Trudy explained. "I just mean, in a way, this is an adventure. Cooking on the open fire. Sitting here on the beach. The kids are certainly having fun."

Ruby obviously didn't share Trudy's enthusiasm for their surroundings, their 'adventure'. In fact, she took offence at

Trudy's apparent lack of concern or worry for Slade. Trudy was being overly happy, Ruby felt, unnaturally so.

"Come on, Ruby. Can't we just take our mind off things, just for a minute?"

"What? And stick our head in the sand, pretending that everything's alright? Because it isn't!" Ruby replied disdainfully.

Then she felt guilty, knowing that Trudy was trying as hard as she could to keep her emotions in control and spirits up. They were all struggling in their own ways, she realized. But Ruby felt there was nothing to gain by pretending that things weren't as bad as they really were.

"Mister Claw Claw!" Brady shrieked, thrilled at noticing a crab moving across the sand.

"Be careful with that 'thing'," Trudy shouted, "I don't want you to get hurt."

"You're pathetic, Trudy, you really are! Talk about being selective with your concern." Ruby couldn't help herself. She felt Trudy was being insensitive, not seemingly showing any care for Slade.

"How dare you speak to me like that!" Trudy snarled at Ruby. "Who do you think you are?!"

"Hey - you two going to cook up some seafood?" Darryl called, trying to diffuse the argument between Ruby and Trudy. He was still working on the shelter nearby and put his fingers to his lips in anticipation at his imagined meal. "Crab thermidor - magnifique!"

Sammy appeared from the undergrowth looking a bit sheepish.

"Well? You look to me like someone who feels... 'relieved'." Darryl said.

"Shhhh. No need to broadcast it, Darryl!" Sammy snapped.

"And there's no need for you to be embarrassed, Sammy boy. When someone's gotta go, they gotta go. Least with all that jungle back there, there's no chance of the toilet overspilling like it did on the boat."

"I wouldn't bet on it," Sammy groaned, rubbing his stomach.

Gel suddenly shrieked out, dropping a pile of branches she had cradled in her arms.

"I chipped a nail!" she bellowed.

Lottie let go of the ropes she was holding to secure the shelter Darryl was putting together and crossed to Gel nearby.

"And I've got calluses and blisters all over my hands - look!" Lottie said.

"Oh, poor you!" Ruby mocked. "Not as bad as some others around here if you'd only take the time to notice!" She cast an angry glance at Trudy.

Darryl focused on the shelter, its frame slowly taking shape, carefully tying on a palm leaf, wrapping it around the flimsy branches. But now, with Lottie no longer holding the base in place with the rope, Darryl froze. In one swift motion, the shelter they had worked on for hours collapsed like a house of cards around him.

He turned and glared at Lottie and Gel, who both sighed.

"It's not our fault!" Gel said helplessly.

* * *

Jay and Ram wound their way through the dense jungle, the air humid and moist. It was incredible just how thick the undergrowth was, the shade from the massive trees overhanging providing some relief from the otherwise almost impossible heat.

The jungle was alive with the sound of insects, the buzzing almost deafening, piercing the ear.

Ram waved at his face for the umpteenth time as more mosquitos swarmed around his exposed features.

"They obviously like you," Jay said, leading the two of them.

"Doesn't everybody?" Ram said, swatting at more bugs biting into his neck.

Jay also had many bites but he was trying to ignore the irritation, knowing that once you started, it was nearly impossible to stop scratching.

"I just hope they don't have malaria or some other - diseases," Ram grimaced, itching an ear with his finger.

"Think yourself lucky we haven't seen any snakes. Yet. They've probably seen us though."

"Can we go back now?" Ram pleaded, nervously looking at the jungle all around. "Doesn't seem to be any sign of anyone."

"Yeah, we'll head back. But not until you've talked."

"I told you - there's nothing to talk about!"

"And I told you - I don't believe you. I know you better than you think I do. And I can tell when you're keeping secrets."

"What do you want? A medal? A promotion, Jay?"

He had once, long ago. When the two had worked closely together in the Technos, Jay as Ram's general, Ram making an allusion to their past. But that was in a different life, Jay thought. It was all history.

"I want the truth, Ram. About why you were so keen to change your clothes, get out of your uniform, scratch away your Techno markings..."

"That's my business," Ram insisted.

"Oh, I don't think so. And you'd better tell me why it's been so important to you to want to go back to the city we fled. Why? Is there something out here - that you know about? Come on, Ram. Your behaviour's been extreme from the moment we arrived in this God forsaken place!"

Ram sighed, staring at Jay. Frustrated by his continued suspicions. His probing and persistence.

Ram gulped nervously, looking around the mysterious jungle environment, his eyes darting. Scared. There was definitely something about this place that was getting to him.

"Let's go back, Jay. We've come far enough."

"Not until you're finally ready to talk."

Ram bit his lip in growing unease.

And before Jay knew it, Ram was off, sprinting, finally tripping over the thick tumble of plants and branches on the jungle floor, struggling to keep his footing.

Like a panther chasing down its prey, Jay grit his teeth, moving in on Ram at top speed, determined not to let him get away.

Ram was panic-driven as he picked himself up and continued running quickly, desperate to escape.

But with Jay's longer stride and athletic prowess, it didn't take him long to close the gap and he launched himself at Ram's legs, rugby-tackling him to the ground, Ram shouting in disappointment, frustration at being caught.

"Get off me!" Ram struggled.

"Think I need any more proof!?" Jay grabbed Ram by the scruff of the neck, dragging him to his feet. "Something's going on, Ram! And it's about time you explain exactly what it is!"

Powerless, Ram began to laugh. Was he just trolling? Doing it to annoy Jay? Or had he lost it completely, going mad? Jay would find out, he promised, soon enough.

"So? What is it!?" Jay demanded.

"Don't look at me," Ram said, a manic glint in his eyes as he laughed uncontrollably. "I think you'd better look up, Jay. There's something in the trees. And it ain't no bird!"

Unsure exactly what Ram meant, Jay kept his grip on Ram so he couldn't escape, then cast his eyes upwards.

There, perhaps thirty feet off the jungle floor, visible through the thick undergrowth, he could see the wreck of a huge grey-coloured military cargo plane, stuck in the mighty boughs, covered slightly by the massive trees and vines. It looked like a Hercules or Tupolev, its enormous wings spanning across, blocking out the sun. The titanic-sized trees and density of foliage supported the bulk of the aircraft, which lay on an angle, as it must have done when it crash landed.

"What the hell?" Jay said, in awe of what he was seeing.

"So what about it, Jay? I reckon you should forget about me," Ram said, cackling to himself. "Don't you? Because I'm not your mystery. This land is."

Jay suddenly felt uneasy about leaving Amber and the others behind at the camp. But he couldn't head back now. He had promised Amber he would return with answers from Ram. And Ram was right, the plane added another mystery to the equation.

There was so much they didn't know. And maybe Ram knew more than he was letting on.

"You'd better start talking, Ram, if you know what's good for you. I mean it," Jay threatened, tightening his hold on Ram.

Ram considered Jay for a long moment. His laugher gradually subsided, then he nodded.

* * *

The waves pounded all around, surging across the rocks, exploding in a mist of spray.

Heads down, Salene, Ellie and May continued to scan the beach, as they had done for several hours now.

It was like finding a needle in a haystack. There were so many pieces of debris, bits of metal, broken objects of all sizes, from the wreck of the Jzhao Li, edged between the rocks, caught up in the gaps between.

Ellie was carrying a plastic drinks cooler that had been washed ashore. As well as searching for Zak, she was gathering up any other potentially useful medical supplies the girls had found throughout their search.

The drinks cooler was getting increasingly heavy as additional items were thrown into it. They had accumulated a good many packets of paracetamol, some bandages, bottles of disinfectant, cans of food.

But there had still been no sign of Zak. Only the girls, alone in this section of the beach, and in the distance, a good way off, Camp Phoenix.

Out in the ocean, the immense hull of the container ship lay on its side like a prehistoric monster from the deep, stranded on the reef from where it had run aground.

The sound of the surf was accompanied by the occasional noise of metal creaking, grinding and twisting from above and below the waterline, the Jzhao Li groaning as it slowly continued to be broken up by the pounding of the changing tide.

The girls had considered at one point diving underwater, to swim into the wreck to see if they could find some additional medical supplies. Or any sign of Zak. But they had abandoned such notions as being too dangerous, fearing that they might get stuck in the wreck and risk drowning.

"We should probably head back," Ellie called out.

"I'm not going anywhere!" May shouted. "You can go if you want."

"But we can't leave you here alone," Salene spoke loudly over the roar of the waves striking the rocks. "We don't know who - or what - is out here."

"I've got to find him, Sal!" May replied, the determination in her tone clear.

Seagulls squawked as they flew by, floating on the breeze, angling their wings, scavenging for any food.

Salene let out a scream. A piercing cry.

Ellie and May followed her gaze, and then they too, recoiled.

Caught between two rocks, Zak's body twisted in the movement of the water, like a lifeless doll. The colour had drained from his skin, his eyes shut, his features bloated.

"Oh, my God!" May screamed and began running towards the shallows, followed by Salene and Ellie.

* * *

The jungle seemed to be alive with the noise of so many insects as Jack followed Lex, weaving their way through the thick green undergrowth, with nothing else visible but the countless plants above them, under them and all around. They were engulfed and Jack shuddered to think of all the millions of tiny insect eyes staring at him that very moment.

A wild whooping sound rang out from some of the massive trees above, startling Jack even more.

"What do you think that is? A monkey?" Lex asked.

"Either that or maybe Trudy's having a panic attack," Jack smirked, trying to find the humour in the situation, like he always did, and to settle his nerves with a joke.

"Ha, ha, very funny," Lex replied. "But it sounds a bit too calm for Trudy. Man, I've been bitten so many times I'm surprised there's any blood left in me. I feel I've been attacked by a vampire."

"Well, let's just hope that's the extent of it. And we don't get attacked by anything else."

"Doesn't seem to be anyone around but the two of us," Lex said.

"And a bazillion insects," Jack mumbled.

"Some closer than you think," Lex said, putting his finger to his lips, indicating Jack to be quiet.

Wondering what Lex meant, Jack looked down to where Lex was gazing - towards one of his legs. Crawling on Jack's shin was a gigantic spider, slowly making it's way up Jack's leg.

Jack mouthed a silent scream, a look of anguish on his face.

Snapping a branch from a plant, Lex knocked the spider to the ground.

"You are such a wuss, Jack. I wonder what Ellie would say if she saw you now. Don't faint on me."

Relieved to be spider free - for now - Jack thought he heard noises around them, a branch swishing, the sounds of movement, and he spun around, nervously scanning the trees.

"Jack, would you please relax?" Lex said, then continuing on, suggested, "How about we take a break for a while? Have something to eat."

They stopped and opened a bag that they had placed their food rations in and snacked on some asparagus and tinned vegetables which they had opened earlier, before they left.

"This is the life, eh, Jack? Out here in the wide open spaces."

"Don't know about open spaces - I feel like this jungle's strangling me," Jack said wearily gazing around with a growing sense of claustrophobia and being engulfed by so much foliage.

"Chill, Jack. Calm down. We'll be alright. It's no big deal."

"Aren't you... scared?" Jack wondered.

"Nothing much scares me anymore... not these days," Lex said.

It was true. He wasn't just trying to raise Jack's failing spirits. He had experienced a lot, surviving back in the city on the streets since the adults had all perished.

"Then what is it?" Jack asked, noticing Lex gazing ahead.

He had spotted a dead bird. But all the feathers had been plucked.

"That's weird," Lex replied. "Check that out."

Lex and Jack moved towards the carcass.

Lex sniffed at it and resolved that it hadn't been dead for too long and didn't seem rotten.

"Look - there's another one over there," Jack said, gazing in growing intrigue.

"I'm sure Ellie will give you something special tonight when we arrive back with this fresh meat," Lex mocked, looking forward to a feast of something other than the canned rations which had been gathered back at base.

The other dead bird has also been plucked of feathers, which again confused Lex as he swaggered over to grab it. Then he suddenly disappeared, the ground beneath him giving way with a whoosh as he fell into a wide hole, the branches covering it imploding under Lex's feet.

"Lex!" Jack yelled out, gripped by panic.

But it was too late. Lex had gone.

CHAPTER EIGHTEEN

Bray wondered what his captors had in store for him, confused at the mixed signals he had received.

He had been kept in the room for several days now, his hands and feet bound. That he was their prisoner, was in no question. But he had also been treated well, his infected leg regularly cleaned so that now the wound had pretty much healed. He had been fed and watered several times each day. This was so different compared to his incarceration under Eloise with all the mental and physical stresses he had suffered. Yet he was still a prisoner. They were keeping him alive - but why?

Bray was genuinely baffled by the intentions of his captors. In the times that they visited him, he had managed to gradually piece together a picture of who they were. Where he was. They had been guarded with him, trying not to be too friendly, but in conversation a few clues and details had slipped through, Bray attempting to ask some subtle questions here and there, probing for information.

The young boy's name was Shannon, and the girl was called Tiffany. They were brother and sister, Bray discovered, and had been very kind to him on their visits, bringing and clearing away food, feeding Bray since he could not do so himself with his hands bound. They were so young, Bray felt a sense of protectiveness towards them. Just as he did to the other younger Mall Rats like Patsy and Chloe in the city so long before. And he considered what kind of future lay in store for them all in this dangerous world they all found themselves in after the demise of the adults.

The leader of the captors was undoubtably Emma, the blind girl, who Bray had learned was the older sister of Shannon and Tiffany. Emma had been less friendly to Bray, suspicious of him, wondering in turn what his motives were and who he was.

Bray had been able to gauge from his conversations with Emma, Shannon and Tiffany that they were all surviving in the remnants of what had once been called Arthurs Air Force Base. It had been used in World War 2 as a refuelling station and seemed to have been reactivated when the pandemic was reaching its peak, spreading globally.

All Shannon and Tiffany knew, they had told Bray, was that Arthur's Base had seen major building work and activity just before the 'virus' killed the adults. They themselves were far too young to remember much detail but it gave some kind of explanation for the construction machines and massive hangars Bray had spotted when he stumbled into the base, as well as the military aircraft left behind.

Apparently a lot of United Nations personnel from all around the world had spent time in this remote base, adding new hangars, buildings. For what reason, Shannon and Tiffany were unsure.

The small 'amusement park' itself had been introduced, Bray had been told, so the military personnel stationed there could enjoy the facilities with their families, the rides and fairy tale setting put in place as a break from whatever activity the

United Nations teams had been carrying out. Also schools and accommodation blocks were built with the area being prepared as an evacuation camp to house several thousand children.

According to Tiffany and Shannon, both far more talkative and less guarded than their elder sister, they had been told that the base was also to have been used by the adults as a makeshift hospital in the days when the 'virus' struck. And nearby in the area now known as the 'wastelands', there was a huge burial ground of mass, unmarked graves. But Tiffany and Shannon didn't seem to know too much detail about that either. Emma never liked to talk about it. The younger kids were not allowed to visit the 'wastelands' because Emma said it was far too dangerous to set foot there. The whole area was off limits because it was contaminated. But they didn't know by what.

Though the amusement park had been visited by other kids and teenagers since the adults died, trashing it in the process, apparently the fact that the base had once housed a hospital now worked in its favour. Likewise, that it was located near the 'wastelands'. It had a 'taint' from the past, that it wasn't safe, perhaps even still having traces of the 'virus' or some other diseases, its reputation ironically providing a safe place to stay.

Bray couldn't decipher if Emma, Tiffany and Shannon were the only ones now living at the base. Emma and the younger kids didn't give any detail. And Bray was determined to try and discover more. Then it might shed light on what they wanted of him.

Bray felt that they weren't going to hand him in. He had been there for so many days they would have had ample time to arrange for his return to Eloise's compound, if they were somehow connected to her forces. But equally, although he was gaining Tiffany and Shannon's trust and was beginning to know more about their set up, he still didn't want to take chances or have a false sense of security with any flawed assumptions. He needed to get some more facts.

There were so many questions floating around in Bray's mind. It would soon be time, he hoped, for some answers.

Bray's thoughts were disturbed as the door to the room was unlocked and swung open - by Tiffany, the young girl stepping aside so Emma could enter the room.

"Thank you, Tiffany," Emma said, entering. She clearly knew the layout well and gradually made her way towards Bray, carrying a glass of water in one hand and an open tin of baked beans in the other, a spoon sticking out of it.

"You may go," Emma instructed Tiffany, the young girl casting a furtive uncertain glance at Bray before closing the door and locking it from the other side.

Emma sat down on the side of Bray's bed and slowly inched the glass of water to his face.

"Thirsty?" she asked Bray.

"Thanks. But I don't understand," he replied. "You feed me, clean me up, but keep me under lock and key. Why?"

"We've been wondering the same thing," Emma answered carefully, putting the glass of water down on the side table next to Bray's bed that she knew was there.

"I just don't get it, Emma. Is it your idea to show hospitality by taking hostages? You got anyone else locked up here? The three of you seem nice. You've treated me well. But still, here I am, your prisoner."

"And lucky you are, too. You should be grateful."

"I am in a way. But not totally. You going to keep me here forever? You enjoy doing this or something? What's your plan, Emma? Please - let me know, what's going on!"

"You have no idea - about anything - have you?" Emma seemed flustered, agitated.

"All I know is, this isn't the way to treat people. What kind of world are you wanting? For Shannon and Tiffany? You giving them a crash course in kidnapping and imprisonment?"

Emma angrily threw the tin of beans, spilling their contents.

Bray sat back in his bed. Part of him worried what Emma would do to him, she was fuming. Upset. Tears began to well up in her opaque eyes.

"Do you know how hard it's been? I mean, look at me!" Emma said, pointing to her eyes, staring, unseeing at Bray. "How am I meant to look after the little ones when I can't even see?"

"What happened?" Bray asked.

"As if you care," Emma said, bitterly.

"If I didn't - why would I be asking?"

Emma wiped at her tears, breathing deeply to compose herself, trying to keep her dignity.

"It's a long story."

"Seems I'm not going anywhere," Bray ventured.

Her face scrunched up in thought, Emma blinked her tears away.

"Where to begin...."

"How about you tell me how you lost your sight?" Bray asked.

"How about you just keep quiet?" Emma replied.

"Please..." Bray asked after a moment, sensing that Emma was about to open up.

And after a long moment, she eventually did.

"When my Mum told me she was sick, my whole world caved in. I needed her. So badly. She was everything to me - and suddenly, she was gone."

"The virus?" Bray questioned.

"No. She had cancer. Not long after she died, we were evacuated here. Just before the 'virus' hit. We had no idea where we were going. We were put on a ship, like animals, and sailed for many days. My Dad... he was in the military. There were a lot of other kids, just like us. Their parents also serving their countries. We were all so scared. Missing families and friends back home. We were told we had to stick together. Safety in numbers."

"I know how that feels. I was in a tribe of my own."

"Not long after we arrived here, my Dad also died."

"How? Was it the virus?"

"I don't know exactly. All I know is that he was with other servicemen who went off. They were on high alert. All the adults at the base were. All the children... we were supposed to stay in the bunkers. But I wanted to see what was going on. And I did. Until the explosion, that is. The light was so intense. Ever since then, all I've known is darkness."

Bray considered her in growing concern.

"Explosion! So what happened exactly?" he asked.

"I don't know. My Dad never came back. Neither did any of the other adults. None of them made it."

"What about the other evacuees?" Bray carefully probed.

"You ask so many questions," Emma pointed out suspiciously.

"I need to know, Emma. Not just for my sake. I'd like to help you, and your brother and sister. If you'll let me. Along with anyone else around here."

"If you're trying to find out how many people are still left, Bray, then... there are at least a couple of hundred of us."

"That's odd. I haven't seen any sign of any of them."

"You think I'm - lying?" Emma said.

"Are you?" Bray enquired.

"I could be. Then again..." she shrugged.

"You know what I think? There are only the three of you."

"You're wise, Bray. Very wise. But maybe not wise enough," Emma said.

"Why don't you just tell me, Emma?"

"Of all the original evacuees," Emma finally revealed, "most who survived split into different gangs. Some went away to explore. Others decided to stay. In our group there were about thirty of us. We called ourselves the Roaches."

"So these Roaches still live here, in the base?"

"They've gone, Bray. You're right. It's just the three of us left now. Me, my brother and sister."

"What happened? To the other members of the Roaches?"

"I was hoping you might be able to tell me," Emma answered. "Most ended up as slaves, I think."

"I never told you I was a slave," Bray reminded her.

"You never said you weren't either," Emma replied.

Bray could see she was wistful, staring into the distance in a reverie. She was sad, mournful.

"Have you ever heard of a tribe called The Fallen?" she asked.

"The Fallen?"

"We thought that if we traded with them, that they'd leave us alone. And for a time, it worked. But after a while, they made it clear it wasn't just food they wanted from us. But people. That's when they began to take my friends. One by one. Our little group, our family that had grown so close, pulled together to look after one another, began to be picked apart. I thought I'd never lose a family again. But I did."

"These Fallen? Had they been evacuated here?"

"I don't know. For sure. I doubt it. They didn't seem to know much about the wastelands. After I told them about what it had really been used for... burying so many people... they didn't seem that interested in taking any more of my friends or visiting here. Again. Pretty soon after, they left us alone. And haven't been back since."

"What about your friends? Any more of them still around?"

Emma considered Bray, even though she couldn't see. It was as if she was searching by instinct to establish whether or not she could trust him.

"If you must know... all my friends... they died. All of them. Including my elder brother. He would have been about sixteen then. And now, like I said, it's just the three of us."

She was trembling with emotion and it made Bray feel distraught.

"I understand how you must feel," Bray said. "I also lost my brother. I know all about the pain when those close to you die. Or are taken away."

What he said struck a chord with Emma, looking deeply in Bray's direction through unseeing eyes, which streamed more tears. Perhaps Bray and she had more in common than she had thought.

Bray felt truly sorry for her. Before in their encounters, Emma had seemed confident, in control. But now so vulnerable, which endeared her to him.

"Why don't you let me help you, Emma? If you let me go. Believe me, I can help. I don't mean you any harm."

Emma shook her head. She gathered her composure and once again, the barriers were raised as fast as they had been dropped.

"No... I can't do that, Bray. Can't risk it."

"Risk what? Release me and I'll help you!"

"What would do in my situation, Bray? I might be blind but I'm not stupid. You say you stumble into our lives, as if by chance. And that might be true. But if I let you go so you can walk out the door - would you really just walk away and leave us alone?"

"I told you, Emma. I'll help you!"

"What? Help us get captured by The Fallen? Traded?"

"No. I'd never do that," Bray replied.

"I'd be worthless as a slave anyway," Emma went on. "But I've still got to try and protect Tiffany and Shannon. Whereas you, Bray. You might have a value. So maybe we should hand you over to The Fallen if they ever pay us a visit. Perhaps they'd be interested in getting their hands on someone to trade, like you."

"Emma! You can't mean that! You must know this is wrong," Bray insisted.

"You say you arrived from the north... I told you I'm not stupid, Bray. I've heard tales of what goes on up there. And to someone, you must have been of value. Once. And who knows, you could be of value again. If we ever decided to trade you, that is."

Emma stood up, crushing the tin of baked beans beneath as she accidentally stepped on it, making her way unevenly towards the door, which she knocked on, giving Tiffany on the other side a signal to open it.

"I have to do what I have to do to protect what's left of my family. To survive. I like you, Bray. But I'm sorry. You're not going anywhere."

CHAPTER NINETEEN

Lex had gotten himself out of a few holes and tough places in his life but so far he was well and truly stuck.

The pit he had fallen into was a good ten feet deep. It was obviously man-made. Lex could see it wasn't natural, due to the chips and marks in the earth where the symmetrical shaped circular hole must have been dug.

"You sure you're okay?" Jack called down from above, peering at Lex.

"For the millionth time, I don't need your help!" Lex shouted.

His pride had taken a fall when he had, and he was determined to get out of the mess he had gotten into under his own steam.

He was now clutching the sides of the earth, trying to climb up, struggling to get various foot and hand holds from the vine roots.

It was no use though. Despite his best efforts, Lex lost his grip and collapsed to the ground, landing on his backside.

Jack winced as he edged closer, at the top of the hole.

"Why don't I find some vines and try and haul you up?"

"Why don't you just shut it?" Lex replied, brushing off the dirt from his fall.

"You got nothing to prove, Lex," Jack said.

"Maybe not to you."

"It's obviously a trap. Bet it's the first time it's captured a wild 'Lex'. It must be designed to normally catch a wild pig - or something," Jack said, his voice echoing from above.

"What's that supposed to mean?" Lex called up.

"Nothing!" Jack smiled mischievously.

"Well, if it makes you feel any better - I hate to admit it, but maybe I do need your help."

"About time. That's all you had to do, was ask," Jack hollered. "I'll see what I can find. Back in a min."

Jack was just relieved that all that seemed to be hurt was Lex's feelings - he must have landed on his thick head, Jack chuckled to himself, as he scrambled away from the hole and scanned the undergrowth for something Lex could cling to.

Lex paced around the muddy floor of the hole, looking up at the darkening sky directly above, just visible through the overhanging thick jungle of trees and plants. They had been gone from Amber and the others for some time and it would be completely dark soon. He just hoped the two of them would be able to find their way through the jungle to the beach. It would have been hard enough remembering the way in the daytime, let alone at night.

Jack better not tell the others about this, Lex fumed, embarrassed at being unable to take care of himself.

Suddenly, a twisted tangle of vines dropped down from above.

"Thanks, Jack. I owe you!" Lex called up.

Lex grabbed hold, feeling the strength of the vines, and he felt sure they would be able to support his weight. He was continually impressed by Jack's practical skills, his ability to make mechanical devices out of basic items - and this improvised rope made of 'vines' seemed perfect.

Lex began to clamber up, hauling himself, his arms straining on the vine, trying to assist his ascent with a better foothold in all the vine roots.

But suddenly, to his surprise, he was making rapid progress towards the surface as if he was in an elevator.

"Whoa, Jack," Lex admired, he would never have thought Jack had it in him. "You been working out?"

As he neared the surface, the sounds of the jungle life getting louder with him getting closer, Lex was thrilled to be finally regaining his freedom.

But as he arrived at the top and out of the hole, he gazed in sudden unease.

Jack was squirming, trying to call out a warning, though his cries were muffled, a big hand clasped over his mouth. He was being held by a huge 'native' looking figure, daubs of war paint on his face and body.

"Get off him!" Lex barked, his anger rising.

Lex was going to rush to Jack's assistance but as he scrambled to his feet, he noticed other similar looking natives and was quickly overpowered.

The last thing he saw was Jack's wild, panicked eyes, before a massive hand covered Lex's eyes and another his mouth, muffling his own shouts of frustration and resistance.

CHAPTER TWENTY

It was so strange to be back on dry land, Amber thought, as she looked up at the twinkling stars above in the night sky.

It had been her routine before bed, to stare up to the Heavens, taking a moment to gather her thoughts. She had done that every night during their voyage in the ocean, when they were first on the trawler, then the Jzhao Li. Normally Jay would accompany her, the two of them having some quiet time together to try and make sense of everything.

And now Jay had gone and Amber was worried. Jay and Ram hadn't returned back to camp yet from their excursion. There had also been no sign of Lex and Jack.

At least the girls had returned earlier, to Amber's relief, bringing back more medical supplies with them from the wreck of the Jzhao Li - and most importantly, Zak.

It was a miracle. He was alive. Just. His pulse was weak and he hadn't regained consciousness. He had obviously nearly drowned, hitting his head, a huge swelling visible on it. Amber and the others feared that they wouldn't see him again, suspecting the worst had occurred when Zak heroically lowered the lifeboat, allowing them all to escape the cargo vessel, becoming trapped on it when it ran aground.

May lay beside Zak's prone body, huddling herself against him, determined to remain by his side.

Similarly, Ruby was still keeping a close watch on Slade, inside the makeshift shelter. Slade let out an occasional murmur of pain from the wound in his side, Ruby doing her best to ease his plight. But thankfully the blood loss had been stemmed from Amber treating the wound earlier. Now they had to watch for infection.

The temperature felt as if it was dropping as the night advanced but it was due to the wind from the ocean.

"It's cold," Lottie said nevertheless, through chattering teeth, sitting as close as she dared to the heat of the fire they had made.

"First it's too hot, then it's too cold," Darryl muttered, trying to get some sleep, Lottie irritating him, not to mention the swarms of mosquitoes. Darryl waved his hand, trying to shoo away the insects that seemed to have a fondness for him. They continued to buzz in the humid night air and Darryl sighed to himself. He wouldn't call this cold. What did Lottie expect - snow? And that she would be building snowmen in this region, which was clearly sub-tropical?

"Ellie - Jack and Lex know how to look after themselves," Amber said, trying to reassure Ellie, who paced up and down the sands around camp.

"They're taking too long!" Ellie said, her anxiety all too clear.

"I'm sure they'll be back before too long," Amber insisted.

"Jack..." Ellie broke up in sobs on saying his name.

"He'll be okay, don't worry," Salene said, giving Ellie a hug.

"You hope!" Trudy said, as she gazed around uneasily at the dark jungle bordering Camp Phoenix. "You won't fall asleep on watch or anything, Amber?" Trudy continued.

"No, don't worry. I'll keep awake. So why don't you all settle down and try and get some rest."

Trudy nodded, then lay down near the little ones, already lost in slumber.

Clutching a roughly-made spear she had fashioned earlier, Amber crossed to where Sammy was sitting, also supposedly on watch. But his head was drooped forward and he was emitting a loud snore.

Amber touched the point of the spear to his neck.

Sammy awoke with a start, then sighed with relief. "Oh, it's only you, Amber."

"And a good job, too," Amber replied disdainfully. "No point in taking a shift on night watch if you sleep, Sammy. If you're really that tired, off you go."

"Sorry," he said guiltily, then scampered away nearer the fire to join the others as Amber embarked upon her own shift.

It was an eerie night, the moonbeams casting an unnatural glow, the waves rolling onto shore incessantly, the water a strange palour of grey, illuminated from the bright moon. The wind rustled through the foliage. They were all so exposed. So alone.

What was this place, Amber wondered as she gazed around at the endless rows of palm trees bristling in the wind, the dark outline of the jungle full of mystery. Just what or who was out there?

Amber gripped the spear tighter in her hand, readying it in case she needed to spring into action at any time and tried to dismiss her growing worry for the continued absence of Lex and Jack. And Jay and Ram.

But this unknown land wouldn't get the better of them, Amber resolved, vowing that whatever was in store for them all, she would be ready to face it and reassured herself that the other four would be alright and would return soon.

* * *

"Ground control to the Technos. This is Ram. Over?"

"Earth to Ram. Just what the hell are you doing?" Jay asked.

Ram was sitting in the pilot's seat in the cockpit of the massive cargo plane, spinning the wheel and pressing buttons on the instrumentation panel like a happy child playing with an oversized toy.

"I thought you wanted to get some sleep?" Jay continued. "If not, we can always talk now."

"Maybe you're right," Ram said, slumping back in his seat. "It's getting late."

He had promised to go over a few things with Jay in the morning but Jay was beginning to have suspicions that Ram was intentionally drawing it out, avoiding matters. He apparently had a headache and reassured Jay that there was nothing of much importance which couldn't wait until morning.

Jay was eager to find out the reason for Ram's unusual behaviour but felt tired himself and thought it might be better for them both to grab a few hours sleep while they could.

The priority had been to discover the mysteries of this aircraft and then he would deal with the mysteries surrounding Ram.

The two of them had climbed up earlier to check out the interior of the downed plane, stuck high in the trees.

They had searched the cavernous hold. Which had been empty. There was no cargo. Just the aircraft, with its onboard built-in equipment still reasonably intact.

Thankfully, there hadn't been any bodies. Presumably the crew would have bailed out, Jay considered. Or escaped the wreckage when it must have crash landed, ditching in the jungle. Someone must have obviously been piloting the plane and since there was no telltale signs or any skeletal remains, Jay concluded that the occupants might have survived.

The aircraft had United Nations insignias on its tail.

What the plane had been doing and why it crashed still remained a mystery though, as did so much of the final days of the adult times.

Jay wondered if there could be some connection between the cargo plane and the Jzhao Li. Perhaps it was involved somehow in the United Nations Pacific Fleet that Dr Jane Gideon's journal had mentioned. Was it part of some last ditch effort to escape the 'virus'? Or something else?

Despite their efforts to find out by clambering into the wreckage, Jay and Ram hadn't discovered any answers, however.

There were no maps, no paperwork. The power to the onboard computers had gone. Ram was unable to reactivate them. But Jay was aware of Ram's continual eagerness to at least try, which reinforced Jay's suspicions that Ram was avoiding revealing information regarding his irrational behaviour of late.

Jay cast a glance at Ram, beginning to snore in the pilot's seat, and couldn't help but smile slightly. The former leader of the Technos had really enjoyed being in the plane, reacquainted with technology, the only sign of happiness he had shown for some time.

For all of Ram's eccentricities and manic intemperance, Jay liked him. And in many ways admired him. They had met just before the 'virus' struck when they were streamed into a boot camp during the height of the pandemic. Amidst all the panic, the authorities had began emergency evacuation for those uncontaminated and aged under 18. A survival program had been implemented. It was known as S.E.E.D, an acronym for Survival Education Endurance Development.

Basically the rational was that various segments within the demographic of young people would be streamed during the course of the evacuation so that they would spend some time in boot camps, where they would be trained in all manner of areas.

Different regions specialised in different skills.

The camp where Jay originally met Ram focused on working with those with a flair for computers. Jay had always been interested in programming but knew from the first time he encountered Ram that he was no match. Ram possessed abilities right off the scale. Though his biggest skills seem to have been dating Siva and Java at the same time, both of whom had also been evacuated to the same camp, excelling at Information Technology.

During the course of the induction, all at the boot camp were taught in the limited time available a range of matters which were thought to be crucial to aid any chance of survival. Such as programming electricity grids. Or rebooting sewage and other infrastructures.

In the aftermath of the adults dying, Jay felt drawn to Ram's vision of starting his Techno tribe - though he didn't entirely agree with his ambitions to dominate and control, resulting in invading other sectors.

Ram justified his ambitions, feeling that society could benefit from the expertise of the Technos but had a contempt for those he considered to be 'virts'. All those illiterate and uninterested in the marvels of technology. The one constant being that Ram was someone of great extremes. Cunning. And brilliance. He excelled strategically but as with his beloved computers and all inanimate technological objects, seemed to be devoid of any 'human' feelings. Other than displaying stubbornness. He was certainly a complex individual.

Jay knew something was troubling him since the time they left the city but so far Ram had avoided explaining anything.

Jay had a stubborn streak of his own and was determined that he would get Ram to open up.

A wave of fatigue washed over Jay. Before long, he fell asleep.

As soon as his eyes closed, Ram's own eyes opened widely. He knew now was the time.

Jay had tethered Ram's wrists with vines on the dashboard control panel in the cockpit in case Ram tried to run off again.

Casting a careful glance to make sure Jay was asleep, Ram began to rub the vines against the instrumentation panel.

Who was Jay to think he could keep Ram bound? Didn't anyone know by now Ram made the rules? He decided the fate of others. Not the other way around.

With a grim look of determination, Ram worked the vine, trying to not make too much noise, resolving that he would soon be free.

* * *

Jay turned, shifting positions, aware of noises in his semi-dazed slumber.

There was constant creaking as the wind blew against the hulking wreck of the Hercules aircraft, which shifted slightly, suspended high within the trees.

Somewhere, in the recesses of his mind he was also sure that Ram had stopped snoring.

Squinting a tired sleepy eye open to check on Ram, he was jolted by a sudden unexpected vision of Ram staring down at him, just inches from Jay's face.

"What the hell are you doing, Ram?!"

"Trying not to disturb you...so you didn't disturb me," Ram drawled, all too pleased with himself at showing Jay he had managed to get out of Jay's bonds. "You were sleeping soundly, Jay boy. Just like a baby."

Ram settled back into the pilot's seat, stretched and yawned before considering Jay. "And you wanna know something, Jay? You really hurt my feelings. Tying me up. What is it, don't you trust me?"

"Well, that's one way of putting it," Jay smiled, despite himself.

"I could have clambered out of here, down these trees, and escaped. Or 'attacked' you, Jay, taken you out without you even knowing it," Ram grinned.

"So why didn't you? Worried I would wake up? Catch you in the act?"

"No need to be so hostile, Jay. I didn't choose to escape. Because I don't want to. And I don't want to 'fight' you either. We're on the same side. You should know that by now. I wanted to prove you can trust me. I'm still here even though I don't need to be... I'm not gonna run from you - or myself - not any more..."

Jay sat up and was now leaning his back against the metallic wall of the plane's hold, staring at Ram with a degree of fascination.

"You do my head in, Ram, at times. You really do."

"I do my own head in, Jay, if you want to know the truth. It's not easy living with a mind like mine." Ram pointed at his head. "This brain, can you imagine how many petaFLOPS I've got swirling around, processing quadrillions of files? What might take a computer a second, might only take me a millisecond. If only we could have programmed software, eh Jay, the way God programmed humans, then maybe this world wouldn't have ended up in such a mess."

"So you admit - you are human after all?" Jay smiled affectionately.

Ram was suddenly intense and began sweeping his hand through his hair nervously. "Yeah, I'm human. I wish I wasn't. I wish I was a computer. At least a computer doesn't have a conscience."

"Go on," Jay encouraged warily.

"You're right, Jay. I have been keeping something from you. I've even been trying to keep it from myself."

He started patting his head with the palms of his hands in growing frustration.

"These damn petaFLOPS. I can't programme them to stop what I've been thinking. And I've been thinking... a lot. You wouldn't believe what's been going through these data files these past few weeks. I thought, when I tried to get away from you earlier, I could run from my problems. Or keep them hidden somehow, pretend they didn't even exist. But I realize - now we're here, well and truly stuck on this land - I can't just trash all the files. And above all, I can't get through just by myself. I need your help, Jay. We're in this together."

"In what together?" Jay replied, intrigued.

"There's... a lot of things you need to know. I've been keeping a few 'things' from everyone. I've been doing it for everyone's good. Protecting you - as well as Amber and the others. But it's time you know the truth."

At last, Jay thought. He could hardly believe Ram was opening up to him this way. In Ram's own way. And he felt sorry for Ram because he was clearly suffering, patting his head obsessively, anguished by some inner turmoil.

"Where do I begin?" Ram yelled. "Let me try and recover a few things from limbo! Just hope I don't get caught in an infinite loop! We wouldn't want this old brain of mine to crash now, would we!? Or we might not be able to reboot!"

"Why don't you just tell me everything?" Jay said.

"In order to do that, I need to go back to the beginning. And it's one hell of a bedtime story, Jay."

Ram seemed to be hyperventilating now, his eyes flicking, his head twitching like he had a nervous tick while he processed information embedded in the deep recesses of his mind.

"Me! You! Everyone here! We're all in terrible danger!"

CHAPTER TWENTY-ONE

The cruiser towing the lifeboat ploughed through the water. Ebony, bound in the net, gazed uneasily ahead, noticing a towering silhouette in the distance. Flames poured out of the top, glowing in the dark night sky. The infrastructure stood on four legs like some colossus. It was gigantic. Ominous. And the cruiser was heading directly towards it. Ebony suspected it could be an oil rig.

The cruiser arrived just over an hour later. Ebony was in awe of the rig's size, let alone its existence. She was amazed that out here in the middle of nowhere, far from land, this behemoth stood as if defying everything Mother Nature had to throw at it. The wind had picked up, the waves increasing in size, sweeping against the massive struts that supported the immense infrastructure, like they had no impact on it at all.

She noticed that a larger vessel had already arrived and was moored on a dock surrounding the base of the rig. Prisoners were disembarking, herded by a wild, feral-looking bunch of thugs. Like most of the tribes Ebony had encountered back in the city, they all were about the same age. But few she had ever come into contact with looked as menacing as this bunch.

Ebony was as confused as she was afraid, wondering how the military-looking boarding party who had captured her were connected to these vagabonds.

It took some time for Ebony and her fellow group of captives to climb several stories of metallic stairwells of the oil rig. When they reached the summit, arriving on a helicopter deck, their ankles were bound by metal chains.

Some of the group begged to be released, others wailed in self-pity as the vagabonds marshalled all the prisoners in lines. It seemed they were being separated by gender and into different age groups.

The military-looking types watched impassively as if they were some kind of overseers, checking on the progress of whatever was being planned.

The pit of Ebony's stomach churned. She had no idea of her fate, the intentions of her abductors.

"Over there!" one of the vagabonds bellowed, kicking a boy from behind into place. The petrified child seemed as if he was about to erupt into tears, struggling to keep his composure for fear of any repercussions.

The first group was the largest. They looked to be the oldest, strongest, biggest, the most physically fit, Ebony reasoned. All were male.

The next group was quite the opposite, comprised of the smaller and younger members of the prisoners assembled. They were scrawny. Some of them didn't look well at all. They were clearly malnourished and must have been living rough for a long while to be in such a state. They were comprised of both males and females.

Ebony formed part of the last group, with only six other girls. And she wondered why they had been singled out.

Satisfied they had arranged the prisoners in the right order, one of the vagabonds crossed to the leader of the military. "We're all done," he said.

"Stand by!" the leader replied. Then he spoke into a walkie-talkie. "Ready when you are, Commander Blake."

The wind howled on the open deck.

Ebony and her fellow prisoners shivered in the cold night air but also in growing anxiety at what was to happen next as a shadowy outline appeared on the outside walls, dimly lit by flaming torches.

Tall, well built, intimidating... Ebony and the captives gazed transfixed by the shadow, which was soon revealed to belong to a young man, striding confidently across the helicopter deck.

He, like the boarding party, was dressed in black with a similar balaclava, which had been rolled on top of his head. But unlike the others, his hair wasn't close cropped. On the contrary, a mane of blonde locks tumbled across his shoulders, rippled in all directions as the wind howled. He was also unshaven with stubble on his broad jaw. But it was his eyes that Ebony noticed. And which unsettled her. They were deep blue, intense, as he paced around, surveying the prisoners as if inspecting them on a military parade ground.

There was a utility of motion and emotion in him. An undercurrent of energy and impatience. He exuded power. An ominous power. He ticked like a bomb. No doubt that he had to be the alpha male around here.

He was good looking, Ebony had to admit. Very much so. Despite her loathing of her captors, she had never been one not to ignore any male physically attractive. And this dude was hot. His magnetism and presence took her breath away. She surveyed him like a lioness, as if he was to be her prey.

He seemed to be around the same age as Ebony and the military-looking boarding party but unlike their regimented behaviour, was more relaxed, casually eating a ripe apple.

"One hundred and twenty-two intakes, Commander Blake," one of the vagabonds said in deference, proudly over the cold wind. "We exceeded our quotas."

Blake nodded, clearly impressed, and took another bite of his apple, his eyes scanning back and forth, analyzing all of the assembly.

Then he turned to the leader of the boarding party. "Axel - what have you got to report?" Blake asked.

"There was only one on board, Sir! A female. She's in the third group."

Axel indicated, then led Blake to where Ebony was standing.

Blake eyed her up and down, examining her hair, ears, teeth.

"So you're the 'blip' on the radar screen, eh?" Blake said.

Ebony smiled coyly, uneasily.

"My name's Ebony."

"I didn't ask your name!" Blake snapped in sudden anger.

Ebony's smile quickly disappeared as Blake turned to Axel.

"I was hoping for a few more. But she'll do," Blake said.

He examined the hair, eyes, teeth and ears of the others in Ebony's group.

"Have any of you ever been pregnant?" Blake asked.

"Why?" one girl replied, confused by the question, as were the others in their group, including Ebony.

But they were astounded by what was about to transpire.

Blake lifted the girl with ease over one shoulder, her arms and legs flailing as he crossed towards the railings - and casually thew her over the side.

Ebony and her fellow prisoners listened, terrified, hearing the receding wailing cries of despair as the girl fell, plunging into the ocean far below.

Blake casually took another bite of his apple, then threw the core into the ocean.

All watched intensely, petrified, as Blake returned and addressed the assembly.

"I don't ask much during your time with us. But I would strongly suggest never to answer a question - with a question.

When I - or any of my team - ask anything, we expect an answer. Understood?"

A murmur spread through the prisoners.

But Ebony yelled at the top of her voice. "What's the matter with you all? Can't anyone speak? You heard the man! Tell him you understand!"

Blake cast a surprised glance at Ebony, a glint of amusement in his deep blue eyes while the other prisoners shouted out in unison, indicating that they were fully aware of his instruction.

Ebony raised her voice loudly above the chorus. "Don't forget - Sir! Let me hear you all now!"

"We understand, Sir!" the prisoners replied.

"Nice one!" Ebony said.

Blake sighed to himself, then addressed the assembly as if purposefully ignoring Ebony.

"So you must remember one thing! All of you! You obey. Or you suffer!" he bellowed to the cowering prisoners.

Then he crossed briskly to Axel, indicating impatiently. "Get them out of my sight!"

"What about the girl, sir?" Axel asked, glancing at Ebony.

"Bring her to me," Blake ordered. "I'll deal with her!"

* * *

Ebony, accompanied by guards and manacled by her leg irons, shuffled as she walked down a long corridor of the living quarters.

Axel tapped politely on the closed door before him. So strange, Ebony thought for a moment, to see mannerisms of the old world still being observed.

"Come in," a female voice replied.

Axel opened the door and Ebony was pushed inside by the guards.

Blake sat behind a huge oak desk.

The grotesque girl with the scars running down her face who Ebony had seen earlier during her initial capture, stood behind Blake, gently caressing his shoulders, giving him a massage. She glared disdainfully at Ebony, then nodded as Axel spun Ebony around like she was on display. Which she was.

Blake sipped on his glass of wine and examined Ebony. He was in the midst of eating a meal.

"Get your hands off me!" Ebony snapped, squirming in the grasp of her captors.

Axel raised a fist to strike.

"That won't be necessary!" Blake said. "I don't want any blood spilled in my quarters. Not while I'm eating. You and your men are dismissed, Axel. Thank you."

Axel nodded, then left with the other guards.

Blake continued eating, sipping on his wine, the disfigured girl still massaging his shoulders.

From what she had witnessed earlier on the helicopter deck of the rig, Ebony decided it would be wise not to be the first to speak.

The silence seemed to go on for ever, with Blake almost ignoring Ebony. She started to feel faint, standing motionless for so long.

After a while, the silence was broken.

"Why?" Blake probed, without looking up, spooning the remains of his dessert.

Ebony didn't now exactly what he was referring to, suspecting though that he was seeking details of how she ended up drifting on the lifeboat, but wasn't about to give any information. Not until she had a better idea of just who exactly these people were.

"Why not?" Ebony replied. "Philosophically speaking, that is. I'm not answering a question with a question...Sir. Just trying to engage in some friendly conversation."

"Who are you?" Blake said, topping up his glass of wine.

"Why don't you try and get to know me a little better and you might find out," Ebony said, unbuttoning her blouse.

The hideous girl cast Ebony a pathetic look.

Blake reached out for a small toothpick and started cleaning between his teeth, sucking out the remnants of food, seemingly oblivious to Ebony stripping before his very eyes.

"Why would I want to do that?" he asked.

Ebony removed her blouse and began undoing her bra.

"I can bring skills to that table of your's. Skills like you would never imagine," she said seductively.

"Can you now?" Blake replied, taking another sip of wine. "Well, isn't that interesting?"

"Why don't you release the creature of the deep - and we can discuss it? In greater detail?" Ebony said, dropping her bra to the floor.

She was desperate. She had no idea who these people were but had to make an impression and take her chances while she still could. And instinctively, this was the only way she knew how.

She was aware she was attractive and she was going to use anything and everything in her considerable arsenal she had to in order to survive.

"That sounds like a sensible suggestion. Leave us!" Blake commanded casting an appreciative glance over the upper parts of Ebony's naked body.

"You can't be serious!" the disfigured girl protested.

Blake spoke quietly, tapping the girl on the hand reassuringly. "Please."

The grotesque girl sighed to herself, then reluctantly left the room, closing the door behind her.

"Hungry?" Blake said, indicating the spoils on the table.

"Ravenous," Ebony smouldered, shuffling towards him. "I've got one hell of an appetite. And I just hope you can satisfy it."

She sat on his knee, cupped his hand on her breast and started to kiss him gently at first, then with increasing passion.

CHAPTER TWENTY-TWO

Bray slumped on the bed, wiggling his ankles and moving his wrists, trying to get the circulation flowing in his bound limbs. His tethers had been tied together well, he had to give Emma and her siblings credit. He had done everything he could to try and prise himself free but doubted if even the most flexible contortionist would be able to extricate themselves from the bonds keeping him a prisoner.

Just what was Emma going to do with him?

He felt pity for her. It couldn't have been easy with her disability, struggling to survive with her much younger brother and sister. And if Emma's story was true, they had endured their share of heartache and suffering with the gradual erosion of their tribe, the Roaches, reduced to just three members. Would they hand Bray over to The Fallen? Or ever let him go on his way?

He wouldn't stop trying to persuade Emma that he meant no harm to them, hoping she would set him free. Then Bray could formulate a plan to discover just exactly where he had been held all this time, and how he could get back to his friends and tribe in the city.

The sound of screaming from outside jolted Bray out of his reverie. It sounded like a young girl crying, calling for help, in great distress. Was it Tiffany?

Bray braced himself. There was danger out there, alright. Something was wrong. And here he was, powerless to help.

The door to the room was unlocked, then opened, revealing young Shannon entering, tears in his eyes, with his older sister Emma following.

"Is he there? Is he still there?!" Emma shrieked.

"Yes! He's here!" Shannon yelled back, panicked.

"What's happening?!" Bray called out as Emma stumbled slightly, following Shannon headed back towards the door.

Emma stopped, turned and gazed at Bray through her opaque eyes.

"I thought it was you at first!" Emma cried. "That'd you gotten out, were going to hurt Tiffany... or hold her ransom."

"What are you talking about?" Bray yelled, frustrated at Emma's continued suspicions of his character and intentions.

He could sense her very feelings of helplessness as no doubt she was sensing his despair. Emma nodded. Shannon flicked a switch. The security monitors suddenly displayed various images of a wild-looking gang moving through the base.

"The Fallen?" Bray enquired.

"Yes," Emma replied, in mounting unease. "And they seem to have Tiffany."

"You can't fight them on your own. Set me free, Emma! I'll help. I promise!"

Emma's mind was racing. She didn't have much time. Was it a ruse? Could she trust him? Would he turn against her if she let him go? Her face betrayed the tormented emotions she was feeling of doubt and agonizing uncertainty as Tiffany's cries for help outside continued, though the revolving security camera didn't pick up any images, displaying only members of the gang entering various buildings, searching.

"She needs help! I can help her!" Bray yelled out.

Reluctant, with no option, Emma nodded to Shannon. The young boy ran over to Bray, pulling out a small knife from his pocket, the blade glinting in the light.

For a moment, Bray wondered if Shannon meant to use the knife against him - but his anxiety about that was put to rest when Shannon cut the bonds securing Bray loose, the ropes falling to the ground.

Bray didn't say a further word and angered by whatever harm had happened to Tiffany, he raced past Emma and Shannon, both recoiling as he brushed past them in full flight.

Tiffany let out another piercing scream. Emma shuddered, terrified, feeling helpless, young Shannon hugging his big sister as Bray disappeared out the door.

* * *

"Where's your good-looking sister?" a member of the gang yelled. He was standing outside the accommodation block where Bray was being held, twisting little Tiffany's arm back painfully, a grimace on Tiffany's face as she did her best to resist.

"Here!" Bray shouted, gazing around for any sign of the other gang members.

"You don't look like Emma to me!" the gang member said. "Who the hell are you?"

"Your worst nightmare, if you don't let her go," Bray replied, threateningly.

"I could either do that. Or break her arm!" the gang member replied, backing away slightly, forcing Tiffany's arm up more.

He was clearly threatened by the imposing figure of Bray who looked like a guy who could take care of himself.

Other members of The Fallen appeared.

They were all dressed in black grungy clothes, with self-inflicted scar marks on both sides of their faces from where they must have at one stage cut into themselves the shape of the letter "F", indicating their tribe. They looked gothic, each with dyed black hair, red make up outlining their eyes and mouths, as if they were smeared by blood. They had chains with skull jewellery and adornments.

"What have we got here?" one asked. She was the only female member of the tribe Bray could see and must have been the leader. The others seemed in awe of her as she surveyed Bray.

"A hero, Belle," the thug holding Tiffany replied, "Least that's what he thinks he is."

Belle considered Bray and suddenly lunged forward snarling, like a wild animal.

Bray recoiled.

Belle started to laugh manically, smacking her lips as if she was savouring an imagined taste.

"Oh, I don't think so! Doesn't look to me like any hero. Besides, heroes never taste too good! I prefer my meat a little more raw!"

She and the others were now converging on Bray, circling him menacingly.

Bray suddenly noticed a red laser dot moving across the face of Tiffany's captor. Emanating from one of the windows of the living quarters. It was Shannon, using a small keychain laser, trying to help in his own way. And as the light pointed into the eyes of the captor, Bray quickly took his chance. In one lightning movement, he twirled and unleashed a powerful kick into the gang member holding Tiffany. It was enough for him to release his grip.

Tiffany took off, running as fast as she could to the living quarters.

Bray sprinted in the opposite direction, The Fallen in pursuit. Now all were snarling like wild animals, hunting prey.

Bray arrived in the amusement park area and noticed buildings on the other side beyond the roller coaster.

Roller coasters had never been his thing, and they certainly weren't now. But this was crucial to the plan Bray quickly formulated in his mind.

Clambering the rickety wooden frame, Bray could feel the fragility of the structure beneath him, fearing that it would collapse at any moment.

Soon he was a good fifty feet off the ground, clutching the outer frame at the top of a loop de loop. A piece of the wood he was clinging to ripped away from the railing, the rotten timber twisting as gravity pulled it downwards. Bray felt dizzy, glancing at the the piece of wood as it plummeted to the ground far below. It was another reminder, as if he needed it, that the slightest mistake and he too would fall to his doom.

The Fallen gazed up, their eyes wild as they focused on Bray.

Belle indicated. A member of the gang rushed into the nearby control booth, pulling levers.

To Bray's surprise, carriages began to move. The ride was obviously still operative and now posed another threat as carriages gathered speed and would soon crash into him as he clung to the tracks.

Bray climbed higher, higher, hoping that at least he was providing a distraction to enable Tiffany, Shannon and Emma to escape.

The carriage was approaching closer. Closer.

Within seconds of it arriving, Bray leapt spectacularly on to the roof top of the hangar building located opposite the roller coaster infrastructure. He tumbled to one side as he landed to try and break his fall.

Then he clambered down the side of a drainpipe.

Belle and The Fallen appeared round the other side of the building and converged on him.

Once again, Bray was now a captive.

CHAPTER TWENTY-THREE

They had obviously gone back in time. Either that, or they were in a movie set.

Something had to explain it, Jack thought, peering out as best he could from the mud hut in which he and Lex were being held. Their hands were tied by thick vines, wrapped around their wrists, attached to wooden poles driven into the muddy ground, which supported the mixture of grass and leaves that formed the roof of their hut.

It was so strange. Such a bizarre sight compared to what they had been used to with their old lives in the city.

Jack could see many 'natives' wandering about the primitive camp outside, along with other huts of various shapes and sizes.

The 'natives' themselves - for that's how Jack and Lex had referred to them - were made up of males and females. Some of the oldest - and biggest - were about the same ages as Lex and Jack. They had to be the warriors of the group, Jack reasoned. They were certainly imposing physical types, the muscles on their bodies rippling, showing their strength, which had been enough to subdue Lex and Jack and bring them to this village.

Other 'natives' sat on the ground, girls singing an unusual melody in a language Jack had never heard before, as they weaved together flax and plant material. Very young kids, probably two years old, raced around the camp playing. Some stopped by to cast an occasional intrigued glance into Jack and Lex's hut, fascinated by the two strangers inside.

"It's just like being in one of those documentaries I used to see when I was a kid," Jack said. "One of those travelogues. Either that, or I'm dreaming."

"You must have some pretty weird dreams," Lex replied, pulling with all his might on the vines binding his hands to the massive wooden poles.

"What do you think they're going to do with us?"

"I dunno. But I'm not planning to stay and find out," Lex said, inching forwards toward Jack as closely as he could, leaning so he could get a better glimpse through the open door which had been cut out.

"If I could only get loose. I reckon I could take on a couple of those warriors..."

"Leaving just the rest of the village to me," Jack interrupted, the skepticism showing on his face at any notion of escaping.

Darkness had fallen. In the centre of the village, a pig was being roasted over an open fire.

"Man. I am so hungry," Lex said, the aroma of the cooking wafting through. "They might have a lousy sense of hospitality. But it sure seems they can cook!" he continued, breathing in the aroma of the roast wistfully.

Then he considered Jack, preoccupied with a sudden thought.

"I just hope we're not on the menu. You don't think they might be cannibals? Do you?"

"Well, that's food for thought," Jack joked.

Lex deadpanned. "I know."

"Don't you get it, Lex? Food? For thought?"

"Yeah, I get it. I just hope they don't get us!" Lex replied, but was in no mood for Jack's jokes. He poked his head toward the doorway as far as he could.

"Hey, you!" Lex yelled at some of the natives passing nearby. "I'm talking to you!"

The villagers ignored Lex, continuing on their way with what they had been doing.

"Answer me! Are you deaf!?" Lex bellowed in frustration. "You can't keep us here! What are you going to do to us? Who do you think you are!?"

"Um, Lex - maybe they're not answering - because they can't speak our language."

"Well, that's their problem, Jack. But lucky for us, I speak the universal language."

"Which is?" Jack questioned, wondering just what Lex had in mind.

Lex wolf-whistled at one of the native girls kneeling near the fire, turning the spit roast.

Puckering his lips, Lex's bizarre behaviour and noises attracted the attention of the girl and she looked at him out of the corner of her eye.

Achieving contact, confident he was making inroads, Lex winked roguishly, blowing her a kiss.

The girl raised an eyebrow dubiously and shifted position, turning her back on Lex.

"Well, I'm impressed. That was effective," Jack muttered sarcastically.

"Give it time." Lex protested, his pride knocked. "She's just playing hard to get. I'll rely on my charm to get us out of here. You'll see."

The clatter of an arrow thudding into the ground by the entrance to the hut startled Lex and Jack, both of them recoiling back further into the interior of their confinement.

Three huge warrior figures appeared at the entrance, staring down at their prisoners, brandishing weapons threateningly.

"Obviously don't like you hitting on the women," Jack whispered.

"Let us go - and we'll just forget about it!" Lex ordered, staring defiantly at the warriors.

The warrior in the centre replied in his native language. But from the contemptuous look on his face, it was clear whatever he was saying wasn't friendly.

"What's your problem, pal? All this because of a couple of lousy chickens? What's so special about them anyway!? They looked well and truly - plucked!!" Lex bellowed.

Jack cast Lex a glance, reacting to the innuendo, widening his eyes as if to say don't go there.

Then he gazed in unease as the main warrior who had been speaking drew an arrow back in his bow, aiming it directly at Lex - who froze submissively, finally silenced by the prospect of the arrow pointing at him.

The disdain and hostility towards Jack and Lex was clear as the warriors glared threateningly.

Jack swallowed nervously, dreading what might now occur.

But as quickly as it had started, it was over.

The main native pulled away the bow, glowering at Lex, and the warriors moved off, leaving Jack and Lex alone in their hut.

"Next time I'll do the talking!" Jack insisted, breaking the silence. "You really have a way with people - not!"

"Shut it!" Lex insisted, slumping down onto the dirty earthen floor of the hut, taking stock of what had just happened. "This is crazy!" he continued. "I mean, what have we done wrong? What did we ever do to them?"

"Apart from offending them, you mean!" Jack said.

For once, Lex was silent, staring up at the roof of the mud hut.

That had been too close for comfort.

Whatever they had done to upset the 'natives', Lex knew for sure that he and Jack were obviously in a whole heap of trouble.

CHAPTER TWENTY-FOUR

Jay felt like he wanted to either thank Ram and be grateful for what he had told him the night before - or that he was going to kill him.

They were retracing their steps through the jungle, the blazing sun burning down as they tried to find their way back to Camp Phoenix.

"You're quiet," Ram said, his eyes shifting to and fro, anxiously surveying their environment while they walked.

"After all you've told me, Ram - I've got a lot to think about," Jay replied with a degree of contempt in his tone.

"Now you know how I've been feeling... why I might have been a little 'tense' lately..."

Jay went through the story once again in his mind that Ram had explained in the Hercules aircraft the night before.

Ram had told him that before he even formed the Technos, in the days when the adults were still alive... that Ram had been a prolific geek. No surprises there, Jay had thought.

But what did surprise Jay was when Ram revealed how he had been in contact with a number of other like-minded computer-obsessed people of all ages, based around the world.

They had met online, gaming, Ram forming teams that competed in professional competitions. He had boasted to Jay of the achievements of his guild and the status he had as a role player. Ram's dream was to either become a computer engineer - or a pro gamer. Jay was aware that technology was Ram's life and that he had never been able to relate to people, understanding the logic and structure of the computer, feeling like he thought like one himself.

But he was unaware that beyond gaming, Ram and his online friends kept in touch through the Internet. And that they had tried their hand at hacking. First, into school computer networks. Then, harder to crack businesses. Finally, Ram and his associates had broken into the computer systems of major corporations, taking them down, perfecting their hacking skills. There was nothing philosophical driving them, just the challenge of it all. Their next targets were government agencies. Eventually the military. They could hack into anything, they felt.

Ram's point in telling Jay all this was that he became particularly close with one online friend. Someone who hid behind their online identity of 'KaMi-1314' - or as Ram called them affectionately for short, 'Kami'.

Ram thought initially that Kami was a girl, the two of them flirting at times online - but he eventually discovered that Kami was a guy. He couldn't be exactly sure of who he was or where they lived, Kami just revealing that he and his friends were based somewhere in the Far Eastern Region. Ram used his own online identity when they communicated, calling himself infinIT-Ram, an allusion to being infinite with Information Technology, and having a memory of no limits. Ram felt that described him perfectly.

When the 'virus' descended upon the world, Ram formed the Technos Tribe. That part, Jay obviously knew. He had been recruited not long after the Technos came into existence.

Ram had worked hard building the tribe under his leadership, with the assistance of his close friends, Java, Siva and Mega.

But what no one was aware of was that Ram had hacked his way through automatic security systems of the military. And obtained information on some advanced hardware and weapons.

In those initial days when the adults began to perish, Ram still kept in touch with 'KaMi-1314' through the Internet, until it eventually shut down as the pandemic spread.

He then resorted to hacking into the UNANET, along with 'Kami', to continue their online relationship. UNANET was a successor to the old ARPANET that had gone so long before, which had been developed by the military in the event of a nuclear attack. UNANET stood for 'United Nations Agency Network' and was designed to enable communications to continue around the world in the event of any catastrophe by transmitting data through old copper telephone lines - almost like a more modern version of the 19th century telegram.

What Jay also didn't know was that this Kami contact Ram befriended online, became leader of an alliance of Tribes that became known as 'The Collective'. Drawn mainly from friends initially in his guild.

Their plight had been similar to what young people were experiencing in most of the major cities throughout the world in the wake of the pandemic, with smaller 'tribes' beginning to form from the scattered survivors. Whereas the tribes in Amber's home city had been at war, with Zoot and the Locos the most dominant among them, in Kami's home city the tribes had recognized the need to co-operate under his leadership, forming a powerful coalition of several tribes.

He had been inspired when studying the historic globalisation which had occurred. Where countries had formed alliances into unions. Thousands of years before, of course, scholars were fascinated - as was Kami - with the structures of ancient Rome, which grew from a city state to become a vast empire. And no doubt Kami had ambitions in that respect, too.

The 'Collective' insidiously and ruthlessly were able to seize raw resources such as fuel, vehicles, food, medicines and any useful technology they could get their hands on. Neighbouring communities were taken over by them, the smaller fragmented tribes and strays who lived in them unable to defend themselves against the superior numbers and forces of The Collective. They had no option but to go along or they would be eliminated.

According to Ram, The Collective had discovered classified files during the time when they were hacking at the height of the pandemic, revealing that governments were implementing a repopulation program. And Kami himself was intrigued to use this as a springboard to embark upon his own 'breeding' initiative, aware that he required a critical mass in his quest to dominate and eventually rule.

Ram had told Jay that The Collective had also hacked into a United Nations system, the data files of which showed that in anticipation of trying to survive the deadly 'virus' and mitigate its effects - along with any other potential threat -governments had co-operated in a top secret plan where they established a series of military bases dotted in key strategic points around the world.

Each base contained a compound. A place where top scientists and leading members of the government, as well as talented minds from academia to the arts, could be protectively housed, hoping to outlive any danger ravaging the world, sealing them off from the outside until it was safe to re-emerge. The bases were customised from earlier designs for nuclear proof bunkers and shelters from the 'Cold War'.

The adults assigned to each base were going to continue their research on combating the pandemic, trying to find a breakthrough, a cure. Substantial resources and funds were poured into this classified project as it was vital to prevent the possible extinction of humanity.

There were other similar but ocean-based approaches undertaken, with fleets of 'Noah's Arks' brought together, carrying important cargo. Some top secret. The Jzhao Li vessel that the Tribe had so fortuitously stumbled upon, was probably part of one of these fleets, Ram suspected, under the guise of just providing medical support. But in reality, there were a lot more objectives which probably many of the crew were unaware of.

Perhaps there were even isolated groups of adults who still survived, Ram had mused, living safely to this day, in the thick protected walls of the bases, atmospherically sealed off from any apocalypse, waiting for the day they could re-enter the world outside.

The Collective also uncovered a program of propaganda designed to drip feed information as the governments saw fit, so as to minimise panic.

Jay knew enough about history to realise that in the past, previous pandemics that decimated humanity had mutated and returned many times in waves. This had been the case with the Black Death in the medieval era - it didn't happen once but was a series of outbreaks, each one slightly different than the other. Similarly with pandemics of Influenza that had destroyed significant populations around the world.

But while Ram agreed with the potential threat of the virus mutating, he advised that Kami had a lot of theories and was beginning to suspect that there was more to the 'virus'. He saw references to bacterial warfare in some documents. Also genetic engineering. Even threats from germs from outer space, which resulted in the aged NASA program being stopped, with space station activity occupying the major focus. Kami wondered if the entire planet would be evacuated at some point. And if so - why?

Ram had tried to obtain more information, feeling that Kami was holding a lot back, fully aware that knowledge was power and that he wouldn't reveal all to Ram, choosing to maintain his own series of classified information. Equally, he might have shrewdly been sending out false signals through his own propaganda to throw anyone like Ram off his scent.

Jay was always aware of Ram's germ fetish since the first time they met and reflected that his phobia must have been heightened by not only the pandemic, if indeed that was the reason for the adults being wiped off the face of the Earth. But he wondered if Ram was being totally honest with him and that he, too, had his own series of 'classified files', just as he had accused Kami, and that Ram himself was holding something back.

"Jay, look," Ram indicated as they noticed a clearing which had been carved out of the jungle.

Ahead of them was the first of many vehicles they could see stretched on a makeshift road, which had been cut through the jungle.

The wind rustled through the foliage as Ram and Jay cautiously moved to examine the wrecks.

"Where do you think they were headed, Ram?"

"I think we'd better ask the grim reaper," Ram replied.

Not the answer Jay was looking for. Ram could be so weird at times.

There were no bodies inside, Ram and Jay noticed, as they checked out each vehicle that they passed.

Both of them felt like they had emerged almost into another dimension, a glimpse of the past, like a moment had been frozen in time and they wondered what had happened to the occupants of each vehicle and the reason for this long line of traffic. Especially why the vehicles had been abandoned.

Deciding to try and head back to Camp Phoenix, Jay questioned Ram more about his online contact, Kami, and discovered that Ram had hacked into The Collective's computers, furious at being kept in the dark by his enigmatic friend.

Previously unknown to Jay or any other member of the Technos, The Collective leader had tried to recruit Ram into joining Kami's team.

Kami had proposed that if Ram and his Technos joined The Collective, they could then be an advanced force, using their technology to invade the very same city where Amber and the Mall Rats had lived, securing it for The Collective.

Ram had found in his hacking that The Collective believed the observatory at Eagle Mountain near the city was actually an underground military compound, potentially bristling with secrets and equipment kept hidden away.

Jay remembered Amber telling him how she and the Mall Rats had gone there in the past, hoping to find an antidote for 'the virus' as well as more clues which might reveal exactly what happened to kill off all the adults. At the observatory, Amber and the Mall Rats had heard adult 'voices', Jay recalled Amber saying, having made contact with some sort of satellite before an explosion went off, killing one of the Mall Rats and nearly taking Amber's life in the process.

What Jay hadn't realised was that Ram was expected to carry out other invasions but felt he couldn't trust Kami or The Collective anymore, beginning to realise that Kami was keeping information of magnitude from him.

He was anxious, Ram told Jay, that he was just being manipulated, used, and had ambitions of his own for the Technos. He wasn't satisfied for them to be just a junior partner if Ram accepted Kami's offer to form an alliance to join the other tribes in The Collective.

So Ram's response had been characteristic. He had come up with a strategy, deciding to move in first, mobilising his Techno forces for the invasion that took place that memorable day when the city fell under Ram's sway, taking all the spoils - and Eagle Mountain, with its potentially hidden military compound - for himself.

"You're not mad at me, Jay?" Ram asked suddenly.

"You've got to be joking," Jay scoffed. "I've got all kinds of feelings inside, Ram. And yes, anger is one of them. As well as betrayal, distrust. Regret. I could go on."

"I did what I had to do."

"You should have told us before. Told me," Jay said.

He had believed that the Technos invaded the city to take the next step in making the world a better place. That's what Ram told them was the motive for their invasion. They were going to force peace onto the warring tribes who lived there, help the people build a new world through harnessing technology, Ram the architect of the future. For all involved.

Jay was completely unaware of this power struggle with The Collective. He didn't even know they had existed.

"Don't blame me for Kami trying to take over the world," Ram said. "I was just making sure there was just a little piece left for ourselves. So you should thank me, Jay. Not criticise. I mean it hasn't exactly been easy for me knowing that I had a price on my head."

"Don't try and pull one of your sympathy tricks on me, Ram, because it won't work!" Jay said.

"I thought you were a friend," Ram replied, wounded. "And after all the sacrifices I've made."

"Sacrifices!" Jay scoffed.

"Yeah, sacrifices," Ram reiterated. "I could have been right up there. In a position of real power. But I turned down the offer to join The Collective. For us, Jay. You, me. All the other members of the Technos. People who wanted to join."

Jay scoffed again, knowing only full well that Ram's brazen act in invading the city was first and foremost to probably turn it into his own fortified personal kingdom.

Ram explained he actually thought Slade was a bounty hunter retained by Kami to search for him and had been so relieved to find refuge in the little town of Liberty, rather than having his head delivered on a plate to the head of The Collective. But, of course, Slade had his own reasons for using Ram, to help him get to his brother, Mega.

Ram advised that he just had to keep the fact he was persona non grata among The Collective a secret. Ram was paranoid about any one of the highest ranked figures, Jay included, and that they might start a coup against him. That they would hand him in.

Kami was fascinated with the Roman Empire. If he considered Ram to be a potential Caesar figure, then he would have loved to have seen someone acting as Brutus. Stabbing the Technos' emperor in the back. And thought if anyone else discovered The Collective existed - and that Ram was their enemy - this would prompt a call for a change in leadership and only lead to a rebellion in the ranks. In the end, it had been Siva and Java, Ram's own wives, who had conspired against him, deposing Ram from the very tribe he had founded.

"I don't feel safe out here," Ram said, gazing around at the jungle as they retracted their steps back towards Camp Phoenix. "I'm taking a huge risk. For all we know, The Collective could be crawling around."

"What - here?" Jay asked. "God - if there's anything else, Ram, you'd better let me know. I mean it!"

Ram revealed why he was worried this land could now be under the influence and control of The Collective. When he hacked into their computers, Ram had seen plans for future expansion phases, which included a string of islands, one of which Ram suspected they were now in.

Like Eagle Mountain near the city, Ram claimed that The Collective had uncovered secret military compounds in other areas. He didn't know the exact locations but was sure he recalled the co-ordinates which he had noticed displayed on the Sat Nav back on the Jzhao Li.

Ram was beginning to panic, sure that he and the Mall Rats were accidentally drifting straight into enemy territory, with Ram being the most endangered due to the bounty The Collective must have placed on him. So he was desperate to obscure his features, protect his identity, just in case he was right and encountered members of The Collective who might so otherwise easily recognize him.

"You know, this is all your fault, Ram," Jay admonished him. "If you had just said something about it, maybe we would have listened and turned back, instead of drifting on the ocean. We could have avoided coming here if you had said earlier."

"Yeah, well nothing like hindsight, is there?" Ram grumbled. "Let's imagine for a moment. Back on the trawler. I say, "Hey everybody, let's go back to the city we fled from because The Collective could be lurking on some islands in the middle of the ocean. And they're real nasty pieces of work"... If I said that, would you honestly have believed me and decided to turn round and try and head back from where we had come from?"

"I don't know if I believe you now," Jay admitted honestly. "You could be making all this up."

"Believe me, Jay, for your sake and the others, I'm telling the truth. I can't say for sure but I reckon we might have drifted straight into the lion's den. There's no shopping mall to hide behind. We're not in the city anymore. Not now. If The Collective's really out here, we're all in danger. Not only me!"

CHAPTER TWENTY-FIVE

The sun continued its climb into the clear, deep blue sky, the heat increasing. All around in the palm trees lining the beach, the birds and insect life emitted a noisy dawn chorus.

Amber sat on a huge log that must have been washed up onto the beach long ago. It made the perfect seat now for what she needed, as Amber balanced a large drinks container retrieved from the wreck of the Jzhao Li, which sat unevenly on her lap.

She was tired, having found it difficult to sleep during their first night on the mysterious land. As the night had gone on, Amber and the other's imaginations had gone into overdrive, Trudy's in particular. All the Tribe felt vulnerable, unsure of what was lurking out there, in the jungle beyond.

Amber had stayed awake most of the night, keeping watch, never far from the improvised spear she had made, vigilantly on alert for any signs of danger.

Something had to explain the continued absence of Lex and Jack, Ram and Jay. None of them had returned to Camp Phoenix.

Amber had tried to keep the morale of everyone up, reminding them to trust in the abilities of those who were missing. They were all skilled, having survived in the dangerous city that used to be their home, and Amber was sure that they would all be safe out there - wherever they were - and would come back soon.

In the same way Ellie missed Jack, her love, Amber in particular felt the pangs of separation from Jay. She hoped he was alright, with the unpredictable and untrustworthy Ram as his companion.

Trudy hadn't helped matters. And had become slightly hysterical about the disappearance of the others, sure that they were dead. And that before long, all would suffer a similar fate. Amber had managed to get her to stay rational, at least as rational as Trudy could ever hope to be. They would never survive if they gave up hope.

Zak and Slade remained critically ill. Something had to be done for them, urgently.

"Let's see what we've got in here," Amber said to herself, peering through the contents of the drinks cooler, seeing what other medical supplies they had at their disposal.

Already earlier that morning, she had worked with Ruby to replace the gauze bandages covering Slade's wound, after first cleaning it with disinfectant from the bottles Ellie, May and Salene had brought back. While being treated, Slade had roared with pain, wincing with each touch Ruby made. He was mostly unconscious. Ruby knew her efforts were better than nothing and she just hoped they would go at least some small way to help Slade. She had to at least try something, she felt.

Amber's concern, as the day before, was that infection might be setting in. She recalled her parents once had gone on vacation in the tropics and her mother had cut her foot while snorkelling in the shallow waters. The infection from the coral in the reefs had made her terribly ill for weeks. Without expert medical help, she surely would have died.

Whereas Slade's wounds were visible, Zak's situation was a lot more problematic, difficult to discern. Since he had been found trapped in the rocks near the wreckage of the Jzhao Li, Zak had spent most of the time unconscious. Salene, trying to remember her own basic first aid training from school, had felt a pulse when his body was discovered initially and given him the kiss of life, Zak spewing salty sea water from his lungs. But that was as active as he had been since they found him.

May continued to watch over him, distraught. All the colour had drained from him and they were all uncertain what exactly was wrong. Amber suspected it must be some sort of internal injuries sustained when the Jzhao Li ran aground. There were certainly few signs of any obvious external wounds to explain why Zak remained unconscious. But one thing for sure. It looked like his very life force was slowly fading from him.

Amber wondered, if due to his head injuries, that he might even have lapsed into a coma.

Treating Slade and Zak wouldn't be easy. None of them were doctors. They didn't have the expertise or knowledge, let alone a hospital and proper medical equipment, to give the care Slade and Zak so clearly required. Thankfully though, they had recovered more medical supplies that Ellie, May and Salene had brought back to the camp. At least it was something.

"We've got 14 tablets of Morphine... maybe 40 paracetamol and these look as if they're some form of antibiotics," Amber said, examining bottles and counting the contents.

"There might be something more that we missed laying around," Ellie responded, feeling bad that despite scouring the beach, that was all they had managed to recover. There had to be other medicines to be sure but most of them were either submerged in the wreck, or if they had washed ashore, were now drenched in salt water, dissolving the tablets and liquids that had once been inside.

"You did great," encouraged Amber.

"So what do we do now?" Salene asked.

"I guess - we share it out between them," Amber suggested. "They're both in a lot of pain. Let's split it up. Seven tablets of Morphine each. And we hope for the best."

"It'll be difficult getting any tablets down Zak's mouth," May thought out loud. "I guess I could crush them up, force them in. Until he gains consciousness."

"I can't believe I'm saying this. But..." Ruby interjected.

"But what?" Amber wondered.

"I don't think we should be wasting any medicines on Zak," Ruby explained, almost ashamed to admit what she was tbinking.

May scoffed. "What are you talking about!?"

"I know how much you care, May, about Zak..."

"Do you?" May replied warily, looking at Ruby in anticipation of what she was alluding to.

"But... I mean, face it. He's not going to come round. We have to be real here, deal with the facts. Zak could be in some sort of coma. I wish it were otherwise but from the looks of him, he won't be for this world much longer. I'm sorry, May, I know you're going to feel angry with what I'm saying but we have to use all the medicines on Slade. He's got the best chance of making it and pulling through."

May was shocked. She was actually speechless for a moment and could hardly believe what she had heard.

"You - bitch!" May spat out, bubbling over in fury. "How dare you even think such a thing, let alone say it!? Have you forgotten? We owe Zak. He risked his life, as did Slade, to free us all. Without Zak, none of us would be here today. We would have been stuck and gone down with the ship! Maybe for some of us, that would have been the best thing!"

May stared at Ruby with venom in her eyes, like she was going to attack her.

"Cut it out you two!" Amber shouted, stepping between May and Ruby. "I hear what you are saying, Ruby. But I disagree with it."

"Amber," Ruby appealed. "We've got hardly enough medicine as it is!"

"Which is why we have to use it carefully," Amber insisted. "We can't leave either Slade or Zak just to die. And the only way we can help the two of them is by sharing the medicine we have, 50/50. That's the fair - and only - way we're going to go about it."

"What's fair about wasting medicine on Zak? Denying Slade what he needs?"

"Were not going to 'deny' Slade," Amber interrupted. "Or anyone else if they get sick. As well as the morphine to help his pain, we'll have to give Slade some of the antibiotics. He's bound to have infection setting in."

"Amber, I respect you. But can't you see how wrong you are on this?" Ruby went on. "If we don't focus all we have on Slade, we could be needlessly condemning him to die! Zak is done for - there's nothing more we can do for him!"

"That's right, Doctor Ruby," May snapped furiously. "You're real impartial about all this, aren't you?"

"I'm only suggesting what makes sense! Focus what we have on the one most likely to survive! Save Slade! It's better to risk one life, than two."

"How dare you!" May screamed.

Amber had to physically restrain May, so enraged was she.

"May, stop it!" Amber urged, slapping May's face.

The shock of it caused May to calm down but she was still clearly worked up, glaring intently, dangerously at Ruby.

"We are not going to give priority to either of them!" Amber insisted. "We're going to be absolutely fair about this. We split the medicines equally. Is that understood!?"

Ruby shook with emotion, frustrated at not getting her way.

"Do you both understand? We share what we have. And I don't want to hear anything else, Ruby, about Zak or anyone else dying around here! Alright?!" Amber emphasised her point again.

"Then you can all go to hell!" Ruby exploded into tears and stormed away down the beach back towards Slade.

"Ruby!" Salene called out after her but to no avail.

"That went well," Ellie muttered.

"Who does she think she is?" May complained, staring with bitterness at Ruby. "What a nerve!"

"I'll go and talk with her," Amber said, concerned at what had transpired. "Will you keep an eye on the medicine, Sal? Make sure nothing happens to it?"

"Is that supposed to be a dig at me?" May snapped.

"For God's sake, just settle down will you? Please!" Amber said. "I was merely suggesting that we have to make sure we don't lose any of it. It's all we've got. And we're all we've got as well, and need to look out for each other."

May exchanged glances with Amber, then nodded.

"I'd better get back to check on Zak."

Sammy was taking his shift beside Zak while Darryl had relieved Ruby, watching over Slade.

Salene closed the lid of the plastic drinks cooler to protect its contents.

Amber smiled her gratitude to Salene then headed off to Ruby, passing Trudy, who was cooking some fish on the open fire.

Brady was playing in the sand while Amber's baby was fast asleep under the shade of a palm leaf.

"This smells good," Lottie said. "But I'd prefer cornflakes for breakfast rather than crab."

"Just be careful with anything you're preparing to eat," Amber called out to Trudy. "Make sure that crab's fresh. We can't risk all of us getting sick with any shellfish that's been left lying around. Not in this heat."

"What - you think we might get poisoned or something?" Trudy replied, gazing at the skewers of crab placed in the fire.

"Calm down, Trudy," Amber called back. "None of us will get any food poisoning - as long as we're careful."

Trudy gazed at the crab she was preparing then removed the skewers, pieces of fish, and buried them in the sand.

"No need to get paranoid," Lottie said, her stomach rumbling. "Otherwise we'll all starve to death."

"Well, I'm not taking any chances," Trudy replied, frantically throwing more and more sand over the crab meat she was burying.

* * *

Ruby sat on the beach, shoulders slumped, heaving with emotion, her face buried in her hands.

Amber could hear her crying as she approached.

"Ruby..." Amber said, unsure what to say. "What happened back there? I'm on your side, you know. We all are. It's just what you were suggesting, pragmatically, might make sense but none of us can ever decide who might live. Or die."

Ruby broke down sobbing uncontrollably.

"Come on, try and not get yourself so upset," Amber said.

She put her arm around Ruby to offer comfort.

Ruby buried her head into Amber, bawling tears, Amber hugging her to try and give whatever support she could.

"This isn't like you," Amber said, rocking Ruby back and forth slowly in her embrace. "You're normally so cool and level-headed."

"Not anymore!"

"What's got into you?" Amber wondered. "If it's me, I didn't mean to get you upset. Believe me, I want Slade to get better, as well as Zak. There's no favouritism or anything."

"I know... and I'm sorry for shouting at you," Ruby explained between sobs.

"That's alright. I understand how you must feel," Amber said.

"I don't think so," Ruby replied, trying to gather her emotions. "It's just something else you said earlier, Amber, which really got to me. About deciding who lives and dies."

Amber considered Ruby, aware that there was something else troubling her. Deeply troubling her.

"Do you... want to talk about it?" Amber asked.

There was a long pause, then after a while Ruby exchanged glances with Amber.

"How does it feel? Being a mother?"

"To the tribe, you mean?" Amber smiled. "At times I feel like everyone's mother around here. And it isn't easy, believe me."

Amber's smile made Ruby smile slightly and she wiped more tears.

"No. I wasn't just meaning the tribe. But baby Bray?"

Amber thought for a moment, unsure of how she could ever begin to explain motherhood.

"That's an interesting question, Ruby. I remember someone once saying that love... well... it's like someone else's happiness and wellbeing is central to your own. So you always put yourself second. Especially being a mother."

Ruby broke down again in wracking heaving sobs, but this time convulsing her entire body.

"What is it?" Amber probed.

"Back in the city, I was pregnant once. And I didn't want to go through with it. I didn't really care for the guy. It was just a casual relationship. So I... terminated."

"That's your decision," Amber said gently. "Every woman's right."

"You don't understand," Ruby replied, trying somehow to contain her emotion. "This time I want it. I want it so badly, Amber!"

Amber considered Ruby. She recalled back in the city, days before they embarked on the fishing trawler, that Ruby thought she was expecting but the makeshift pregnancy test was negative.

"You're pregnant?!" Amber asked, delighted and surprised.

Ruby nodded.

"Are you sure this time?"

"No doubt about it," Ruby said.

"Slade?" Amber enquired.

Again Ruby nodded then gazed down at Slade and stroked his head gently.

"Does he... know?"

"Not yet. And I don't want anyone else to know either," Ruby replied. "I just couldn't keep it bottled up inside any longer. I can't take it anymore!"

"Don't worry, I won't say a thing," Amber said gently, extending one arm around Ruby. "Not until you're ready to tell everyone yourself."

"Slade's his own person. I wouldn't want to tie him down, make him feel I'm some sort of burden. That he has to be with me because of some sense of 'duty' or something."

"It's obviously up to Slade to speak for himself. But from what I've seen, he really cares for you, Ruby."

Amber watched sympathetically as Ruby gently caressed Slade's hair and wiped at tears flowing from her eyes.

"I can't let him die. He has to live. Our baby will need him! And I do, too!"

CHAPTER TWENTY-SIX

Blake wrapped one of his massive arms around Ebony as she leaned on his chest, running his fingers through her hair.

It had been quite a night. In another time, another place and situation, she could have really got into him in a big way. But this was all about survival. Her survival. She just hoped Blake had at least enjoyed himself and she had done enough to make an impression.

Blake started to get out of bed but she pulled him back.

"Do you have to go?" she said, kissing him. "I'm still hungry."

"I've got 'things' to do," Blake replied.

"Like what?" she asked, then suddenly caught herself in mock concern, a hint of melodrama in the tone. "Sorry. But sometimes it's difficult not answering a question. With a question."

"You seem to be more than capable. Of knowing what to do. Or say," Blake said, gently running a finger down the side of her cheek.

She wondered if that was a compliment or if he was letting her know that he was suspicious of her. He was unpredictable, capable of exploding at any time and she would have to tread with care, rely on her innate survival instincts. And charm. Then maybe she could find out any information and be better equipped to come up with a plan. It was essential to know more about what she had gotten herself into. She knew she was in a precarious - though where last night was concerned, not entirely unenjoyable - position, and just had to try and find out more information about who Blake and his people were. Information was power, Ebony had come to realise, during her time ruling over Zoot's Locos tribe in the city. The more knowledge the better.

He slapped her on the backside then climbed out of bed. "Come on. You've got 'things' to do as well. You've not been fully categorised as yet."

"Categorised?" Ebony replied, as she pulled herself up and watched Blake putting on a robe over his naked body. "What - are you interested in checking out how greasy my hair is or something? I mean, you and your people out here in the middle of nowhere searching for oil? Or is this rig used for something else?"

"You'll find out. All in good time."

"Why don't you tell me more about it now?"

"What business is that of your's?"

Ebony decided to back off, not wishing to push her luck. "Got you. Answering a question - with a question. But don't worry about it. You're forgiven," she beamed, trying to ingratiate herself while she climbed out of bed and placed a robe around her own nude body. "Any chance of me coming back later - for dessert?"

"You're persistent - I'll give you that. Yeah, there might be a chance for some desserts tonight. After you're categorised."

"Sounds like fun. Look forward to it," Ebony replied carefully. Then added, as if in a casual afterthought, "What does it involve?"

"Let's just say it's getting to know you a little better," Blake said, pouring himself a glass of orange juice.

"After last night, I reckon you already know me pretty well."

"Not well enough," Blake said, turning to gaze at Ebony coldly, handing her an orange juice he had also poured.

Ebony kissed him on the side of the cheek coyly. "I'm just a poor, lonely shipwrecked girl. Worried about what might happen to me, that's all."

"Sure you're not playing... some kind of game?" Blake said, eyeing her intensely, searching to read her expression.

"I could be," Ebony replied, poker-faced, deciding to change tactics, testing what buttons to press to draw a more favourable reaction, realizing the sympathy card wasn't going down well. "Maybe I even wanted to be captured. And am here by choice."

"Is that so? Well, maybe I've been expecting you."

"Really?"

She realised he was toying with her just as she was toying with him and wouldn't put it past him that he was enjoying seeing her squirm in unease at the prospect of what might lay in store for her.

He was sure one smart cookie. Shrewd. She was going to have to be very shrewd herself if she had any hope to come through this. Alive.

As much as Ebony tried to gain some kind of control, she was painfully aware that the only person fully in control of this situation was Blake. And that he wasn't giving anything away, leaving Ebony deliberately hanging in the uncertainty of her fate.

There was a knock on the door.

"Enter!" Blake said.

The door opened. The disfigured girl came in, nodding to Blake respectfully but also giving a quick glare of jealousy and distrust to Ebony.

"They're ready for you, Blake. On the helicopter deck."

"I'll be there in about half an hour. After I take a quick shower."

"What about 'her'?" the hideous creature asked in disdain.

"Why don't I just stay here? I could do with a shower myself," Ebony ventured.

"You can shower. But you can't stay here. You're a new intake. Everyone needs to be categorised. No exceptions," Blake replied firmly.

* * *

Outside, the waves had picked up, crashing into the colossal rig, its huge steel legs holding firm against all nature had to throw at it.

On the helicopter deck, the slaves were in a terrible plight, Ebony could see, as she arrived with Blake and the hideous creature.

It wasn't that they looked to have been mistreated. All seemed to have been cleaned up and Ebony wondered if they had been fed. It was more the agony in their expressions, the fear, the uncertainty about their futures. She knew exactly how they were feeling, mirroring her own concerns. She felt sympathy for their plight. It was a wretched spectacle. At least she wasn't bound and manacled, unlike all the others assembled, with the military-looking guards and vagabonds all around overseeing whatever was about to occur.

There was no way she could escape. Not yet. There was nothing she could do. Except bide her time, see what was going to unfold.

"A ship will be here in a few days!" Blake called out, addressing the assembled slaves, shouting so his voice could be heard over the wind howling across the open decks of the oil rig.

A ship? From where, Ebony wondered, as Blake continued.

"And you will all be transported. But right now we've got to categorise you. It's painful. But don't resist. Otherwise you'll know what pain really is!"

Ebony and the prisoners braced themselves in growing fear and anticipation.

A vagabond put on a glove and picked up one of several iron forks that had been sticking in an urn, bubbling away with hot tar inside boiling over.

It had a letter 'M' shaped on one end of it. Other vagabonds steadied a young boy and in one swift movement, pressed the steaming fork against the boy's face, the youngster's cheek sizzling while the fork imprinted the letter 'M'. The boy passed out from the agonizing pain and had to be dragged by two other vagabonds, steadying him, before carefully laying him in a recovery position on the deck.

Over the course of the next hour, other prisoners were branded 'M'. Ebony wondered just exactly what it signified. Until Blake addressed the segment of the group, all clutching at their cheeks and groaning in agony.

"In any roll call - remember you're all categorised 'M'. Manual workers."

He cast his gaze on another group. All female this time. But rather than just six the night before, more girls had been added. Ebony was unsure if they had not long arrived.

"All of you," Blake advised the group. "You are to be assigned to the breeding program and categorised 'B'. Remember if anyone asks your identification - it's 'B'."

Another vagabond removed a fork from the steaming cauldron and approached the group of females. Ebony watched nearby and could feel the cries of agony permeate into her very soul as the group were all branded. She couldn't stop herself watching and wondered what the hell she had gotten herself into. Sickened by the brutality of it. But equally, she admired the efficiency of it.

Overall though, the gruesome nature of it all repelled her. And she was right smack in the middle of it. She was also aware that Blake had been casting an occasional glance at her so she tried to suppress her reaction, not wishing for him to know how it affected her.

"Ebony," Blake said, crossing to her. "Now it's your turn."

"I've got just one request," Ebony said, overly casual. "If I'm going to be branded - I'd prefer it on my backside. I've always been proud of my complexion. Would hate to have it ruined."

Blake smiled slightly at the gall Ebony displayed, requesting this. But once again, Ebony was conjuring up a plan in her mind, deciding that this gruesome event might provide her with an opportunity of impressing Blake.

"Can I do her?" the hideous girl said, striding up to Blake.

"I'd prefer not," Ebony said. "If she's done herself, I'm not impressed with the result."

The disfigured girl lashed out, slapping Ebony's face.

Ebony struck back, flooring her with one punch, blood oozing from the girl's nose as she sprawled on the floor.

"Don't mess with me, sister! I mean it!" Ebony snarled before faking a slight smile to Blake. "Sorry about that. You got a thing about answering questions with questions? Well, I've got a thing about my face. So if you want me branded, I'd prefer it somewhere more interesting for you to notice."

Blake considered Ebony, clearly intrigued, as the hideous girl climbed to her feet.

"Back off, Karin," he said. "I'm sure you'll get a chance to repay our friend, Ebony, here. At some point."

The hideous girl glared at Ebony, who watched as Blake crossed to the cauldron, removing an iron fork with the letter 'L'.

"What do you think this stands for?" he asked the remaining group.

"Loser?" Ebony offered up.

Blake crossed back to her. "What did you say!" he snapped threateningly.

"If you think I meant you, then obviously... it would be 'Leader'. But they all look like a bunch of losers to me," Ebony replied, trying to defuse matters.

"And what about you?" Blake asked.

"Only one thing 'L' could stand for with me - 'Lover'."

"Could be," Blake said, sabre-rattling further. "There again, it might be labourer. Or even... liar."

"Oh, I don't think so," Ebony replied.

She exchanged glances with Blake and tried to mask her tension as he added, "in which case 'L' could also mean... liability."

"The opposite of that, is asset," Ebony tried to reassure him. "And you'd better believe it. That's what I could be to you and your team, Blake. If you'd let me."

"Prove it," Blake ordered Ebony.

"How?" Ebony was genuinely perplexed.

"I couldn't help but notice, that despite all this bravado of your's..." Blake said, eyeing Ebony coldly, "throughout the branding so far... you seem not to 'enjoy' it. What is it? As well as having a 'thing' about your face... do you have a thing about seeing people in pain?"

"Doesn't bother me," Ebony said. "Not in the slightest."

"Then maybe you'd like to assist?"

"Glad to."

Blake removed the glove from his hand and passed it to Ebony.

Now she had a chance, Ebony figured, putting the protective glove over her hand. She was so tempted to pick up the steaming fork, use it as a weapon against Blake. Perhaps she could hold him hostage, somehow make good her escape. But decided against that. For the time being. The disfigured girl and the military team were far too efficient and would no doubt spring into action. Though she reckoned she could take out some of the vagabonds. But not enough of them.

"Right, then. Who's first?" Ebony said, realizing that this could be some sort of initiation for her.

Blake led Ebony to a group of assembled prisoners who were overseen by Axel and some vagabonds.

Ebony glanced at a slave trembling in line. A girl perhaps thirteen or fourteen years old, quaking with terror, waiting to be branded. She looked straight into Ebony's face, her eyes pleading. Urging, as if hoping to make some kind of contact, beg her to either make it quick and get it over and done with, or take her away somehow from the fate inevitably unfolding.

"Close your eyes," Ebony said.

The girl did this.

Ebony pressed the fork against the girl's face, the steam singeing, and Ebony almost threw up, smelling the searing of human flesh. The girl screamed in intense agony throughout the branding process with the glowing red hot poker bearing into her cheek. Ebony tried as hard as she could to mask any sympathetic reaction, well aware that she was being watched closely by Blake and his men.

"There you go," Ebony said to the girl. "That wasn't so bad, was it?"

"Why don't you decide - when it happens to you?" Blake suggested.

"Can't wait. You know what they say. No pain, no gain. Let's get it over and done with."

She unbuckled her pants, dropping them.

Blake smiled. "Would you like me to assist?" he asked, reaching out for the poker. But Ebony yanked it back.

"No," Ebony insisted. "I'm quite capable."

She gritted her teeth, pressing the scolding poker on the side of one cheek of her backside, determined not to give Blake or any of her captors the satisfaction of hearing her groan or cry out. And managed through her gritty determination to retain a smile throughout the long, painful process. Then Ebony hurled the poker back into the cauldron, removed the glove, drew up her pants.

"That feels a lot better. Nice one. Why don't you try it? See for yourself?"

She gazed at him intensely as if she had just offered a challenge.

He returned her stare evenly.

"That won't be necessary," he finally said.

Ebony knew she got him. Finally. He backed down, not rising to her challenge.

At last she was beginning to seize some control. And recognized something else during what had occurred. For all that Blake had clearly been taken aback at her actions, Ebony was in no doubt at all that he had also been impressed.

CHAPTER TWENTY-SEVEN

Jack strained with all his might, trying to loosen the tight vines tying him to the wooden poles inside the mud hut. He had given it everything and he kept pushing, using every fibre of strength in his body.

Exhausted at his effort, Jack collapsed to the ground, panting heavily.

"It's no use. Seems we're going to be stuck here forever. There's no way out," Jack said breathlessly.

"If I can't break those vines, and I've got these babes," Lex said proudly, pumping up his biceps, showing his muscled arms, "what makes you think you could break them?"

"I had to try. At least I tried," Jack replied despondently.

"Jack, for a clever guy, you can be pretty stupid sometimes. Why don't you just leave it to me? I'll get us out of this. I promise."

Lex crawled along the muddy floor as far as his tether would allow, looking out at the natives, continuing with their activities, busy weaving, sharpening weapons, cooking, seemingly oblivious to Jack and Lex's very existence.

Lex took a deep breath.

"Hey, you!"

A native warrior cast a glance at the hut as Lex continued.

"Yeah, I'm talking to you!" Lex bellowed angrily. "If you don't get someone to release us, I swear I'm going to take those spears of yours... and stick them in a place where the sun don't shine!"

"Lex - that's probably not helping!" Jack insisted, uneasy at Lex's bluster.

"Answer me!!! What do you want from us?!" Lex hollered, then sighed as he withdrew from the door. "It's no good."

"They want you to be quiet," a female voice said.

Lex and Jack were startled as a girl, around about their own age, walked into the mud hut, ducking her head as she entered. She was tall, gangly, and wore a pair of thick glasses over her piercing green eyes, one of the lenses covered in scratches. With long curls of blond hair ruffled over her shoulders, she wore a Tribal costume similar to that of the other native girls. The one startling difference, however, was that she didn't look like the rest of the 'natives', beyond the dress she was wearing. More like a girl of European origin.

"All your noise! You sound like a big baby," the girl said, Jack noticing her accent.

"Me? A baby?" Lex protested.

"Are you the leader of this Tribe?" Jack asked, as the girl stood over Jack and Lex.

"No, not at all," the girl laughed off the idea as ludicrous.

"You're not from round here, are you?" Lex blurted out the obvious.

"So you must be the smart one," the girl teased.

"I am, actually," Lex responded in all seriousness, Jack giving him a funny look.

"I was born in Germany, if you want to be precise. But I live here now."

"Well, guten tag," Jack smiled, trying to be friendly. "It's just nice to finally meet someone who can understand us," he continued. "What are you doing here? What's going on?"

"I'm here to translate, to talk and find out the same thing from you. So... tell me. Who are you?"

"I was about to ask you the same question," Lex shot back, turning on the charm, "what's a good looking girl like you doing in a place like this?"

"My name is Lia. That's all you need to know... For now. You don't look like some of Blake's people?"

"That's because we're not. Whoever... this 'Blake' is," Jack explained.

"Really?" Lia retorted, suspicious of Jack and Lex. "You could be some type of spies."

"We're not 'spies'... secret agents or superheros. Just prisoners. With no idea why," Lex said, casting an admiring glance down Lia's figure.

"It's true," Jack insisted. "We've done nothing wrong - Lia. Honestly. All we were doing was tying to get some help. We were shipwrecked. My friend, Lex, here - he's always thinking with his stomach..."

"That's offensive, Jack," Lex interrupted.

"He saw some poultry, couldn't resist the idea of a free meal... fell into a hole and next thing we knew, this Tribe showed up and brought us here. We don't mean anyone any harm. So if we could just be let go, then we can head back to the others."

"Others?" Lia asked. "There are others of you?"

Lex cast Jack a look to keep quiet, not to say anything more. They couldn't necessarily trust this girl, whoever she was.

"Yeah, there are others," Lex clarified. "If you don't let us go, before long they'll come and rescue us. They're armed. Dangerous," he bluffed. "So you better listen, 'Lia'. If you want to spare some bloodshed, save a few lives, the last thing you want is the others to arrive and break up this party. They'll tear this place apart. And anyone dumb enough to hurt me - or Jack, let alone touch one hair on our heads. So why don't you just have a word with whoever is in charge, will you? Let Jack and I go, and we'll say no more about it."

"Was that a threat?" Lia scoffed.

"You're obviously not such a good translator," Lex scoffed back.

"Because if it was, you haven't done anything to help your case, believe me," Lia said. "I'm to report back what I have learned. Every single word."

Lia turned her back, ducking to head out of the mud hut.

Jack gave Lex a look - then called out.

"Lia - please!"

Lia stopped in her tracks at the doorway to listen.

"Lex was just trying to 'impress' you. He's bluffing. There is no threat from any of us. We truly mean no harm. Honestly. The reality is we've got injured and sick people back where our shipwreck happened. We're a long way from home and we need help."

"I'll tell that to the Priestess. It's not my decision."

"What are we meant to have done? Why are we tied, cooped up in this hut?" Jack pleaded. "We're here by accident."

"You have trespassed on our land. That is undeniable. And for all we know, you could be spies for Blake, though you deny it. The Priestess will know what to do."

"What does that mean?" Lex asked, choosing his words carefully. He was frustrated but realised he was in no position to bully his way out. "And this Priestess... who the hell is she? What does she do around here?"

"If you are guilty of trespassing, you will be punished. Broken. You have tainted the Tribe's sacred lands."

"Then what?" Lex couldn't help butt in.

"Believe me. You don't want to know."

Lia turned on her heel and walked out of the mud hut, leaving Jack and Lex, who exchanged concerned glances.

CHAPTER TWENTY-EIGHT

After the initial joy at their safe return to Camp Phoenix, Jay and Ram wasted no time in calling the Tribe together for a meeting. Ram told Amber and the others - with a bit of prodding from Jay - about Kami. And The Collective.

"So the sooner we find a boat and get as far away from this island as we can, the better!" Ram concluded, after relaying all the information.

The Tribe were seated around the fire they had lit as the night descended. For a moment, all that could be heard was the crackling of the embers and the waves rolling onto the sands. Everyone was absorbed by what Ram just told them and were trying to assimilate it all.

"You're crazy!" Trudy broke the silence.

"Well, you should know," Ram threw it back at her.

"What are you going to tell us next?" Trudy carried on. "That you've been abducted before by little green men? Hitched a ride on Santa's sleigh? I don't believe a word of it, Ram, and I don't believe you!"

"There's a surprise," Ram said caustically.

"It does sound a little far fetched, you've got to admit," Amber pondered. "I mean - some mysterious leader... you never met. Who you used to communicate with. But only on your computer?"

It was clear Amber didn't trust Ram now, anymore than she had before. And the others seemed to share the same sentiment, though Lottie and Sammy stared wide eyed.

"This 'Collective' group... you don't think they can morph, do you, Ram?" Sammy asked. He was being serious and Ram thought about it.

"'Morphing?' Now that's an interesting concept," Ram said, considering the notion.

"What do you mean, Sammy - 'morph'?" Lottie probed.

"I mean, who knows? They could be watching us right now. In the trees. They might even BE the trees - "

"Oh, stop, Sammy. Please, for goodness sake!" Amber interrupted.

"At least someone seems to believe me around here," Ram said in disdain, but also was clearly hurt. All present were having great doubts about all he revealed.

"Sure you're not a member of the Collective yourself?" Darryl wondered. "Come to think about it, if they CAN morph - maybe they could have infiltrated any one of us!"

There was a hint of melodrama in the tone. Darryl couldn't keep a straight face and burst out laughing.

"This is no time for jokes, Darryl. Working with the Technos, and especially Ram, I'm well aware of all they could achieve. We have to take what he has to say seriously," Jay said. "If he isn't being truthful, then we've got nothing to lose. But if he is -"

"If you have been telling the truth - how dare you!" Ellie interrupted. "If this land might be under the control of this 'Collective'... that could explain why Jack isn't back yet, with Lex... They could be in danger!"

"That's true, too," Ram agreed.

"And you said nothing about it until now!? You let them go, like innocent lambs, wandering off into enemy territory?" Ellie said.

"Lex - an innocent lamb?" Ram scoffed.

"You are so selfish!" Ellie screamed. "If something's happened to Jack or Lex, I'll make you pay!!"

"The way the Collective operate, they'll consume you, for nothing. But you'll never be free," Ram shuddered at the thought.

"Where's your proof, Ram?" Salene joined in. "There must be some way you can back up what you've claimed."

"You want proof?... Let me think!"

Ram paced around the camp, running his fingers through his hair. Then he started patting his head with the palms of his hands, the others exchanging incredulous glances.

"What's he doing?" Gel asked.

"Just processing. Give me a few seconds till I examine all my files," Ram said.

After a while, he spun around, addressing them all, a manic glint in his eye.

"I've got it! What about Paradise and reality space?"

"What about it?" Amber said, watching Ram, as puzzled as all the rest.

"Kami might have tried to take credit for programming it. But it was me. I put it all together. One of my greatest accomplishments."

"I don't know if others would agree with you," Trudy muttered, well aware of the devastating effect Ram's virtual reality program had on all those back in the city. "That's nothing to be proud of!"

"I understand how you feel, Trudy," Amber said. "But why don't we just let Ram try and explain? And you'd better, Ram. I mean it. You owe it to us to tell everything you know."

"After we invaded, we checked out the observatory at Eagle Mountain and found the military complex The Collective wanted."

"What?" Salene said. "You were at Eagle Mountain?"

"That's where the virtual reality technology came from," Ram continued. "And Kami was desperate to get his hands on it. But I adapted it. Using the protons I needed, otherwise I'd never have known if what I had in mind could work."

"Are you saying The Collective were involved in the invasion?" Amber asked.

"No," Ram replied. "Just the Technos. One of our objectives was to check out Eagle Mountain and try and obtain this equipment. Without it, all we had was a theory. But Kami knew... and above all, I knew, that we needed the right technology to bring it all into existence."

"And why would it have been at Eagle Mountain?" Salene asked, sceptically.

"It's obvious, isn't it?" Ram answered. "It was being hidden. In the military base. Kept under wraps. So the adults could use it. To try and develop it themselves and presumably conduct their own simulations, eventually."

"You forget, Ram. We went to Eagle Mountain too," Amber said. "And there was no sign of any hidden military base. Just the observatory."

It brought back painful memories for Amber, remembering the tragedy when the compound erupted in an explosion which had also nearly claimed her life.

"But you obviously didn't go underground, did you?" Ram explained. "We did. We found this entrance, bypassed its security. And discovered an underground facility. Still there, beneath what's left of the observatory. Just like the information Kami had obtained when he hacked into the government computers. And to think, you didn't even know it existed. It was there, right under your feet..."

"That's not exactly proof though, is it?" Salene demanded.

The others murmured in agreement.

"Tell them about the hibernation chamber," Jay said to Ram.

"Hibernation chamber?" Trudy exclaimed, exchanging more incredulous glances with Amber and the others.

"I found one of many. Right there at the complex in Eagle Mountain," Ram continued. "So I also adapted the chambers. Who knows, I could have lived forever."

Ram had always been paranoid about his health throughout his life but no more than when was in charge of the Technos, forever obsessed with germs of all varieties, in the aftermath of the pandemic. The possibility that the 'virus' would mutate in particular. But had planned to survive whatever other threat he might also have encountered by making sure he was protected. In hibernation, Jay explained, recalling Ram's anguish at being forced back into the real world when he was showing dangerous signs of preferring reality space, along with all the other population of the city, through the use of Ram's Paradise virtual reality network. Most had become almost as addicted as Ram.

"There's another thing you should know. We found adults inside the chambers," Ram continued. "Their bodies, anyway. Don't you see? They must have tried to seal themselves away as a desperate last resort to escape the 'virus'. As much as I'd like to take credit for inventing that myself - I didn't. The military did. I just adapted what they had put in place."

"That's not exactly proof that a base was hidden away there," Amber stated.

"Tell them, will you, Jay?" Ram sighed, frustrated.

"Yes - why don't you tell us, Jay? Everything you also know about all this," Amber said, considering Jay suspiciously. "Are you saying that you also went to Eagle Mountain? If so, why on Earth didn't you say anything about it before?"

"Because I never went there," Jay replied.

"He didn't. I did" Ram clarified. "Jay was no longer a member of the Technos by then, having thrown his lot in with you. And I'm telling you, Ebony and the rebels reeled you in like a fish."

"If the Collective really wanted to take over the city and all the sectors," Amber asked, "and you and the Technos got there first - why didn't The Collective ever show up? To try and take back what they wanted? And get their own back on you?"

"Because I scared them away," Ram said.

"What - with your face!" Gel suggested.

"I sent messages. Through my computer," Ram continued, ignoring Gel's taunt. "I told Kami it wasn't safe. To come to the city. That the 'virus' had returned with a vengeance. If they arrived, there was risk they would all be wiped out. So they did stay away. It worked - for a while."

"And...?" Salene enquired, eager to know more.

"They got suspicious. Kami's so smart, believe me. I knew it wouldn't take long for him to cotton on that it was just an excuse. At that time I was trying to hack into his system and unleash a virus of my own. To get him off my trail. Once and for all. But he countered. And I've got to admit, it was brilliant."

"What was?" Amber asked.

"The Collective sabotaged the Techno computers. No doubt about it."

"What are you talking about?" Trudy probed.

"Resurrecting Zoot... Remember? It all started to get out of control. I'm telling you, it bore all the marks of the type of thing Kami would do. Pure genius. And it sure as hell got you all spooked."

"That was Mega," Trudy said.

"Was it?" Ram replied.

All were now gripped by what Ram was saying, starting to believe that there was some plausibility in it all, well aware of the disruption and confusion the virtual reality Zoot had caused throughout the city.

Then they were astounded when Ram suggested that the Collective could have been responsible for unleashing the chemical attack.

"Now that's stretching it a bit," Amber said. "You seriously expect us to believe that?"

"You really think Mega or I were so slack that our systems would go out of control? At least give us some credit, please."

"What are you saying - exactly?" Amber asked.

"Believe me, there's only one person who could have possibly made those computers fail. 'Kami'. And his Collective," Ram stated.

"But the Virus Mark II... Mega owned up to it," Salene pointed out. "He said it was him."

"He might have thought it was him. That's why it was all so brilliant. Don't get me wrong. Mega had such great potential. But he was my apprentice. I was his master. And I don't believe for one minute that he was intentionally going to wipe everyone out. Himself included."

"So what are you suggesting happened?" Trudy asked uneasily.

"I can't say for sure. All I know is after I was kicked out of the Technos, Mega was playing in a different league. When I was working with Kami, I could match him. Even better him in some areas. But you can bet when that virtual reality Zoot started to go out of control, Mega must have known something was going on. But he might have not had the skills to realise just exactly what. And you know what I think?... His systems were sabotaged..."

"What - by the Collective?" Amber enquired.

"Think about it. There's only three possible things that could have happened. One. That Mega rigged up a system to launch those chemicals into the air. Or two, that he wanted someone to at least believe that he did."

"Why?" Salene asked.

"So they'd be under the impression that the city and area was contaminated," Ram explained.

"You're not seriously suggesting that it was all a bluff?" Amber demanded.

"It might have been. Initially. Either that. Or if The Collective did breach Mega's security, option three would be that they triggered it all. Which means that it was either a real chemical attack. Or just a lot of hot air was released into the atmosphere. Not germs."

Ram was referring to the release of the deadly chemicals upon the city which forced the Tribe and everyone else to flee in the first place, with Ram and the Mall Rats escaping on Zak's trawler, beginning their drift out to sea. Leading up to that, the Techno computers, with the virtual reality Zoot, had been going out of control. The electrical grids were playing up. And throughout Zoot's apparent resurrection, there were a lot of unexplained events prior to that fateful day when everyone escaped the city.

Ram tried to explain all the technicalities, that within Mega's master control centre, he could have discovered his systems were being compromised. And might have tried to retaliate. Sending out false messages. But it was either a bluff. Or, if for some reason he did want to unleash chemicals into the region, he must have realised that his plan had backfired and that ironically, it was tantamount to committing suicide. He was clearly trying to oppress the region with some kind of threat. But why? In Ram's logic, it didn't make any sense for him to do it just for the sake of it, and that he was trying to send a clear signal to The Collective that it wouldn't be safe for them to ever come to the city or any of the sectors. Maybe he had even rigged up something so all he had to do was press the button. So that if anyone was trying to threaten him and the Technos, then they'd destroy themselves in the process. Just like in the old days when countries used to send out nuclear threats. So if The Collective did hack into Mega's system... Ram couldn't say for sure.. but he suspected that they were responsible and not Mega - for what eventually transpired.

"Just one thing I don't understand," Amber asked, considering Ram. "If what you're saying is correct, this theory of your's. Then why were you so keen to get back?"

"Like I say. Mega might have hooked up something but I got to know him really well. When I was training him. And no way he would have destroyed everything in existence, himself included. So we could have a situation where The Collective thought the city was in danger. Even if the odds were 50/50 and those chemicals unleashed were active and posed some form of threat, then it might have been only confined to a radius. Other areas might not have been contaminated."

"That's a pretty big gamble to take," Amber said. "I'm not sure I'd like those odds."

"I'd prefer them rather than encounter the Collective somewhere like here."

"What makes you think The Collective... could be here?" Trudy asked nervously.

"You just don't understand, do you?" Ram sighed, frustrated. "Just believe me. Throughout the time the adults were being wiped out and we were hacking into some of the government systems, we discovered several military bases. Just like Eagle Mountain. In strategic places. And no, I can't say for sure that there's a base here. Because I don't know the exact co-ordinates. But on that death ship we all ended up on, there's no doubt in my mind that whatever that United Nations Task

Force were doing, they were clearly active in this region. Now we're marooned here."

"I know it's a lot to take in," Jay spoke up. "And Ram's been very brave to open up like this..."

"Brave?" Amber retorted. "More like deceitful!"

She and the others were still outraged. They had already so much to deal with, such as Lex and Jack's disappearance, the critical conditions of both Slade and Zak. And with Slade unconscious, they couldn't check if he knew anything about it. Amber wondered if he might have any detail regarding who he worked for when he was on the trail of Ram back in Liberty, and that might help shed some light on it all.

She felt so overwhelmed. Above all, angered why - and how - Ram chose only now to reveal all of this. Amber just couldn't understand what made him tick, why he hadn't said any of it before.

"Are there any other secrets you've been keeping away from us, Ram?" Amber demanded bitterly. "Anything else you care to tell us about?"

"Yeah, there is..." Ram glared, not liking Amber's tone. "I hate spinach - and I've got a big mole on my backside! There, you happy?"

"Spare me the sarcasm for once, Ram! That is so typical of you, isn't it? Are you sure this isn't all some kind of game to you? Like another of your precious computer games you said you used to play? Is that what you're doing? Playing with us? Are you enjoying this? Getting some kind of thrill out of others' misfortune and suffering? If not, you've got a lot of nerve to reveal all this stuff! After all this time!"

"And here we go, more moral pronouncements from the lips of Miss Sanctimonious!" Ram snapped. "You don't ever do anything wrong, do you, Amber? So squeaky clean. If only the world was as perfect as you are. Too bad not everyone can live up to your high and mighty standards!"

"High standards? You call being truthful 'high standards'? It's common decency, Ram! How dare you put your own safety ahead of others? You ask us to believe what you say - but how can we trust you now? After all, you've proven yourself to be nothing more than a selfish liar!"

"Well, that's up to you, Amber!" Ram said. "As well as the rest of you. You can either believe what I've told you or not. I'm not some moron. I was the leader of the Technos. We could have done so much if it wasn't for Kami and The Collective. And all I've been trying to do is protect all of you. Not just myself. After all, most of you... you've become like friends now."

"With friends like you, Ram..." Trudy said.

"I'm not an enemy. There's only one enemy we should be worried about. That's Kami. And The Collective."

"I wouldn't be too sure about that," Amber said, trying to contain her anger. "Sure you haven't overlooked anything else! Like what happened to Bray and the others who disappeared after you just happened to 'invade' our city?"

"I had nothing to do with anyone's disappearance. That was Mega's department. He was in charge of all the prisoners! I had more important things on my mind - than all the small details!"

"Small details? They were human beings!" Amber cried out. "You had no right to ruin innocent lives!"

Amber and Ram stood head to head, eyeballing each other. Jay crossed to Amber, who looked as if she was ready to strike out at Ram.

"Amber, please calm down! We have to listen to Ram. Everything he's saying. You're not being reasonable right now."

That did it.

Amber slapped Jay hard, stinging him in the face, surprising herself, as much as Jay, along with the others, by her sudden outburst.

She was utterly dismayed and deeply hurt by the insensitivity of Ram, and now Jay.

"I'm not being 'reasonable', you say?" Amber repeated Jay's words, wincing as she said it.

"I didn't mean it like that!" Jay insisted.

"What? I'm wrong or something... to ask what happened to the person I once loved? The father of my child, who got snatched away!? Along with others who were special in this tribe?"

"Amber... that's not what I meant!"

"How could you?"

Amber shook her head in disbelief and began crying, as she strode away, Jay following on after her.

"Great! Just what we need, for them to fall out!" Trudy said.

"I'm so glad to have you back, Ram!" Salene added sarcastically. "Thanks for everything!"

The meeting broke up, the others dispersing from the fire in the centre of camp, going their separate ways in the wake of Amber and Jay's row.

"You'll all wish you had thanked me for telling you the truth if The Collective show up!" Ram bellowed out into the night. "Unless we come up with some kind of a plan - believe me, it's game over! For all of us!"

CHAPTER TWENTY-NINE

"It's party time!!" Belle yelled, the rest of The Fallen whooping it up at the prompting of their leader.

The crazed tribe were leaping around a swimming pool. But Bray had no way of knowing. He could only listen. Which he did in a mixture of disbelief and disgust. They were a despicable group, he felt. Sub-human. Totally unstable. And more frighteningly, unpredictable.

Not long after being captured back at the base, Bray had been beaten. The leader, Belle, took great delight in licking blood, then sucking it, like a wild animal, as it oozed from his wounds. He was then taken, blind-folded, and bundled into the back of a military vehicle along with Tiffany, Shannon and Emma. Sadly they hadn't been able to escape.

The Fallen probed if anyone else was left. Emma reassured them amidst her panic that despite Bray and her brother and sister, there was no one else around. For a moment, Bray was uneasy at the prospect that they didn't believe Emma and that she and her two younger siblings might even become victims of torture to obtain information.

"There's no one else here. I swear! I promise you! If there was, I'd tell you!" Emma had pleaded, amidst her tears.

"How would you know anyway?" Belle had teased. "Least you don't need a blindfold!" she taunted, while masking tape was wound around the eyes of the petrified Tiffany and Shannon. The same had occurred to Bray earlier, shortly after his capture and beating.

Bray felt he had let Emma, Tiffany and Shannon down. If only he hadn't climbed up the roller coaster and had run somewhere else, maybe there would have been a better chance for him to have made good his escape. And Emma and her brother and sister might have gotten away.

He had tried to provide a distraction, luring The Fallen further from the accommodation quarters and into the amusement park area so that Emma, Shannon and Tiffany at least had a chance.

Shortly after his own capture, he realised that it had all been to no avail.

Belle didn't believe that Bray had made it across the wastelands. And pressed for detail of where he had come from. But of course, Bray didn't know much other than he had been held by Eloise's forces. And he wasn't about to reveal this, suspecting he could have a bounty on his head, preferring to take his chances, rationalizing that even if he had provided detail, there would be no guarantee that it would result in being better treated. Not from the extraordinary inhumane behaviour he had experienced so far from his new captors.

Throughout the long ensuing journey, Bray began to appreciate more what life must have been like for Emma. With his sight totally obscured by the blindfold, he had to rely solely on his hearing to gain any idea at all of what was occurring. He also tried to calculate just exactly where they might be heading and thought they must have driven in the military vehicles for at least ten hours. But again, he had no way of knowing for sure.

Emma whispered that they were probably being taken to The Mirage, a once thriving resort in the south which was now the home base of The Fallen.

Bray pondered why they should have returned to the military base. And had now taken the last of what was left of Emma's tribe, the Roaches. He hoped they weren't connected to Eloise and that he was somehow responsible for all this. Due to his escape, and inadvertently getting Emma and her siblings involved.

There was no chance of obtaining any more information. Members of The Fallen accompanied Bray, Emma, Tiffany and Shannon in the back of the vehicle, instructing them all to remain silent. But Bray managed to decipher from elements in The Fallen's conversations that they were running out of 'human' flesh to trade and were desperate to meet their quota.

Bray couldn't comprehend what they meant and shuddered to think what Belle and her Fallen tribe were involved with, primarily what they had planned for their hostages. Were they really to be traded? Or was there something more chilling in mind?

They clearly had a sadistic streak, one that would have done Top Hat and Tribe Circus or any of the other crazies Bray had encountered back in the city proud. Everything Emma had warned him about The Fallen was true. They were certainly dangerous but Bray hadn't expected them to have been so wild, almost feral.

There had to be some way out, Bray thought. Something he could do. But he realised for the time being at least that he, Emma, Tiffany and Shannon were all helpless.

His natural sense of justice was enraged at being once again held prisoner. Which was enflamed, knowing that Emma and her siblings were suffering the same fate. Especially when he heard one member of The Fallen ask if he could 'play' a little with Emma when they arrived at their intended destination before handing them over.

"I've never had a blind girl," the tribe member had said. Bray could hear Emma struggling, heaving, and Bray's frustrations and feelings of helplessness were unbearable. He tried to prise himself loose but his hands had been tied so securely with thick packaging tape, just as taut as it had been wound around his head, covering his eyes.

It was a surreal experience to rely solely on what he was hearing as opposed to seeing what was unfolding. And Bray was unsure if it was better to leave it all to his imagination and not see. Or see, without his imagination distorting matters.

"She bit my tongue!" the tribe member cursed. "I'll kill her!"

"Back off," Belle had warned. "Remember there's one value for the living. And another for the dead."

Bray couldn't bear to even think about what they were referring to.

From the conversation, he knew that Belle must have started kissing the tribe member. The one who must have tried to kiss Emma, with her biting her assailant's tongue in the process.

What Bray found disturbing was that rather than being concerned for any injuries, The Fallen seemed thrilled that there was so much blood which must have been dripping from the tribe member's tongue. Belle had demanded that she be the lucky one to indulge herself before the wound congealed as if she was intoxicated by the taste of blood. Bray wondered if these people were really even sub-human after all, or through their struggles to survive in the post adult world had been reduced to behaviour normally exhibited by wild animals.

Now, he was one of eight other prisoners - along with Emma, Tiffany and Shannon - standing blindfolded in The Mirage resort.

Unbeknownst to them, The Fallen were circling the frightened group, snarling and yelling, taking delight, deliberately intimidating their prisoners.

Bray could hear what sounded like the ocean, with waves pounding a beach.

What he did not know, along with the other hostages, was that they were indeed being held in a resort area, as Emma had mentioned earlier. The decaying buildings of what had once been a hotel were now covered in graffiti and had been ransacked. Looted, long ago.

Flaming torches cast looming shadows across the walls. Had they all been able to see, the prisoners would have known that The Fallen were dancing merrily around them, howling like wolves.

Bray suspected some kind of insidious initiation ceremony was occurring.

"Smile!" Belle yelled over the cacophony of noise. "You don't have long here - so smile! Come on! Show how much 'fun' you're having."

Any prisoner who did not co-operate received a stinging backhand slap and tried somehow to provide weak smiles while The Fallen continued howling, but were now grinning themselves, enjoying the surreal reactions as they continued circling their captives standing helpless in the darkness.

Suddenly Belle turned and ran towards the pool, leaping off the cracked, tiled edge of the patio, and diving into the water, disappearing under the surface. The water was so disgusting, darkened with green algae. Belle vanished from sight, traces of diluted blood visible within the pool's density.

Bray and the other prisoners recoiled, straining to use their instincts for some kind of idea of what was occurring, hearing the splash, water spraying over them.

And for the first time since escaping from Eloise's mountain compound, Bray wondered if he was once again participating in a virtual reality program. Had he really met Emma, Tiffany and Shannon? He was definitely aware that they must have been feeling great fear through the intimidating events from hearing their whimpering, sobbing. And from the sounds of the other prisoners, they, too, were clearly suffering.

Bray tried to concentrate his hearing as the howling subsided. Unbeknownst to the prisoners, The Fallen had stopped their frenzied ritualistic dance and were now staring at the pool as if they were worried at what might have happened to their leader.

Seconds passed.

Suddenly Belle exploded through the surface of the pool, a mad look of delight on her face, to the jubilation of her tribe, who began cheering her return. In her mouth she had a human ear, which she tossed to members of The Fallen, who proceeded to fight among themselves while trying to catch it.

Bray and the prisoners flinched at the frenzied noises, then braced themselves as they struggled to comprehend what could be occurring as Belle screamed over the hysteria.

"Anyone fancy a dip?! It's very refreshing!!!"

"Let me, Belle," a member of The Fallen replied. Then, encouraged by the others, with the howling continuing again, he dove into the water. Through the spreading algae after his entry, glimpses of bodies were visible, which would have repulsed Bray, as well as the other hostages, had they been able to see. The Fallen seemed to be devoid of any respect for the sanctity of human life, any and all things living.

"Well?" Belle said, drying her hair with a towel as she surveyed the prisoners, her eyes wild in expectation. "Anyone want to join him?"

"Please! I don't know what you're doing but whatever it is, have some mercy on us. I beg you! Especially for the younger ones!" Bray said, hoping to touch even a degree of humanity, which was so obviously absent from this tribe.

"Good idea!" Belle snapped. "Wouldn't want you to think we're 'inhospitable!' So what about you, Shannon, or you, Tiffany - fancy getting 'cooled off'?"

"No! Please don't harm them!" Emma said.

"Why?" Belle scoffed disdainfully.

"I can't swim!" Shannon yelled.

"Then you should have learned!" Belle snickered. "You'll find lots of other people in there. I seem to remember... they couldn't swim either! What was it with you Roaches - didn't enjoy sport or something?"

The other members of The Fallen howled, encouraged by the panic of the stricken prisoners.

Bray was desperate to think of a way he might assist, fearing that any moment The Fallen would hurl them all into what obviously was a pool, he had concluded, and that they would suffer a slow, agonising death by drowning, unable to swim with their arms and legs bound.

Then he heard another voice shouting out.

There was an abruptness in the tone. Even concern. Definitely a threat.

"That's enough! Back off! Or you'll have us to deal with. And I wouldn't recommend that, especially if we've had a wasted trip!"

Bray and the other prisoners had no way of knowing but a team of about a dozen military-looking figures dressed in black, with rolled up berets perched on their clean shaven heads, had arrived, marching briskly toward Belle.

They were about the same age as The Fallen but unlike the tribe, exuded discipline, efficiency.

"Don't mean to break up your party," one said. "But we're here to collect. How many have you got for us!?"

"You're early!" Belle replied.

"Good job we're not late," the military figure smiled slightly, gazing around, then noticing glimpses of bodies through the

251

spreading algae of the pool. "Looks like you've had a bit of... 'collateral damage'," he added.

"What's that?" Belle asked.

Bray knew, as he listened. He was aware of the term from the old times before all the adults perished.

"The dead!" the military figure replied. "And we're only interested in the living. Not body parts this time."

CHAPTER THIRTY

Life was strange at times, Ebony thought, resting lazily on Blake's bed, caressing the soft, silk pillows and enjoying the comfort of the smooth linen underneath. Here she was in the lap of luxury whereas only weeks earlier she had been stuck with Amber and the Mall Rats on their trawler, starving and drifting. There were so many twists and turns in life, Ebony reflected - and now it was her turn for an upside, she hoped.

She was alone in Blake's quarters, a huge smile on her face, pleased with her accomplishments.

When Blake had 'tested' Ebony, she turned the tables and had utterly surprised him. As well as impressed him. Elevating herself from being a likely candidate for a slave, as when she had first been captured, to now taking the important next steps of being Blake's mistress - and who knows what else.

One scintillating night of passion, along with her gutsy display during the time all the slaves were being categorised, had revealed Ebony's character. That she was tough. Uncompromising. Like Blake. And Ebony hoped that if she could take more steps, he would begin to come to realise that there was far more to her than just a pretty face.

Ebony stretched out, reached for a glass of wine and silently raised a toast to her absent new admirer before sipping from the glass.

I could get used to this, she thought, gazing around Blake's quarters. He was living the high life, relative to what Ebony had experienced on the streets after the virus. Blake had accumulated many precious goods, his quarters full of wine, spirits, even a gymnasium. He liked to work out. She had certainly given him more than enough to challenge his physical capabilities. And it might continue to be a real pleasure. For her. As well as him.

Her instinct told her that Blake was clearly infatuated, at least enough to want to get to know more about her. Ebony was as equally intrigued by Blake. Wondering just exactly who he was. Who he worked to. Or was he solely in command? What was the story about this rig? And all her fellow prisoners who had been categorised for manual labour, breeding and God knows what else.

She hoped she was luring Blake in with her fawning displays of affection, pleasing him in every way she could think, and that this would enable Blake to believe he could trust her.

As it was, the day had progressed well. Things were moving in the right direction. If she could keep this up, perhaps Ebony could rise up the ranks. After all, she had done much the same thing before back in the city with Zoot. And knew there was no future back there. She had to carve a new life now. And if Blake was the King, Ebony was determined that before long she would not only be his mistress - but she was beginning to have aspirations of becoming his Queen, and who knows, eventually rule alone.

Any prospect was certainly a better option than being marooned in an unknown world. She was pleased that she decided to abandon the Jzhao Li, along with the Mall Rats and those stranded on the vessel.

She had managed to decipher during a meal earlier with Blake that he and his team had been stationed on the oil rig for no more than a couple of months. They were apparently a member of a tribe called 'Legion'.

Blake revealed that the name was representative of what he wanted to achieve. A legion of warriors, which is what he considered himself to be. He demanded strict discipline of his inner circle, never questioning his orders. And the vagabonds were some new recruits being inducted. When they had proven themselves, acquiring a necessary level of skill, then they could join. But not until they deserved to do so.

He mentioned that as the reputation of 'Legion' spread, he was sure they would be seen as being fearsome adversaries, with a status like some of the greatest warriors or militia from a bygone age.

Ebony could see that his inner circle were utterly loyal to their leader and his bidding. He had shrugged modestly, advising that he would expect nothing less with the rewards they received from being by his side in combat.

Blake alluded that his late father had been in the military when Ebony admired a long broadsword displayed on the wall. It was clearly a treasure to Blake. And he seemed to be genuinely touched when he revealed details. That it originally belonged to his great grandfather and had been passed down through successive generations. All had achieved high status within the military forces. No doubt the name chosen for his tribe reflected that somewhere in his psyche he was paying homage to that.

But he seemed reluctant to provide any detail when Ebony pressed for more information. She knew anyone in the military had been put on high alert at the height of the pandemic.

When Ebony tried to ingratiate herself, appealing to the obvious vanity Blake possessed by saying that he must be very proud of his father and perhaps had taken after him, Blake seemed offended. So she quickly avoided the topic.

Blake seemed reluctant to reveal much detail about his mother. But she did manage to squeeze out of Blake that he had met his inner circle at boot camp during the streaming the authorities put in place at the peak of all the panicked evacuations, when the virus struck. She discovered that Blake and his cohorts were put through the rigours of a survival course at that time and wondered if he had adapted some of the methods, 'categorising' all the slaves being held as prisoners.

Blake certainly wasn't a trader, as such. But a facilitator. Looking after the transportation, working to someone, whoever they might be. She knew at this point that there was no way he would reveal any more detail. He was far too shrewd for that. But so was she. And she felt confident that one day she'd squeeze more information out of him. She just needed to be patient. Give it time. And then she would find out more about Blake's 'superiors'. For that's how he referred to them.

There was something about the information Blake revealed so far which bothered Ebony. At least enough for her to question if he was being honest. And she wondered if he was feeding false information to put her off any kind of trail.

He said he was concerned, not fully trusting his superiors, wondering if he had been deployed to the oil rig as a 'guinea pig'. He appeared to be almost paranoid if he had been despatched to this land as nothing more than a human test subject. Exposed to an alien environment so that he would be checked on how he adapted.

He had questioned her and she explained nothing more than the fact she and some members of a tribe had fled the city on a trawler, long after the virus occurred. And had embarked upon the Jzhao Li. Which was drifting. All of which was true.

But Ebony embellished it all a bit by saying that they were looking for somewhere new to settle. There was a terrible storm and she had managed to escape on the lifeboat but didn't exactly know what had happened to the other members of her tribe.

She didn't go into any detail about any 'virus Mark II'. She'd save that. Take it one step at a time. She also didn't mention much about her past life in the city, though she knew from the impression she had made that Blake was beginning to realise that she wasn't just a run of the mill survivor in this post adult world. And had a lot more to offer. She decided she'd reveal only bits of information. When she had fully sussed what Blake was all about. No way was she going to lay all her cards on the table and let him know what she was all about first. Not when he was also playing it all so closely to his chest.

One thing that puzzled Ebony was why Blake and the rest of Legion would willingly accept an assignment on this rig if they believed they were in any danger themselves. And were being tested. She couldn't understand what kind of danger they could ever be in. Not with the control Blake had, which was plainly evident.

"Everyone is in danger if they don't obey 'superiors'," Blake had said with a veiled threat, considering Ebony, fascinated how her reaction would be. But she didn't rise to the bait and tried to find out more about this region.

He revealed nothing more than that this region could prove to be valuable. When Ebony asked why, Blake was the one to quickly change the subject this time. It was alright for him to answer a question with a question, she thought. He was certainly adept at doing that. She was sure there was something more to it and she was determined that she'd eventually uncover the mysteries.

But was pleased that she had managed to squeeze even this amount of information out of him like the freshly-squeezed orange juice he was keen on drinking, which also intrigued

Ebony. He seemed to follow a strict diet, was health conscious, keen on staying fit, keeping in shape.

Ebony was above all keen to try and obtain more information on the slaves and the ship which was due to arrive in a few days, to transport the prisoners who were being held in makeshift compounds in various decks below.

She pitied them. No doubt some would be used for agricultural work, all manner of labour. But they would have gotten off lucky, Ebony felt, compared to the weaker of the slaves who were to be used for 'medical' purposes. And had hoped that her own brand on her backside would continue to be 'L' for 'lover' when she had learned that in the end, 'L' was actually for 'laboratory'. Blake wouldn't reveal any kind of detail on what anyone destined to end up would suffer. And she had no intention of finding out. So she decided for now not to pursue questioning.

Ebony clambered off the bed and gazed at her reflection in a full length mirror. Then she applied more lipstick, flicking her hair seductively. She sure was an enchantress, she felt, gifted - with striking looks. And was experienced and cunning enough to know how to use them, resolved that she would make Blake spellbound. Draw him in. Captivate him. Without him even realizing. And even if he did realize, Ebony felt he would soon become addicted and want more and more.

Crossing to Blake's desk, Ebony refilled her wine glass, then spotted a laptop, it's 'sleep' light blinking on and off.

She sat down in the mammoth, leather office chair, opened the lid, awakening the computer from hibernation, then hesitated for a moment, wondering if she should take a look. If Blake suddenly returned, she already had an excuse and would just say she was looking for something to entertain her. But she'd be ready to entertain him with something better than any computer could ever offer.

She noticed some directories with files which had been segmented into 'the pandemic'.... 'military installations'... 'orders'... 'prisoner status'...

Ebony went through the directories in mounting intrigue, suspecting that the rig was more than just a way station for slave transportation. It was obviously a floating fortress, the perfect place for an outpost, offering a sweeping panoramic view of the ocean around it. And rather than any exploration of oil, which it had apparently been used for once according to Blake, Ebony was intent on trying to discover more detail, sure its current operation wasn't limited to housing human cargo.

When she tried to gain access into any file, she was blocked.

Suddenly a live 'feed' activated and Blake's face appeared on the screen.

"Looking for something?" he said, his cold voice audible through the small speaker.

"No," Ebony replied, swallowing nervously. "If you can hear me - I wasn't doing anything, Blake. Honest."

"Oh, I can hear you very well," Blake replied. "In fact, I've been watching you. Closely. If you wanted some wine, then you should have asked. Likewise if you wanted to access classified files. Unfortunately, I think you'll find that you don't know the password!"

The screen went blank.

Ebony stood, bracing herself uneasily, listening to the sound of brisk footsteps approaching, echoing in the outer corridors.

She backed away, noticing the door handle beginning to turn.

Then she recoiled as the door opened, revealing Blake, who once again smiled, but it was ice-cold.

"Hi, honey! I'm home!"

Ebony continued to back away as Blake advanced, enraged. Finally unable to contain his simmering anger, he seized her by the neck with one hand, almost lifting her off her feet, pinning her to the wall.

She struggled to get her breath, writhing, trying to defend herself, scratching his face with her nails.

"Get off me!" she screamed. "I promise, I wasn't doing anything wrong!! I was just passing the time!"

He ran his own nails down Ebony's face, gouging her cheek. Slowly, deliberately, his teeth gritted. Then he released his grip, lowering her back down to the ground.

"One thing you should know about me, Ebony," Blake said quietly, but there was an intensity in his voice. "If you ever strike me, then I'll strike back. If you ever cross me, then that would be very foolish. Anyone who's ever tried never took long to realize that it was at their peril. And if you ever try to disobey or deceive me... then I'll destroy you."

"I think I get the gist of what you're saying there, Blake. And I'm just the same. Be nice to me and I'll be nice to you," she said, rubbing the welts on her neck from his clutch.

He considered her and couldn't contain a slight smile. He shook his head. "You're something else. You really are. Like an alley cat."

"Somehow that doesn't sound much like a compliment."

"Well, it is. I hate to admit it... but you know... I'd probably have done the same if I was in your situation," Blake replied. "And in a way, I admire that."

"You were setting me up, eh?"

He nodded proudly. "And you took the bait. 'I was just passing the time'," he mimicked Ebony's voice.

"I wasn't trying to pry into anything."

"You disappoint me," Blake said matter of factly. "I would want to know everything about any opponent."

"I'm not an opponent!" Ebony interrupted. "And that's why I wasn't snooping or anything. I don't consider you any kind of opponent of mine. And the sooner you realize that, the better. I can be useful to you, Blake. But I can't do that... unless you let me."

"In a way," Blake replied, "you might be right. You might end up being very useful. Having a higher value. A value beyond my wildest expectations."

"Oh?" Ebony said, unsure of exactly where he was coming from, what it all meant. But she knew deep down that she had to try and defuse matters as Blake continued.

"So why don't we just see what eventual category you fit. Just let me warn you, Ebony. If I find out I can't trust you, then it is 'L' for you, for sure. Laboratory!"

"And what does that entail?"

"Just trust me. Don't go there."

"You don't have to worry about that," Ebony replied. "I think we know each other well enough by now. Why don't we just stick to 'lover'?"

She pressed her lips on his and they passionately began to undress each other, hardly able to contain their desire.

CHAPTER THIRTY-ONE

The moon was bright, shining down on the surface of the water, the gentle waves retreating on the sands as the tide drifted out. The relaxing sounds brought Ruby some comfort. She was alone, several metres away from Camp Phoenix, needing some time and space away from the others to gather her thoughts.

"What am I going to do with you?" Ruby spoke to herself, as if asking the baby she was carrying.

When she had confided her secret to Amber previously, Amber had asked Ruby if she was sure the father was Slade - and Ruby had been emphatic. Apart from a few relationships - and one mistaken, drunken one-night stand - she didn't sleep around.

How ironic that the pregnancy test she had taken back in the city was wrong, Ruby reflected. Very wrong. She took it before the tribe had been forced to flee the 'virus Mark II' released by Mega. At least she thought it was Mega. She, like the others, was feeling a little confused by what Ram had revealed.

But there was no doubt about it in her mind that she was expecting and who the father was. During the first few days of the voyage on the trawler, Ruby thought she was being seasick. Every so often she was overcome with nausea. But it must have been morning sickness, she concluded, discovering once again that she had missed her period.

Her life had been turned upside down due to the discovery of the life she was carrying inside her. Pregnancy tests weren't 100% accurate, she knew. There had been articles, she remembered, browsing when she was younger through her mother's stack of women's magazines, revealing how some mothers were surprised to find they were pregnant after having a negative test. And Ruby was more than surprised to know she was indeed carrying a baby. She was absolutely staggered.

New emotions were beginning to surface, along with the hormones.

She would face difficult times. In this post-apocalyptic world. She knew that. But also knew that in Amber and the Mall Rats, that they would be with her every step to give her any support she needed. Amber and Trudy had been there before as mothers themselves and Ruby would no doubt be grateful for any assistance they, along with the rest of the tribe, would provide.

Her overwhelming need right now was to keep it secret. So that Slade would know. First. Then Ruby would also know if he would stand by her. She didn't want him to feel obligated in any way. And above all, needed to know that Slade shared the same feelings she had for him.

She had never fallen in love before. But was sure that it must be the real thing. She had never felt this way about anyone and couldn't bear the thought of losing Slade.

Poor Amber, Ruby pondered, thinking back to the falling out that had happened hours before when Ram revealed his own 'secret' to everyone, about The Collective. But Ruby believed Jay and Amber would make up. Eventually. They were such a close couple.

Ruby would have to take it all one step at a time, she reasoned. Whatever unfolded on the island. The pregnancy. Her relationship with Slade, which had been further complicated by the fact that Slade's heart once belonged to someone else, with Ebony being the walking proof of that. And Ruby needed to know how Slade truly felt for her without any elements of duty of being a father clouding matters.

The most important thing for Ruby was that Slade survive his injuries. Or there would be no future for them together.

Also, Ruby was still distraught at the confrontation she had with May when she suggested how best to share out the limited medical supplies.

She wondered, going over everything in her mind, if she had she been right to insist that only Slade be treated with the medicines they had. Or if May was right, and she was being unfair.

Ruby didn't want to reduce Zak's chances of pulling through by denying him any medicine but she strongly felt there was no other choice. Zak was barely breathing, his weak pulse testament to the awful condition he was in. Ruby wished she could wave a magic wand, make both him and Slade better. But there were no quick fixes, she knew. She felt Zak didn't have much time left on this earth. So what was the point in wasting the precious limited medicine supplies that they had on him?

Yes, it was better to focus on Slade, Ruby was sure. Give all the medicine to him. At least he was semi-conscious, not in some coma, and though his wound was severe, he was surely in a stronger position than Zak to pull through.

Her thoughts drifted back to the old times when she was sitting in the waiting room in the hospital. It all brought up similar emotions. She would have been about ten years old. And she remembered the day like it was yesterday. Her grandmother had been admitted after suffering a massive stroke.

She was unconscious, in a coma. Ruby had cried more tears than she knew possible. Ellen was her favourite grandparent. The doctors had entered the waiting room with a solemn look on their faces and Ruby had overheard her parents discussing Grandma Ellen's plight.

There was nothing they could do, the doctors had told them. Grandma Ellen was technically alive but without being on life support, was in reality clinically dead.

Ruby's family had decided to accept the inevitable, to reluctantly agree with the doctors' recommendations - that the life support machines be switched off, resulting in Grandma Ellen drifting from this world to the next.

Ruby vowed she would never forget Grandma Ellen - and neither would she forget the manner of her passing.

That episode in her younger life brought back painful recollections. Zak was surely going to follow in Grandma Ellen's steps. Their situations were so similar. There was no point giving Zak medicine. It was too late for him. But not for Slade.

For all of her stance, Ruby couldn't help but feel pangs of guilt as she reflected on her argument with May earlier. And the look in May's eyes when she was sitting, refusing anything to eat, the light from the bonfire back at camp reflecting flickering, dancing flames in her eyes. She looked to be so lost, eager to get back to taking her shift to watch over Zak. As eager as Ruby had been to check on Slade, both still being sheltered some distance away from the main camp, being too unwell to be moved.

Ruby wondered if she had become sensitised. To death. She had experienced so much of it throughout the pandemic. With news initially of hundreds, thousands, then millions passing away as the 'virus' spread. Before long, the impact seemed to evaporate. Death became routine, just like the struggle to survive, to live, to get through another day.

Salene was now taking a shift to watch over Slade and Ruby welcomed the chance to try and gather all her thoughts together as she waded through the shallows, gazing at the wreck of the Jzhao Li, silhouetted in the distance against the dark sky.

None of them had dived inside the wreck itself during the search for more medical supplies. Ruby suggested they check it out but had been overruled by the others, feeling it would be far too dangerous.

But she was a good swimmer. During her vacations while at school, Ruby worked as a lifeguard, plucking many people from the water, having got themselves into unnecessary difficulties.

It was all about minimizing the risks, Ruby knew, finding the right spot, being sensible.

The ocean was calm tonight, the tide gentle.

Wading deeper and deeper into the waters, a part of Ruby wondered whether or not she should continue on. Then, when she was waist high, she took a deep breath, lunged forward and started to swim towards the wreck.

Kicking her feet, harder, she submerged herself, the cold water gurgling around her ears, and proceeded toward the sunken hull.

She was lucky she was still physically fit, not so far advanced in her term that she was unable to do anything. On the contrary, she was still slim, her tummy almost flat, the baby she was carrying not yet showing as a 'bump' though she knew it was there, inside her. She just knew.

Ahead of her, the accommodation tower of the Jzhao Li now came into view, laying on its side in the moonlit waters, motionless. Ruby remembered seeing in one of the cabinets in the bridge a mammoth first aid kit when they were onboard and now was determined to see if she could retrieve it, to check if there was anything salvageable.

Her legs drove her to the surface. She inhaled, desperate to obtain air, gazing around, making sure of her bearings. Then she took a huge breath, her cheeks puffed out by the air they stored, and dived under the surface again, the beam of the waterproof flashlight she had recovered during Salene's search illuminating the way ahead, guiding her further downwards, deep into the wreck of the Jzhao Li.

CHAPTER THIRTY-TWO

Lia stooped under the low roof as she entered the mud hut, a bundle of ripe fruit in her arms, which she dropped to the ground in front of Jack and Lex, the two of them pausing for a moment, staring at the fruit. They hadn't eaten for ages and it was a tantalising sight.

The sound of insects and animal life of the night reverberated through the native camp and jungle beyond.

"Go on," Lia encouraged. "It's not poisoned, if that's what you're worried about. Eat it!"

Grateful, Jack and Lex scooped up the fruit. Though still bound by the vines, they were able to hold the selection of what was on offer and gleefully started consuming it.

"Why are you doing this?" Jack asked between mouthfuls.

"I thought you'd be hungry. And thirsty."

It was true that it was sweltering in the hut and Jack and Lex were beginning to feel dehydration set in, as well as hunger.

"There's few better things in the world than a girl bringing me food," Lex said philosophically, dribbling juice down his chin.

"Lia, why are you helping us?" Jack asked, as Lia knelt down beside them.

"I might wear glasses," she said, tapping her thick lenses, her green eyes peering through, "but I can still see that both of you could never be Blake's people."

"Why's that? Cause we're good looking - and they're ugly?" Lex suggested.

"They're nothing but bad news. But you two? I think my old pet rabbit must have been tougher than either of you! You're no match for Blake's forces, that's for sure."

"Must have been some rabbit," Lex retorted, slightly offended.

Since they had first met, Lia had gotten to know Jack and Lex better. And she liked what she saw of them, believing they were two innocents who meant no harm and were telling the truth, the two of them stumbling by accident into the world of the natives.

She was determined to help. She felt sorry for them and had earlier given them an insight into the native tribe and why there had been such antagonism displayed towards Jack and Lex.

Lia had explained that the natives were survivors of the pandemic, as was anyone else who was still living and breathing since the adults perished.

As indigenous people of this land, they had a longstanding resentment against the international community who had brought many diseases. Their people had suffered for centuries, losing their independence when the settlers first arrived and took over their lands. Trampling on customs, dishonouring their culture, tainting the sacred soil. But the tribe never lost their dignity or desire to continue the way of life of their ancestors, passing down their knowledge and traditions through the generations. And this surviving generation was no exception.

Lia described how the outside world began to creep in, with roads being carved through the jungle, as well as a small airport being built many years ago, to accommodate an influx of tourists who had discovered these paradise islands. There were no cities or towns. Just a few scattered resorts for holidaymakers to fly in and spend some time marvelling at the natural world, fishing, exploring the reefs, lounging on the stunning beaches.

The village existed in its own 'pocket', isolated far from the tourists, thankfully, so that little infiltration had occurred to further affect the culture.

In a way, the camp, as well being a home, had almost been located as if it bridged two worlds. Between the traditional way the 'natives' were so desperate to preserve and the 'modern' lifestyles of the outside.

So the tribe resented the presence of outsiders long before even the 'virus' occurred. And as all the adults began to die off, tried to seal themselves away so that they could embark upon trying to carve out a new future, paying homage to the old and all their people who had gone before.

During the height of the pandemic, Lia had told Jack and Lex, there had been a sudden build up of new activity with foreigners, the military arriving. A massive oil rig had been towed into position off the coast. Construction machinery arrived on enormous ships. An old abandoned air base from World War 2 was reactivated and developed. Many more vehicles were brought to the land. Supplies. Equipment. Soldiers and defence personnel soon outnumbered the indigenous population. At one point there was more aircraft than birds flying around, the natives felt.

It seemed as if these lands were going to be overwhelmed and the indigenous tribe were fearful of their way of life disappearing forever, like a tsunami of foreigners from overseas was threatening to engulf and wipe everything away.

But the danger was far greater than even the 'natives' anticipated. When all the foreign people in their midst began to die off. And then so did the adult members of their tribe. One by one.

When they perished, the tribe believed it was due to the way the international community had treated the world as a whole. Throughout history, they had tried to extend their empires. Greedily pillaging nature's resources with their pollution, oil rigs and spills. And perhaps the 'virus' was nature's way - or God's way - of handing out its natural justice, with the old adult world being purged, paying the price for all the wrongs that had been committed. Unfortunately the native adults had been swept away as innocent victims, they all believed.

As survivors of the plague, now the answers to their future lay in their past. In the wisdom of their ancestors. In the life that was taught to them by their forbears. So they were determined to return to the old traditional ways, to their culture, to guide them through uncertain times.

"And what about this Blake?" Lex asked.

"I don't know much about him. Or his forces. Except that they raided once. Not long after they arrived, taking away many of the villagers."

"To where?" Jack probed.

"No one knows where they end up for sure. But I think they trade in slaves. And if his men ever come back, we'll be ready if he tries to set foot on the sacred lands," Lia replied.

"What about us then?" Jack asked. "I mean, if the tribe thought we did."

"That's not a matter for me," Lia replied.

"Then who?" Lex enquired, before letting out a huge, satisfied, impromptu belch, having finished his fruit, Jack also wiping his own juicy hands on the ground.

"Honestly - you are just like one big baby," Lia teased Lex, a twinkle in her eye.

She was obviously attracted to him, though she tried not to show it too much. But Jack could see that, as always, Lex seemed to have a way with any female he encountered. And this girl was no exception, falling victim to his roguish charms.

"You should see how he can get. On a bad day. Right now he's on his best behaviour," Jack added, sensing that it might help if he could play the Lex card, though Lia seemed to be as kind as she was concerned for their well being and didn't need any extra motivation. But Jack thought it couldn't hurt.

"What is this? Pick on Lex day or something?" Lex protested.

"Just a little fun, Lex," Jack replied. Then he turned back, considering Lia. "So if it isn't a matter for you - who decides? About us, Lia?"

"The Priestess will see you soon. Your fate will be decided then," she replied.

"Do you think she'll let us go?" Jack asked.

"It is up to her. But just know, the way you treated everyone since you have been here - shouting at them, calling them names. Threatening. It hasn't helped. They are suspicious of outsiders enough as it is."

Jack sighed to himself, wondering if perhaps trying to use the 'Lex charm card' was such a good idea after all.

"I still don't get it," Lex said, slumping down on the dirt like a lion after a feast. "If these people hate all things 'foreign' so much - what are you doing here? Why aren't you a prisoner? Like Jack and I?"

"I was - once," Lia replied. "My home was in Frankfurt, originally."

"Well, that explains everything," Lex scoffed sarcastically.

Jack interrupted, not wishing to inflame matters with Lex going off on a tangent. "How did you end up here?" he asked Lia.

"My Mum and Dad were both doctors. With the Red Cross. As a little girl, I was sent to boarding schools. All over the world. But when the pandemic occurred, I was with my parents. They were going to be part of a medical mission. With the United Nations Pacific Fleet."

Jack and Lex exchanged a discrete glance, recalling Doctor Gideon's journal, as Lia continued.

"We were an international force, the last effort supposedly to save humanity. By keeping people away from the land, quarantined in ships, the idea was they would be safe. Like Noah's Ark. And one day, everyone would return to the land and rebuild civilisation."

"So what happened to this ship of yours?" Lex asked Lia carefully.

"The 'virus' happened. It spread throughout the entire fleet. My Mum and Dad put me in a liferaft. Along with some of the other children, and set me adrift. I never saw my parents again."

Lia hesitated, her eyes clouding over in pain at the memories, reliving it once more.

"They devoted their lives to saving others. And made sure I would have a chance to be saved... After many days alone at sea, I was washed up. On this land. I don't know what happened to the other children. But I think some of them might have survived. Joined other tribes. Some, not indigenous to our land but made up of foreigners."

"So you were shipwrecked yourself?" Jack enquired.

Lia nodded.

"Well, at least you know how we feel," Lex said.

"Wandering around the jungle, lost, I was taken in. At first, as a prisoner. Like you. But the Priestess's younger sister was sick. I saved her life, using my Dad's old medical kit. It wasn't anything serious. I think maybe even a cold. But some of the villagers thought I had healing powers. Sure the

Priestess's sister was suffering as a result of the pandemic. So I was allowed to stay. The strange thing is that I probably wasn't even responsible. They have their own cures they use. From the land. And probably saved the Priestess's sister themselves. But they gave me credit. Since then, they've been like a new family to me. I learned their language, their customs. And decided to say good bye to the ways of the old world that I had known."

"So where does that leave us?" Jack questioned, trying to gain more of an insight into what might lay in store.

"I've recommended to the Priestess she be lenient with you. But as I say, it is not my decision. Just remember everything I've told you. Show respect. If the Priestess can see the good in you that I can see, there's every chance you will be fine."

"And if she can't?" Lex asked.

Lia was silent for a moment, unsure what to say.

"Please...," Jack said. "We're grateful for everything you've done. But we need to know. Where do we stand?"

"Unless the Priestess decides otherwise, today could be the last day you are alive."

Jack blanched. Lex looked at Lia, bravely absorbing it all.

"Well, if she has so much power around here... let's just hope she's in a good mood," Lex said wryly, but could barely mask his unease.

* * *

Jack and Lex were led through the village, their feet squelching in the mud, powerfully built warriors clutching their arms either side. Flaming torches illuminated the camp.

The entire tribe had come out to witness the spectacle and were assembled, shouting at Lex and Jack in their native tongue as the two outsiders passed by. It was a language, of course. Neither Jack nor Lex understood, though from the hostility clear in the expressions and tones let alone the jeering, it was obvious they didn't think much of Jack and Lex, other than contempt.

"What you think they're saying?" Jack whispered innocently to Lex.

"I dunno. But somehow I don't think it's how handsome I am," Lex muttered back, trying to keep his humour.

They were dragged towards a massive hut in the centre of the village where a large fire crackled, spitting out hot embers, and around it a circle of younger girls and warrior boys danced, ululating wildly, their arms flailing.

It had to be a ritual, some ceremony, Jack realized. And he and Lex were the focus of it all.

He looked around for Lia, hoping she might give some indication of just exactly what was happening, but noticed she had disappeared into an impressive dwelling.

Pushed to the ground, Jack and Lex remained kneeling as a huge warrior stood near the entrance of the mud hut Lia had entered, a conch shell grasped in his burly arms.

Suddenly the warrior blew into the conch, a loud, primal bellow reverberating around the entire village. The native crowd who had gathered to watch quietened down in anticipation.

"Remind me to never go off exploring with you again," Lex whispered to Jack.

Jack didn't smile. He was terrified by the ordeal, at being on public display. It felt like some sort of show trial. "If anything happens to either of us... it's been nice knowing you, Lex," Jack said sincerely.

Lex nodded. "Sorry about all those times I used to bully you. I didn't mean anything. You've always been a good friend." Lex seemed as if he wished to redeem himself in some way, equally sincere, before sighing to himself, "Though I can't say it's a pleasure spending my last days with you."

Lex and Jack braced themselves as a figure emerged from the dark confines of the large hut, stepping into the night and drawing gasps of awe from the crowd.

She was taller than the other villagers and wore bright multi-coloured feathers in her dark hair. She moved so regally, graciously. On her face were markings, daubs of decorative lines indicating some hidden meaning, unknown to Jack and Lex. She had a commanding aura, surveying first the crowd before her, then turning her attention to the two captives kneeling under her gaze.

Lex drew a sharp intake of breath, contemplating the Priestess. She was staggeringly beautiful. Charismatic. Svelte. Sensual. She possessed an extraordinary magnetism. She was about the same age as most of the girls Lex had bedded in the Mall Rats. And right now, his dying wish was that if this was to be his last night on earth, then he would spend it with her. She took Lex's breath away. For a moment he almost forgot that she had the power over his and Jack's life, so lost was he, mesmerised by her presence.

The massive warrior put down the conch shell and in the ensuing silence the Priestess stared at Jack and Lex, sizing each one up with her determined eyes.

Lia started speaking the native tongue, a guttural sounding language with a few clicking noises here and there. What a contrast to the voice and European accent they had gotten so used to, Lex thought, wondering how Lia could have ever even learned such a language. It sounded so complicated.

Lex and Jack wondered what she was saying.

Thrusting an arm forth, the Priestess silenced Lia. She had heard enough.

Addressing the crowd of onlookers, the Priestess began speaking. She spoke in a smooth, rhythmic tone. She wasn't shouting, just speaking as if in conversation. But so quiet were her subjects, so focused on her every word and gesture, so still was the atmosphere, the Priestess's words carried over the air for all to hear.

Lia began to translate, whispering to Jack and Lex.

"She's saying that the two strangers here among us are a curse. From the foreigners. She is sure you are both demons, sent to cause destruction."

"I think I need a lawyer," Lex mumbled.

"Bow your head in respect!" Lia urged him. Lex did as she suggested as Lia went on translating. "The Priestess claims you are both people of Blake. That you are here to spy on the Tribe. Assess its strengths and weaknesses. Before capturing more of the people, committing them to a lifetime of slavery. Like your kind have done before. You exist to pillage and plunder. Nothing will stop you going about your ways... except..."

The Priestess glowered at Jack and Lex, her eyes full of venom and spite as she continued addressing the crowd of villagers.

"Except what?" Jack whispered to Lia, desperate to know what she was saying.

"The Priestess feels that there is only one way to stop you and the rest of your kind. And that is to send out a warning. To Blake. And his people. Along with anyone else who dares step uninvited into the tribal sacred lands."

The Priestess shrieked suddenly, her high pitch call piercing the air. And the villagers erupted into ululations, the energy palpable, electric.

Backing into her hut, bowing to the stars that twinkled above, saying something in her native tongue to the night sky, the Priestess disappeared from sight.

"Is that it?" Lex asked Lia.

"What - they're letting us go?" Jack questioned, hopeful at the answer. "They want us to take some kind of message with us?"

Reluctantly, Lia shook her head. The sadness in her green eyes gave it away, all the sparkle normally shown in them now gone.

"I'm so sorry," Lia began to cry, sniffing through tears. "Tomorrow morning. At sunrise. You will be sacrificed. And your remains given to Blake and his men if they ever set foot in the sacred lands again."

CHAPTER THIRTY-THREE

Amber patted her baby on the back. He had woken up minutes earlier, crying into the night, and she was trying to comfort him. Though in effect, he was giving her the comfort she needed that moment, even though he didn't know it, Amber thought, hugging her baby lovingly.

She was still upset with Jay after Ram had explained all about the information about The Collective, Jay being the only one of the Mall Rats so far who seemed to believe Ram's story. Fully.

Jay had every right to express his opinions, Amber had always felt. That wasn't the issue.

She never wanted to be cynical. To think the worst of anyone or anything. But there was something about Ram she still couldn't put her finger on. Was he being truthful now about The Collective? Or was he holding something else back?

"Amber..." Jay whispered, stepping tentatively towards her. "Can we talk?"

"You tell me. Can we?"

"I didn't mean to get you upset before."

"Well, you succeeded. Or am I overreacting? Not being 'reasonable' enough for you?"

"Amber, please," Jay pleaded. "The word just slipped out. It was the wrong thing to say. You have every right to question Ram about what happened to Bray... and anyone else in the tribe who disappeared for that matter. Just because I might believe him and his story - that doesn't mean it's a blank slate, and the past is all wiped away. Clean. Ram still has a lot to answer for."

Amber looked at Jay, studying him. She couldn't believe that she was beginning to question even his integrity. But he had been Jay's 'general' after all, the one who planned the main invasion that led to the Technos taking over the city. Jay had always denied he knew what happened to Bray and the others, why they were taken. She had believed him. Jay eventually turned against Ram's rule of tyranny once he had been exposed to all the realities and had helped Amber lead the rebels to freedom. They had so many things in common, with their ideals and principles. It was hardly surprising they entered into relationship.

But still, Jay seemed to be siding with Ram. Amber hoped it wasn't the start of a slippery slope that would end up with Amber losing him, which would certainly be the case if he was going to do Ram's bidding. Becoming his 'general' once more. Amber couldn't bear even the thought of it. That Jay would ever reunite again with Ram. And if he ever did, she knew her relationship with Jay would be over. She could never begin to forgive Ram for all the pain and hurt he had brought to the city and sectors. For all that he protested his innocence. She was always a good judge of character and could see through people. At least that's what she thought. But now was beginning to have some painful doubts if Jay was involved in any way. If so, she had been totally taken in. He wouldn't have been the man she thought he was.

Jay knew Amber well enough to realize what must have been going through her mind. And that he might have been tarred in her view with what Ram had been saying.

"When Ram first told me about The Collective, I didn't believe a word of it," Jay said. "I thought that's it - he's finally lost it, teetered over into the brink of madness, that it was all in his head... But the more I thought about it, piecing it together... it does all make sense."

"Well, I'm glad it does. To you." Amber replied.

"All I'm saying, Amber, is that I believe Ram about the existence of The Collective. Nothing more. Nothing less."

"And these 'underground adult bases', like the one at Eagle Mountain," Amber probed. "You sure you didn't know about all that? Or anything else?"

"You know all that I know, Amber. Please. Believe me. And if Ram's right, we could all be in great danger here. If The Collective are somehow involved in these islands."

Amber considered Jay, then sighed.

"I don't mean to doubt you, Jay. It's just a lot to take in."

"That's for sure," Jay agreed, then he continued, sadly. "After what happened to Ved, I know how it feels to lose someone special."

"I know," Amber said, gently stroking Jay's arm.

Then she indicated the baby, now sleeping in her arms.

"I'm just so worried about our future. My baby's future."

"That's why I wanted you to listen to Ram. I'm as concerned about the future for you, me, the baby. Everyone. I wasn't trying to shut you up, tell you what to do. And I wasn't choosing to side with Ram. The wrong words slipped out of my stupid mouth at the wrong time. I'm so sorry, Amber."

Jay ran his fingers through her hair as he continued on gently. "You don't really think I had anything to do with Bray's disappearance? Or any of the others?"

"I had to check, Jay."

"What? If I'm a liar?"

"No. I know when it comes down to it, you're not that. I'm sorry. And I'm sorry I slapped you."

"So am I. You've got quite a right hook. If The Collective are out there somewhere, they'd regret crossing you, Amber."

Amber smiled, then looked at Jay uneasily. "Do you really think they could be out there?"

"I don't know what I think anymore, Amber. But we've got to tread with care. Ram can be a bit like a loose missile at times. But for all his faults, he just had his own agenda for the Technos. Ideologically."

"Well, I don't agree with them. I never have," Amber replied firmly.

"Well, that's your opinion and you're entitled to it. But don't you see - whoever he is, it doesn't matter if you're right. Or I'm right. Ram can still be a valuable asset. He knows more about The Collective and how they operate than anyone. Now it doesn't mean to say that I'm his best friend or that I'm working for him again, by me saying that. Or even against him. It just means that, thinking strategically, if we're going to have any kind of chance and The Collective do exist - we might need Ram."

"I understand," Amber agreed, seeing the sense in what Jay was saying. "But let's keep our eye on him."

"Now that sounds 'reasonable' to me," Jay said, kissing Amber tenderly on the cheek.

Amber smiled as well and kissed him back.

"I'm so glad that nothing happened to you. Even Ram, believe it or not. And now that you're back, we'd better think about sending out a search party for Jack and Lex. They're long overdue and Ellie's really struggling."

Amber's expression clouded, as did Jay's, as they noticed Salene.

"Amber!" Salene called out, racing towards them.

"What is it, Sal?" Amber replied.

"I think something must have happened to Ruby. There's no sign of her back at camp!"

* * *

It hadn't all turned out how she had expected, Ruby thought, gasping for breath.

She was trapped inside the wreck of the Jzhao Li. The underwater flashlight she had brought with her to guide her way in the murky depths, had stopped working several minutes before. Most likely its battery had gone.

Now, all around, it was pitch black. There was nothing she could see. Just the empty darkness that was all encompassing.

And Ruby felt terrified.

Panic gripped her. As hard as she fought to push it away, it just kept coming back.

This was her worst nightmare. Drowning, alone, in the unforgiving sea. She had many recurring dreams about it when she was a little girl. It was the very reason her parents had given her swimming lessons in the first place. And her fears had subsided, having become such a proficient swimmer, eventually a lifeguard. Now all those anxieties had returned. Ironic that she had saved so many lives in her time as a guard but was unable to help herself, her unborn baby. And Slade.

Ruby had swam into the wreck through one of the broken windows in the bridge, and had managed to find what she had been searching for. The medical kit was still there, fastened to its wall hanging, and in the air pocket.

The Jzhao Li was unstable, however. While Ruby was inside the bridge section, the hull of the ship had continued creaking, its groans reverberating under the water like a whale's song, though Ruby wondered if each shift of the vessel was going to be a death knell.

The bridge window that Ruby had entered was now inaccessible, the wreck having turned on its side several degrees so that Ruby would have to find a different way out.

The ship was resting in a good thirty feet of water and Ruby knew her air pocket wouldn't last long. She was floating inside the dark confines of the bridge, her face pressed to the ceiling, feelings of claustrophobia and a fear of drowning combined, filling Ruby with an awful sense of doom.

She wouldn't give up, though. Clutching the medical kit in her hand, fighting back cramp, her legs aching from the cold salt water, Ruby was determined to give it everything she had. A deep grinding noise moved through the hull of the Jzhao Li, stuck precariously on the reef, signifying to Ruby that the wreck hadn't finished its capsizing movement yet. It was a terrifying sound, like the gates of hell were being opened for her, a foreboding screech of rending metal that permeated through the water, through the essence of Ruby's entire being.

Taking a huge gulp of air, she managed just in time to submerge under the water as the air pocket disappeared, with the wreck shifting.

Under the water, in the dark, Ruby prayed she would be able to rise up under the bridge and find another air pocket once the wreck settled.

Panic rising through every fibre of her body, Ruby struggled to keep calm. But knew she needed to find another precious intake of breath. Soon. Would this breath be her last? Was this really how it was meant to be? Had she brought this upon herself, foolishly venturing into the water alone, underestimating the risks?

Seconds passed. The awful sound of the Jzhao Li shifting in the unstable depths subsided.

Time to kick up to the surface, Ruby thought, her lungs feeling like they were going to burst. It was now or never.

Ignoring the cramp that constricted her leg muscles, her calf throbbing painfully out of control, Ruby gave it all she had, kicking, desperate to find another air pocket - or even a window so she could escape rather than be trapped in this watery grave.

But her worst fears were realized when she reached what was once a wall, and now a temporary ceiling, due to the angle of the sideways leaning bridge section of the Jzhao Li. There was no pocket of air this time. Just the cold metal wall.

Her chest feeling like it was on fire, her lungs under protest, her mouth instinctively, desperately wanting to open to breathe, her entire body was weakening, her life ebbing away.

She was terrified at the thought of her unborn baby being starved of oxygen, along with herself. She couldn't yield though and kept her mouth clamped shut. Stars appeared before her eyes. She realized that she was drowning, losing the young life she carried inside her in the process.

Twin beams of light burst through the murky darkness, like Heaven had sent down angels to welcome her.

Ruby focused weakly. Who was this? Her Mum and Dad? Her Grandma Ellen? The baby she had terminated? Friends who had perished in the apocalyptic pandemic?

The bright beams of light cut through the darkness, enveloping Ruby, losing consciousness, swallowing the salt water.

But a feeling of total tranquility, peace, replaced her panic.

There were angels, after all.

Her body fell limp. Ruby let go of her thoughts, as well as the side of the metal wall, and floated towards the bright light, a slight smile on her face, a strange feeling of calm prevailing. Somehow everything would turn out well in this new world, beckoning her.

* * *

Blinking with uncertainty, Ruby opened her eyes.

Amber's warm smile gazed down above her face.

"Thank God!" Amber shouted for joy. "Are you okay?!"

Ruby couldn't talk and coughed up more salt water.

"We were so worried about you!" May cried out, thrilled.

"I'm... alive?" Ruby questioned in uncertainty.

"Thanks to May - yes!" Amber and Jay explained.

Ruby slowly discovered, coming to her senses, that she was laying on her side on the sand in the recovery position. She was coughing and spluttering, spitting out water, illuminated by flashlights being held by other members of the Tribe gazing down in concern at Ruby being assisted to sit under the circle of light shining down on the beach.

They explained that once her absence from the camp had been noticed, Amber split everyone up so they could search the beach and undergrowth.

May was sure she had noticed Ruby wading into the water and decided to accompany Amber and Jay swimming out to the wreck. Plunging into the murky depths, she noticed that Ruby was trapped inside the Jzhao Li.

"I was so stupid!" Ruby said. "What have I done?"

But she wasn't just referring to her search for medicines to complement the precious little that they had. She was focused, in particular, on May, who nodded and smiled slightly.

"It's water under the bridge," May quipped.

"Amber!" screamed Lottie.

The others turned in the direction of the cry, noticing Lottie sprinting towards them in the distance.

"Tell Trudy and the others that they can stand down. We don't need to search anymore. We found Ruby!" Amber shouted out to Lottie.

But Lottie continued in full flight, her shoulders heaving from the exertion of the run, and sobbing uncontrollably. "He's dead!" she screamed.

CHAPTER THIRTY-FOUR

It was such a beautiful night, Jack thought, staring up at the Heavens, the stars twinkling through the gap in the entrance to the hut he and Lex were imprisoned in. What a night. Was it really going to be the last night he would ever see?

How he missed Ellie, Jack reflected. She loved the stars. The two of them used to gaze up at them in the city, considering life, talking about the meaning of existence, their hopes, dreams, futures together in the post-adult pandemic world.

And now it was just him. Contemplating what little time he had left to live, knowing that in a few hours he and Lex were to be executed.

Was this how the adults all felt when they got the virus, with the clock ticking until they succumbed?

Jack strained on the tight vines, twisted in knots, trying to free himself. Yet the harder he pulled, the closer the vines wound around his arms and legs, further constricting him.

"We could try biting them?" Lex suggested, pulling at the vines with all his might, getting nowhere.

"Why not?" Jack replied. It was worth a try. Anything was. Their situation was desperate and called for desperate measures.

Lex bit into the vines binding his arms and yelped, the prickles and spines protruding from the flaxen sinking into his tongue.

Jack noticed a shadowy figure approaching outside and whispered, panic-stricken, "Lex! Someone's coming!"

Lex froze, spitting out the tangled, twisted vines that were his bonds - before slumping to the dirt, Jack doing the same. The two pretending to be asleep so as not to arouse suspicion from whoever was approaching.

The polished stone surface of a spear end glistened in the moonlight.

Lex stole a glance out of the corner of his eye, noticing that it was Lia, and instinctively recoiled from the sharp weapon she was holding as she crouched down.

"What are you doing?" he asked.

"Ssh!" Lia hushed him. "What do you think I'm doing?"

To Jack and Lex's relief, Lia began to work on the tangled vines, the sharp spear sawing through their bonds.

"It's such an injustice!" Lia continued. "So wrong! You are both innocent!"

"I knew you liked me," Lex grinned.

"We're not out of it yet," Jack whispered, sighing in contentment, rubbing his hands together, now cut free, feeling the circulation once more flowing in his limbs.

Lia was clearly in some emotional conflict as she crossed to cut the vines securing their legs to the wooden poles. She felt caught between her loyalty to the native tribe, who had fed her, given her shelter and support for so long - and her new-found companions, Jack and Lex, who she just knew were wrongly accused of guilt, having committed no crime.

It was her principles that guided her, and where her pleas to the Priestess to release Jack and Lex had failed earlier, she reluctantly realized she had to resort now to more direct means, even if it meant endangering herself.

"There - done!" Lia whispered happily, cutting Lex free.

"If we get out of this - I won't forget," Lex promised, staring into Lia's green eyes, beams of moonlight flowing through the cut-out windows in the hut, reflecting off her glasses.

Lia wondered if Lex could see that she was blushing.

"So...what now?" Jack whispered, climbing to his feet.

"We stay here and hope all the villagers find us," Lex scoffed, casting an incredulous glance at Jack. "For a smart guy, you still got a lot to learn."

Jack faked a smile to Lex, then considered Lia. "Well...?"

"Follow me... and don't make a sound!" she urged softly.

Lia led Jack and Lex out of the hut and they moved furtively through the native village.

It was quiet. Eerily so. All the villagers must have been asleep.

Lia waved Jack and Lex on, indicating the way ahead.

Jack was petrified. One false move and he knew they could awaken the entire village, alert them to their escape. He noticed some warriors sleeping outside huts, their massive barrel chests heaving up and down as they dreamt, while at the same time Jack scanned the dirt in front of him, making sure he didn't step on anything which would cause a noise.

Tiptoeing quietly, they finally made it, miraculously, to the outskirts of the village.

Lex grinned at Lia. He liked her. A lot. She was brave and was putting herself on the line for them. And she was pretty slinky too, noticing the way she moved, cat-like.

"Which way now?" Lex asked.

"I don't think there'll be any signs to the beach," Jack said, getting his own back on Lex.

Lia held a finger over her lips as if to shush Jack and Lex, reminding them to keep quiet, to focus.

A loud, whooshing sound through the night air surprised the three of them, and a huge spear embedded itself into the ground, the end of it wobbling from the momentum of it being thrown.

Jack, Lex and Lia stared at the weapon wide-eyed, full of fear.

"I get the 'point'. That's the only sign I think we need, Jack! You as well, Lia. Run!" Lex urged.

And they took off in full flight, Lia glancing back, noticing the Priestess at the perimeter of the village, now glaring in disappointment.

Lia wondered for a moment if this spear was a warning shot or an actual attempt to injure one of them, with Lia being the closest target to where the spear had landed. Did the Priestess mean to hurt them? Lia in particular? Or just show her displeasure?

A loud banshee scream escaped from the lips of the Priestess, as if giving Lia her answer.

Jack, Lex and Lia continued to run for their lives, receding into the dark jungle, conscious behind them of light from flickering flaming torches as the villagers began their pursuit, responding to the Priestess's call.

"Split up!" Lex shouted urgently. "It's our only hope!"

Lia and Jack nodded, then took off in different directions, realizing that they might at least have a one in three chance of getting away if the villagers in pursuit were distracted.

Alone and running as fast as she could, Lia felt like a traitor.

It was the look on the Priestess's face. She had let her down. Betrayed the entire tribe.

Pushing themselves on through the dense, dark jungle, Lia, Jack and Lex continued, panicked, their pursuers slowing, gazing around, looking for any sign, sound, so they could choose a direction to take.

CHAPTER THIRTY-FIVE

Blake extended one arm, offering a chicken drumstick to Ebony.

As she reached out, he quickly withdrew it and started gorging on it himself.

They were sitting at his desk in his quarters, having a meal. But only Blake was eating. Ebony was sitting opposite, unsure of what would unfold.

There had been no sign of the disfigured girl for a while. Ebony wondered if she had perhaps answered a question with a question and had 'gone for a swim'. Or suspected that the girl might have been some kind of servant. And now Ebony had that role.

It had been a close call when he discovered her checking out his computer and she was still unsettled by Blake's volcanic temper, hoping that he was still intrigued enough by her to keep her as his mistress for more time to come.

They had certainly made mad, passionate love after his attack but she was unsure if it would still be enough to save herself.

He licked his fingers, lifted another drumstick.

"Any chance of getting something to eat?" Ebony asked, prodding to try and establish where she stood. Although she suspected he was still infatuated enough with her to want her to share his bed, an overwhelming uncertainty engulfed Ebony. Since the situation with the computer, she was aware that he was cold.

"One thing you need to realize, Ebony," Blake said, between taking bites of food. "You're in no position to ask for anything."

"If you're still mad at me about the computer - honestly, I wasn't trying to snoop around or anything."

"What were you hoping to find?"

"I was just interested in knowing if you were still connected to a network. I mean, not many people are these days. Please. Just trust me, Blake. There was nothing more to it than that."

"So... it wasn't what it seemed," Blake smiled slightly.

Ebony knew he was toying with her and being so volatile, wondered if he would erupt at any moment.

"If I'm going to be of any use to you, that's up to you to decide, Blake," Ebony said, changing tactic. "I mean, you said yourself you'd do the same thing that I did. So if you were setting me up, how do you know - that I didn't? Know. That you're giving me some kind of test. And I'm not the type who would ever want to fail."

Blake considered her and smiled. "Nice one. Like it," he said.

"I was trying to please you. Make an impression. You're the man around here. All I ask is for the chance to be your woman."

Ebony's hopes were once again being raised, feeling that if this dude was some kind of control freak, then she'd let him think he was in control. But she knew it was important to keep him on the end of the hook, feeling that she was capable of controlling matters herself. Otherwise, she would be of no use to him in his organisation.

She needed to get more of a handle on just exactly what he was up to. She was still unsettled by his earlier references that she might be destined for the 'laboratory'. She was determined the only place she'd end up was in his bed. At least for the time being, until another opportunity presented itself. Her core aspiration was to survive.

"You've got an impressive set up, Blake," she said, looking for a way in to steer the conversation to what he and his forces were involved with. She reached out for the chicken drumstick he was holding - and this time he didn't withdraw it. Now she was making progress, she thought, sinking her teeth into the meat as if it was some kind of prey she had just caught. Blake's chosen the wrong one to fool with, Ebony thought to herself, devouring the chicken, viewing the mere fact she was even eating to be an important step in her seizing back a bit of control.

"I'm glad you 'approve'," Blake said, continuing eating, but still studying Ebony.

"Oh, I do," she replied. "And I'd like to be a part of it. Like I've been telling you. I can bring skills. Not that you might need them, of course. I mean, you seem to have everything working really well. But I've also had experience. Being a leader."

"So I gather," Blake replied, gazing intently at Ebony. Then he casually added, "The Locos, wasn't it?"

Ebony was floored by that revelation, wondering how he knew. She didn't recall saying anything about it at any time when he asked her what she had been up to back in the city. But maybe she had, and had simply forgotten. But if not, he clearly knew more about her than she ever thought. The question was, how? She decided to play it cooly until she found out more. If he did know anything, then she would have to tread very carefully. She didn't want to give away any unnecessary information. But equally, the consequences could be catastrophic if he knew that she wasn't revealing all... she knew.

"Yeah, the Locos. I started out as the mistress of the head of the tribe."

"Zoot - wasn't it?"

Ebony's mind raced. This guy was good and really was in control. He had all the power with whatever information he had uncovered. So she would need to keep her story straight.

"That's right. Zoot. Then after he was killed, I took over. I'd never have been able to do that if Zoot was alive. And would have never wanted to either," Ebony added, not wishing Blake to ever think that she might be a threat and the type to try and seize control. Though characteristically that was certainly the case.

"How do you know all this?" she asked Blake matter of factly, trying to mask her concern.

"Just a lucky guess," he smiled, enjoying himself and waiting to see Ebony crack under the strain. Which she was determined not to do.

"Bet you're an ace in a quiz," Ebony smiled as well, making light of it all. "I'm pretty good too. Can you imagine us being on the same team? We'd be formidable."

She could see that he wasn't entirely unaware of that from the glint in his eye. She took another ravenous bite of the chicken, casting him a seductive smile. He responded with a wild bite of his chicken drumstick, as if matching her. "Anything else you'd like to know?" Ebony asked. "Or maybe we should just think of going to bed. All this food...it's making me 'hungry'. From the first time I ever saw you, Blake - I think you must know by now that you 'whet my appetite'."

"Why don't you tell me more about the Jzhao Li first?" Blake continued to probe, ignoring her suggestion.

"I don't know that much about it."

"I do," he smiled.

"Then maybe you'd better tell me," Ebony replied, enjoying the verbal sabre rattling more and more. "You obviously know a lot more than I do."

"I wouldn't be too sure about that," Blake replied.

"Honestly, Blake. What I told you earlier is true. We fled our city on a trawler, found the ship drifting, boarded it so we could try and survive. In the midst of the storm, the ship was abandoned. I got in the lifeboat. And I want you to know I'll always owe you and your guys for saving me."

"And the others? Who else was on board?"

Ebony decided she'd better come clean. This guy had one hell of an intelligence network. So it would be wise to provide all the detail she could. Including Mega's attack, which caused them to all flee in the first place.

"This Techno tribe. What else do you know about them?" Blake probed.

"I don't know where they originally came from. They just invaded the city. They were led by this guy - Ram."

Ebony realized from Blake's expression that something about the name registered in a profound way, though Blake was clearly trying to mask his reaction, not wishing to give anything away.

"Ram?" he said, as if to himself. "That's an interesting name." But his demeanour was now cold. He seemed irritated at even hearing the mere mention of the name 'Ram'.

"Have you ever known anyone...with the same name?"

"You ask too many questions!" Blake replied.

Ebony decided to back off. She was pressing the wrong buttons.

"No problem. You're the man. In control. If you ever fancy telling me, then that's up to you, Blake. If not - no skin off my nose," she said, trying to defuse the tense situation.

There was a knock at the door.

"Enter!" Blake called out.

Axel came in, nodded his head respectfully. "Sorry to disturb you, Commander Blake," he said, casting a glance at Ebony. "But I thought you'd want to know. The next intake has arrived."

"I'll be right there," Blake responded.

Understanding he was dismissed, Axel left.

"More categorising?" Ebony asked, sensing that this might be an opportunity for her to consolidate her position. "Any chance I can help? All that branding... I think I could really get into it."

***

On the helicopter deck the clear moon illuminated a fresh intake of slaves being arranged into position. The wind howled. Ebony discovered that these slaves were the last batch due to be processed before the ship arrived, which was due to take them away to wherever they were to be taken.

They were a pathetic-looking bunch, Ebony thought, as she and Blake arrived, crossing the helicopter deck towards the assembly. They all looked absolutely terrified, quaking in fear, the metal chains biting into their ankles, clanking, as they shuffled themselves into place for Blake to examine them, as if on display like pieces of meat.

Suddenly Ebony stopped and gazed in pure disbelief. Standing amidst the group of slaves, she noticed a figure next to a teenage female, and a younger boy and girl. They were all blindfolded. Ebony was stunned. He may not have been able to see her but she could see very clearly and there was no doubt in her mind that it was him. Bray.

CHAPTER THIRTY-SIX

The shipwrecked survivors were in a circle, arms linked together as they stood around the grave, a small pile of rocks stacked, marking the headstone of the deceased, buried deep under the sands of the beach.

May shed aching tears of loss as she knelt down beside the grave, placing her bracelet on the rocks.

Zak had passed away the night before, losing his battle for life.

While the Mall Rats had split up to try and find out what had happened to Ruby, Gel had stayed back at Camp Phoenix with Lottie and the little ones. Sammy was watching over Slade while Zak, who never regained consciousness, slipped away, Trudy taking her turn to keep watch over him, was with him when he died. She had felt for a pulse, feeling none, and tried to revive him, desperately beating on his chest as if to reawaken the life that had once been inside, trying to resuscitate him. But he had gone. There was nothing Trudy or anyone could do for him any more. And it left Trudy absolutely hysterical.

May had become resigned. She was expecting it, for all that she tried to convince herself otherwise. It was a painful irony though, May felt, that she had left Zak's side, going off with Amber to try and find - and then rescue - Ruby from the depths of the Jzhao Li, at around the same time in the night Zak would have departed the world.

All present knew they owed a huge debt to Zak when the Jzhao Li ran aground. He paid the ultimate sacrifice, leaving Slade also critically injured in the process, enabling all the others to have a chance on the lifeboat to survive.

United in grief, even Ram felt emotion. Bonding in adversity, all had been through so much on their long ocean voyage, first on Zak's trawler, then the Jzhao Li.

Ruby's shoulders heaved as she shed her own tears, her anguish fuelled by her sense of guilt. Zak's death may have actually vindicated Ruby's judgement, yet she still was so ashamed of how she had devoted herself on fixing Slade's injuries and wondered if she could have done more to help Zak. But it was too late now. They would never know, Ruby sobbed to herself.

Amber stood next to May, supporting her as her head slumped, resting on Amber's shoulders, her eyes cascading tears.

"Somebody should say something," Jay whispered quietly out of respect, feeling it was important for Zak to be given the send-off he so deserved.

"May?" Amber asked softly, to see what May would like to do, how she wanted to proceed.

But she couldn't contain all the pent up emotion any longer, wailing.

"I just don't understand!" May blabbed through tears. "It's not... fair! What did he do? What had he ever done to anyone?"

"It should have been Ram," Gel pointed out. "If anyone deserves to die - it's Ram."

"Excuse me? I'm actually standing right here, if you haven't noticed," Ram protested, glaring at Gel. "You really are stupid, aren't you? Think I can't hear?"

Gel glared at Ram. He was starting to really get to her. While the others had broken away to search for Ruby the night before, she had been questioning him more about The Collective during their meal at Camp Phoenix being cooked over the open fire Darryl had made.

"I still can't understand," Gel had said. "These Collective... what do they collect?"

Sammy scoffed. "Duh! It's just their name!"

Gel had poked her tongue out at Sammy before Ram interrupted, adding, "Gel's not as dumb as she looks."

"Oh - thanks," Gel had replied, clearly unsure if it was a compliment or an insult before Ram had clarified.

"They do 'collect' people in some ways. All the tribes who work to them. That's why they're called The Collective."

"And we're what... collectables?" Gel had considered.

"I don't know about you, but I sure as hell am not!"

Now at the ceremony, Ellie cut in, still deeply concerned about Jack.

"Gel's right! That should be you in there, Ram. Not Zak. For all the pain you've caused others! And if this Collective has done anything to Jack, I'm warning you. You really will pay!"

"Stop it, you two! Don't start now, of all times, please!" Amber insisted.

"Leave it, Amber. If that's how everyone feels - I'm outta here!" Ram snapped, glaring angrily at Gel and Ellie. "I'll pay my respects in my own way. I'm sorry, May, but it seems my presence here is only making things worse."

Ram stormed away back to Camp Phoenix.

"Ram!" Jay called out, encouraging him to come back. But Ram waved Jay's protests, continuing on.

"That was a terrible thing to say," Amber chastened Gel and Elli.

"I'm just being honest," Gel replied petulantly.

"And I'm just worried about Jack," Ellie said.

"We're all worried about Jack, Ellie. But please. Try and have some consideration." Amber nodded towards May, who was struggling, with her emotions threatening to overwhelm her.

"Zak wouldn't have wanted this. All this in-fighting! He would want us to stick together! Help each other..." May said.

"Trudy, would you?..." Amber asked Trudy, who shook her head, sure she would be unable to find any appropriate words to honour Zak.

"Why don't you, Amber? I think it's right that you say something, being the leader," Trudy suggested.

Amber stepped into the centre of their circle as Salene moved to take Amber's place, supporting May, comforting her, the others readjusting themselves to fill in the gap where Ram had been standing.

"None of us choose how we enter this world. Or how we leave it," Amber began, searching for words, the right thing to say. "But we do choose how to live our lives. And Zak chose how to live his life well. He gave so much. Without him, and Slade - their efforts back on the ship - perhaps none of us would have been here today. It is because of Zak that we continue. We live on. As a result of his heroism. His sacrifice. And we owe it to his memory, to make it his legacy, that we go on. And survive. We live our lives the best we can. Anything less... would be a stain on what Zak did for us all. As well as dishonouring all our loved ones who have gone before."

Ellie began to cry. Moved by the occasion, Amber's words. And still worried desperately about Jack.

Trudy comforted Ellie as Amber looked down at the grave. She was sure that all present were reflecting in silence, recalling all those special in their lives they had also lost when the pandemic swept across the globe.

The waves lapped onto the shore in the distance, the morning sun ascending, the hum of insects and choir of birdsong ringing out in the palm trees and jungle beyond.

With the virus bringing so much pain, suffering and death and all the anguish of all those present to honour Zak, it reinforced the sanctity of life, Amber reflected, her words giving comfort to all assembled. But to May and Ruby especially. The purity of life was so precious. But also fleeting. Amber only had to look at her son to be reminded of the wonders of life and was determined that whatever his destiny would be, she would do all she could to ensure he had a future. They all had a future. All her friends. All of her Tribe.

One life had ended, in Zak, Amber continued, stating that another had been saved - through Ruby. And Amber couldn't help but think - though she didn't say - that one more life waited patiently, being the unborn baby of Ruby and Slade, for the day when he - or she - would emerge and take the first steps of their own journey in this strange new world the young inhabited, since the adults had perished.

"Zak. Rest in peace. You will be missed. But you will not be forgotten. You will live in our hearts. In our memories. You made this world a better place. Nothing more can be asked for any of us, in our own lives. God bless you."

Jay smiled slightly to Amber. She had said what needed to, articulated for all within Camp Phoenix, providing much comfort. And hope.

Little did Jay - or any of the others know - that they were all being watched.

* * *

Fascinated by these strangers, his eyes peered out from the cover of the thick jungle undergrowth.

Hidden from sight, the watcher stared at the group gathered on the beach conducting the ceremony for Zak.

What were they doing here in this land? Who were they?

Counting the number of them, as well as those who stayed behind at their camp with the younger ones in the distance, the watcher was satisfied he had seen enough.

Like a shadow in the trees, he moved away quickly, silently. With the wind rustling the leaves that had seconds before been his cover - like a whisper in the breeze, he had gone.

CHAPTER THIRTY-SEVEN

Lex struggled, straining his body with all his might. He was strong, no doubt about it, and if there had been two, maybe three of them, Lex could have stood a chance.

As it was, he was seized by five of the huge native warriors, lifting him by his ankles and hands, while they carried Lex, squirming, over to the Priestess's hut.

Jack and Lia were already being held by other natives nearby, both of them resisting as best they could.

Lex gave everything he could to try and escape, but there was nothing he could do as the warriors snarled, restraining him.

"And people say I have no manners!" Lex bellowed to his captors.

He knew - as did Jack and Lia - that they didn't have a chance, recalling their failed escape the night before.

They had split up, running quickly through the dark jungle. But outnumbered by their pursuers, who obviously knew the area intimately, the position of every tree and plant, Jack and Lex had been caught, overwhelmed by the superior forces of the natives.

Lia had been the last of the escapees to be captured. Living with the native tribe so long, she too had a better awareness of the layout of the land. Upon hearing Jack and Lex's cries when they had been apprehended, Lia had gone back towards them, rather than carrying on to save herself. They needed her help. She alone would be able to speak with the tribe in their native tongue, she surmised, and hoped she would be able to negotiate with the Priestess on not only Jack and Lex's behalf - but make a case for her own defence as well.

All Lia's hopes were dashed, however, by the Priestess's insistence that the original sentence be carried out.

The escape attempt had hardly done Jack and Lex's cause any good, Lia recognized in hindsight. She had undermined the Priestess's authority by rebelling against her, trying to release Jack and Lex.

And now Lia was going to be forced to watch the execution of first Lex, then Jack. The Priestess would decide afterwards what punishment Lia would face for her treachery.

Determined to show her authority, that the customs and traditions of her tribe be upheld, and still sure that Lex and Jack were somehow connected to Blake and his forces who had recently arrived within the environs of their island, the Priestess stood outside her hut, the sharp polished stone of her dagger gleaming in the morning light, the sun continuing to rise up over the horizon.

"Let us go!!" Lex shouted, as he was pushed to the ground, forced into a kneeling position by the warriors.

The Priestess stepped forward, slowly, holding aloft the ceremonial stone dagger so the assembled crowd of villagers could see it clearly. It was hundreds of years old, a connection to their ancestral past, Lia explained.

"Do they think I'll be flattered!? Being wiped out by an antique?" Lex shouted.

"This is it!" Jack said to himself in disbelief. "I've got to wake up from this nightmare! Can't you do or say anything?!" he implored Lia.

Lia bit her lip nervously, wondering exactly just what she could do, then called out suddenly in the native tongue.

"This is a terrible mistake!"

Lex and Jack turned their heads, staring at Lia. What was she saying? All they could hear was the strange guttural sound of the native language flowing from her lips.

Unknown to them, Lia was begging the Priestess for mercy, insisting Jack and Lex were innocent, shipwrecked with their friends. They didn't mean any harm, had no connection whatsoever with this new foreigner who had arrived, instilling terror when he visited the islands, referring to Blake and his forces.

The Priestess shouted back, enraged at Lia's disrespect.

The two white men were criminals, the Priestess shrieked venomously to Lia, in her ancient language. All the tribe had seen what harm could befall them if they studied their history and had seen how foreigners had brought diseases for hundreds of years, just like those in the military and all the people they brought during the height of the pandemic. But even placing that aside, the Priestess felt that it was no coincidence the two strangers were there, obviously spies working with Blake's men who were probably preparing to attack and to gather up more villagers to enslave. Jack and Lex had to be made an example of. And to show that her people are brave warriors who will resist any threat to the bitter end.

Lia tried to argue her case further but the Priestess called out suddenly. One of the warriors clutching Lia thrust his hand over her face, covering her mouth, so she could speak no more, though her garbled cries showed she was continuing to try, wriggling in an effort to get free, desperate to throw herself on the mercy of the Priestess.

"Get your damned hands off her!" Lex threatened, staring at the Priestess defiantly, as the warriors around prevented any more movement from him.

"Some justice!" he spat out with disdain.

The Priestess glared back at Lex, her contempt for all things 'foreign' from the western world, for Lex and Jack, plain to see. Lex thought it was strange how such a striking-looking girl, a picture of perfection, could show so much hostility, hatred, act so violently to others. Be so imperfect, blinded by her beliefs.

Lifting the dagger higher above her head, preparing to strike, the Priestess waited a few more seconds as the sun rose higher into the sky.

Lex prepared for the inevitable blow to arrive. He had never been religious. But he found himself saying a silent prayer anyway. Maybe he was wrong and his Mum and Dad had been right about God - and that he would see them in the afterlife. Soon.

He flinched as the Priestess took aim, ready to strike.

Then she suddenly hesitated.

A native warrior ran into the village at top speed, crying out, calling for attention.

A murmur of unrest, surprise, swept through the villagers.

"What's happening?" Jack asked Lia. He could tell the mood had changed. It was subtle but he, along with Lex, instinctively felt the atmosphere was different even though they didn't understand a word of what was being spoken around them.

The native warrior raced up to the mud hut, panting, out of breath. Then he fell to his knees, bowing before the Priestess in respect, relaying some kind of information.

The Priestess lowered the stone dagger, withdrawing it away from Lex, to his relief, and looked shocked by whatever the native warrior was telling her.

Lia began to cry.

"Is it that bad?" Lex asked.

Jack pleaded. "What is it, Lia?!"

"It's good," Lia said, overjoyed. "It's so good." She could hardly believe it, trying somehow to contain her tears of joy.

* * *

The sun was high in the sky, the intense heat of the day blazing, birds calling, a myriad of other animal and insect life chattering.

Jack never thought he would have seen or heard such a thing again. And it looked, and sounded, beautiful. He had honestly expected to die, earlier. Now, he was thrilled to be alive and couldn't get the grin off his face.

Lex was strangely quiet. By his standards. He hadn't said much since the Priestess had ended the ceremony, allowing him, Jack and Lia to live.

"Thanks for everything, Lia," Lex whispered, touched by the sweet girl who had risked so much on his and Jack's behalf. He gently patted her on the shoulder in gratitude.

Lia caught Lex's admiring glance and blushed slightly.

The three of them were invited into the Priestess's hut and now stood still as the Priestess entered.

Around were ornate carvings of animals from the forest, idols of the spirit world, with which the Priestess communed for guidance.

She knelt on the floor, and compared to the outright hostility she had showed earlier that morning, was now looking serene, with a peaceful countenance. She was deep in thought, searching for answers, and began meditating.

After a while she flicked her eyes open and began to speak in the native language, Lia translating into English after a few seconds delay so Jack and Lex could understand.

"It is all different now," Lia began, explaining what the Priestess was saying. "Everything has changed. Our scout, Kalyut, returned with news that your story was true. He saw others at the beach. People like you. The ruins of a mighty ship nearby. There was a baby. A very young girl. Some people sick and injured. It was as you described. That you are who you said you are. He saw everything that you said. She is now satisfied that you are not a part of Blake's people and mean no threat."

The Priestess took a moment, gathering her thoughts.

"Now we're getting somewhere..." Lex quietly said.

"Kalyut is one of our most trusted warriors," Lia whispered. "He had been sent to check but was late in returning. So the Priestess was sure he had been abducted by enemy forces. He's the one you owe your lives to, for he ran back faster than the wind to bring the news of your innocence."

The Priestess spoke once more.

"You are allowed to go, both of you... back to your people," Lia continued, happy at what she was relaying.

"That's great!" Jack beamed.

Lia's expression began to alter, however, as the Priestess went on, telling Lia everything the animal spirits had told her, of what had to happen now.

Jack and Lex both picked up the change in Lia's demeanour. She looked concerned, worried.

"Lia? Why have you stopped?" Jack whispered.

The Priestess stood up, walking towards Lia, her voice getter louder as she neared.

She was angry now. Shouting into Lia's face.

"Hey - leave her alone!" Lex insisted protectively.

Lia listened intently, showing her respect to the Priestess, absorbing all that she was being told so audibly and at such close range. It obviously wasn't good news.

"What's going on, Lia?" Lex asked.

The Priestess glared at Lia and suddenly yanked off the shell necklace Lia wore, which had actually been made by Lia herself years ago when she was first accepted into the native tribe, and it burst into pieces now as it fell.

The Priestess unleashed a venomous backhanded slap across Lia's face. Lia recoiled, the momentum of the blow knocking her glasses off her face, which also fell onto the floor.

Jack was gobsmacked, stunned at the sudden turnaround.

Lex stepped in front of Lia, trying to defend her.

"If you touch her again, I'll -"

"No, Lex!" Lia insisted, pulling him back.

Jack picked up her glasses from the dirt, blew dust from the lenses, and handed them back to Lia. The one broken glass lens had completely shattered.

Lia began to cry, struggling to keep her composure, obviously shaken by whatever the Priestess had told her, as well as the slap across her face.

The Priestess shrieked, raising her arms as if she was going to lash out again at Lia, at all of them, if they stayed.

"We have to go - now!" Lia said, backing out of the hut, watching the Priestess carefully, her expression showing the hurt she felt not just at what the Priestess had done, hitting her - but what had been said.

"What was that all about?" Lex asked as they stepped outside, dabbing his hand gently on Lia's cheek where she had been struck, wiping away a trickle of blood from her mouth and tears from her eyes, overspilling down one cheek.

Standing outside, the three of them were being totally ignored. Shunned by the other villagers who continued with their daily activities, weaving, cooking, deliberately not paying any attention to the three while they made their way cautiously through the village. The Priestess had shouted so loudly inside, the villagers outside had heard everything.

Lia kept her dignity, fighting back more tears, nobody trying to prevent them now from leaving this time.

"What's happening, Lia?" Jack asked, desperate to know.

"I'm an outcast," Lia admitted, shamefully. "She told me I betrayed her... all of them. I've been expelled from the tribe for treason. I can never return."

"I'm sorry," Lex said, supporting Lia as she staggered now, overcome by emotion, the three of them heading into the jungle, the village receding into the distance as they walked on. Free at last.

"What about us? They're still letting us go - right?" Jack asked.

"You are to take a message back to your friends," Lia said. "The Priestess is sympathetic to your plight but won't sanction anyone being on sacred land. You will have to leave. Get far away from this territory."

"And if we don't?" Lex asked, his inner fire burning. He felt that this was another injustice. The Mall Rats didn't mean anyone any harm and couldn't help being shipwrecked on the island.

"Then you will have insulted the land, the spirits, by your continued presence."

"What does that mean? What happens if we don't leave?" Jack wondered.

"The Priestess would need to cleanse the land of your intrusion, the taint upon it. If you are still at your camp by sunrise tomorrow, or anywhere near the native land, she and the tribe will come for you. They will deal with you. Every single one of your friends."

Jack and Lex were stunned, taking in the news.

"Well, what are waiting for? - Let's go and warn the others!" Jack cried out, doubling his pace as they made their way through the jungle.

"Everything'll be okay, Lia. If we have to, we'll fight. We know how to defend ourselves," Lex promised, trying to reassure Lia.

Lex just didn't know what they would be up against though, Lia thought to herself. Far outnumbered by the native tribe, from what Jack and Lex had told her of their numbers, Lia feared that if Jack and Lex's friends tried to resist and put up a fight, it would be a massacre.

CHAPTER THIRTY-EIGHT

Ebony walked down a twisting, metallic stairwell leading into the bowels of the rig where all the prisoners were being held, pending being transported to God knows where. And for the first time in a long while she had got the bounce back in her step.

She had been absolutely stunned to see Bray earlier on the helicopter deck. There was no doubt in her mind it was him. But what was he doing here with this new intake of slaves, being paraded before Blake and their masters?

Bray's disappearance had been a source of mystery to the entire city. And it wasn't just Amber who worried about what had happened to him. Along with the other members of the Mall Rats, of course.

Despite the troubles they had shared in the past, and although they had crossed swords on a number of occasions, Ebony always had a spot in her heart for Bray. From the very early days at school.

When he went missing after the Technos invaded, Ebony expected the worst and thought he had to be dead, surely.

And yet there he was for some reason amongst all the other prisoners, returned to her like a ghost resurrected from her past.

Now by some miracle, their paths were about to cross again.

She wondered if this was another test concocted by Blake. Letting her interrogate Bray. Not only was he highly intelligent and a strategic thinker, Blake obviously had some kind of impressive intelligence network. He had to, Ebony was sure. How else would he have known so many details about Zoot and the Locos? How much did he know about Ebony?

So she thought it was better for her to come clean and mention she knew one of the new intakes from her homeland. Just in case Blake knew. She wouldn't put it past him, to have some insidious scheme planned with the arsenal of cards he seemed to hold up his sleeve. Ebony had long decided she would need to play her cards carefully and use every bit of cunning in her own arsenal if she had any hope of survival, to elevate herself up in the ranks to work alongside Blake. There was little other option available than to forge an alliance. At least it might keep her from the slave camps.

Blake had questioned her, probing for details of her long lost companion and suggested that she look after the interrogation. He wanted to discover just exactly where Bray had come from prior to being traded. Ebony agreed, promising to report back every detail.

Ebony, forever calculating, decided she would massage any facts if it suited her plight. And was intrigued herself to know just exactly what had happened to Bray since he went missing in the city after the Techno invasion. But one thing for sure. She would selectively reveal whatever she was about to uncover. If it was some kind of test, then this was her chance. To show Blake that he could trust her. Even if he did know more than he was letting on. If not, then she was in a win win situation, feeling she could manipulate matters to her own benefit. With the bonus being she would get more of a handle on this region by finding out how Bray fit into it all.

Ebony stopped at the entrance of a cell.

"I've come to interrogate one of the latest intakes," Ebony said to the two burly guards standing outside while glancing around discretely, checking if there might be a camera and if Blake was watching. Or even listening somehow. If so, it was important for her to let him know that she was on his side.

She was met with silence, the guards looking at her suspiciously.

"Well? Aren't you gonna let me in?"

"This deck is out of bounds unless authorised," one of the guards replied.

"If you know what's good for you, don't answer a question - with a question!" Ebony shouted.

She was laying it on thick in case she was being observed, sure Blake would like that, flattered that she was carving herself out of his own control freak mould.

"What - do I have to go and explain to Blake that his men don't follow orders? I am his woman, do you understand? And he's the man! He sent me to interrogate and I can't do that standing here now, can I?! Open the damn door so I can go inside. Or do I have to smash it open using your thick heads?"

The guards exchanged glances with each other and one probed cautiously. "You were sent by the Commander?"

"There you go again. I'm the one supposed to ask questions. So if you know what's good for you, just open the door, will you? Then I might put in a good word about you both with Blake, when I see him tonight," Ebony continued, reminding them of her status.

The guards unlatched the heavy bolt and pushed open the door. Ebony entered, kicking it closed and stared at Bray, taken aback by what she saw.

He was being kept in solitary confinement.

He had apparently been 'difficult', refusing to follow orders, co-operate, and had been beaten for not showing respect.

Now Bray was hanging in the centre of the darkened cell, his arms stretched above his head and secured to girders in the ceiling, numbed by the chains which had been bound around his hands, the manacles biting into his wrists painfully.

He was still blindfolded. Ebony felt a wave of sympathy. He looked in a mess, his face bruised, swollen, his lips cracked and smeared with matted, congealed blood.

"Well, look what the tide's washed in. Fancy seeing you here," Ebony said, checking out the prison cell for signs of any lenses, still unsure if she was being observed.

"Eloise?" Bray whispered quietly, weakly, a degree of unease in his tone.

"Eloise? No, it's me, Ebony. Don't tell me you've forgotten all about me?"

Bray wondered once again if this was a simulation. Ebony was just as confused as he seemed to be, as he continued, as if lost in another world. "Is Martin here?"

"Not unless you're in Heaven," Ebony replied, bewildered.

"Ebony... Is that really you?"

"Last time I looked in the mirror."

"What are you doing here?" Bray said with sudden interest as the realization was settling in amidst his disorientated state.

"I was about to ask you the same question," Ebony replied, deciding not to use the word interrogate, feeling she would probably get more out of Bray that way.

Bray was struggling to remain conscious after his beating but Ebony managed to decipher that rather than being uncooperative just for the sake of it, he was trying to look out for Emma, Tiffany and Shannon, who were separated on another deck. He seemed deeply anguished, pleading for any news, desperate to know that they were alright.

She promised she'd check it out, reassuring him that they would be fine and no harm could come to any of them. As long as he answered her questions.

"You're not involved with these people, whoever they are, are you?" Bray asked weakly.

"Not yet," Ebony replied, gazing once again around for any lenses and hoping if Blake was listening he'd be pleased as she continued. "But I'd sure like to be."

"Who... are they?" Bray asked.

"They're more interested in finding out more information... about you, Bray."

Bray was finding it all increasingly difficult to comprehend, struggling through his pitiful state, revealing that he had tried to ask for Emma to remain with her younger brother and sister, pointing out that Emma was blind, and received a beating for speaking out of turn prior to being led to the cells and held in solitary confinement.

On another floor, on higher decks, Bray was sure he could hear the distant whimpering and wailing from all the prisoners, in obvious distress, being held in different parts of the sprawling rig. It was an awful chorus of sobbing, pleading, panic. But he couldn't distinguish if he heard Emma, Shannon or Tiffany, which seemed to add to his concern. He was totally disorientated, forever asking if this was a simulation.

Ebony reiterated that there was no virtual reality programming here and that it would be wise for Bray to co-operate. To tell her all about what had happened to him. But she couldn't get any sense other than he had been traded as a slave.

She asked if that meant he had been categorised. Before. He didn't reply. His head had slumped forward, leaving Ebony suspecting that he must have passed out.

She reached up, checking his neck for a pulse, his skin for any sign of branding. Then ripping his shirt, she noticed on the side of his shoulder the letter 'L'.

She lifted a pail of water and hurled the contents at him. The shock brought him around, though he was still in a semi-conscious state.

"What about the others?" Bray asked weakly. "Amber...?"

So typical of Bray, she thought. He hadn't changed one bit since she last saw him, all that time long ago back in the city. Always putting the interests of others ahead of his own. Especially where Amber was concerned.

Ebony had fallen for him in a big way in the old days before the 'virus' wiped out all the adults. He had been the Captain of the basketball team at school. And she was in competition with Trudy, who had tried to get her claws into him. If opposites attract, Ebony was certainly drawn to all the standards he seemed to set himself, his strict moral code. She found it boring at times. And was always attracted more to the bad boys. But couldn't deny there was something about Bray which had always intoxicated her, finding him not just physically attractive but admiring all his qualities and traits, his great strength of character.

Even so, she found herself equally drawn to his brother, Zoot, and had used all her skills manipulating events, quickly rising up through the ranks of the Locos, eventually becoming leader after Zoot's death.

Ebony had always thought it a strange irony how she could be drawn to both brothers, who had become estranged through the ensuing darkness of the post-adult world. And wondered how both could have been born from the same parents. As if one was driven by the forces of light. And Zoot? Well, Ebony never believed he was evil. More of a rebel. She was mindblown by his ideology of 'Power and Chaos' from the first time he rose up at school, battling against any and all forms of authority. Ebony could relate to that. In some ways, even Bray was a rebel, refusing to conform to anything other than what he perceived to be right, the best way forward.

Ebony decided to steer any conversation away from the Mall Rats. She didn't want herself to become implicated in any negative way. Assuming Blake knew about them. If he did, he was certainly shrewd enough not to provide any unnecessary detail.

Ebony probed more about this Eloise person Bray had referred to. And was gripped by an awful sense of fear, wondering if Blake was somehow involved in all this through his references to 'L' for 'Laboratory' branding. There seemed to be a link with the small letter 'L' marked on Bray's shoulder. Ebony smiled slightly to herself, wondering what Bray might think if he only knew she was also marked the same way on one cheek of her backside. Who knows, one day he might even see for himself.

Bray, through his deeply confused state, revealed that he had been subjected to so much virtual reality simulation he had difficulty knowing what was real and what was illusion anymore. All he knew was that he was once held in a compound, which seemed to be exploiting his 'bloodline' for whatever agenda, explaining that there were many within the compound referring to themselves as 'Zootists'. All dressed like his late brother and appeared to have been indoctrinated into his ideology. Ebony wondered if he was hallucinating. He seemed sincere though in his recollections. And she got the gist that Eloise, whoever she was, controlled wherever he had been kept.

Ebony was absorbed by Bray's tale of his escape. How he had ended up in a military base, being saved by two young children and a blind girl, leaving Ebony to feel that maybe Bray had indeed lost it, sure a capable warrior like Bray didn't need to rely on someone like that to survive.

Bray kept asking about the Mall Rats and Amber. In an attempt to avoid any of his questions, Ebony took delight in advising that Amber was probably dead. That would hopefully shut him up.

She had always despised Amber. Not just for what Ebony perceived to be her piety. She had caused Ebony no end of problems in the past throughout all the scores and clashes since the days of the Locos.

It had been a much more personal matter though - the fact that Amber and Bray had fallen deeply in love, Ebony perceiving way back when that Amber had actually taken the place of Ebony. She had desperately wanted Bray for herself.

Secretly though, Ebony had difficulty suppressing that she felt a sense of jubilation. Not at seeing Bray hurt. But that he was still alive. And especially that they had been reunited.

Destiny seemed to have done her a favour, as it had a habit of doing. With Bray showing up. In exactly the same place as her. And she was almost orgasmic, thinking that she could drive a wedge between him and Amber. It was an exquisite feeling. Revenge wasn't just sweet. It was beautiful.

And the bonus was she could use it all to elevate her own position.

She had never been lucky in love. Now she wondered if she might be more lucky in hate.

"You've been sensible, Bray," she said, raising her tone in case Blake was listening. "Telling me all you have. I'll report back to my man and might come back another time if I need to clarify anything."

"This is real - isn't it?" Bray asked, still disorientated. "Not just some simulation?"

"Oh, it's real alright," Ebony replied, casting a discrete glance at what she suspected was the small lens of a camera high in the ceiling.

"Good seeing you again. Hope you enjoy your stay!"

She drew back her arm and unleashed a powerful blow into Bray's face, blood oozing from the wound on his lip, which opened up.

He slumped his head forward, his body swinging back and forth slowly as if he was a human punch bag while Ebony stormed out, nodding to the guards, who swung the heavy bolt back noisily to secure the door.

CHAPTER THIRTY-NINE

"I am so glad to see you!" Ellie gushed, wrapping her arms lovingly around Jack, giving him a close hug.

"If this is the kind of reaction I'll get - I might have to go missing more often," Jack quipped, enjoying Ellie's attention.

"Don't you dare... you have no idea how much I've missed you! We were so worried."

Jack and Lex had returned to Camp Phoenix a few hours earlier and their reappearance after several days missing was just the good news the entire Tribe needed to raise morale and lift spirits, following the tragic death of Zak.

The others had filled Jack and Lex in on what occurred while they had been away. Both were saddened to hear of Zak's passing. Since they had missed the Tribe's funeral ceremony, the two had already visited Zak's grave to pay their personal respects.

May was further down the beach, having gone off from the others so she could spend the time she needed to grieve and try to come to terms with the loss. While Amber called the others together for a meeting so they could discuss their options in light of Jack and Lex's return. Especially all the details they revealed of their captors, along with the ultimatum to abandon Camp Phoenix by sunrise.

They also filled Lex and Jack in on all the information about The Collective and why Ram was so uneasy, claiming that they might even be lurking menacingly on the island, that it could just be a matter of time before their paths crossed.

"If there's any truth in all of it," Lex had mentioned, "maybe we should just gift wrap Ram and hand him over as a present. He's their enemy. Not our's."

"You're wrong, Lexy-boy," Ram had replied. "Believe me. The Collective are a threat to us all."

Amber and the others tried to check if the native tribe could somehow be involved with The Collective, linked in some way.

Lia dismissed any such notion. She had been kneeling on the warm sands by the fire staring into the distance, as if in a daze, still upset about her fall out with the Priestess, worried about the consequences of what she had set in motion by helping Jack and Lex.

Jay asked more about Blake. Lia explained what she had told Jack and Lex, that he and his men had arrived recently. She didn't know much about them. Except that they had rounded up some of the warriors who were hunting, and seemed to be slave traders.

Ram was uneasy by the revelation, which didn't go unnoticed by the others.

"You don't know anything about THEM, I hope?" Amber had enquired.

Nothing would have surprised her with Ram anymore. But he reassured everyone he had never heard of anyone called Blake. Though that didn't rule out that he could be involved with The Collective. Along with some of the other tribes. Lia doubted that, advising that in the aftermath of the pandemic there were other pockets of survivors within the surrounding islands who formed themselves into various tribes. And apart from one known as The Fallen, most were trying to live in harmony. Like the Roaches, who based themselves on the other side of the island in an old World War 2 military base.

Ram questioned Lia for details of the base. It didn't sound like it would have been a hidden compound like the one in Eagle Mountain.

Lia mentioned that in the far north, there was talk of mysterious goings on in the mountainous region. But she didn't have any other detail. Just rumours that whoever was in the area had also recently arrived and were trading slaves. Ram certainly wasn't reassured that this meant they weren't involved in The Collective.

"The thing you've got to all realise about The Collective," Ram had explained, "is that they gather all kinds of people. Some might be used as slaves. But they are also after leaders, the best brains -"

"Well, that rules you out," Lex interrupted, sure that Ram wasn't so smart if he had gotten himself involved.

Ram agreed. That if he knew then what he knew now, there was no way that he would have become involved with Kami and his network. He was aware from their online relationship when Kami was a member of a guild, that he was always trying to expand, inspired by some of the greatest empires in history. Like the Spartans. But had no idea that he'd use the same strategies after the pandemic.

"I understand some of you might not have agreed with what I was trying to achieve with the Technos. And it's just the same. I didn't agree with the way Kami wanted to operate with this Collective of his. But by then, it wasn't just a matter of walking away," Ram said.

"I still don't understand what he was involved with?" Gel said.

"You don't want to know," Ram continued. "The full extent of it. He even had plans to try and repopulate. Just as the adults were going to do -"

"How can you be so sure? 'Repopulate'?" Jack interrupted.

"And how can you be so sure you can 'trust' everyone around here?" Ram asked, casting a discrete glance at Lia.

"What's that supposed to mean?" Lex snapped angrily at Ram.

"I just want to be careful. With anything I say. Especially with any 'strangers' around."

"If you've got anything else you need to say, then you owe it to us. Owe it to everyone. To let us know," Amber insisted.

"I've told you all I know. I promise. It's just, when Kami and his people were hacking into the government computers they found some files about some plans to repopulate. And I think it gave Kami some ideas. He was even thinking about developing breeding programmes. So don't for one minute just think that slaves would be clearing the land, labouring."

"You mean some... might spend all day 'doing it'?" Darryl beamed, in growing interest, intrigued just by the thought of it.

"No. Not just any kind of people. But those with the right kind of DNA. The right kind of brain. Skills. And don't even think about what he'd do to anyone if they crossed him!" Ram shuddered as he considered the consequences. "I'll have a hell of a price on my head!"

"Well, let's just hope it's as BIG as your head," Lex replied.

"Not now," Amber stated. "Please, Lex. Our priority is to deal with all that Lia has told us. And with this deadline of her tribe, we don't have long."

Trudy agreed and was becoming almost hysterical, wondering what might happen. "They seem like a bunch of savages, from what Jack and Lex told us."

"I wouldn't call them 'savages' exactly," Lex said.

"Well, they hardly seem to have been friendly, threatening to sacrifice Jack and Lex," May stated, in mounting unease.

This was far from a deserted paradise, everyone debated, realising that the island they were marooned on was considered to be sacred land.

Jay wondered if it might be an idea for them to try and travel to one of the other outlying islands in the region. Or even to go to another part of the island, if the Priestess and indigenous tribe were a threat. But he agreed with the others that they couldn't very well travel with Slade. And they all resolved that they were in this together and had no option but to stay.

Though Ram thought what Ruby had earlier suggested concerning Slade and Zak might be a wise resolution so that they could get out of there as far as they could. While they still could. May was horrified, as was Ruby, along with everyone else, that Ram could be so ruthless to even suggest that they just abandon Slade, leave him to die, with Ruby ironically stating that from hereon in, it would never be an option for her. Ever again.

Sammy felt terrible about it but was so scared that he thought there were some merits in what Ram was suggesting, sure that the needs of the many outweighed the needs of the few. Ram didn't like it any more than anyone else but it had always been the way of the world, he reflected. None more than now in the post adult world. They could either choose to move on. Or stay and fight. But he didn't fancy their chances. The tribe of Lia's seemed to be capable adversaries.

Everyone took a vote. The majority decided that they should stay. And if the indigenous tribe showed up, hoped that Lia might translate their appeals to give more time until Slade recovered so that they could then at least have a chance to find somewhere else to settle. Away from the sacred lands, which they all respected, fully aware of how proprietorial they felt about their shopping mall that had once been their home. So they could well imagine how Lia's tribe must view their lands, which had been their home for centuries.

Lia was taken to the nearby shelter that the others had built, rudimentarily constructed with branches and palm leaves providing some measure of protection from the sun and elements for Slade inside. He had remained unconscious for several days now. All were deeply concerned how much longer he could last, how long he would stay alive.

His wound had been regularly re-dressed and was showing signs of healing. But Amber and the others were still unsure if he was suffering from septicaemia, if infection was travelling through his entire bloodstream.

Lia suggested that she and some of the others gather a selection of native plants, revealing to them - as she did to Jack and Lex previously - that her parents were conventional doctors within the United Nations Task Force fleet. And that Lia herself had learned a lot from her time with the indigenous tribe, who used homeopathic medicines to cure all manner of ailments.

The Mall Rats didn't need much convincing, recalling Tai San's gifts and abilities. She, too, had been in tune with the natural world and was able to concoct different remedies for different problems. Lex was affected as he thought of Tai San and really missed her. As did all of her friends. Especially in this situation.

Like Tai San, Lia seemed to know what all the plants and juices from them could do. Though privately, Amber wondered if Lia could deal with blood poisoning, if indeed that's what was affecting Slade. She felt he would probably need to remain on antibiotics. But they had a limited supply, with the amounts Ruby had managed to recover from the wreck of the Jzhao Li soon to also run out. But it was worth a try.

While Ruby and Salene worked with Lia in her attempts to assist Slade, the others agreed with Amber that it might be sensible to try and implement some form of defence plan. As a contingency in case the Priestess and indigenous tribe were unsympathetic to their plight, refusing to give them an extension to the deadline before they had to leave. Or worse still, unleashed an attack.

Lex wouldn't put it past them from all he had observed. But thought they might still have a chance. The survivors were outnumbered by the population of the village but most were females or children, with many warriors having been seized by Blake to be traded as slaves.

Lex thought that they might have a chance to repel any form of attack, especially when Lia advised that the Priestess would never leave the village unprotected. If an attack occurred it would come from a raiding party rather than the entire warrior contingent.

It still didn't provide Trudy with much comfort but Amber seemed more concerned and offended by Lex's chauvinistic reference to the female members of the indigenous tribe being purely in charge of more domestic matters.

Lia tried to calm matters, explaining that within the culture no female was expected to fight. Their duty was to care for the children as well as prepare food and look after their men.

"I suppose you enjoyed yourself, did you, Lex?" Amber asked, knowing full well that it would be the type of structure he could fit into quite easily.

"As a matter of fact, I did. In a weird way," Lex had replied. "And no, not because of having a bunch of girls looking after me like servants. I just liked their way of life."

Lex had encountered many warring tribes back in the concrete jungle in the city, initially oppressed by the Locos. As had all the sectors through the warring tribes.

But this indigenous tribe who had taken in Lia didn't seem to be the type who would invade. Not like the Technos. They just wanted to be left alone. To follow their ways. And Lex respected that. They had no ambitions to conquer and rule, to expand their empire. They weren't like this 'Collective' Ram had gone on about.

Lex had been dragged up in the gutters on some very mean streets. And in many ways he felt all the people he had dealt with throughout the anarchic days that followed the pandemic seemed to be more primitive and untrustworthy than the people who had held him captive.

Jack intimated that Lex seemed to have the hots for the Priestess, leading everyone to suspect if Lex had in reality been touched by the way of life the indigenous tribe seemed to strive for. Or whether or not the Priestess represented a conquest Lex had in mind, which was fuelling his blurred fantasy of living with nature.

Lex couldn't help but admit that the Priestess was statuesque and had something really mysterious about her. She was like a Goddess.

"With a capability of killing people," Trudy added, recalling what Jack and Lex told them all, that they only had minutes to spare before their throats would be slit by a ceremonial dagger, which caused Ellie to shudder about the mere thought of it.

Lia confirmed that it would be unwise to underestimate the Priestess. Or the reactions of the village. They would always be prepared to fight and die for all they believed in. And would also kill to protect their way of life as well.

Amber tried to motivate the others after the meeting, feeling that having come this far they couldn't give up now and had to give it everything they had. She was still hopeful they could reason with Lia's people. But if not, she was determined they be prepared as much as they could.

The majority of the group began to fortify Camp Phoenix, making improvised spears, Amber showing them what she had learned during her time with Pride and the Eco tribe. More tree branches were stripped, the ends of them sharpened against rocks to make spears. The Eco tribe had used them for fishing and hunting, and Amber dreaded the prospect of having to use them as weapons.

They gathered coconuts, which Jay thought would be useful as other weapons.

And began even building an improvised defence perimeter with large branches, which were shaved into protruding points over barricades of metal, which had been washed ashore amidst the flotsam and jetsam sprawled along the beach from the hull of the wreck of the Jzhao Li.

"It's not all bad, is it, Lex?" Gel asked, as she searched debris littering the sand with Lex beside her, also looking for anything which might be of use in building their defence. "Look!" Gel continued, noticing a pile of plastic toiletries. "I've run out of shampoo! This must be my lucky day! "

"Brilliant, Gel. That's just what we need," Lex said sarcastically, smiling slightly while watching Gel lift the containers. "If those warriors show up and you offer to wash their hair, or give them a beauty treatment - I'm sure they'll surrender. Immediately."

She poked her tongue out, gathering as many toiletries as she could while Lex hauled mammoth sheets of debris toward the barricade.

If Lia's tribe wanted to mix it up, then at least they would make sure they were ready to give as good as they got.

CHAPTER FORTY

The sky was like a planetarium, filled with stars.

Ruby kept up her relentless vigil, laying near Slade in the makeshift shelter.

The others tried to sleep as well but most within Camp Phoenix were restless, wondering what events would unfold when the indigenous tribe arrived at dawn. Though Lottie, Sammy, Brady and the baby were lost, deep in slumber.

Amber had agreed to take the first shift on night watch and would soon be replaced by Jay. After the events of the day she welcomed the opportunity to be alone, gathering her thoughts, reflecting on all that had occurred. And what might transpire. But she, like the others, was relieved that at least Jack and Lex had returned safely and was pleased for Ellie, knowing all too well the pain suffered by the disappearance of a loved one.

Amber was keen to try and grab a few hours sleep, feeling particularly drained, exhausted. Physically. As well as mentally. Sleep, at least, provided some refuge from the world young people now inhabited. At least the past could be relived through dreams, when the world had been a better place, before the adults had all perished during the pandemic.

Amber had also met up with Bray through her dreams but invariably woke up with a start, disappointed that it wasn't real. Since Jay came into her life, her dreams - and memories of Bray - had never subsided. And had always left her feeling guilty. That she was betraying Jay. But rationalised it to herself that Bray would always be by her side either in dreams or memories, and that was the right way for it to be, given that he was the father of their child.

Suddenly Amber heard a sound and gazed around, uneasily.

She couldn't see anything. It must be an animal or bird, rustling the leaves of the trees. Or maybe in her sub-consciousness, she was just tense, wondering what the dawn would bring when Lia's tribe were due to arrive.

There was another sound. But this time Amber noticed figures through the darkness, moving quickly in the undergrowth.

Before she had even had a chance to bang the metal warning device to raise an alarm, Amber knew that they were under attack, and she shouted out a warning.

"Jay! Lex! Everyone!" she shouted, panic-stricken.

The others sprung into action, Trudy protectively gathering up the little ones and screaming hysterically as Axel and his men appeared from the undergrowth, converging on the camp.

Lex grabbed one of the makeshift spears they had fashioned earlier that day and tried to strike out at one of the attackers. But another attacker was on him, seizing the spear out of Lex's grasp.

Lex was nevertheless able to unleash a powerful kick into the attacker's groin, doubling him, before striking out another blow at the other attacker.

"Amber!" Salene screamed in warning while climbing to her feet, noticing another attacker knocking Amber to the ground, then pressing the full weight of his massive forearm into Amber's throat, preventing her from moving.

Behind Salene, yet another attacker appeared, grabbing her.

Darryl was immediately there, striking the attacker with a log. Although the attacker sunk to his knees, other members of the raiding party quickly overwhelmed Salene and Darryl, having the benefit of surprise.

Amber struggled, desperate to get up and to her baby, to protect him.

Unexpectedly her attacker released his hold, having been smashed in the head with a coconut which Jay had hurled, before spinning to confront others in the raiding party unleashing vicious blows.

Ram scrambled and dove behind a log, as if he was trying to be invisible, his own safety being paramount to him.

Jack, Ellie and May were putting up strong resistance, Ellie hurling flaming branches at their attackers. But in no time at all they were subdued, as was Sammy, who was lifted up by the scruff of his neck but still swung wildly.

Ruby, in the makeshift shelter watching over Slade, was standing at the ready as two attackers arrived, managing to floor one with a punch. But the other seized her. Ruby bit into his arm but apart from a groan, it did no good. Her attacker had her fully restrained.

Trudy continued her sustained wail, clutching desperately at Brady, Lottie running to gather Amber's baby in her arms.

But the baby was yanked away.

Amber couldn't believe her eyes.

It was Ebony.

It felt to Amber that time had stood still. And that she was alone, oblivious to all the panic around her at the height of the ambush. All she could focus on was her son, her precious baby, who meant more to her than anyone else in the world. And there he was, clutched in Ebony's arms, crying. He needed his mother. He was calling. Frightened by Ebony holding him prisoner. Amber dreaded to think what would happen if she reached out and tried to get him.

Ebony took great delight in Amber's pained expression, then gazed around, shouting.

"If you know what's good for him - for all of you - back off, everyone, and do exactly what I say!"

She looked as if she would drop the baby on its head, which caused Amber to freeze in her tracks, still trying to come to terms and gather her composure from the sudden surprise of the attack.

Gel was laying sprawled on the ground, having fainted when she first noticed the raiding party.

All that the others noticed was that they were outnumbered and never stood a real chance.

Lia had put on her glasses when the ambush first occurred and was now trying to fix her gaze through the one good lens as more and more of Axel's men were arriving and rounding up the members of Camp Phoenix, all gazing unbelievably at Ebony giving Axel instructions, identifying who was who.

A spear thudded into the sand.

All present recoiled as more spears sailed through the air, the sounds sibilant like whistling wind.

Native warriors from the indigenous tribe appeared from the jungle undergrowth, ululating, causing Trudy to scream even more hysterically, accompanied by Brady and Lottie. Even Sammy was struggling to contain himself and was crying out in fear.

"Lia - what's going on!" Amber shouted.

"I don't know! I don't know!" Lia replied, deeply concerned, unsure of what was happening herself other than the warriors were engaged in combat with Axel and his raiding party, who were now in turn being outnumbered.

"I don't know what the hell is going on, but it seems to me that either the natives either set their alarms early - or they're here to help us!" Lex called out, unleashing a blow against one of Axel's men before rushing to Jay and Amber, who were converging on Ebony, backing up.

"Let the baby go!" Amber pleaded. "Please, Ebony! Let him go!"

"Sure!" Ebony said, "No problem," realising that Axel's raiders were losing the fight.

Ram, peering over the log, stood, then nodded to more warriors rushing past and shouted out a friendly greeting to them.

"Hey! How you doing, guys? Am I glad to see you! The name's Zak," he added for good measure.

Then he crouched again, tried to hide, realizing that the warriors didn't seem to be that friendly and were purely intent on their task of subduing whatever resistance they encountered.

Before long, there was no resistance.

Lex noticed the Priestess approaching, her feathers rippling in the wind as it blew her long hair, a spear clutched in one hand.

Behind her, other warriors followed, looking fierce, daubs of warpaint and tattoos covering their faces and well-built bodies, all of them similarly armed with spears.

Finally arrriving into Camp Phoenix, the Priestess's gaze was riveted on Lia.

Unexpectedly, she called out in her native language, a melodious flow of sounds mixed with guttural inflections, clicking noises. It was as if she was calling like a bird in the jungle, her voice carrying over the wind and hysteria of sobbing from Lottie, Sammy, Brady and baby Bray. Though Trudy seemed to be gathering her composure and stood gazing around unbelievably at what was transpiring, as did her fellow Mall Rats.

"What's she saying?" Lex shouted to Lia, confused as the warriors continued to assemble Axel's raiding party.

"She is saying that the actions of the tribe should show what loyalty really means. I might have been treacherous, but that is not the way of the Priestess and her people."

Lia continued translating, advising that although the ultimatum for them all to leave the sacred lands had still been put in place, one of her hunters had noticed a large boat approaching, which he knew belonged to Blake. And despite all Lia had done, the Priestess could never allow her to be taken as a slave, as had occurred to some of the warriors of the tribe previously.

Ebony crossed to Lia. "Thank God for that! At last I've met someone with common decency! Tell her, will you? Go on, tell her that I might be able to help. I know all about Blake!"

Axel and the others in the raiding party cast Ebony a surprised glance, as did the Mall Rats.

Ram peered again over the log and swallowed nervously as the Priestess hurled the spear she was holding, which thudded into the ground near Ebony.

"Somehow, I don't think she believes you," Amber said. "And you don't need any translator to let you know neither do we."

Ebony, thinking quickly, tried to plead her case. To let everyone know what had happened to her after she left the Jzhao Li. How she had drifted, been captured by Blake, a tyrannical tribe leader, and only by the skin of her teeth had recently been able to make good her escape, accompanying the others on a boat from the oil rig where Blake and his people were based.

"This guy, Blake - he's crazy! You've got to believe me! After all I've gone through, I'm lucky to still be alive!"

"Well, that serves you right for abandoning ship, doesn't it?" Jay snarled.

"I didn't abandon ship," Ebony pleaded. "I was trying to get the lifeboat prepared. Not just for me. For everyone. But when I climbed aboard, the ropes gave way. It wasn't my fault. I got stranded. And if you think it was easy for me drifting alone for days at sea before being picked up by Blake and his thugs, then you're as crazy as he is!"

Lex and the others scoffed. Not buying Ebony's story of being a damsel in distress, even if she did break down sobbing when relaying all that had happened. She was tougher than this and was clearly trying to make a meal out of the situation.

"How can anyone not believe me?" Ebony said.

"They've had a lot of practice," Ram cut in, casting a disdainful glance at the others. Then he suddenly stopped and gazed uneasily as the Priestess spoke up, in her native language.

"What's she saying, Lia?" Amber asked.

"She wants to talk with you. All of you."

* * *

When the dawn broke, the sky was ablaze in a multitude of colour. Few could have foreseen what the new day would bring.

Having prepared to face the ultimatum given by the Priestess and the indigenous tribe, the Mall Rats had unexpectedly encountered Ebony. With Ram uneasily wondering if her cohorts were a part of his long lost adversary, Kami, and The Collective.

Lia translated while Amber provided details of the Mall Rats and their past.

Lex interrupted occasionally, boasting of his exploits, advising that he was a mighty warrior back in the city and that the Priestess's group would have been impressed if they ever saw him in action, even if he was taken by surprise. On his own patch, he was formidable.

Much to Lex's disappointment, the Priestess didn't pay much attention, preferring to focus more on what life was like for them in the 'uncivilised' world, still highly suspicious of foreigners and struggling to bridge the cultural gap, unable to understand why there were so many warring tribes in their homeland.

Amber made a good case that not all of their people were like that. Explaining that the Mall Rats, at least, were certainly different. They had hoped to build a better world out of the ashes of the old, introducing social charters, educational system for the young, even a judicial framework. Representing remnants from their old world. From what the adults who had gone before had sought to put in place. And that in many ways the Mall Rats were no different to the Priestess and her people. Honouring the past and their ancestors in their attempts at building a better future.

The Priestess softened the more Amber spoke. Encouraged by her reaction, Lia prompted May, Salene, Trudy, Jay, Ellie and Jack to tell the Priestess how they felt, confirming all Amber had said. Even Lottie and Sammy were invited to speak up about what life was like being a Mall Rat. And even Gel inadvertently made an impression, intrigued by and complimenting the Priestess on her hair and make up design. The Priestess considered Gel for a long moment, then nodded gratefully, as Lia translated what had been said. Gel cast a look at Lex, proud of herself, and Lex faked a weak smile. Talk of hair and make up was the least of what he had expected as he listened to Lia telling Gel that the Priestess thinks her hair was lovely as well.

Only Ram was prevented from speaking too much, with Lia being unsure of where he really stood, given his account of The Collective. She was aware that he had invaded the city and that would hardly endear him to the Priestess or her people, who had suffered from the invasions of foreigners themselves throughout their long history.

Ebony, Axel and the raiding party were being held in an empty container. Ebony had tried again to retrieve her position, pleading that she had been taken prisoner and had no option but to go along with them. But had tried to devise a plan to help the Mall Rats. Everyone. And was on the point of shouting out to warn them of the ambush, but was restrained.

She mentioned that she had seen Bray, sure that this would be her ace card in especially winning Amber back on her side. But Amber was having none of it. Not from the same person who, years before had tortured Bray, along with the other members of the Mall Rats, with the false information that Amber herself had died during the explosion at Eagle Mountain.

Ebony was devastated and continued pleading to be given a chance before she, Axel and the party were locked up in the container while Amber and the others had a chance to decide what they might do with them.

Lia translated that the Priestess felt they should be sacrificed for their treachery. Particularly if Ebony was once a member of their tribe and had turned against them. Ram believed there was some merit in that.

There was a moment when Lia felt that the Priestess might also be sending her threatening messages that she might suffer the same fate.

But Lia finally relaxed, sensing that the Priestess was warming to her again, the more she heard the Mall Rats giving a good account of who they were, what they aspired to achieve for their Tribe. A fair and just society. Freedom and equality for all.

That was the way of the old world, Amber reiterated. And although an ocean might have divided the Priestess and her tribe geographically and they couldn't speak the same language, philosophically they were on a similar plane.

Amber made sure that Lia let the Priestess and her people know that they were grateful for their assistance. And had they not intervened, they shuddered to think what might have occurred had Ebony and the raiding party succeeded in their mission.

All the Mall Rats made a point to also let the Priestess know that they didn't mean any disrespect by being on sacred lands. They were here by accident. Not choice.

Lex wanted Lia to emphasise that destiny could have been responsible. For bringing them all together. And if the Priestess got in tune spiritually, then she would see that had the indigenous tribe not captured Lex and Jack in the first place, then they wouldn't have been able to have helped the Mall Rats. And if that was the case, then the prisoners wouldn't be now being held in the container. So even Lia played a part. And with the dawn breaking across the sky, if she really thought about all he was saying, then she would know that it must have been meant to be.

Jack smiled slightly to himself as he listened, sure that Tai San must have made a real impression during her time together with Lex. Either that or Lex was referencing all she had taught him in an attempt to connect with the Priestess.

Ram was even impressed with the way in which Lex was speaking. It didn't take a genius to notice a degree of flirtation in Lex's entire demeanour, but there was a wisdom as well in what he was saying.

Ram asked Lia to check with the Priestess if she knew of The Collective. Or if she thought the raiding party being held might even be involved. Lia didn't think it was a good idea to get into that area at all. It might only inflame matters.

The Priestess was furious enough that foreigners had invaded and had taken some of her warriors as slaves. This sparked an idea in Amber, who suggested that there might be a way for the Mall Rats to repay the Priestess and her people, along with securing the position of both tribes.

Lia confirmed that the Priestess said she was open to hearing any proposition. And the others were just as eager to discover what Amber had in mind.

CHAPTER FORTY-ONE

Blake stomped down the twisting, circular metal staircase and into a corridor, his heavy boots echoing throughout the cavernous deck as he crossed to the cell.

Flanked by two huge guards who obediently followed, Blake was silent, deep in thought, his face a mask of concentration.

He regretted giving Ebony the assignment.

Blake had met enough people in his life to know if someone could be trusted. Or, so he thought. A large part of him still doubted her. But he had to admit that she was starting to sound as if she might be genuine.

And if not, then Axel and his raiding party should have been sufficiently well-trained and capable to 'deal' with her in a double-cross.

Blake just couldn't understand what could have happened. The raiding party was long overdue. And he was furious at himself but just couldn't help being lured into the web she had spun. She was an animal in bed. Fiery, independent, enigmatic, bright. Posing a real challenge. And Blake always rose to a challenge.

Unlike all the other females he had encountered, Ebony wasn't so easy to dominate. She could have been a worthy mistress. A useful advisor. A mixture not only of beauty but great cunning.

For all his simmering anger, a part of him even admired that she had tricked him. If indeed that is what had occurred.

Blake arrived outside the cell, commanded the guards to open the heavy doors, then he entered, gazing coldly at Bray before him, dangling from the girders above, shackled by his arms.

Bray had still refused to co-operate with any of Blake's people but Ebony had managed to obtain some information. Blake was concerned now though if the information she had given was false.

He nodded to the guards, who removed Bray's blindfold.

Bray focused his eyes weakly, finding it difficult to see, having been blindfolded for so long.

"Enjoying your stay?" Blake asked, with more than a hint of disdain.

"What do you think?" Bray answered weakly, defiantly.

"I think -" Blake replied, examining Bray's features, then noticing the 'L' on his shoulder, "that you've been categorised before!" At least Ebony had told the truth about that.

"I don't know what you're talking about!" Bray responded.

"I'm talking about the brand. On your arm!"

He continued to survey Bray as if he was assessing him. Bray seemed to be about the same height, weight. And from the small tattoo on the side of his cheek, seemed to match the identification from the reports he had recently received.

"I gather from your friend, Ebony, that your name is Bray. Is that correct?" Blake continued.

Again Bray considered Blake, unsure of who he was, what was going on.

Blake sighed to himself, impatient at Bray's silence and suddenly unleashed a powerful blow into Bray's abdomen.

Bray groaned in pain, but at least being suspended from the overhead chains meant that it softened the impact and he swung slowly back and forth from the momentum of Blake lashing out.

"Okay, if you don't want to talk about Ebony. Or yourself. Why don't we talk about your brother. Zoot? Or Martin, wasn't he?"

"Who are you?" Bray asked, in a mixture of mounting confusion and suspicion.

"Life. And death," Blake smiled. "And the one asking the questions. So don't play any games. I've been studying your file. You seem to have quite a value. At least, according to Eloise."

"You're involved with that monster?" Bray snapped, in disgust. "I should have known! You seem to be exactly the type."

"And you don't seem to be the 'type' to have escaped. Across the wastelands. You can't be that good. Or you wouldn't have ended up here," Blake sneered, surveying Bray in a cold, calculating manner, thinking about his next move.

"And where's here?"

"Oh, don't worry. You'll be transported soon. When the ship arrives. If you board, that is. Either way, you won't be with us for long." There was a veiled threat, menace in Blake's tone.

"What do you want with me?" Bray asked.

"Payment. That's all you are. A name on a manifest. And a wanted name at that. You should be proud of yourself, Bray. In some ways, I should thank you. You'll provide a good bounty."

Blake moved closer to Bray, leering into his face, his teeth clenched, trying to control a simmering anger boiling within his manic intemperance.

"If you really want to know, if it was up to me - I'd kill you. Right now. But Eloise? I don't think she'd be very pleased. There again, as long as she has some other members of the bloodline to work with. Like your brother's... little daughter."

Bray was stunned by what he was hearing. He just couldn't understand why this person seemed to know so much about him.

"You... don't have Brady being kept here?" Bray asked.

"Not yet. But I've been working on it," Blake smiled, an excited glint in his eye.

He lunged forward and screamed.

"Power and Chaos!"

Bray recoiled, sure he was in another simulation.

"What is it? You don't like the word of... who is it... Zoot?"

Bray exchanged glances with Blake, who sneered in mock concern.

"Sorry. I didn't mean to use Zoot's name in vain."

Blake glared contemptuously, then turned, indicating Bray to the guards. "Get him down! Now!" he snapped.

The guards lowered Bray, unwinding the pulley attached to the chains.

Bray slumped to the ground, rubbing his wrists, numbed from having been suspended for so long, while the guards unlocked Bray's manacles from his ankles.

Blake indicated. One of the other guards tossed a spear fishing gun he was holding, which Blake grasped, stroking its sharp jagged razor's edge, which drew blood, and he licked the trickle, running down his finger.

"Gotta be careful with a weapon like this, Bray. It can do a lot of damage. Unless of course, you're as good as you might think you are."

Blake nodded to the guards, who yanked Bray to his feet.

"There you go. That's better now, isn't it? You're... free."

"Somehow I don't think so," Bray responded defiantly.

"You've got no-one but yourself to blame. You see, if you play games with me when I question you, then that leaves me with no option... but to play a game with you."

Bray swallowed nervously, wondering what on earth might be coming next, and his unease made Blake burst out in laughter.

"What's the matter? Never played first person shooters? Never got into any kind of game like that? Or weren't you into gaming? In the old world? Because I was. Oh, yes. In a big, big, way!"

Bray didn't respond and continued to watch uneasily as Blake's laughter subsided, his demeanour turning ice-cold.

"The rules are very simple. I'm the hunter. You're the prey. It's so much more 'fun' with a moving target. Let's see how good you REALLY are. I'll give you a ten second start."

Bray looked at Blake, abhorrent and stunned as he noticed Blake removing a small spear from the quiver, which he inserted above the barrel.

"One..."

He indicated the doorway.

"Two..."

Bray braced himself.

"Three..."

Bray ran flat out, leaving Blake yelling in a manic intensity.

"You've run out of time, Bray! Ready or not - here I come!"

CHAPTER FORTY-TWO

Ruby and Trudy sat gazing into the fire. Ruby was preparing something to eat but didn't feel hungry. Nor did Trudy. They were both far too worried what might transpire, what the night would bring.

Ruby turned skewers of fish, then settled back and glanced at Trudy, who was cradling Amber's son.

"Can I hold him?" Ruby asked.

"Of course," Trudy spoke softly, so as not to waken the baby.

Seeing Amber's young child only reminded Ruby of the baby she was secretly carrying inside her. Slade's baby. She felt a connection. After all, she was a mother-to-be.

Giving him a hug, baby Bray remained asleep, oblivious to his environment. Ruby imagined what it would feel like one day to be holding her own child. And hoped that Slade would be able to experience that joy. His condition seemed to have improved since the medicines he had been given by Lia.

For the first time since the adults had died during the pandemic, Ruby was beginning to think that she might have a future. If only they could get through whatever lay ahead.

"I hope the others are getting on alright," Ruby reflected.

"You don't think they'll end up being taken themselves?"

"I certainly hope not."

The thought of it sent an involuntary shiver down Trudy's spine.

"If so, you know what that means, Ruby. We'll be stranded here!" Trudy cast an uneasy glance at Ram, who was sitting nearby on a log, lost in some private reverie, clutching his head in his hands.

Sammy was wading in the shallows, trying to get some respite from the blistering heat of the night.

Lottie was looking after Slade, in the makeshift shelter.

Gel was trying to file her nails with a stone, the rhythmic sounds almost in time to the noises of the wildlife and insects emanating from the depths of the jungle.

A contingent of warriors were standing outside one of the containers which had washed up from the Jzhao Li, but which had been emptied and was holding Ebony, Axel and his raiding party.

The others had left several hours earlier. In the cruiser which had transported Ebony, Axel and his men. And although everyone left behind knew the mission had dangers, there was no other option but for the Mall Rats to accompany the warriors to the rig in an attempt to release the slaves. Including other warriors of the indigenous tribe who were being held.

They had been able to get some kind of an idea of the size of the forces on the rig. And even if Axel and his men weren't telling the truth, they knew that strategically they had a good chance of their night assault succeeding.

Amber and Jay had planned it all out carefully before they left, then briefed the others. Going over all the details several times. They would attempt to infiltrate the rig, get to the cells so that they could gather strength in numbers, releasing the slaves and warriors being held, to assist in overcoming whatever resistance might be met.

There was room on the cruiser to transport enough people to carry out the operation and they knew there were other vessels, including Ebony's abandoned lifeboat, to facilitate the return.

They had carefully chosen who would participate in the mission. And especially who they would leave behind. Trudy was a capable fighter. She had proven that throughout any clashes the Mall Rats had with tribes back in the city. But was better suited to look after the younger ones. That was important, especially for Amber to know that her baby would be well taken care of in case anything went wrong. Trudy could be histrionic at times, but there was never any doubt that she was a loving, caring mother.

Ruby volunteered to go. But Amber thought, given that she was also to become a mother, that it would be too risky. Besides, she would need to be near Slade, as well as remain to keep a close eye on Ram. For all that she was pregnant, she was still characteristically feisty, level-headed, and could take care of herself, as she had shown many who were out of order in her saloon back in Liberty.

Lia was needed so that she could translate orders during the mission and had also left strict instructions to the warriors who were left behind that they also needed to watch out for Ram.

Ram himself wasn't keen on going at all. Lex had accused him of being a coward. But Ram quickly agreed with Jay, who felt it would be wise for him to stay in case they encountered anything unexpected and Blake's forces were somehow connected to The Collective. With Ram being a wanted man, at the top of the list of their leader, Kami, they couldn't be too sure of what or who they might be dealing with. His presence could be a liability.

Now Ebony started banging loudly from inside the container, demanding food and something to drink.

"Come on, give me a break!" she yelled from inside the container. "It's sweltering in here! Never thought the Mall Rats would stand by and let one of their own die! I've done nothing wrong. I'm innocent! Doesn't anyone believe me?"

Ruby scoffed. "She just won't give in, will she? What does she take us for?"

"You don't think there's a chance she COULD be innocent, do you?" Trudy reflected.

"What - Ebony? You've got to be joking."

Trudy sighed, clearly torn. On one hand, Ruby was right. It was always difficult to know just exactly where Ebony was coming from. She had shown a capability of changing sides when it suited her. But before the incident with the lifeboat, she seemed that she was settling and keen to be a member of the Mall Rats.

Ebony banged again on the container. "I can hardly breathe in here! There's no air! Have some mercy. Please!"

"Keep quiet, will you!?" Ram yelled, irritated at the constant banging and shouting. "I can hardly hear myself think!"

"Maybe we should at least give them all something to drink," Trudy suggested tentatively.

"I wouldn't."

"What happens if they do die in there?" Gel asked.

Ruby cast a glance at the container and sighed to herself, sharing the same concern. She had resolved that she would never try and play God again, deciding anyone's fate and whether or not they lived or died.

"They should have more than enough still left to drink," Ruby concluded. "Ebony would stab herself in the back if she thought she could benefit. So don't let her get to you. Because I'm certainly not going to let her get to me."

"Ruby!" Lottie screamed from the distance. "Quick!"

Ruby leapt to her feet, running flat out towards the makeshift shelter where Lottie was standing, with a huge grin on her face.

Back at Camp Phoenix, inside the trailer, Ebony winked at Axel and the others, then banged again. "Have some mercy! Please!" She started to emit melodramatic, choking sounds.

Trudy and Gel exchanged concerned glances, then gazed at the container.

"Are you alright... in there?" Trudy asked.

There was no answer. Just Ebony's choking.

Oblivious to all this, Ruby arrived at the shelter and thought she was imagining what she was hearing.

"Ruby...?" Slade called, his voice still weak.

"Oh, my God!" Ruby said, tears filling her eyes as she crouched to lean over him, thrilled, as was Lottie, that Slade had regained consciousness. He had been gone for some time now and Ruby was anxious, believing that Slade might have also slipped into some sort of coma, just like Zak did before he died.

Laying on his back, Slade gazed up, trying somehow to focus on Ruby, peering down at him.

"Just relax! Don't try and talk! You're going to be alright!"

But Ruby looked more to be the one who needed to try and relax, hardly unable to contain her excitement and joy, evident through her tears.

She glanced up at Lottie. "What happened?"

"One minute it still seemed like he was fast asleep, then the next minute... he just opened his eyes and groaned," Lottie shrugged.

Ruby turned back and gently stroked Slade's hair.

"I can't believe it. I thought we lost you... I had lost you."

"I... need to tell you something," Slade said, flinching, still in pain.

Ruby leaned down closer, placing her ear near Slade's mouth so she could listen, make it easy for him.

"I love you," Slade declared with a slight smile, which made Ruby smile through her tears of joy. Then she was concerned at Slade, trying to prop himself up on one arm.

"What's going on!" he said weakly, staring disorientated at Camp Phoenix.

Lottie and Ruby turned, following Slade's weak gaze.

Then Ruby suddenly leapt to her feet as she heard Trudy emitting a long, hysterical scream. Brady and Amber's son also started to cry with the commotion.

Sammy stared wide-eyed in the shallows, frozen in fear.

Ram was backing away.

Ebony and Axel's raiding party were exchanging blows with the warrior guards. There had been a clear flaw in the briefing, with Lia translating to the warriors that they needed to watch Ram very carefully. But they didn't mention Trudy.

Trudy had taken some fruit to the container. Ram had followed, concerned by Trudy's actions. The warriors took a step forward towards him, ignoring Trudy, who undid the side metal door slightly to leave enough room to pass some fruit inside. Ebony, Axel and the party seized their chance, shouldering the door, which burst open, the logs tumbling which had been left to secure it.

Now, having floored the warriors, they were dragging Ram, who was yelling for help in growing panic, toward the jungle.

Another member of Axel's party grabbed Brady and Trudy but Gel released a burst of hairspray into his eyes. He ran off, following the other members of Axel's team, noticing the indigenous tribe warriors climbing to their feet.

Ruby indicated Slade to Lottie. "Stay with him!" she said, then started running towards a distraught Trudy, still screaming hysterically.

"Oh, my God! I was just wanting to give them some fruit! Something to drink! I had no idea this would happen! What have I done?!"

She stared helplessly, but there was no sign of Ebony, Axel and the raiding party, or Ram, who had disappeared deep into the jungle.

CHAPTER FORTY-THREE

Bray ran flat out along a metallic corridor in the bowels of the oil rig. Above, on the upper decks, the sobbing and whimpering of other slaves echoed through the catacombs of the mammoth infrastructure, the desperate sounds adding to the surreal situation Bray now was finding himself in.

He arrived at the end of the corridor and stopped for a split second, gazing left then right, wondering which way to take. He could hear the rhythmic pounding of Blake in pursuit, then took off, hurling around the right hand side and into another corridor.

Blake, the hunter, had several advantages over his prey. For that's what Bray now realized he was. Even though he couldn't quite understand why. And unlike Bray, Blake knew the layout of the oil rig, whereas Bray had no idea whatsoever where each of the metallic corridors he was running down would take him next.

Should he make a stand and fight, Bray thought, rushing around another corner and into yet another long, dimly lit metallic corridor.

His mind was a swirl, relying on his instincts and senses to rapidly assimilate all he could about this environment, hoping to find the slightest element he could use to his advantage.

Bray stumbled as he took off his boots and socks while he ran, hoping that continuing on in his bare feet would dampen the sound of his running.

It worked.

Blake, in another corridor, stopped. Listened. With the acoustics taking on another dimension.

Up ahead, Bray's skin was now being torn on the steel of the deck.

Taking a split second to gather his breath, his shoulders heaving from fatigue, Bray considered that the longer he stayed out in the open, in the corridors, the less of a chance he would have to stay ahead of Blake. He had to change the terrain, somehow.

"You can't run forever, Bray!" Blake's voice echoed ominously, threateningly, his approaching footsteps pounding as he approached closer. Closer.

Bray gazed around, noticed steps, then ran as fast as he could towards them, leaping, ascending each step, which led him into another deck. And another metallic corridor.

Bray continued on to the end, hurled around another corner, passing doors, which he tried to open. The first one was locked. Likewise, the second one. The third door creaked open. Inside, Bray could see shelves of processed food, bottled water, alcohol. These rooms were obviously where the crew kept their provisions.

Blake heard the echoey sounds of a thick, steel door being shut and smiled to himself. This was too easy.

He had always had a competitive edge since he was evacuated during the height of the pandemic. He had been identified as a suitable candidate for survival training at boot camp. Where he excelled, quickly becoming a leader, meeting

Axel, along with the others of his inner circle. That was the birth of his tribe and Blake had great ambitions, to build them into a force to be reckoned with in the post-apocalyptic world. To expand, extend his power base, build an empire.

And who knows, even better what his father had been able to achieve before the pandemic struck.

Blake was never close to his father. His mother had died giving birth and he had always wondered if he was somehow to blame. He suspected his father thought that to be the case.

Being in the military, Blake's father had always been a hard disciplinarian. Blake had struggled with that. And rebelled against it. Much to his father's chagrin. At least he had been able to make an impression. Succeed at something. But in the eyes of his father, he was a total failure.

Blake had always regretted that his father could never see what he really could have made of himself, if given the chance. Even as his father was approaching death during the height of the virus, Blake was criticised. For not showing up at the hospital earlier. They were the last words he had heard. And he couldn't help but feel a sense of relief, even delight, as he watched his father's life ebb away.

He stared coldly as the sheet was drawn up over his father's face. And even had difficulty providing comfort to his elder sister, who was sobbing uncontrollably, affected by every fading, last gasp of breath her father struggled to take.

In a way, Blake enjoyed it all. He had hoped in many ways that he could reconcile their differences. With some kind of deathbed revelation. But painfully realized there were too many scars which would never heal.

His father had been a Four Star General in the military, fuelling Blake's determination that in his own life he would become more. He wasn't interested in just becoming a general. But having his own army.

Meeting his friend, Kami, online just before the virus spread, his instincts told him that Kami could be the key. Kami wasn't just a capable gamer. But had organised an impressive guild, with members from most countries. When the darkness fell in the post-adult world, Kami reactivated his online friends, tracked Blake down. And Blake was determined to prove his worth.

Which is what he had done so far. Throughout his past assignments. And he was quickly rising up through the ranks. He only had a few more months to go on this assignment, then he was due to travel to the Far Eastern Region to eventually meet Kami. Get more of a handle on what he was planning with The Collective.

No matter what - Blake's plan was to make sure that he was a candidate for Kami's inner circle. Which would provide the gateway to power through Kami's expanding empire. And one day, Blake was determined that rather than Kami, Blake himself would become number one.

Now, crossing towards the door where his latest prey was hiding, Blake sighed to himself, slightly disappointed. He had hoped that Bray would have at least given him more of a workout. But he didn't seem up to the challenge. And decided that he would take him out and report back that his prisoner had been killed while trying to escape.

He knew Bray had some kind of value. For Eloise. And probably through her, a value for even Kami. Although he was unsure of just exactly what, Blake suspected from his earlier encounters with Ebony that there was some kind of a link to the experiments Eloise had been conducting. Above all, a link also to Kami's number one adversary - Ram. Blake still didn't know what had occurred. But Ram had a price on his head. Just like Bray. Being from the same bloodline of his brother, Zoot. Power and Chaos might have been an interesting ideology for Kami to nourish and spread 'the word'. But Blake thought the way of the warrior far surpassed anything that any religion had to offer. Zealots might become indoctrinated by faith but everyone could be dominated and controlled through fear.

Blake swung open the door, stepped inside and moved stealthily down each row of shelving.

Suddenly Bray appeared, unleashing a blow, sending Blake sprawling, before rushing out.

Blake wiped at a thin line of blood trickling from his mouth. He was encouraged, rather than angered. At least Bray might provide some kind of challenge after all. He clearly had skills to make it across the wastelands. But Blake, too, had skills and knew it was only a matter of time before he came out on top of this 'leader board'.

He took a breath, then ran out of the room in pursuit.

Bray hurled around a corridor, leaping up more metal steps which led to another deck. And ran along a corridor, passing cells each side where prisoners were reaching through the bars, clutching at him, their eyes wild, disorientated, all screaming for help. They were living in sheer hell. Which was in itself a vision of hell.

Bray couldn't comprehend where he was. Or just what was going on as he sped past.

One again, he suspected he might be trapped in a simulation, especially as guards at the end of the long corridor didn't bother to try and apprehend him, which surprised Bray. He had expected them to put up some kind of fight. But they just backed up, pressing themselves against the cells, allowing him to pass.

Little did Bray know that the guards knew never to interrupt Blake when he was indulging himself in any kind of 'hunt'. And Blake was clearly in pursuit.

Bray arrived into yet another metallic corridor, gazed around unsure which way to go but pushed himself on, casting an occasional glance behind. Then turning back. He had arrived at a dead end.

He noticed a row of switches and began flicking them.

Suddenly the dim fluorescent lights went out. Bray stood, rigid.

Backing up against the wall, daring not even to breathe as he heard the footsteps of Blake echoing, signalling that he was approaching, closer. Closer.

"Come on! This is too easy! You're starting to become a 'bore'!" Blake laughed, taunting.

Bray lunged forward, realizing Blake was almost on him, hurling him to one side, and ran on in full flight, retracing his steps, stealing looks behind as the fluorescent lights were switched on again.

Blake turned from the wall socket, raised the spear gun and yelled manically.

"Any last words, Bray?!"

Bray caught a fleeting glimpse of Blake's shadow moving across the wall as he pursued his prey.

But Blake wasn't running. He had slowed to a walking pace, while raising the spear gun, closing one eye, taking careful aim at Bray, visible in the cross hairs ahead.

Blake fired.

The spear shot out from the barrel of the spear gun, soaring through the air with a loud whoosh, embedding itself into the side of Bray's arm.

Bray winced and staggered slightly, yanking at the spear, removing it, while continuing running in full flight.

* * *

On the far horizon the silhouette was unmistakable.

The Mall Rats and warriors on the large cruiser were all watching in nervous anticipation of what they would encounter as the vessel sped, bouncing over the waves.

Jack was at the helm, gripping the wheel, trying to steady himself from the momentum.

On the deck, Amber and Jay were giving a final briefing, going over one last time what had already been planned. May, Ellie, Darryl, Salene and Lex nodded that they understood, while Lia translated to the warriors of the indigenous tribe, who also indicated that they were ready.

"Don't forget - the priority is to get as many of the prisoners being held out as we can," Amber said. "That way they can be of help to us. If we need extra help."

"Darryl and Salene - it's just so important for you to stay at the dock. In case we need to abort and get out of there," Jay reminded them.

"Lia - maybe you can go over one last time what your warriors need to do," Amber instructed. "Make sure each group know which one of us they're assigned to. And what we've all got in mind. We can't have any breakdowns in communication with anyone who doesn't stay with your group."

Lia nodded and began to translate.

Then all aboard gazed in mounting tension as the mammoth structure ahead in the distance seemed to grow larger and larger in size, the closer they approached. A remnant of the old world, a technological monstrosity that once harvested the second most important liquid in the world after water - oil. But now, people. Also an important commodity in the new world without adults.

"It's almost time," Amber whispered. "You all know what to do!?"

Once again, the others on board nodded, then gazed at the rig looming before them, preparing themselves for what lay ahead, realising that if there was ever a time that they needed to perform, then it was now.

They were about to shape their destinies. The outcome of their entire future and any hopes of survival, was at stake.

CHAPTER FORTY-FOUR

Blake bounded up more metallic steps, taking two, three at a time, following trails of blood, which had been dripping from Bray's shoulder wound.

Arriving at the top of the stairwell, he noticed a guard rushing toward him.

"Commander! Axel and his team are approaching."

Blake felt pleased though slightly surprised that Ebony had proven to be trustworthy. He wondered if she had really risen to the test. But if she didn't, no doubt Axel would have. Blake could always rely on him. And would be delivering Ram. Blake would receive a valuable bounty. But that was less important than the impression he'd make with Kami and The Collective.

"Tell Axel I'll be with him as soon as I can. This hunt shouldn't go on too long," Blake said, stroking the spear gun gently, excited by all the prospects which lay ahead.

"And Miss Ebony?" the guard asked tentatively, aware that Blake was ready to move off.

"Tell her to wait in my quarters. And I'll be with her shortly. I'm kinda 'busy' right now."

The guard nodded, understanding he was dismissed, and ran off.

On an upper deck, Bray was ripping at his shirt, and tried to tie a tourniquet to mask his trail of blood while he ran. Feeling exhausted and unsure of how long he could keep going on, disorientated from all he had suffered, Bray's eyes were full of utter confusion and fear as he heard Blake in the distance.

"I'm getting closer! But don't worry, Bray. Some of your friends will soon be here! Just a pity that you won't 'see' them!"

Bray stole a terrified glance behind him, then turned back, leaping up another stairwell, desperate to stay ahead of his crazed pursuer.

* * *

Even Blake himself might have been impressed with the irony of his strangely prophetic warning. He had fully expected Ram to be boarding by now. Along with Ebony. Perhaps even the daughter of Zoot, as well as the child's mother. But he - and especially Bray - had no way of knowing that Jack was carefully steering the cruiser towards the large dock surrounding the lower struts of the rig.

Jay leapt onto the dock, followed by the Mall Rats and warriors of the indigenous tribe.

Salene and Darryl stayed on the vessel, its engines idling, while they stood by at the ready, and the raiders moved quickly, stealthily along the dock, finally climbing metal ladders leading into the bowels of the mighty infrastructure looming over them.

* * *

Bray continued pushing himself on, up another metallic stairwell, the skin from his bare feet being torn with each panicked step, feeling his only hope was to try and get away from the maze of corridors and search for a window, a doorway, any portal into the outside world of wherever he was.

Blake was gaining on him, his eyes fixed as he relentlessly pursued. Pushing himself harder, harder, his teeth clenched. A glint of triumph at what he knew would soon lay ahead.

Bray had given him a good workout. Now he had other more important matters to attend to. It was time to move in. For the kill.

* * *

The Mall Rats and warrior raiding party entered the mammoth infrastructure, illuminated by dim fluorescent lights on all walls.

Amber noticed huge fire exit diagrams outlining five storage decks and the living quarters and upper mechanical and helicopter decks.

She indicated to Ellie and Jack, her voice in an urgent undertone.

"You take your group, check out deck 1. Lia, you go with them. Tell the others in Lex and May's group they'll need to secure deck 2, while Jay and I head to deck 3."

"Got it," Lex nodded as Lia whispered her translation to the warriors.

Ellie and Jack's group headed off.

Lex and May's contingent set off to another stairwell.

Jay suddenly spotted a guard at the end of the long corridor who had clearly noticed them in turn and rushed to a control panel, pulling down a lever, activating an alarm, the sound pulsing along with the dim fluorescent lights.

Amber, Jay and the warriors quickly ascended their stairwell while other guards converged at the end of the corridor and ran flat out in pursuit.

* * *

Outside on the dock, Salene and Darryl, aboard the cruiser, gazed up, hearing the shrill alarm, the pulsing lights from the cavernous infrastructure flashing, casting looming shadows across the surface of the water.

"Sounds like - it's on!" Darryl shouted to Salene, who was gripping the safety rail of the cruiser as it pitched up and down on the rolling waves while Darryl steadied the throttle of the idling boat.

"I hope they're alright!" Salene replied, craning her neck upwards, searching for a better look.

She felt like clambering up the stairwells surrounding the dock to be with the others but fought her natural instinct, sticking to what had been planned. She and Darryl had to remain on standby for when the Mall Rats returned with the influx of slaves. At least, that's what Darryl and Salene hoped. But if the operation had to be aborted in any way, then they would be ready for a quick getaway to transport the raiding party.

Salene dreaded to think of any other option as she continued to gaze eagerly at the rig for any sign.

"Come on... come on," she urged.

* * *

At the very top of the rig, Bray burst through the doors and gazed around at the helicopter deck. For a moment, he felt as if he was back in the city, on top of one of the skyscrapers where he regularly scouted for glimpses of tribes and activity, especially during the Locos' rule of the sector.

He stopped for a few seconds, heaving, trying somehow to catch his breath while he tightened the tourniquet, the screeching of the alarm and flashing fluorescent lights further disorientating him.

Suddenly he noticed Blake appear through the doorway.

There was a hint of uncertainty in Blake's expression. He decided he'd better end the hunt and head back below to check out what was happening, sure the alarm must have been set off accidentally. But a part of him instinctively knew that was not the case, though he couldn't even begin to assess the reason. They couldn't be under attack. The guards would have been alerted much earlier to any approaching vessel. Maybe there was a fire. But if so, Blake thought his men were more than capable of dealing with that.

Bray noticed Blake inserting another arrow. And seized his moment, springing forward into action, lunging at Blake, unleashing a powerful blow, doubling him.

Bray grasped for the spear gun, yanking it from Blake's arms.

Blake spun, kicking the spear gun, which shot out of Bray's hands, and landed, skidding across the open deck floor.

Bray tried to run again, to get away.

Blake lunged forward, pounced on him like a wild animal, bringing him down.

Yanking Bray by the hair, Blake smashed Bray's head on the deck. Once. Twice. He was in a frenzy now, his teeth clenched, his sadistic eyes bearing down on Bray as if into the depths of his very soul, like the Devil incarnate.

Bray gathered up all his fading strength, raised one leg and with all his might unleashed his knee into Blake's groin, then he elbowed Blake in the throat, hurling Blake from him.

He leaped to his feet, ran towards the gantry, then started climbing up the struts, his bare feet ripped to shreds, his face battered, bruised, blood oozing from his wounds, the tourniquet unable to stem the flow from his arm.

He knew he didn't have long.

Blake knew it, too. As he climbed slowly to his feet, gazing ahead at Bray in excited anticipation, Blake decided now was the time to finish the hunt... with his bare hands.

* * *

Jack and Ellie, followed by Lia and the warriors of the indigenous tribe, ran up a stairwell, then arriving at the top, scanned the labyrinth of metallic corridors.

"Which way now?" Ellie shouted, fuelled by adrenalin.

"Let's try down here," Jack replied, straining, concentrating, listening intently to another noise the group heard amidst the sound of the pulsing alarm.

They followed the noise, which got louder and louder with each step they took. And it had an ominous effect on even the warriors, normally so brave.

Although it was the sounds of cries, wailing, distressed pleas for help, it all blended into a cacophony, like some unearthly choir of ghosts from the other side, calling out from the afterlife.

Arriving at a huge doorway, the group carefully nudged the door open, stepped through.

And all were unnerved to see prisoners trapped in cells, tormented, sobbing, some reaching through the bars, clutching at Ellie, Jack, Lia and the warriors. Others sat idly on the ground, staring blankly.

At the opposite end of the corridor, guards arrived, outnumbering Jack and Ellie's group.

"How do you say we've got to do something - fast - in your language!?" Jack asked Lia in an undertone, not fancying their chances with the amount of guards approaching.

Suddenly Ellie - to Jack, the warriors and Lia's amazement, stepped forward, smiling politely.

"Hi!" she said casually.

The guards were confused as she swaggered towards them, hips swaying, chewing imaginary gum.

"Well?" she asked, seductively. "Where do we go? We're here to... pleasure you."

The guards exchanged more incredulous glances.

One female guard scoffed, indicating Jack.

"Him - pleasure us?"

For all the danger, Jack was deeply offended.

"Sorry to disappoint!" he muttered, his ego bruised.

The female guard wasn't part of the militia but the vagabonds and was wearing a belt that looked to be full of mounds of human hair.

"Pleasure us, eh? I don't think so," she said menacingly.

Then as the guards arrived, much to Jack's astonishment along with the native warriors and Lia, Ellie lunged to aggressively kiss one of the male guards on the mouth before reaching into his belt, carefully removing a set of keys, which she tossed behind her.

Jack caught them and began opening the cell doors, Lia indicating and yelling in her native language for the warriors to attack. Which they did, while Jack behind them swung open door after door.

"If you know what an uprising is - now's your chance!" Jack shouted. "Come on! We can't help you unless you help yourselves. And us! Move it, move it!"

The slaves poured out of the open doors, rushing to help the warriors and Ellie exchanging blows with their adversaries.

The female guard removed a blade from her belt and grabbed Ellie. Then sweeping up Ellie's hair, sliced through it, holding a clump of her long flowing locks in one hand, her arm around Ellie, backing her up, the point of the blade held at Ellie's throat.

"Back off! All of you! I mean it!" the female guard yelled, realising that her group were being overpowered.

Ellie gazed down nervously at the blade. Jack turned from opening a door, watching, terrified, as Ellie began to cry.

It wasn't just the danger she was encountering, but bizarrely she could see the clump of her hair out of the corner of her eye. She had been growing her hair long, ever since the 'virus' struck, with her sister, Alice, being the only one allowed to go near it - apart from Jack. And now that special bond, so symbolic with her past and her missing sister - had been so viciously taken from her.

But what no one could comprehend for one brief moment, the horrors of what she had witnessed in the cells brought back painful memories of Alice. She couldn't bear to think of her being held in such a way. The thought repulsed her. And it was all manifest by the clump of hair.

As well as distress her, it also angered her and she unleashed a vicious elbow into the female guard's stomach, causing her to release her grasp. Then Ellie turned, pulled back one arm and swung a wild blow, carrying all the simmering anguish, hatred and fear she was feeling. The female guard spun as the blow connected to her jaw and slumped to the ground.

The warriors and slaves didn't take long to overcome the guards, marshalling them into the cells as fast as they were emptying, with more prisoners being released.

Jack rushed to Ellie, who lifted her clump of hair and gazed at it sadly.

"Remind me to never try and meet you in a dark alleyway," Jack quipped, throwing his arms around Ellie for comfort.

Then Jack stepped back, considering her. Between her sobs, she plunged the clump of her beloved hair into her own belt.

"Hey - it suits you. I mean it. Really!" Jack said.

It didn't, of course. Her hair hung ragged, uneven. She knew it and overwhelmed by all that she had witnessed, continued to sob, nestling her head on Jack's shoulder while he embraced her.

"It's gonna be alright. Everything's gonna be alright, Ellie, I promise," he said, gently.

CHAPTER FORTY-FIVE

On the second deck, Lex, May and the warriors ran through a maze of metal corridors, arriving at a door which they inched open, revealing more cells filled with slaves.

Lex, May and the warriors were also greatly affected by the spectacle, overwhelmed by pity. Thankfully there was no sign of any guards. At least not so far.

"Keys! There's gotta be keys!" May said, yanking open a cabinet, before finally discovering some, which she tossed to Lex.

Both went from cell to cell, matching each key, while the warriors assisted Lex and May, opening doors, reassuring the prisoners that they were now free.

The prisoners could hear a wave of noise from the decks below, signifying the uprising, and also started shouting in cheers of jubilation. In the last cell, Lex noticed two small children sobbing, clinging to an older girl. They were all standing, rigid with fear.

"What's the matter with you?" Lex said. "Come on, you're all free. Can't you see?"

"No!" Emma replied, reaching out, searching the features of her younger brother and sister to make sure they were there and drawing them closer, under the protective care of her arms.

May exchanged a glance with Lex, who was staring mesmerised, not only by Emma's natural beauty and the opacity in her strangely beguiling eyes, but her poise and dignity.

"Here, let me help you," he said gently, taking Emma's hand while May comforted Tiffany and Shannon.

"Come on, sweetheart, everything's okay. No need to be afraid. Neither of you. We're here to help."

* * *

Amber and Jay, with their contingent of warriors, were now checking the living quarters, having secured the earlier decks, releasing more slaves, instructing them to assemble at the entrance dock with the others who had already been released.

They could hear the sounds of the cheering reverberating throughout the infrastructure of the rig. Any guards they encountered were surrendering, with little or no resistance.

Amber and Jay eventually arrived at Blake's quarters. Heading inside, they were astounded to see such opulence compared to the degrading conditions of those who were being held captive.

"Talk about living in the lap of luxury," Amber said, gazing around.

Jay was equally appalled by the difference. "I wonder who this Blake guy is - more importantly, where he is!"

"No sign of him here," Amber replied, searching the quarters.

"Let's try and salvage anything which could be important," Jay said.

Amber joined him, searching through drawers, cabinets, cupboards, removing paperwork, files, discs, a laptop, which they handed to Jack and Ellie, who arrived with other warriors.

"What on earth happened?" Amber said, noticing Ellie's ravaged hair.

"It's a long story," Jack interrupted. "You should have seen her - you'd have been proud."

"Any word from Lex and May?" Amber asked.

"They're both fine. Everyone's fine. We've lost no one. No injuries," Jack said.

"Thank God for that," Amber sighed, relieved.

"Luckily no one seems to be hurt. Except maybe for Ellie's pride," he said sympathetically, casting a glance at Ellie before turning back to Amber.

"Just one thing - there's more prisoners than we imagined. Just hope there's enough room on those boats."

"Check it out will you, Jack?" Amber suggested. "And we'll try and get finished up here. Come on. Move. Let's get out of here, while we can!"

* * *

Bray climbed slowly, carefully, along the huge steel struts, hoping that it all wouldn't result in the same way it had when he had ascended the roller coaster.

But he had little choice. It was his only hope to try and shake off Blake, who continued to pursue him relentlessly.

Bray cast a weak glance behind and could see that Blake was closing on him, ready to move in.

Blake, in turn, was gazing intently at Bray with more than a manic degree of excited anticipation. He knew that the very essence of life was fading from his prey and that Bray would soon succumb, if not from any final attack, certainly from the horrific injuries he had suffered.

Bray turned back, searching deep into the resources of his heart, his very soul, to find the will to keep going. It was all that he had left. His will. Now he barely had the strength even to move.

With the alarm still pulsing, the sounds now mixing with an avalanche of noise amidst the whistling wind, a rushing chorus and cacophony of jubilant cheering, it all further disorientated Bray, being totally unaware of what it all represented. He still had no idea where he was. And what was happening.

But Blake knew and wondered what had occurred, resulting in his cargo of slaves being set free. For there was no doubt in his mind that the chorus of cheers, electric, alive, had to be the sound of freedom.

Bray suddenly slipped and gripped as hard as he could, while clinging to a girder, sure he had no strength left, his legs dangling in the air.

Blake smiled slightly and accelerated forward, stomping his heavy boots on Bray's hands, resulting in one losing its grip.

Searching for every fibre of will and resolve, Bray hung on desperately, knowing that he didn't have much, if anything, left to give. He could give no more. But had to try.

Clinging with one arm, he wiggled his legs to gain even a bit of momentum, which was enough to gain a foothold on another girder. Then he reached up, yanking Blake by the ankles, and he, too slipped - but managed to cling while Bray hauled himself higher, propelled by more footholds he managed to find within the metal struts.

Blake and Bray were just a few feet apart now and gazed exhaustedly at each other.

"I underestimated you!" Blake said, finding a foothold and hauling himself onto the girder, climbed slowly to his feet.

Bray gazed up weakly, bracing himself for what was to come and struggled to remain conscious.

"I just wish we might have met up, another time, another place. You're a true warrior! And so am I!" Blake said, in a mixture of admiration and pride. "But now, it's too late. We're both going to die!"

Bray watched weakly as Blake stood, raising his arms aloft, and began screaming up to the Heavens above, his outline silhouetted against the flames billowing above into the dark sky.

"You hear that! Me! Blake! No matter what you thought! I was a warrior! And I never failed!"

Blake began to sob, much to Bray's confusion, further fuelling his disorientation.

Blake tried to compose himself and closed his eyes, his arms still spread, held aloft.

Even in defeat, he would find victory. It would be a warrior's death. He had taken his enemy with him, knowing that Bray also would soon die.

Blake was determined that he wouldn't fall at the hands of mere slaves intent on vengeance. Or the mighty, unforgiving Collective, if Kami had ever gotten a hold of him.

Blake had always been master of his domain. He would choose his own end.

In an instant, Blake was airborn.

Bray gazed down as Blake receded quickly in the distance, falling towards the churning ocean below, ready to accept Blake into its embrace.

Crashing into the surface of the water, Blake disappeared from total sight under the waves, which rolled over where he had impacted the water.

Blake was gone.

* * *

Amber stepped through the doorway onto the deserted helicopter deck, followed by Jay, both casting a quick glance around.

"Looks like there's no one up here," Amber said.

Jay nodded. "Let's go! We'd better catch up with the others!" he replied.

Amber considered Jay, who had noticed sudden movement in the lower girders above them.

"Wait a minute - look!" Jay indicated.

Amber gazed across the open deck, following Jay's puzzled stare.

Ahead, through the darkness, they could just about make out the silhouette of a figure climbing slowly, weakly, down the girders before finally losing his grip and slumping to the deck.

Amber and Jay watched as the distant figure climbed unsteadily to his feet.

Bray tried somehow to focus his eyes as he noticed the distant figures standing by the doorway.

It can't be.

He quickly dismissed it all, sure now more than ever that this was another simulation.

But it was no simulation.

A hint of unbelievable recognition was also evident in Amber's expression, which registered with Jay.

She stood staring. In silence. Speechless. A part of her wondering if what she recalled Ebony saying earlier was true, a larger part of her unable to even comprehend that it could even be true.

"Bray!?" she whispered to herself.

At the opposite side of the large helicopter deck, Bray also just stood, staring in pure disbelief. Was this really just a dream?

But there was no doubt about that voice. And who it belonged to.

This was no dream.

And yet it was a dream that they had both clung to for so long.

"B-R-A-Y!" Amber screamed out, her voice and entire being charged with emotion.

She ran flat out towards Bray, breaking down in wracking, heaving sobs, convulsing her entire body.

"It is you! It is! Oh my God! B-R-A-Y!!!"

Bray fought to contain his own emotion, his clothes torn and ravaged, blood still oozing from his wounds, his eyes swollen from his injuries filling with tears, overspilling down his battered, bruised face.

A surge of adrenalin raced through his entire body. And he, too, started to run, stumbling, still weak.

Jay stood motionless by the doorway, watching as Bray and Amber finally connected, each throwing their arms around the other.

Neither could speak. They were so overcome. And clung tightly to each other.

It was so moving that even Jay had difficulty in containing his own emotion while he watched Bray and Amber locked in their embrace, a cast iron grip, as if now they had been reunited here, of all places, and had found themselves, they would never let each other go.

* * *

Salene and Darryl stood either side of a gangway, helping the endless stream of slaves board the cruiser. Further along the dock, Jack was assisting Lex and May, doing the same, cramming as many of the prisoners as they could onto the lifeboat of the Jzhao Li.

An automatic rising temperature gauge inside the rig triggered more alarms.

All gazed around, unsure of exactly what was happening as flames were suddenly visible, shooting from one side of the upper decks.

The Mall Rats stared open-mouthed as they noticed Amber and Jay steadying Bray between them, stumbling down the steps leading to the dock from the main entry point above.

There was an explosion somewhere within the infrastructure, adding a dimension of added panic now to all assembled, from the initial relief of being only minutes from completing their escape.

"Bray!" Salene shouted, while Amber and Jay approached along the dock, almost dragging Bray between them. He was barely conscious and Amber could see that as well as her surprise, Salene was deeply affected at the pitiful state Bray was in.

"Now's not the time for any questions, Sal!" Amber said, glancing up at smoke billowing from the rig above her.

"Help us, will you?... Easy! That's the way!" Amber continued as Salene steadied Bray, who was laid gently down onto the deck.

Jay and Amber leapt aboard.

Then Darryl, extending a long pole to the side of the dock, pushed the vessel away.

On the lifeboat, May and Lex were doing the same while Jack started the ignition and the engine burst into life. He spun the wheel, punching the throttle to maximum, as did Darryl on the cruiser.

The propellers at the back of both vessels kicked into the waves, spraying up foam, the engines unleashing all their horsepower.

Both vessels pulled away, picking up speed, while behind them the rig was being consumed by the cataclysms erupting within, a series of what sounded like small explosions.

In the midst of the battle, a steaming cauldron had been overturned, causing a small fire, which in itself wasn't a danger. Some of Blake's guards quickly extinguished the flames. But the embers overspilling into a shaft had precipitated what was about to occur.

The flaming debris had ignited some gasoline tanks on the lower decks of the rig, the flames spreading to a massive storage tank, which the adults had towed to the converted oil rig in the last few months of the virus.

The rig had more than enough fuel to supply the visiting ships used to transport slaves since Blake and his forces had used it as a base. But some of the submerged pipes also led to thousands of tonnes of natural gas stored inside - intended to provide a lifetime of energy for the adults, who were to have been stationed on the island as part of the efforts to survive the pandemic that was sweeping the world.

Now, that energy was being consumed by the fires raging out of control and igniting all the combustible gases.

As the boats sped away, all the occupants clung, trying to steady themselves with the vessels bouncing along the waves, while behind them the superstructure of the rig was simply being torn apart by a chain reaction of explosions, huge flames spreading throughout all parts of the rig, fuelling an inferno.

The night sky was illuminated by all the devastation, casting an eerie glow across the water.

A creaking, groaning sound could also be heard as two massive cranes began toppling, their bases surrounded by flames.

Suddenly a massive explosion erupted, the shock wave felt by all the frightened occupants of both vessels, who watched and instinctively ducked as a towering pillar of flame shot high into the night sky from the very heart of the oil rig, dark smoke billowing.

The headquarters of Blake's operation was in its death throes.

Buckling under the shifting weight and with all balance gone, the oil rig began to tilt as one of its legs slowly gave way, melting from the intense heat.

The ocean was now reclaiming the doomed rig as another cataclysmic explosion occurred. The rig slipped slowly under the surface of the water - which seemed to be boiling - as more underwater eruptions ignited and the rig sank deeper and deeper towards the murky depths, the surface of the water ablaze.

EPILOGUE

The stars shone down. The moon was bright, bathing the native village. It was a magical night.

The villagers were singing in close harmony, clapping their hands, stomping their feet, bashing sticks against the sides of their makeshift drums.

Gel was helping some of the natives girls weave flaxen plants as hair extensions attached into the remnants of Ellie's long blonde locks. Jack sat nearby, assessing each stage. And liked what he saw.

"Ellie - I think it suits you. I really do. I might even get my hair done the same way," Jack said.

"It's my turn next," Gel moaned.

"Don't worry, I was only joking," Jack replied - then added quickly, so as not to offend Ellie, "not about this new hairstyle of your's - but mine."

"You just stay exactly the way you are - you're perfect!" Ellie reached out, taking Jack's hand and kissing it.

Lottie, Sammy, Tiffany and Shannon were playing with some of the native children, throwing coconuts to each other.

Lex was feasting on wild boar, turning on a spit over an open fire. Lia was next to him, translating tales of some of his past battles he had back in the city to the warriors, who were eating and listening intently. But Lia wondered somehow if Lex's boasts were more designed to impress her - or the Priestess - who stood watching Lex, listening intently. Although Lia wasn't experienced in male and female rituals and had never had a serious relationship, her instincts told her that Lex seemed to be sticking very closely by her.

Jay arrived. Lex offered a coconut filled with liquid.

"Here - try some of this. And you'd better hold on to something. Tight. I don't know what they put in it - but it's got a hell of a kick."

Jay took a sip. "I see what you mean," he said hoarsely. after he swallowed. "My throat feels as if it's on fire."

Lex grinned and was getting a little intoxicated by the liquid himself, hoping that all present throughout him holding court would also be intoxicated by his tales. He asked Lia to let the warriors know that Jay had once been an adversary, invading Lex's homeland city, but now was a friend. And Lex hoped the same would occur with all the warriors - and villagers - who Lex really respected. And admired.

He cast a glance down the Priestess's figure, winking at her.

"Don't push your luck," Jay said.

Then Lex relaxed and smiled to himself, noticing the Priestess winking back, with Lia advising that the respect was mutual.

"The Priestess said that she is looking forward to learning more about you and your culture," Lia explained.

"Me, too," Lex replied, downing the rest of his drink.

"Why don't you go and slip into something a bit more comfortable?" Lex suggested. "And who knows, I'll show you how we dance. Back home. Just as long as you teach me how you guys dance. Back in a tick," he added, smiling at the Priestess and Lia, while he led Jay away.

"What is it?" Jay asked, sensing something was troubling Lex.

"I don't know if it's this firewater I've been drinking and it's playing tricks with my mind... But one thing I've been thinking about. When you were with the Technos... you never met up with The Guardian, did you?"

"Not that I know of. I knew about him. And his Chosen, of course... But no, I never met him."

"I don't mean after the invasion. I mean BEFORE the invasion," Lex pressed.

Jay thought for a moment, then sipped on some more of the intoxicating liquid in the coconut shell. "I don't know what you're getting at."

Lex explained that he had been thinking about what Bray had told everyone. Especially about the time he was held in Eloise's compound. And all the references to the 'Zootists' confused Lex - as it had the others - when Bray recounted the despicable events he had suffered during all the virtual reality programs.

"It's just, I remember one thing The Guardian said. Before the Technos arrived. And I've never been able to figure it out," he continued, hiccuping and belching.

"Figure what out?" Jay probed, glancing at Lex, intrigued, and smiling slightly at his drunken demeanour.

"When The Guardian was being held captive at the Mall, he gave me a warning. I remember his exact words. "They're coming, Lex. The true bringers of Power and Chaos." If he didn't mean you guys - and had nothing to do with the Technos - then who he was talking about? I mean, the Technos were never involved with anything to do with Zoot and the Locos, right?"

"I see what you mean," Jay said, in equal confusion and concern.

He suggested that once they went over all the data and intelligence they had recovered from the rig, it might throw up more information. Jack had started to go through it thoroughly and so far there was nothing. Except some communiques which linked Blake with Eloise. But he could see why Lex was so disturbed by what The Guardian had warned.

"It was more than a warning," Lex replied. "More like a prophecy."

Darryl and Salene were dancing, the recent events drawing them closer together. Salene laughed as Darryl started to participate in an indigenous dance the villagers were doing. They whooped it up, encircling Darryl and Salene, amused as Darryl played to the gallery, exaggerating his movements and facial expressions and she joined in, exhilarated by the joyful reactions.

Whatever she thought of Darryl, she couldn't deny that he always brought a smile to everyone he encountered and helped brighten up the day. Certainly Salene's days. And she was becoming more fascinated with him, intent to delve beneath that comic facade and get to know who else was there.

May was sitting near Trudy, trying to comfort her. She was still blaming herself for inadvertently releasing Ebony, Axel and their raiding party.

"Come on, Trudy. This is a time for celebration, not blaming yourself. Because no-one's to blame," May said.

"I just feel so bad. And especially for Ram. I just hope he's alright," Trudy replied, wracked by guilt.

May shared her concern, as indeed did all the Mall Rats. They all felt badly that they had not believed Ram's story. And were stunned how Ebony had managed to get herself involved with Blake's people and that they could have been a part of The Collective.

Trudy shuddered to think what might have happened had Gel not intervened, and in so doing, saved her. And Brady. She was uneasy why they were trying to seize them, as well as Ram.

May gently reassured her that she shouldn't let her imagination run away with her. It must have been because she and Brady were nearby when Ram was abducted.

Trudy sighed, hoping that was the case. But nevertheless, was still having her doubts.

Ruby had told everyone when they arrived back just exactly what had happened. And that Ram certainly wasn't running off willingly but under protest.

All had speculated what fate might lay in store now that he was being held captive and were determined that they needed to try and find out.

The Priestess had decreed that Zak's burial spot would be sacred. And it gave May a lot of comfort when Lia had translated that one day Zak would be an ancestor to future generations. And that the story of all that had occurred would be handed down through the ages.

Slade was recovering well. And was absolutely thrilled by Ruby's news that 'they' were expecting. Both were determined that they would do all they could to ensure a bright future for their unborn child. As well as themselves. And all their friends. Not just the Mall Rats. But their new-found friends they had met within the indigenous tribe.

Since the assault on Blake's oil rig citadel, Bray had also recovered well from the appalling injuries he had suffered. But was still fragile. After hearing all that had occurred, no one was surprised, realizing that he would need time to become accustomed to any resemblance of a so called 'normal' life, having been incarcerated for so long and subject to so much physical and especially mental torture.

The mere fact that Bray and the Mall Rats had become reunited fuelled speculation and hope that others long lost might one day be found. Bray recounted that he had heard some talk amongst many prisoners, alluding that KC and Alice were being held themselves somewhere. As slaves. From Bray's horror stories, Ellie was alarmed at what Alice's story might be. Likewise KC. Tai San. And all the others. But at least the Mall Rats had hope that their friends and loved ones might one day come back into their lives. As had occurred with Bray.

Bray was caught up on everything that had happened since his disappearance. He was told about the invasion of the Technos, culminating in the eventual need of the Mall Rats to flee their city. All wished more than anything that they had Bray by their side during all the troubled times. They all missed him. Lex, especially. For all that Lex and Bray were occasional adversaries, they were still buddies when it came down to it. And all the Mall Rats knew, along with Lex, that when anyone's back was against the wall, there was no-one better than Bray to face any danger which was thrown at them.

It was a touching moment for all when Bray was introduced to his son. He thought the baby had Amber's eyes but she disagreed, feeling that baby Bray best resembled his father. Amber was sensitive to all the feelings which must have been swirling around Bray, and ushered everyone away so that he would be left alone to cradle the little one in his Daddy's arms.

Bray had been overcome with emotion, kissing the baby gently on the cheek. It was a day he had long dreamed of occurring.

And although he never imagined it being in such circumstances, it still filled him with such a sense of joy, and he could not contain the tears that flowed.

As well as his son, he had also clung to the hope that Amber and he would also become reunited. Throughout all the dark days, the difficult times, he had never given up. However hard everything had been, no matter what life had thrown at him, he never lost faith. That destiny would bring them back together.

He had relied on that hope, that faith, to focus and sustain him. As if a very life force. And without it, he doubted he could have gotten through every passing day.

Though they had been separated for so long, Bray felt they were never truly apart. They would always be together, bound by the very special love they shared. That extra special connection and bond which had been so evident since the very first time their paths had crossed.

But he could understand and was sympathetic to how it must have been for Amber not knowing if he was alive. Or had died. And he didn't expect that they would suddenly just pick up from where they left off. He had hoped that to be the case. But he was a realist and knew 'things' had changed. Now that she had Jay in her life.

And he was pleased for her. That she had found someone. He genuinely warmed to Jay. Liked him immediately, responding to Jay's quiet self-assured manner. And was especially touched when Jay had a private word, reassuring Bray that if he and Amber wanted to get together again then Jay wouldn't stand in the way.

Bray told Jay that the same applied.

But refrained from mentioning that although his shattered body still ached from the many stresses and injuries it had been subjected to throughout his time with Eloise, and recently Blake, there was no pain greater than the joy he had felt at even seeing Amber again.

No wound could ever be inflicted on him that was deeper than the love Bray felt for her. And just being in her presence, as well as being a free man again, was proof to Bray that anything was possible, punctuating his resilient determination throughout all the time since he had been taken prisoner during the Techno invasion - to never let go. To always cast any doubts aside. To always believe.

Jay was pleased to see Amber so happy, and relieved, along with all the other Mall Rats, that Bray had been saved. And was alive. He had reiterated to her the same sentiments he had expressed to Bray. That although Jay loved her, he would step aside. If that's what she wanted. Truly wanted.

Amber couldn't bear to even think about any aspect of this, let alone discuss it with Jay. And certainly not Bray. Not for a while. Though she knew those matters would need to be addressed, she suggested that Bray needed time to recuperate. And then they could go over it all, along with the other issues the Mall Rats needed to consider, concerning what the future now might lay in store for them all.

Amber was painfully aware that she herself needed some time and space to go over everything. There was so much to think about.

The Priestess had invited them to remain on her sacred lands. Lex seemed keen. And Amber could see why. Living an uncomplicated life in the natural world with nature had once appealed to Amber as well, during her time with Pride and the Eco tribe. Though Amber, like the others, wondered if Lex was more infatuated with Lia, or the Priestess, fuelling some kind of fantasy of living on a paradise desert island. Nevertheless, there was some merit in Camp Phoenix being built into a more permanent base.

Others, like Ruby and Slade, pondered if they should even try and return to the city.

Trudy was keen. Fearing that these islands weren't safe. Not only for her or Brady. But everyone. She was sure that she and her child had also been a target of Axel and his men.

May also wondered if Ram had been right. And their homeland was safe from any 'virus'.

Jack and Ellie agreed that it might be the case. But no-one, at this time anyway, could face the prospect of another long sea voyage. And even if they could, everyone shared Jack's view that the logistics of sailing a vessel back across the vast ocean would prove to be a difficult task. Though not impossible. The recent events had encouraged the Mall Rats that nothing was indeed impossible.

Amber's emotions were in a state of complete flux. Torn one way by the love of her past, Bray. Yet pulled in the other direction by the love of her present, Jay. And it was just too overwhelming to even ponder any kind of future beyond tonight's celebrations.

She was painfully aware, however, that she was now entangled in an eternal love triangle, which had tormented so many through the eons since time began.

Bray was someone she had lost her heart to before fate cruelly took him away from her. He was the father of her child and she had never expected to ever see him again. Miraculously, this had occurred, just as she had hoped one day it might. But in reality, she had always held her doubts, resulting in her entering into a relationship with Jay.

Jay and Amber had experienced so much together. She relied on his honest advice, the strength of his convictions, the two of them sharing many beliefs. She had thought, with the absence of Bray, that Jay would be central to her and her baby's life, their entire future. But now there was just so much to consider. And she needed time.

So tonight, she was determined to put it all out of her mind and focus on the present. Rather than the future.

Amber checked on baby Bray, who was fast asleep next to Brady in the guest hut. Then she stood at the doorway, watching the party. Reflecting on all that had occurred since they left the city. And was enjoying seeing everyone enjoying themselves.

"Are you okay?" Jay asked, arriving from the barbecue. He kissed Amber gently on the cheek.

She nodded, while Jay wrapped his arms around her.

"Everyone seems to be having fun. Except you," Jay said softly.

"I'm fine. Really," Amber replied. "We should all feel so proud, Jay," she continued. "We've come so far. But we've still got a long way to go. And I'm determined - we'll get there."

"I'll drink to that," Jay said. "And so will you. Stay where you are and I'll get you one of these. But I warn you - it's lethal," he said, indicating the coconut, and sipped on the juice while he crossed back to the barbecue area.

Amber leaned against the side of the doorway gazing at all the celebrations and smiled slightly to herself, noticing Bray dancing with Emma. But she couldn't help but feel pangs of jealousy welling deep inside.

Bray was very protective of Emma's two young siblings and had also paid close attention to Emma since they had all arrived. Amber knew that it was natural that they would have bonded. After all they had gone through. Amber shuddered, recalling the news Bray had relayed of his time with The Fallen. And it was typical of Bray to try and help Emma and her younger brother and sister. He had always shown such great compassion and a willingness to help those in need. Particularly those with a special need.

But Amber couldn't deny that Emma exuded something extra special. A haunting beauty and dignity, a poise and bearing which few would be able to resist. She endeared herself to all she encountered. And had certainly had a profound effect on Amber, who admired the innate strength and courage Emma had displayed, simply even to get through every passing day, let alone the way in which she cared for her siblings. Along with all those around.

There was a gentleness about her. As there was with Bray. Amber recalled someone once saying that opposites didn't actually attract. But those displaying similar characteristics seemed to be inextricably drawn together. Bray himself possessed so many wonderful qualities, standards, ideals.

Amber continued watching and felt as if her heart was breaking as she cast a glance at Jay at the barbecue area, getting her one of the coconut drinks, before glancing back at Bray. Emma was laughing, clearly enjoying all the celebrations and especially being with Bray, gently leading her to join Darryl and Salene, encircled by all the villagers, clapping and singing.

Emma and Bray joined in the dance and Amber thought it was wonderful that Emma was participating. No doubt Bray was inspired by it, too. Anyone would be.

The world had fallen into darkness since the adults had perished. But Emma seemed to be guided by an unseen force of light. Fuelling a will to survive. No matter what she suffered and endured. Bray had done the same, throughout all the horrendous things he had to suffer.

Amber, of course, was unaware that she had been Bray's light. And wondered now if she was also blind. Bray was special. And would always occupy a special place in her heart.

But so too, Jay, who now dragged her to join in the dancing and share in all the celebrations of all that had been accomplished.

Trudy was encouraged to join in as well. To get her mind off Ram, Ebony, Axel and his men.

Amber had felt just as bad as all the others that she had ever doubted Ram and was intent in trying to rescue him. And bring Axel and his men to justice. Along with Eloise's people, as well as The Fallen. Just as they had with Blake and his forces.

Bray especially was determined for The Fallen and those working with Eloise to be held to account. He had never been driven by revenge. But had some scores to settle.

There would be many more challenges ahead. As well as decisions which needed to be made. For all concerned.

As to Ebony? Everyone was sure that their paths would cross again and that she would ultimately get what she deserved, being no more than a rat, deserting what she perceived to be a sinking ship when she left the Jzhao Li.

But the Mall Rats were different.

They looked out for each other. Stood by each other. No matter what adversity. And they would work together to build a better world, somehow, somewhere.

They might no longer live in a shopping mall but that would never prevent them from living together as a Tribe, wherever that might be. Keeping their dream alive. They were still Mall Rats, after all...

The Tribe: A New World

A.J. PENN

CUMULUS PUBLISHING LIMITED

COMING SOON

2012

**The next installment in the series of novels
and the continuing saga of *The Tribe.***

CPSIA information can be obtained at www.ICGtesting.com
Printed in the USA
LVOW081130250312

274669LV00001B/4/P

9 780473 199388